DREAM MACHINE

WILL DAVIS was born in 1980 and lives in London. His first book, *My Side of the Story*, won a Betty Trask Award.

DREAM MACHINE

WILL DAVIS

BLOOMSBURY
LONDON · BERLIN · NEW YORK

First published in Great Britain 2009

This paperback edition published 2010

Bloomsbury Publishing Plc
36 Soho Square
London W1D 3QY

www.bloomsbury.com

Bloomsbury Publishing, London, New York and Berlin

A CIP catalogue record for this book is available from the British Library

ISBN 978 1 4088 0111 6

10 9 8 7 6 5 4 3 2 1

Typeset by Hewer Text UK Ltd, Edinburgh
Printed in Great Britain by Clays Limited, St Ives plc.

Mixed Sources
Product group from well-managed
forests and other controlled sources
www.fsc.org Cert no. SGS-COC-2061
© 1996 Forest Stewardship Council

ACKNOWLEDGEMENTS

Heartfelt thanks to Mum, Dad, Tamsin, Seraphina and Dawn for all their advice, support, tips, forbearance and technical expertise.

Massive thanks to my agent Peter Buckman, my editor Michael Fishwick, and to Justine Taylor, Anna Simpson and everyone at Bloomsbury.

'My name's Riana. I'm twenty-three years old, I'm from Watford and I'm an exotic dancer. But please don't let what I do to pay the rent put you off. All I want is an opportunity to prove to you that I've got what it takes. I can do this. I know you're gonna love me.'

Been fantasising about a hot bath all night, but by the time I get in I'm so knackered I end up just flopping down in front of the telly with a packet of Doritos, staring through this blur of tiredness at some crappy old late-night chat show. Shouldn't have done that last line. Might have made the last hour at the club go quicker but now I've got a bugger of a headache and the thought of getting up again to switch on the heating, then of waiting till enough water's dripped out into our bucket of a bathtub to make a bath, is frankly fucking painful.

I close my eyes and drop the Doritos on the carpet. Slowly I ease my feet out of my trainers and kick them over to the pile of my shoes in the corner, which Eddy is always on at me to put away. Where? I always want to know, cos our matchbox of a flat's not exactly full of nice little compartments for footwear. I reach down and start massaging my ankles. Started aching even before I put the heels on tonight, and those pads that are s'posed to cushion the ankles have gone and given me two arse-angry red blisters. You might think that by this time I'd have developed Superman-like skin and be able to wrap them in barbed wire if I wanted, but they only seem to get sorer. So stop dancing in those instruments of fucking torture! is what Eddy always snaps when I complain to her, like I've got any choice in the matter. Like it don't turn her into a bitch on heat if I wiggle around in front of her in nothing but a pair of spikes. Sexiness is a painful business, that's the trouble with it. But it's also my business. It's what I do and what I've always been good at.

There's this piano tune and then these drums, and then all these girls' voices break into my thoughts. Do *you* have what it takes to be the new Purrfect girl? they chorus. I open my eyes. Course it's just the telly, some advert for yet another neuron-eating reality TV series they're putting together, one of those shows where they take a bunch of young hopefuls and film them getting their innocence slowly sucked out of them bit by bit, till only one's left, who then gets congratulated for surviving and given a record contract. On the telly this girl band Purrfect are standing in front of a Hawaiian backdrop all smiling and pointing out from the screen, their bits held in (only just) by bikinis, their arms and legs all wrapped round each other in one of those girl-on-girl could-be-friends/could-be-lovers poses. I could do that, I think to myself, and what's more, I could do it a lot better too. Look at that girl on the left, that Monique or whatever her name is. Someone really ought to tell her to lay off the pasta if she's going to be flaunting it in killer panties. Doesn't she have a PA or whatever it is that's supposed to prevent these celeb types from going out looking like heifers?

I shut my eyes again and try to imagine myself up there on a podium as a pop star stead of a stripper. Mum was a singer. I used to want to be one too, but a couple of years of struggle wore me down. There's nothing more soul-destroying than crooning your heart out in some flea-pit pub to a bunch of beer guts that are only interested in your cleavage. That's why I switched to stripping: least the clients aren't allowed to heckle you, and there's no pretending about what they're there for either. Pays a fuck of a lot better too. I did stick it out for a while, mind. Sent off letters and demos to producers, joined local groups and did free gigs in parks, entered local talent contests and sang at weddings, that kind of thing. I even did busking after I heard how the popular spots sometimes get scouted by agency reps. But the fact is the last thing anyone's looking for is another black female singer, specially one who's already hit the twilight years of her early twenties. And the only other option is the backing route, the kiss of death to a singing career if ever there was one. I'm well fucking versed in what happens when you go down that miserable back alley – sob story of Mum's life, that's what. Still, I never meant to turn to stripping full time. It's just that once I got into it I found out I was pretty special at it. There's a real craft to pole dancing, and to lap dancing, too. Even to something as simple as taking your clothes off. That's what most people don't get, including Eddy, who still reckons all it takes to be a stripper is a bust and a beaver. I'm constantly having to stress to her that actually darling it's fucking hard work, thanks very much.

The chat show comes back on. It's called *My Kid's An Addict With Attitude*. The kind of show I'm a sucker for, which I can't watch when Eddy's around cos they make her so mad. There's some fifteen-year-old chav in a shell suit being slated by his mum and dad because he steals from them to buy crack. His parents list all the bad things he's ever done to them like it's some kind of competition, and when he finally gets the chance to defend himself it's not long before the smug hostess cuts him off with all these bitchy comments of her own. The audience boo and hiss, and everyone lines up to have a shot. But this teenager just sits there and endures it, staring into the air like a statue while everyone tells him what a waste of life he is. It's enough to drive anyone to crack.

There's the sound of a key in the lock. The door opens and closes and there's the heavy thud of storm trooper boots as someone who just doesn't get dainty stomps up our little passageway.

Riana? shouts Eddy. You up?

Hello baby, I call as she comes into the room. Eddy's hands appear on either side of me and touch down on my shoulders as she leans over and kisses me. I reach up and stroke the top of her head, running my fingers over the bristle of stubble that covers it and using my pinky to set the earrings on her left ear jingling like a wind chime. She peers over at the telly.

What crap is this?

Newsnight, I say. Where you been?

At a meeting.

I don't ask for details. Eddy likes to be all mysterious about her SCUM meetings. Every so often she goes out at the dead of night to attend one of these super-secret get-togethers, where they plot mini acts of terrorism, like sending off hate mail to homophobic MPs and planting stink bombs in shopping centres. Pretty juvenile stuff if you ask me, but Eddy's very political and shit, and thinks doing stuff like that makes her a radical. Maybe it does, I don't know. I guess it *is* sort of radical to be letting off stink bombs in Debenhams when you're thirty. I'm pretty curious about SCUM actually, though I've never been to one of their meetings. I did offer once to go with her, but Eddy said I wouldn't like it. I let it slide, but really I knew it was cos *she* wouldn't like it, since her hardcore dykey pals probably wouldn't be too happy about her having a stripper girlfriend who's into skirts and lipstick. I'm her guilty secret. Like she's mine.

I reach up and grab Eddy by the waist. Eddy doesn't usually like being the one who gets manhandled, but she lets me pull her on top of me so she's sitting in my lap and gives me a grin.

How were the pervs tonight?

No more pervy than you are, I tell her, as she places her hand over my right tit and starts to knead it. Loves my tits, she does. I've not told her they're fake cos I don't know how she'd deal with it.

As a matter of fact, I got a proposal of marriage.

Oh? Eddy raises one eyebrow. And what did you say?

Said I live with a violent bastard who'd chop off his balls if he so much as mentioned the M word again. Tipped me twenty quid, didn't he?

Mmmm, good work.

She drops her head forward and starts to kiss my neck. I look down at it and put my hand on the stubble again. Cocoa brown against creamy white. Together we make a mocha. I kiss her there, which is yucky because it reminds me of kissing someone with a beard, back in the days before I knew what did it for me. Just then something catches my eye on the TV screen – that ad again, the one about the girl band looking to find a new bitch for their group. For some reason I'm suddenly intrigued and I grope for the controller to turn it up.

We're searching for a new girl! chorus the girls from Purrfect as I raise the volume, thrusting their busts out like missile launchers and flashing killer wedges of white teeth. If you think it could be you then why not come on down and try out!

Eddy stops what she's doing and looks round.

Oh my Lord, what fucking brainwashing, she mutters, frowning like they're the faces of evil. She climbs to her feet and crunches down on the Doritos. Jesus, Riana, she moans. You're such a slob!

I dunno, I say, unable to resist the urge to needle her just a bit, cos I know how Purrfect are pretty much the opposite to everything Eddy believes in. That one on the left is kind of cute. Think I got that same bikini too.

Eddy frowns and snatches the controller off me, pointing it at the telly and switching the channel to BBC News 24.

There, watch something that won't make you stupider.
Looking all pleased with herself she stomps across the room and into our microscopic kitchen, where I hear her opening drawers and rummaging for spoons to make tea. I turn down the sound and change the channel back, but the ad's already over and the chat show is beginning again. Another fat zitty teenager with a so-called attitude problem is in the hot seat, facing off his angry parents while the audience boo at him. In the old days they'd just have stoned him and been done with it. But I'm not really concentrating on this anymore. Stead I'm thinking about the ad. The old hamster's at it in his cage and I'm thinking, Why not? I'm as good as any one of those bimbos. Do you have what it takes? That's what they all wanted to know, shouting it like it was some kind of challenge. And do you know what? I reckon I fucking do.

'My name's Ella . . . I live in West London, I'm seventeen and I'm still in school. I'm studying French, English and History . . . I sing in the school choir and I used to do ballet when I was nine . . . I really want to be a pop star!'

My plan is to lock myself in the bathroom until they agree to take me to the audition. I take my iPod and go and sit on the toilet for nearly three hours, staring at the wall, listening to Purrfect and imagining myself on stage with them. I picture myself standing between the other girls as they introduce me as their new member, thousands of screaming fans stretched out in the stadium below my feet. Monique is holding my hand up like I'm a champion, and Saffron's got her arm round my shoulders like we're best friends. I'm wearing my pink silk skirt from Lipsy that I had to save up to buy, this white halter neck with a golden swirly pattern on it that I saw in an old Mark Jacobs catalogue, and those new Chloé high heels with real gold on them that cost £2000 a pair. My hair's got amber lowlights and cascades down around my shoulders in this waterfall of bouncing curls, and my eyes have got this silver glitter on them that make them look huge and catlike. I'm stunning and sexy, nothing like the frightened albino rabbit I usually look like. Then the girls start singing 'Ooh', harmonising with each other, Fina doing the high part, and then they start to walk to the sides of the stage and Saffron gives me a gentle push forward. I raise the microphone and the crowd let out a great cheer as I sing the opening line to 'My Heart Is Not Your Toy'.

Then Mimi ruins my fantasy by banging on the door and shouting at me that Rita's just got home from work and says I have to get out of there right this minute. This is the tough part, because Rita still scares me even after all these years. She can be really sarcastic in that way that you can't come back at, and has this tone of voice that makes you feel like the stupidest person on earth just because you forgot to put the cereal boxes away. She wasn't so bad when Daddy was around, but after he died she morphed without warning into this totally evil stepmother who no one dares to cross, not even Mimi who she adores. But I know I've got to do this and so I keep quiet and refuse to answer. Finally Mimi goes away, but not before gleefully telling me how much trouble I'm going to be in. Still, I can hear this grudging respect in her voice which makes a nice change. Some girls look up to their elder sisters, but not Mimi. She thinks I'm a lost cause. And whenever anyone calls us sisters she always has to point out that we're not biologically related to one other, like the idea of being genetically linked to me would be like being related to an amoeba.

I can hear them in the kitchen down the passage, Mimi informing Rita that I'm not talking and Rita's voice rising as she demands to know who the hell I think I am, playing games like this in her house and at my age. Then Jack, who's cooking a mushroom risotto from the smell of it, says something I don't catch but I know it'll be designed to soothe, something like that I'm just a teenager and I'll come out when I'm hungry. But if that's what he does say then he's wrong, because I'm in this for the long haul, and anyway, everyone knows that teenagers can do hunger strikes better than anyone. I put my earphones back in and turn up the volume.

Bathrooms are really great places for sieges. You can totally see why girls are always running into them for refuge in TV programmes after bust-ups with their families. You've got everything you need – toilet, shower, bathtub, mirror and, most important of all, toiletries. The next hour goes by without me hardly even noticing, I'm so busy trying to make myself up to look like the girl in my fantasy. I experiment with some of Rita's Maybelline, the new stuff that separates out your lashes and gives them coal-black definition and extra length. It makes my eyes look like they've got spiders' legs stuck around them.

At half-past eight Rita herself comes and knocks on the door.

'Ella?' she says in her reasonable voice, which isn't really very reasonable at all since Rita's one of those people who's used to just demanding things. 'Come out now, please.'

I stick with my vow of silence. This is mostly because I'm afraid to speak, because if I do I know Rita'll somehow get control and make me open the door. But it's also partly because I don't need to. She knows perfectly well why I'm in here. I cried myself to sleep after she said I couldn't go to the audition, and when I got up this morning my face was all red and swollen like I'd had an allergic reaction overnight.

'Listen, Ella,' says Rita, a rising edge to her voice now. 'You don't want to parade around with a bunch of girls and then get judged for it. I'm not letting you go and that's final. I really don't care how long you stay in there.'

This is rich of course, since judging girls for what they parade around in is what Rita does for a living. But I know it's not really her opinion anyway. It's Jack's. He's the one who said I shouldn't go and Rita always listens to him when it comes to Mimi and me. He said that it was damaging, that all they want to do is turn the girls they get into a product, first for TV and then for some corrupt record company. I said I was perfectly fine about this, but Jack said I didn't know what I was talking about. He said I wouldn't get in, and that then I'll be crushed and he doesn't want me to get scarred by such a stupid process. But that's not the real reason. The real reason he doesn't want to take me is because he doesn't want me to get the attention. He doesn't want to have to acknowledge me, to deal with me, to look up from fawning over Mimi and notice that I'm still here.

'Ella, this is very selfish of you,' says Rita, going all high and nasal, which is how her voice is naturally. 'You know how much stress I'm under. I don't need this.'

Rita is always under stress because she's the deputy editor of *Fascinate!* Every Sunday, the day before the magazine goes out, this stress boils over into fever pitch and she practically has a meltdown, and goes racing through the house looking for things to scream at you for. It's quite frightening actually, but she always calms down the next day and makes up for it by giving Mimi and me loads of the free samples of perfume and cosmetics she gets sent, and sometimes even accessories.

Still I don't answer, though it's really hard because I'm crossing a line and there's no going back. After a few seconds of waiting Rita screeches 'Fine! Stay in there for ever!' and angrily clip-clops off down the passageway in her spikes. I put my ear to the door so I can hear everyone sitting down to dinner in the kitchen. The conversation is dominated by Rita, of course, complaining about some assistant at work and how impossible her deadlines are and how much she needs a holiday. Jack and Mimi eat in silence, except for Jack saying 'Mmmmm' and Mimi saying 'Yuck' from time to time. By dessert Rita's ranting is all about me, how spoilt I am and what excruciatingly wanton behaviour I'm displaying; how I'm my father's daughter through and through, unable to accept it when something doesn't go my way.

I find myself wondering if this is true. I was seven when Daddy died and I know he loved me more than anything else in the world, apart maybe from Rita. I remember him as this friendly giant who never had a bad word to say to anyone. But memory gets chewed up over time, and I sometimes wonder if I haven't gone and made a hero out of him, and if he was really as great as I remember him being. Sometimes, in dreams, I even get confused between him and Jack, which is quite weird, considering.

But I do know that sooner or later Rita will have to cave. She doesn't care enough not to. Sure enough, at ten thirty there's another knock at the door. This time it's Jack.

'It's me, Ella,' he says in his deep gentle voice. Hearing my name coming out of his mouth always gives me a strange feeling in my stomach, like a butterfly has somehow got in and is batting around trying to get out again. I've just put on this mask of pea-coloured deep-cleansing clay that's supposed to provide the ultimate defence against blackheads. It feels like acid on my skin.

'What do you want?' I shout.

'I'll take you to the audition. If that's what it'll take to get you to come out of there and eat something.'

The exhaustion in his voice is hurtful. It makes that flapping butterfly instantly melt into a lumpy sick feeling, like that instinctive heaviness you get in your gut when you know something's really wrong. Suddenly all I want to do is wipe away the clay, fling open the door and throw myself into Jack's arms, sobbing about how sorry I am and that it's okay, he doesn't have to take me. All I really want is to be close to him again, to feel the warmth of his body pressed around me, to see him smile and hear him say it's all right and that he knew I'd come to my senses.

'You'll have to explain it to Mimi though,' says Jack then with a sigh. 'She still thinks we're going ice-skating Saturday. We won't be able to do both.'

Fuck Mimi, I think. It's always Mimi this and Mimi that with Jack now. I don't care if Rita prefers her – like Mimi's always saying, she *is* Rita's biological daughter. But the way Jack organises his whole life around her is disgusting. When Rita first got with Jack *I* was the one who welcomed him into the family, not Mimi. I was the one who made an effort to get to know him, who offered him second helpings when he came for dinner and put his shirt in the wash when he stayed over. Mimi just ignored him. But Jack and me – we were close right from the start. All that stuff I told him, like how hard I found it to make friends with the other girls at school and how lonely I was. And the stuff about Daddy too and how I wished I could remember him better. Now it's like he just wants to wash his hands of me. Now that Mimi's fourteen and getting boobs, she's the one who gets all the attention, like at seventeen I'm already past it.

'Okay, Ella,' says Jack, still in that exhausted tone, like he's got a fatal illness that's preventing him from speaking in a normal way. 'I'm going to bed now. You've won, okay?'

I listen to his footsteps as he goes, and it's like they're in time to the beat of my heart. I just want Jack to come back to me, that's all. So we can be like we were, with Mimi and Rita out of the picture. I turn back to the mirror, look at the warty green goblin before me and force myself to smile. Hundreds of tiny cracks appear in the dried clay like the wrinkles I'll no doubt get when I'm seventy. But underneath I'm still young and still pretty, I tell myself, even if I do look a bit like a rabbit. Soon he'll be begging me to remember him.

'My name's Joni, I'm nineteen and I'm from Reading. Me whole life all I've ever wanted is to be a pop star. Purrfect is one of the greatest bands ever. They're all so gorgeous and talented and I'm just so excited to even be here, I can't tell you what it means to me. It's like, the biggest thing that I've ever done me whole life!'

Me and Wend decide we gotta arrive early cos we wanna be among the first to get seen, before the judges get all bored and stop paying proper attention. We want the best chance possible.

It means getting up at seven and bunking off work, which means I'll probably get the sack since I've already had two warnings and the third is the cruncher. Plus I have to sneak past Mum. She had her posse round last night and the whole kitchen stinks of their horrid fag smell. She's right there slumped over the kitchen table, snoring away, surrounded by empty bottles of cava with fag butts piled at the bottom of them. It ain't no pretty sight, I can tell you. I pour her a glass of water and stick an Alka-Seltzer in it for when she wakes up, so she don't take out her hangover on Baby. She's going to be right pissed off with me when she finds out where I been, but I don't care. Some things, you just got to do.

The whole journey to London me heart's thumping like it's on speed or something, and I can't even concentrate enough to hear what Wend is saying to me. She sees how nervous I am and to take me mind off it she starts singing 'Tied Up For You', which is the duet between Fina and Kharris, the one with the video where they're both in separate cars racing each other. Me and Wend always sing it when we're feeling low. She does Fina's bit and I do Kharris. I'm a good singer, if I do say so meself. Only this time when it's me verse the words catch in me throat and all that comes out is this puny whiny sound. Wend starts laughing but suddenly I'm really shitting meself, thinking I might as well just turn around and go back home, save meself the embarrassment, cept that ain't an option cos we're already pulling into Paddington and it's too late. But right then, just as the train comes to a stop, the sun comes out and shines in through the yellow glass and makes everything look all bright and happy, and I get that Gabrielle song in me head, the one about dreams and how they really can come true if you make 'em, and I know I gotta do this. I gotta try, even if it don't come to nothing.

We get off and go into the toilets, Wend distracting the guard by asking him if she's got a visible bra line so I can duck under the barrier and save us 20p. Every bit helps when you're skint. Then we both nip into a cubicle and get into our dresses. You got to look the part at these auditions, otherwise they won't take you serious, that's what I reckon. Wend is giggling like a mad thing, and I keep having to tell her to shut up in case someone hears.

They'll think we're dykes, I say as I zip her up, now breathe in.

So let 'em, shrugs Wend. Then she turns, leans in close to me and whispers, Maybe one of us is!

She whips up her hand and covers me mouth with it, then starts snogging away at me like I'm fucking JT. I shove her off and that's when I hear this nasty ripping. I look down to see the front of me dress clean torn away from me tits. It's only gone and got attached to Wend's stupid fucking necklace, the one with the big silver heart she nicked from River Island.

Oh my God! I scream. Wend quickly pulls the dress off her necklace, ripping it even more, the stupid cow.

Don't worry, I can fix it! she goes, grabbing it and patting it back into place like this is going to help. It ain't so bad . . . just needs a safety pin or two, that's all.

It's a fucking write-off! I shout.

Forty quid this dress cost me and it's brought me nothing but bad luck. I got it in the January sales, and the first time I wore it was the day that wanker Davy admitted he'd been shagging Shea from the estate over the road. Stupid rag's like an omen or something. I pull it off me and start putting me jeans back on. Kiss goodbye to your chance at being in Purrfect, I think. I give Wend a good glare so's to let her know I reckon this is her fault.

When we've done our make-up we walk up to where the studio is, Wend complaining the whole way and saying we need to slow down cos she's got her spikes on. They're buggers of shoes, those spikes of hers, squeezing the sides of your feet and cutting off the circulation to your toes. I know cos I borrowed them once for a night out and fuck did my feet scream the next day. But that's the price of style, and I ain't got no sympathy for her now that I'm back in me jeans and a T-shirt which ain't even been washed all week. It weren't my fault! Wend keeps squealing, in between saying Ouch! but I just shrug and carry on walking. If she gets this and I don't I'm gonna belt her right across fucking London.

At the studio in Shepherd's Bush there's already this queue stretching all the way down the street. So much for getting here early. Wend lets out a great moan but there's nothing for it so we queue up behind this lanky posh girl who's here with her parents. Her dad's all over her, saying stuff like Remember to breathe, like he thinks his daughter's gonna accidentally forget and fall down dead. This girl's dressed all in black and has her nose pointed at the sky like everything below it is too whiffy for her. She catches me and Wend checking her over and looks up and down at us with this smirk like she thinks we're a couple of right slappers. Wend demands to know what she's looking at and she looks away fast, but she don't stop smirking. Just ignore her, I tell Wend, though what I'd really like to do is give this girl a good clout, cos you can tell she reckons she's better than us. But you got to be civilised, specially when there's a camera crew going up and down the line asking people questions and stuff. When it gets to this girl in front she turns on this blinder of a smile and starts on in this posh voice like the queen about how she's Purrfect's number one fan and has been having singing and dance lessons since she was an embryo or whatever and how she just knows she's got what it takes to be in the band. Real cool and confident. Her mum and dad stand behind her looking all proud, like she's their gift to the world. Then this girl opens her mouth and lets out this string of Ahs, only she goes up and down and all over the place, and instead of sounding like a right fanny like anyone else would of course the bitch sounds just like Mariah fucking Carey. Me nerves start to kick in big time. Don't worry, they'll never choose her, she's got no tits, Wend whispers, but I can see this girl's got her nervous too cos she keeps chewing at her nails.

When the camera gets to us I go all shy and say the first thing that comes into me head, can't even remember what. Wend just giggles like a right twat. You can see the faces of the guy behind it and the one with the mic, like they think we're a couple of tards with no chance. As they move on to the next girl standing behind us I think of Mum and Baby at home, and how I've fucked up yet another job with this stupid idea of coming here. I can feel the sweat prickling under me armpits.

But there ain't no going back. This miserable woman in a shiny pink skirt comes down the line handing out these disclaimer forms and tickets with numbers on them, saying once we're inside we gotta wait till the number gets called.

She's got a face like a dog just marked his territory on her shoes. We're getting closer to the doors and now Wend is practically jumping up and down with excitement, like her feet have just miraculously stopped hurting, or more likely got deadened from the pain. She keeps on singing snatches of songs, and then yelling how she can't believe we're really here doing this. After a bit this girl's dad in front of us turns round and says Do you mind not making that sound right in my ear? to her. Wend's too busy screaming to hear him. Get your ear out of her face then, I snarl back. He looks proper outraged by this, but his daughter grabs his hand and says Just ignore her, Dad, all superior, the witch. I'm about to start having a go at her, like who the fuck does she think she is, when I get distracted by this horrible wailing. Everyone looks up to see this lardy girl coming out the entrance having a total fit. She's all red, tears are streaming down her face and her hands are all clenched up. Some other girl runs out after her and tries to calm her down, but the fat girl shakes her off shrieking, They're wrong! It's not true! I'm a size twelve and I've got perfect pitch! Then she starts running down the street streaming snot all the way, with her poor friend running after her shouting stuff like Sally wait – you're just big-boned, that's all! Wend is pissing herself beside me, but suddenly I've got this need to have a piss properly, and it's so bad me knees are starting to knock.

Toilet, I says to Wend and make a dash for the entrance. Course everyone thinks I'm pushing in, and this group of right bolshy bitches at the doors start having a go at me and trying to shove me back. They're proper Northern lasses, which means built, and I ain't got no chance against them. Luckily the face-ache in the pink skirt comes by and demands to know what's going on. I tell her I gotta go and she says all right and lets me inside, saying Be quick.

Inside the loo this amount of piss comes out like I didn't know I could fit up there. Whole pints of the stuff.

It's bliss and I let out this Ah sound cos I think I'm the only one in here. Then there's this giggle from outside. I flush the loo and go out all mad cos this day's turning into a real experience, and not in the good sense, only to find this blonde girl blubbering away in front of the mirror like a right nut job. I don't know what to do, so I stand there looking at her. Then I go back in the cubicle and get her some tissue.

Here, I go, handing it to her. She takes it with this pathetic look of gratefulness and blows her nose. Sounds like an avalanche, I want to tell her, but I don't in case she takes it the wrong way. She's one of them fragile, dainty types, the sort that look like they'd just blow away if you was to even speak too loudly to them.

I didn't think it would be like this, she goes (another posh-o, I think). I'm so nervous. I feel like I'm going to throw up. What if they hate me? I should just tell Jack to take me home.

Don't be daft, I tell her, but nicely so she doesn't think I'm being mean. It's just an audition. If they don't like you then screw 'em.

This girl looks at me like I'm her fucking saviour or something. Now that she's stopped crying I can see she's real pretty. One of those girls me and Wend are always slating cos they don't know what a proper problem is. But I don't hate her. In fact, I'm quite glad she's like this, all pathetic, cos it makes me feel better about meself. I have a quick squiz in the mirror, check over me make-up and give me hair a pat down. I look all right, even in the skanky T-shirt. And I think, well you got as much right to be here as anybody, ain't you? Then I think of Baby at home and imagine him growing up with a famous pop star for a mum, getting bought all the best toys and being driven to school in a limo. Worth a shot, ain't it? Course it is.

Come on, I go to this girl. Time to get back out there and face the music.

She nods slowly, all serious like we're going to war or something, but she puts on this brave look and follows me out. I see Wend over at the doors and wave to her. Thanks, goes the girl to me as I leave her, and she gives me this look like she really means it. And suddenly I feel real good about meself, cos it's like maybe it was worth it coming up here after all, even if they do think I'm rubbish, just to get that smile. Like you can still do a decent thing in this miserable old world and be appreciated for it.

'I'm Louise, I'm eighteen and I'm from Appledore in Kent. I believe God gives everyone a gift and for me it's performing. I've been singing since I was little and I can span five octaves. I play the piano and I dance, too. I love all kinds of music and I really love to sing, but most of all what I love is to perform. It's what I was born to do.'

'A hundred and six?' barks the sour-faced bee in her cheap imitation Armani skirt. It's my ticket. I turn to Dad.

'Kill it,' he says. It's what he always says. They're the magic words, what I need to hear before I go in there and show them what I'm made of. Mum just hangs on to Dad's arm like the pointless appendage she is, and pulls her usual worried expression at me as though she thinks there's a chance I might actually fail. But I can't think that way. If I do, then there *is* a chance. That's what Mum will never understand. She's not strong like Dad and me. And that's why she's never been good for anything but housework and making pots of tea.

I nod to Dad very slowly, absorbing the positive energy he's giving out. It's what I always do after he says the words. He used to be in the entertainment business himself, way back when I was little, before he saw a gap in the market and went into advertising instead. He knows what it's like: how you can't give just a piece of yourself or let yourself contemplate failure. How you've got to give it your all or else you might as well not even bother.

Dad nods back to me. I turn and stride towards the doors. To one side is the last girl who went in, now being interviewed by a camera crew. She's sniffling and being comforted by her mum. She's pretty, but straight away you can see why they didn't choose her, no matter what she sounded like. It's her posture, shoulders all hunched forward. Desperate. Posture like that begs an audience 'Please like me!' and that's a cardinal sin on stage. You cannot ask your audience to like you; you have to make them.

I give my ticket to the fake Armani woman, doing my best to ignore the lethal rays of bad energy radiating off her. Then, just before I enter the room I reach up and undo a couple of buttons of the shirt I'm wearing so that the lace from my bra peeps out. That's something Dad would never advise me to do, but he always taught me when you're in the spotlight every detail gets noticed. Sadly God hasn't given me much of a bust, but what He did grace me with I fully intend to make the most of. I'm wearing my Victoria's Secrets bra, which is supposed to be able to make even a flat chest look voluptuous. My bra thus doctored, I take a long cool breath and whisper 'Okay God', just to remind Him now is the time in case he's off being distracted by starving Africans (which is completely rightful use of His time of course, but I'm only asking Him to spare me five minutes). Then I go in.

Inside it's not nearly as large or impressive as I remember from last time. It's just a normal-size white studio room, empty apart from a table at one end, with three people sat behind it, a bit like an early series of *X Factor*. Two women and a guy. There are two cameramen dressed in black, one filming on each side. One of them takes a few steps forward and thrusts his camera at me. I hold my head high and give the panel my best winning smile.

'Hello,' says the woman on the left. She's quite glamorous, dressed in a dark blue two-piece with bright blonde hair falling in waves across her shoulders. I recognise her from the girl band Kissy Kiss Kiss which bombed way back in the nineties after just one top ten hit. 'I'm Emma,' she says.

'Hello!' I say, clearly and brightly. 'My name is Louise.'

'Hi Louise, how's it going? I'm Joe!' says the guy on the right enthusiastically, camp as anything. His suit is all shiny and red, like he's come out today dressed as a Christmas present. I vaguely know who he is too – some record company guy who's always doing sound-bites for those programmes that supposedly explore what celebrity means, but which actually just expose how some people will bend over backwards just to be associated with it. But I'm glad to see him. If there're gays in the audience you never have to worry about giving it too much – that's what Dad always says.

Finally the woman in the centre looks up. She's got a face like she's never managed to crack a smile in her life. She's in her forties at least, black and grossly overweight. She wears silver-rimmed glasses with massive diamanté D&G symbols on the sides, which would be a blatant mistake on anyone else, but since she's never going to look good I suppose she can wear whatever the hell she likes and no one's ever going to bother saying anything about it. Beside Emma she looks like a hippo in drag. She doesn't bother to introduce herself either, just grunts. The bee obviously doesn't recognise me, but of course I remember her perfectly. Her name is Tess Roberts and she's the one who put Purrfect together.

'So tell us a bit about yourself,' says Emma, smiling back at me.

I clear my throat and begin the speech Dad and I have been rehearsing all week. I do it word for word, without stumbling or forgetting anything. As the words pass my lips I become convinced by them. They get imbued with meaning and insight, like the words of a really good sermon that pushes all the right buttons in a congregation. When I've finished the panel are all looking at me and I can tell they're impressed. Emma's nodding, her face all serious, and Joe looks positively delighted. Only Tess is frowning, but that's only because she can't find any fault with what I've just said. Of course, that doesn't stop her from trying.

'So you're classically trained then?' she demands.

I give her a quick run-down of my awards and achievements.

'In my experience,' she says, her furry monobrow leaping up above her glasses like a hyperactive caterpillar, 'those with classical training have a hard time adjusting to the pop industry. It's faster, and too cut-throat for them.'

I can feel my cheeks getting hot. I fight down the surge of panic rising from below. *Help me God. Help me not to let her see my face going red. She must not know that she has ruffled me.*

'But pop is what I really love,' I say firmly. 'It's what I listen to all the time. And it's what I've been singing for the last two years. Pop music is what I live for.'

The caterpillar dances over the D&G frames again.

'So,' she says in a quiet voice. 'You consider yourself to be a dedicated fan of Purrfect, do you?'

'The biggest!'

'Huh.'

I can tell she doesn't believe me, though both Emma and Joe are nodding their heads and smiling. It's obvious they think I'm great. I am great, I remind myself. God made me so.

'What are their names then?' says Tess.

It's such a stupidly easy question that I almost burst out laughing.

'Saffron, Fina, Monique, Kharris and . . .'

I trail off. I was about to say Lucy's name, but of course she's not in the band any more. Lucky I stopped myself. It was a shock when she announced she was going solo, and many people thought Purrfect would split up. But they didn't, bouncing back better than ever with that song 'Never Forget' which they wrote specially because of it and which won them the Golden Egg award for best ballad. And where's Lucy now? Debuted at number 22, the stupid bee. Of course I knew her leaving wouldn't stop them, not when they'd been so successful already. To create Purrfect they auditioned hundreds of girls across the UK in a nationwide search for the greatest talent, and all the girls I know wanted to be in it. I remember the first ads for it on ITV: big curly gold letters demanding to know if *you* had what it took to be in the next Girls Aloud. When I saw that question it seemed to me like it came from somewhere deeper than the television screen. Like God Himself was speaking to me. It was the first time I'd ever properly wanted something with my whole heart and not just in order to be the best of the best or to make Dad proud. He actually had his doubts about the contest, but when I explained to him how big it was he agreed to drive me up to the London audition, even though it was a school day and I was underage. But I didn't care about those things. I so desperately wanted to be one of those girls. Emma and Joe weren't on the panel then, but Tess was, right at the centre just like she is now, staring out at me like I was a dirty sweet wrapper blown in from off the street. I sang 'Memory', which of course I know now was a bad choice of song. The other judges gave their verdicts: they said I was good, but they weren't sure if I was Purrfect material. They said it was up to Tess. Her decision alone. I remember those seconds as I waited to hear how the rest of my life was going to turn out. I really thought that I was in, so it was a shock when I heard the words 'Too podgy.' That was all she said. That and 'Next!' It was the first time I could remember ever outright losing something, not even coming in second or third, or at least being awarded a merit for my effort. It felt so horrible I can't even describe it. Worse than anything I'd ever felt in my whole life – even when we found out Gramps had Alzheimer's. I felt betrayed too: I couldn't understand why God would want to play such a cruel trick on me. When I came out of the room I pretended to Dad they'd said I was too young because I couldn't bear the idea of him thinking it was because his daughter was chubby that she didn't get chosen. I shouldn't have lied: a couple of weeks later the series started on TV, and there was a big close-up of my face as Tess said the words and after that everyone knew. At school they started calling me Podge, and I had to walk round with that nickname hanging over my head for the rest of the year. Meanwhile on TV I watched all those chosen girls competing with one another until just five of them were left, the ones who became known as Purrfect. Of course they went straight to number one with their first release. Everyone at school was downloading their single 'I Want To Be Purrfect' and it was always playing on the radio. They performed it on *The Slammer*, *T4* and *Great Selections*, and all I could think every time I saw them was that I should have been on that stage, that I was as good as any of those girls and that I'd been robbed of what was rightfully mine. For being podgy.

Tess folds her arms over her huge sagging bosoms and cocks her head to one side, causing her glasses to slide rapidly down her nose until they come to a sudden halt above her big flared nostrils.

'*Full* names?'

My smile freezes on my face and a horrible lump rises in my throat. I have no idea what Monique or Fina's surnames are. Saffron Grady and Kharris Mitch. But Monique and Fina . . .? Oh God! I scream silently. What the effing eff are the full names of those stupid bees?!

And instantly, just like the wonder He is, God saves the day.

'This is ridiculous! *I* don't even know their full names!' cries Emma. 'Why do you have to grill everyone that comes in here, Tess? This isn't Guantánamo Bay, you know!'

Slowly Tess turns to her, a grimace of icy contempt spreading across her face. I can't help but notice that she glances slyly in the direction of the cameras at the same time. That's professionalism for you. She wants to make sure they're getting this.

'It's my job to make sure candidates are up to scratch,' she says in a high and mighty voice that reminds me of my first-ever singing instructor Mrs Pilch, who used to walk around you with a ruler, slapping you on the neck every time you went off key. 'I was there at the beginning. Those are my girls out there. They work hard and they're dedicated. And I sure as hell don't intend to let them down!'

She looks fierce and triumphant, and Emma looks suitably intimidated. Nonetheless she raises a hand and says she appreciates all that but it would be nice if Tess didn't interrogate the girls since we do have feelings. Tess declares that this is hardly the point, and anyway she can't be held accountable since the girl *she's* looking for will need nerves of steel. At this point Joe joins in and says they all have a duty to be civil, and before you know it they're all arguing away about the issue of responsibility, making catty remarks about each other's conduct, shaking their heads and doing talk-to-the-hand gestures at each other like they do on *Trisha*. All the while I'm standing there smiling, praying that they don't come back to Tess's original question. I'm smiling so hard my mouth is beginning to ache. Inside my stomach a nasty heavy sensation is building up, and I regret throwing away Mum's breakfast platter when she turned her back to pour out the tea this morning.

After the first audition I stopped eating. It's funny all these magazines with women talking about how difficult it is to lose weight, when actually it's incredibly easy. You just have to be diligent about it, that's all. Follow instructions and not stray from the course, and I've always been good at doing that. It was just that this time it was me who was giving the instructions and setting the course instead of a tutor, and *I* don't do things by half measures. Overnight my body shrank. I lost half a stone in a week. I didn't mean for it to get out of hand, but once I'd started I just couldn't stop. After a month I was down to seven and a half stone, and Dad started receiving letters of complaint from parents and concerned phone calls from teachers about my appetite. He said it had to end and I agreed, then went right back to hiding my food in my napkin and coughing the rest out into the upstairs toilet. Then there was that day I fainted and had to go to the hospital, where they told me I had a serious eating disorder. After that Dad sat me down and had a long talk with me. He said he knew why I was doing it, that he knew I had a dream and that he respected me for it. He said we'd do everything we possibly could to make my dream come true. He actually promised me that one day I would be the biggest pop star ever – but only if I started to eat again. I had to trust him, he said, because when had he ever let me down before? It was hard to start again after going all that time without food. Meals became ordeals that I had to get through, and a lot of times I thought I was going to be sick just on reflex. I'd get agonising pains in my stomach, and feel bloated after just a few mouthfuls. There was even some talk of sending me to Rexia Camp, where they force feed you and put you under twenty-four-hour surveillance to make sure you don't exercise off any of the weight you've put on. But I did it off my own bat. I did it and in return Dad got me hip-hop lessons in Canterbury and a new vocal coach, Mr Field, who specialises in pop. As soon as I was out of school, Dad said, we would find me an agent.

Then last year the stories about the arguments hit, and then came the news that Lucy was leaving. But Purrfect were too strong to let it finish them, and a couple of weeks later they released the news that they would go on without her, even though of course they were terribly upset and it wouldn't be the same. And then came the word that they would be doing a hunt for a replacement girl, and that was when I knew God was giving me a second chance. That all along He had been there, on my side, rooting for me. Before it just wasn't my time. But now it is. I can feel it. That's why I know – I just know – that today I'm going to be chosen.

The panel finally stop bickering, Joe and Emma having ganged up on Tess and persuaded her not to ask me anymore of her mean effing questions. The stupid fat bee sits back in her chair and glares at me, obviously hoping I'll be a disaster and prove her gut instinct right. But what she doesn't know is that her gut instinct isn't right. It's never been more wrong in her whole life.

'Well, Louise,' says Emma, leaning forward and giving me a reassuring nod. 'Let's hear what you've prepared.'

Time to kill it. I open my mouth and take a breath. I sing for them LeAnn Rimes' 'How Do I Live Without You?' It's one of the hardest songs to do, partly because it's already been done in an unsurpassable way, and partly because it requires perfect use of tone, range and pitch. The big three. But if you do get it right it's the best showcase a voice can possibly have. I go through the whole first verse without stopping, really feeling that pain that sits at the heart of the song. The man with the camera steps forward and I close my eyes and imagine the close-up of me he's getting, channelling that raw emotion out into my voice, turning the atmosphere around me into a thing of beauty.

When I'm finished there is dead silence for a few seconds. I open my eyes. Emma and Joe are both looking at Tess, who's still staring at me, still unsmiling, her eyes magnified by her silly designer spectacles. She looks like a bulging-eyed lizard, lying in wait for an unsuspecting insect to pass. I watch as she swallows and the muscles in her jaw begin to work, and time seems to suspend itself. There's a great thumping in my head and I realise it's the sound of my own heartbeat. This is it, God. Don't let me down.

I'll kill myself if they don't choose me.

How long does it take to ruin a life?

In they go through those double doors and out they come just a few minutes later, pale and shaking, struggling to hold back the tears. They will never forget what they've experienced in there. It will scar them for ever. With each girl I find myself desperately wishing I could somehow stop her – that I could say something that would make her change her mind about going inside. But what could I possibly say? These girls are so determined. So full of themselves. They'd never listen to what I have to tell them. They believe this is what it's all about – that behind those doors fame and glamour and all the things they have ever wanted are waiting for them. I should know; I once believed it myself.

How long does it take to ruin a life? The answer is no time at all.

'Oh my God! I can't . . . believe it . . . I never thought they'd actually . . . I'm . . . I don't even know what . . . speechless! I can't tell you what this means to me. How it . . . changes things . . . I'm never going to be the same again after this. Never.'

I stand there in front of the camera, crying like I've just given birth. I know I'm making an idiot of myself but I can't seem to stop. Snot is forming in my nose, I can feel it preparing to launch itself on the world and I don't even have any tissue. I've never cried from joy before. It's a weird feeling. The woman in the pink skirt I've seen on sale in Woo-man stands impatiently at the side holding her clipboard, waiting for them to finish with me so she can take down my details for the call-back. There's no sign of Jack and Mimi.

After a few minutes of filming me acting like I've won an Oscar, the guy with the microphone says he's got enough and heads off with the camera guy to film a group of girls in school uniform who are singing a Sugababes song. The woman mutters 'Finally' under her breath and hands me the clipboard. She tells me to put down my contact information. I try to write down my name and address, but I'm shaking so much it comes out like one long squiggly line and she has to tear off the sheet and get me to do it again. She looks thoroughly unhappy, like she probably wanted to be a doctor and never dreamt in a million years she'd end up saddled with this job, but I'm too elated to care. I'm through! I think to myself, trying to believe it. They really liked me. They really want me back.

'Look, just let me do it,' snaps the woman in exasperation as I produce yet another unreadable squiggle. She snatches the clipboard and pen back off me. 'Name?'

'Ella Platt,' I croak through my tears.

'Address?'

I look around again, trying to spot Jack or Mimi. A few feet away the girl who was in before me is sitting watching. Her face is a blotchy mess of tears – just like mine must be. I can't help shooting her a ridiculous smile. As soon as I do she bites her lip and looks down, her whole face starting to wobble, and I realise that unlike me she didn't get through. Right away I feel bad, like I should go and apologise to her. She's here all on her own by the looks of things, and I think how easily that could have been me, crushed because I didn't get chosen. I think about what that woman Tess, with her sharp voice and her bored expression, might have said to this girl, how she could have just decimated that girl's feelings with one single curt sentence. When she told me my nerves were going to be a major obstacle I was bracing myself for it. Then when she said yes I just stood there staring in disbelief until finally the other woman, Emma, got up, gave me a hug and led me to the door. 'It's okay,' Emma whispered to me when I stared at her, all confused because I couldn't believe what had happened, 'you got through!'

Just as I'm giving my number to the woman Jack and Mimi appear at the other end of the room. Jack hurries over, Mimi trailing behind. 'Ella, there you are!' he cries. I'm so overwhelmed by what's just happened that for once I don't feel any spasm inside at the sound of my name on his lips. I've never felt like this. Like I'm going to burst with happiness.

'Where were you?' I say. My voice sounds dry and dead, like I'm traumatised from surviving a 9/11-style disaster, even though the situation is completely the opposite.

'We just popped out for a breath of fresh air,' says Jack. 'Mimi wasn't feeling too hot. Were you, Mimi?'

I look at Mimi, who's yawning. She looks perfectly all right, just bored out of her brain, that's all. I can't help thinking that Jack would never have walked off and left her if she'd been the one auditioning. Come to that, if Mimi had been the one trying out, Rita would be here too.

'I was seen!' I rasp. 'I had my audition!'

Jack frowns.

'You did? I thought they said ten minutes—'

'Does this mean we can go now?' whines Mimi.

Jack peers at my face and assumes the worst.

'Oh Ella,' he sighs.

Ever so gently, like he's afraid of getting too close, he reaches out and gives my shoulder a pat. In the past he would have hugged me tight and assured me that no matter what anyone else said I would always be his girl.

'I knew this would happen. These set-ups are all about vampirising young women and shaming them for ratings on the telly. That's why I didn't want you to do it. I knew you'd get hurt.'

'That's not it—' I start to say but Jack's not listening. Already he's turned to Mimi and is asking if she's still feeling sick and if she wants to get some water before we catch the Tube. I tap him on the shoulder impatiently, and he glances at me.

'Ella, I'm sorry. You'll feel better too, once you've had a rest and something to eat . . .'

At this point the surly woman with the clipboard who's been standing there listening to us takes exception.

'Hey mister,' she practically snaps at Jack's face. 'You ought to be congratulating, not commiserating! Your daughter's through to the next round! How about that, eh?'

Jack stares open-mouthed at the woman like he's just been told the earth is flat. Then he looks at me and I get this mental image of myself through his eyes and it's like he's seeing me again for the first time. I am no longer this pathetic snivelling lost cause but someone talented, important and special. I think of that awful day two years ago when he turned to me in the car and said 'It's time to stop, Ella – it's time you looked for a boyfriend your own age', and how I agreed because there didn't seem to be anything else for it, even though inside it felt like my heart had just been shot into hundreds of tiny pieces. I bet he's regretting that day right now. I bet he's wondering how he can turn it around and take back what he said to me.

The woman looks at Mimi with a big put-on smile.

'How great, huh? Your sister must be good!'

Mimi frowns and squints at me. I expect her to do her usual shtick about me not being her real sister, but instead she shocks me by suddenly throwing her arms around my waist and letting out a blood-curdling scream that virtually breaks the sound barrier. And instead of pushing the little freak off I find myself breaking down all over again, hugging her tightly back and sobbing like a maniac, all the while with Jack staring at me with eyes like a goldfish.

On the Tube journey back to Kensington he's all silent. I think how he must be coming to terms with the news – maybe even realising that he loves me after all. He barely even glances at Mimi the whole time, even when she demands we go to Delphi's for sundaes to celebrate me getting through. Unlike him she can't shut up. She keeps asking me to repeat over and over what the judges said, and then interrupting to go on about how I'm going to be on TV and how she can't wait to tell all her friends. Finally she breaks off and just gazes at me, her big blue Barbie-doll eyes all full of wonder, making me blush and for some reason want to start crying again. I wish our relationship was always like this, her admiring me instead of sighing and shouting for Jack every time I so much as borrow her hairbrush. 'Oh my God!' she cries as the train pulls in at our stop. 'I've just thought! You could actually make it into Purrfect!'

'She won't!' snaps Jack abruptly.

Mimi gasps and I stare at him, shocked. Jack colours and quickly gives the kind of sheepish grin he always puts on after he loses his temper, which happens hardly ever. But it's what he says next that cuts right to my soul.

'I'm sorry, Ella. But it's true. I don't know how you convinced those judges to pick you, but it was a fluke. You were just lucky and I don't think it's a good idea for you to continue with this. You're only going to get hurt and disappointed. There's no way I'm taking you to that call-back.'

For a few seconds I can't breathe. I hear Mimi crying that it's not fair and that I have to go because it could make me famous, and Jack telling her that it's for my own good and he knows best, but they both sound far far away, like I'm hearing them underwater. I'm dizzy, the world is spinning, faster and faster. Then everything goes dark.

It only lasts for a second. Next thing I know Jack's arms are holding me and he's carrying me off the train, and Mimi is asking excitedly if she should call an ambulance and beyond her there's the roar of the train as it takes off out the platform. Jack tells Mimi no, and lays me down on a bench. Curious faces of other travellers peer down at me from all sides, going in and out of focus.

'Is she okay?' an American woman is saying. 'I'm a nurse.'

'She's fine, she just fainted,' Jack assures her. 'Could everyone just give her some space, please?'

But I can hear a note of panic in his voice. It's like he doesn't want all these people around to be concerned about me. As the world begins to settle back into focus I take in Jack's face hovering above, all pale and drawn, and suddenly I realise something. He can't handle it. He can't deal with the idea of me being special, of other people admiring me and believing in me. He needs to think that

I'm a lost cause so he can tell himself he was right to end it between us. With a grunt of effort I push myself up, trying to ignore the lurching feeling this movement gives me.

'Take deep, slow breaths,' the American advises.

'I'm okay,' I pant. 'And I'm going to that call-back.'

Jack glances at the people around me and does his sheepish grin.

'We'll talk about it at home.'

When we get back Rita is at the kitchen table looking harassed, a cluster of half-empty coffee mugs and lots and lots of glossy photo articles spread out before her. It's cataloguing for the next edition of *Fascinate!* She's wearing her glasses, which is a sure sign that you don't want to disturb her if you know what's good for you, unless of course you're Mummy's little girl who can't do a thing wrong. Mimi rushes right over and tugs at her arm.

'Mum, Ella got through!'

Rita turns, her face all contorted with stress. She gives Mimi a pained smile.

'That's nice, darling. Mummy's busy right now, why don't you run along?' Then she frowns and her eyes dart at me suspiciously. 'Got through to what?'

'The audition,' I say. 'I made it to the next round.'

Rita looks from me to Jack like she has no idea what I'm talking about.

'That girl band thing,' he reminds her. 'They picked her.'

'Oh,' says Rita vaguely. 'Well done, Ella.'

She nods at us like she's dismissing us and starts studying the glossies again. Jack clears his throat. Rita's head snaps up again, this time annoyance is written all over her face in big red letters. I can't help but wonder what Jack ever saw in her. I know he doesn't love her now, and she just tolerates him because he takes care of us, but they must have liked each other at some stage just to have started dating in the first place.

'What is it?' she says in a voice that threatens to erupt like a volcano.

Jack looks at us.

'Girls, could you give us a moment?'

I realise he is going to persuade Rita to forbid me to go. She always does what he says when it comes to us. She can't be bothered to take any interest herself, so she just lets him get on with it and okays his decisions like a lazy dictator.

'I have to go to that call-back!' I shout.

Rita stares coldly at me. I feel the tears forming once again.

'Girls – out,' she orders, and of course we do just what she tells us, legs working automatically like robots. I head for my room, close the door and throw myself down on the bed, burying my head in my pillow where I start weeping with anger and frustration. After a while I roll over and look at my animals. I know it's stupid for a seventeen-year-old to still care about her cuddly toys, but I can't help it. Teddy-O, Andy Panda and Snakey have always been my truest friends. They've never made catty remarks like the girls do at school, or ignored me like Rita does, or simply abandoned me like Jack. I've had them since I was a little girl and I can't imagine what my life would be like if they weren't there for me. 'It's not fair,' I whisper to Andy Panda. His little black-and-white face shines with sympathy and I pick him up and snuggle down with him, shutting my eyes. They sting like mad so I open them again. It's because of all the crying. It's bad for your complexion too. I haven't cried so much since Daddy died.

'Ella? Can I come in?'

It's Mimi, poking her head round the door. Ordinarily I would be shocked by the mere sight of her in my room, not to mention the fact that she's gone to the trouble of asking if she can enter it, but I'm too depressed to care.

She comes over, practically on tiptoe like she's scared of upsetting me now I'm this fully blown diva, and sits down at the end of the bed.

'I think it's mean of him not to let you go,' she pouts. 'I'm going to tell him he has to. He'll listen to me.'

I study Mimi's face, full of belief in herself and her power over Jack, familiar feelings of jealousy welling up inside me. But I'm also struck by how incredibly different we are. Where does her self-confidence come from? I've never had it, not even when Jack belonged to me. Is it because she thinks the world revolves around her that it does? I try to imagine Mimi in Jack's arms, him whispering loving things to her about how special and important she is, how she's his little girl, but I just can't see it somehow. Mimi would be laughing or squealing for him to stop, or else describing some pair of roller boots she's seen and wants him to buy for her. What Jack and I had was too special for him to be able to find it with Mimi. He's mine, only mine. He's just forgotten how much he needs me, that's all.

'It's okay,' I say. 'I can fight my own battles.'

I surprise myself with this one, and Mimi looks put out, like the idea never even occurred to her. But I think to myself that it's true. I don't need Mimi's help. And I don't need Rita's permission to go to the call-back, or Jack's either. They liked me in that room, those three judges. They said I had a lovely voice and a sweet personality, that I was charming and cute. They made me feel like I really had something to offer, and to offer what I've got I don't need anyone's permission but my own.

'What I've always wanted to do is to sing. I grew up listening to Aretha Franklin, Annie Lennox and Kate Bush. Tracy Chapman's my idol. You see, I'm not just some stripper. I'm a somebody!'

Had this punter at the club last night who kept on asking me these questions while I was giving him a private. One of those weirdos who insist on chit-chat stead of just concentrating on the business. Not that it bothers me, so long as he pays up – I'll give him my whole life story if that's what he wants. So I tell this guy a bit about myself while I'm giving him the moves, and eventually I get on to how I like to sing. Then I mention about how I'm going down to audition for this gig and that I'm really excited about it, and suddenly the stupid wanker bursts out laughing like it's the funniest thing he's ever heard. Well good luck to you! he gasps when he's finally done creasing himself, cos I hate to tell you this but there's a big difference between taking your clothes off and being a proper star, love. And I can't come back at him cos he's slipping a twenty into my G, but what I really want to say is Oh yeah, and what do you reckon that is then, Mr Genius? And I'd be genuinely interested to know his answer. Cos the more I think about it the less of a difference I can see between what I do and what those girls from Purrfect do. Apart from the fact they make shitloads more money, that is. Those girls, that Saffron and Fina and Kharris and Monique or whatever her name is, what they do is they go on stage, mime a few words and shake their bits around while men all over the country get hard-ons watching them on the telly. It's just another form of prick-teasing.

So here I am at the call-back, standing in line with forty or so other girls, all waiting to go into the pop boutique to see the so-called image consultants and get revamped for this afternoon's second round of auditions. Up ahead the camera crew are getting girls to turn round in front of a blue screen so they can do before and after shots. Some of these girls, they come out looking exactly the same as when they went in, plus maybe a few hair extensions. There's a couple of real sad cases who come out looking halfway decent I s'pose. Be interesting to see what they have to say to me. I've dressed like a hooker for the occasion, boobs out, legs showing up to the arse, leather goods and big gold accessories. Gotta make this stripping gig work in my favour. I knew when I met the judges that if I could make myself over as this sexpot with a shady past that only wanted a chance to make a proper go of it, then they'd want me. Seen enough of these reality pop shows to know that's what they're looking for. It's not just about finding some pop star to replace that silly bitch that didn't know a good thing when it was going for her, it's about making telly that keeps people from flipping the channel. They want tears and they want flesh. They want a singing Cinderella from the ghetto, and I'll give it to 'em and then some if they'll only let me. Won't make it through to Purrfect of course, there's not much chance of that happening. But it'll get my face out there. A foot in the door. And that's what you need in this business.

I have a look up and down the line, inspecting the competition. I'm probably the only girl here that's not surrounded by family or friends. It took Eddy a long time to come round to the fact that I was doing this. A right fucking long time. But when she saw I wasn't backing down she let it rest. Then she even offered to come. Told her no way. There's nothing so sure to jeopardise your chances as a chain-smoking dyke with a buzz cut and a tattoo of a flaming skull on her neck. But now that I'm here I'm feeling kind of lonesome. I'm kind of wishing I'd let her tag along after all.

As I look back at all the parents and boyfriends I suddenly notice something that's so fucking obvious I can't believe I didn't see it already, seeing as normally it's the first thing I'm aware of when I walk into a room. But I'm not with it today, cos of trying to remember my lyrics and to repress the fucker of a headache I've got buried somewhere deep in the back of my brain. What I notice now is that I'm the only black girl. I mean properly black. There's a few caramel colours, but no other real proper blacks, and I stand out like a Christie doll in a row of Barbies. Maybe I can make this work for me as well as the stripper gig. I look up and see I'm at the front of the queue.

Hi there, says this grey-haired geezer holding a sound boom, could you state your name and then give us a twirl in front of the screen?

Out of habit I size him up, taking in the wedding ring and the big purple circles under his eyes. Married with no sex life is my verdict. Sort that's usually in tears by the time you've finished giving them a private, that only ever splash out on clubs like mine to get a bit of sympathy and material for future wanks. I give him my earth-mother/sexpot smile.

Hi, I'm Riana, I say.

I turn to the dude holding the camera, whose face is hidden behind it so I can't give him the once-over too, and do a quick spin, balancing on the ball of my foot and raising my other leg up over my shoulder so everyone watching gets a good gawp at my lacy pink knickers. Didn't go for a thong in the end, thought it would be too much. There's this gasp of disapproval from the parents of some size zero anorexic that's next in line, but the sound geezer's face perks right up and the dude with the camera peeks round his equipment to check it's for real. He's like the sound geezer's identical twin. Pity they're not the judges. If they were I'd be stretch-limoing my way to the bank already.

This chubby woman at the entrance to the pop boutique calls for me to hurry it along, so I flash them some more teeth and let the anorexic take my place while I follow this woman inside. There's two more camera dudes in here, and several movie-star style dressing tables with the lights all round the mirrors and girls sitting at them being made over by other chubby women, all with these long faces of serious concentration. At the back of the room are rows and rows of clothing racks, frocks galore. My own chubby woman looks me up and down, nodding slowly, and I can practically read the word Tart in one of those think bubbles above her head. She pats the seat in front of her mirror and gives me a smile.

My name's Alice, she says slowly in this bright voice, like she's talking to someone very, very stupid. Right then. . .

I take a seat and she puts her hands on either side of my head and stares hard at my reflection, like she's going to telepathically channel a new image on top of me just like that. One of the camera dudes moves in on us, and Alice breaks off from staring to dart this quick look at it.

Well, you've got quite dark skin, she says, smiling all nervous like she's worried that maybe she's being unPC stating the fuck-off obvious, which means you can get away with bright colours. You're lucky.

She starts holding up different colours of eye shadow and testing them against my face, pointing out the pros and cons of Electric Blue as opposed to Neon Rose Pink. I nod, like I'm taking this advice very seriously indeed, though at twenty-three I think I'm pretty much an expert in what colours suit me, thank you very much. It's quite boring, to be honest, listening to her drone on, and once the camera dude moves off I can't be bothered to keep up the act so I just let her get on with it, chatting away to herself, and let my eyes drift up to this poster of Purrfect on the wall behind the mirror. It's a magazine spread of them as a foursome, all in school uniform, ripped tights and shirts tied in knots above the waist, hair in pigtails, plaits and ponytails. The stuff of sex fantasies, no question about it.

I've been studying up on Purrfect – that's to say I've read their bios on Wikipedia – and the truth is I don't think much of them. In fact, more than ever do I reckon they're nothing but a bunch of bimbos who struck it lucky. Most of their music's got a decent beat to it, and a couple of their songs are all right for stripping to, but that's as far as it goes. They're just another one of those manufactured pop groups. I like my music a bit more edgy and a fucking lot more honest. Course, that's not what I said to the bitch with the face like a troll on the panel last week. Told her how much I admired their unique sound and beautiful voices, like any of them have got something worth mentioning. Even pulled the old salty eye trick and said that one of their songs, 'Never Forget', reminded me of my mum, which is enough to get the old lady choking in her grave. I can just see her looking down and shaking her old head, going I didn't work my arse off putting you through school for this, girl! Mind you, it's not like she would have approved of what I do now either. Sorry, Mum, but you always said you gotta pull some dirty tricks to get ahead in this game. At least Purrfect don't seem to take themselves too seriously. Not that they have to, what with that troll-faced bint doing the job for the lot of them.

What do you think? says Alice, standing back so the dude can shove his camera up my nose to get a close-up on my reaction. I force my lips into a big smile, like I'm totally wowed by this new me looking back from the mirror. Far as I can tell Alice has basically wiped off my tart face and then reapplied it only in different colours. She's also taken my weave out of its ponytail and back brushed it, Tyra Banks style. Twenty minutes, this image turnaround's taken her. Sort of thing I'd have to do in five at the club.

Cor, I breathe through my teeth, can't believe it's really me.

Alice grins like she's gone and worked a miracle. Off you go to see the stylist then, she says all proud, giving this quick glance at my mini-skirt and boob tube. They'll fit you out with something a bit more . . . different.

The camera dude follows me over to the clothing racks, where I'm met by this dwarf of a woman dressed all in black, which cos of her bright red hairdo and orange lipstick makes it look like her head's caught fire. This is s'posed to be my style guru. She looks up and down at me.

Oh my, she cackles, we've got our work cut out for us with you, haven't we?

Ten minutes later and I come out for the after shot. I'm wearing fitted black jeans and a black top, which is all right actually and which I'm planning to have a go at nicking, though the cut's a bit high for my liking. But the gold tassels over the bust make up for that, wiggling every time you breathe and drawing the attention right back to the boobs. Amount these puppies cost me, I don't want nobody forgetting they're there.

The face of the sound geezer from before now looks totally blank and sick of all the pretty girls around him. He gives me this real tired smile and asks me to do another turn. Then the unhappy-looking woman from last week with the face like she thinks death would be a mercy appears, this time in a lemon all-in-one that makes her look like a manically depressed Big Bird.

The panel are just getting ready, so if you want to use the bathroom and anything else now is the time to do it, she tells me in a voice that could cut glass, I'm not joking. I gush out an over-the-top thank you, grabbing her hand and giving it a good yank like I owe her my life. She looks repulsed and snatches it away like I've gone and infected her. Grinning to myself, I head for the loo.

There's a whole scrum of girls in here, all fighting for mirror space so they can go over their make-up, several of them singing away at the top of their voices like they're competing to see who can drown out the others. Plenty of noise and distraction. The end cubicle is free so I lock myself in and drop the lid. Quickly, but not too quickly, cos the last thing I want right now is a spillage situation, I take out my blow and shake out a little mound. Carefully I divvy it into two lines. Outside some girl's burst into tears, and another one's saying Never mind – just say you've got your period! I take out my lucky pink straw and reach out and flush the loo to cover the sound while I hoover up my lines in two fast snorts. It sears nicely. I lick my fingers for residue and take a long and sweet breath of oxygen and wait for the effects to kick in. As I stand there, leaning against the cubicle wall, the words of Emily from the club come floating back to me. Emily's the oldest, thirty-something (she won't tell us what), and she's been stripping since before she was legal. She's kind of annoying, a real drama queen, always moaning on about how she's going to be past it pretty soon and forced to flip burgers for a living. If she does get the boot it's more likely to be cos she gets plastered every night before she goes out on the podium. She tries to act like a mother to the rest of us, telling girls off when they do something stupid like going home with a punter, and comforting them when their hearts get broken, which happens pretty much every fucking week. You make a go of it, Riana, she said to me all stern and serious when I told her about this call-back. You get out of this racket while you still can. And even though it was just Emily being all dramatic, looking at her then, eight o'clock and already smashed, I couldn't help thinking to myself maybe there was a bit of wisdom tucked away somewhere inside that pickled old brain of hers. I don't want to be like Emily come ten years. Drinking myself through the nights and telling people how to run their lives cos I never bothered to see what I could do with my own. I don't want to end up a nobody.

Right. One more good long breath and then I'm ready.

'It's like, the greatest thing that's ever happened to me. I'm just beside meself. Totally [bleep]ing stoked – oops, sorry . . . But I'm just so happy – I could kiss everyone in the whole [bleep]ing world!'

It's Mum who comes with me to the call-back. Once I got home on the day of the audition she started mouthing on about how work had called and said for me not to bother coming in tomorrow and what the fuck had I been doing with meself, not the littlest bit interested in what the answer might be. But when I finally got a word in, told her about the audition and them saying I was through, she changed her tune right smart. Suddenly she was going all girly, grabbing me and practically squeezing the life out of me, screaming on about how she knew I could do it and why the fuck didn't I say something cos she'd have come along too, if only she'd of known. Now here she is, hopping from one foot to the other and moaning on about how she needs a fag and why's it taking these judges so long to get themselves organised if all they have to do is sit behind a fucking table?

Do you think Baby's all right? I says to her, trying to distract meself from how painful these pointy shoes are that stylist gave me to wear – they're proper Jimmy Choos, so the pain's worth it, just about. We got one of Mum's mates, Fat Carol, to sit Baby. Fat Carol's so big she can hardly get through the door to our kitchen. Left Baby sleeping up in his room, but now I'm wondering if he starts crying whether she ain't gonna have a fucking heart attack trying to get up the stairs to reach him.

Oh, he'll be fine! goes Mum. Sent her a text five minutes ago and she says she ain't heard a peep. Now where's that geezer with the camera gone?

46

She caused a right scene earlier, insisting that this guy film her against the blue screen after he'd done me, acting all flirty like this contest was about her. Making a right exhibition of herself. I looked round and saw how all the other mums was stood in line with their daughters, all proper and respectable-looking, and meanwhile there's mine, no bra with her tits drooping out of her too-tight T-shirt and wearing a skirt no woman past forty ought to be seen dead in, trying her best to steal the show.

Here, says Mum, you don't half look funny the way she done you in there. Don't you wanna borrow some lippy?

Right pissed herself when I came out of the pop whatsit. I thought I looked all right when I went in there, but this make-up woman just rubbed it all off and started over. Took her fucking ages. And when she was done I looked at meself in the mirror and there was hardly even any make-up on me. The natural look, she said it was, though if you ask me it's more like the non-existent one. We're not trying to make you look like you're in Purrfect, she said, just trying to bring out your character. Fucking delete it more like.

Look, Mum, it could be ages yet. Just go and have another fag, I tell her.

She don't need no more persuasion. Off she goes, swearing she'll be back in two ticks, and not to do anything without her. I call after her to take her time. Embarrassment with a fanny, that's what she is.

I was hoping Wend'd come to the call-back with me, but she ain't been speaking to me all week. After I got through she didn't congratulate me or nothing, just went all silent and said she was going to get a later train back to Reading cos she wanted to go to Top Shop and look at the new Kate Moss stuff. Off she went without even asking if I wanted to tag along. She was s'posed to be keeping an eye on Baby Wednesday night so me and Mum could have a night out, but she didn't fucking turn up. I texted

47

her with me last bit of credit and didn't get no reply either. Fine, I figured, give her the benefit of the doubt – she's probably in hospital or has got some illness that's made all her fingers fall off. Then yesterday morning I see her in the park while I'm taking Baby for a walk with the stroller, talking to Davy, the two-faced bitch, who she knows perfectly fucking well we're meant to be ignoring cos of the way he treated me. Just standing there, smoking a fag and playing with her hair, all flirty, pretending she don't see me even when I go up to her.

All right? I go. What's up with you then?

Oh, hi Joni, she goes back, all casual and not taking her eyes off Davy, like I'm not even worth the effort of noticing. I was practically ready to fucking deck her right there and then, but I got Baby with me and even though he's only two I ain't committing violence in front of him.

All right, Joni, Davy went, smirking away. Heard you got through in that contest. You gonna be on the telly then?

I pretended like I hadn't heard him. Three whole months I went out with the bastard, and only to find he's been shagging that beast from the Shadwell estate, the type who's nothing but a walking bunch of welcome holes. Lucky I didn't catch fucking AIDS off him.

Listen, Wend, I went, deciding to lay it on the line, I know what your problem is and you can drop the act, all right? Just cos they chose me and not you it don't mean you got to act all high and mighty and not even answer me texts. It's life, that's all.

The ho still ain't looking at me though. Just goes, I don't know what you're talking about, Joni. I been busy, that's all, and bats her eyes at Davy enough times to cause a fucking wind.

She has all right! he went, winking.

At this point I lost it a bit, what with Davy with his winking and smirking and Wend pushing her tits out

48

at him and treating me like I was some piece of talking dog shit. Couldn't help meself. Didn't do nothing violent though, I still remembered I got Baby with me, just reached up and grabbed Wend's fag, threw it on the ground and stamped it out. That got her attention.

Oi! she screamed, that's me last one!

You know something, I said to her, I never thought of you as a loser but now I see it. Just cos you can't sing and ain't as pretty as me. Pathetic!

And I never seen Wend's face look like it did after I said that. All white and bloated like she didn't believe her ears. Like she was gonna try and have a go at murdering me right there and then. But before she could do nothing I just turned and walked off with the stroller, me head held high.

I felt good at the time but afterwards I didn't. Wend has been there for me through some tough shit. I've known her since we was at school and she's been a good mate. Why'd she have to go and start acting arsey, ignoring me and talking to that shithead Davy? Don't get me wrong, cos I am sorry she didn't get asked to the call-back. I don't know what went wrong in her audition, but it would of been real nice to both be here, getting ready to impress them. Maybe they'd even of let us do 'Tied Up For You', that one we always sing together. But the way Wend's been carrying on it's like she's got no integrity or something. I mean, can't she be happy for me?

Hello? goes this whiny voice from behind me, making me jump about a whole storey into the air. I turn round with me hand on me heart and fuck me if it ain't that nervous little mouse from last time, all pale and smiling up at me.

Jesus fucking Christ! I go. Don't sneak up on me like that!

I'm really sorry! she cries, going all frightened like she thinks I'm going to give her a slap for it. I didn't mean to startle you! I just wanted to come over and say hello!

All right, all right, no harm done, I tell her, and give her a grin to let her know I ain't really annoyed. That's the thing about these fragile types – you say one angry word and they think the whole fucking world is going to start shitting on them. I look her up and down. She's got this floaty pink scrap of a dress on that shows off her skinny frame. She looks beautiful actually, with her blonde hair all piled up and this silver band round her forehead, like a fairy princess from a kids' book or something.

Not bad, I say.

She gets these spots of pink in each cheek, which makes her look even more beautiful. Some girls get all the luck.

I couldn't believe what that woman was asking me to wear! she goes. There's hardly anything to it! But I didn't have the guts to refuse, and now I feel like I'm naked!

She lets out this giggle, a squeaky sound that's so high-pitched it makes it seem like everything's not completely right upstairs. I give her a look, since if she thinks that's skimpy she ought to see what me and Wend wear down to Utopia on your average Friday night.

You look great too, she goes quickly, I almost didn't recognise you at first! I . . . I don't actually know . . . what your name is.

Joni, I say, holding out me hand.

I'm Ella, she says. And I'm so glad to see you again. I'm . . . I'm not supposed to be here, you see. I ran away!

She gives another giggle, the sort of noise someone who's on the verge of having a fit might make. Fuck knows how she made it through to the call-back with a laugh like that. Must be cos she's so pretty.

Good for you, I says.

Are you here on your own too?

Nah, me mum's off somewhere, sucking on a fag.

Oh, goes this Ella, looking all downcast like she was hoping it'd be different, me on me own like she is. Looking at her I get this sudden protective feeling, a bit like what

I felt when I met her in the toilets at the audition. Some people are like that, make you feel like you got to take care of them. Must be genetic or something.

Attention everyone! goes this voice.

Me and Ella look round to see that miserable bitch from the other week, this time all dressed in yellow like a banana, holding her clipboard and waving at people. The whole room goes quiet as people listen like she's the queen.

The panel are ready for the second round of auditions, she goes. The girls who are in the contest please form a queue at this door behind me and you'll be told your order. Family and friends may sit in the audience and should go to the double doors to the auditorium over at the other end. We'll be starting in a few minutes, so please make sure you've got your songs prepared.

She turns and the room bursts into action, like this explosion of movement, girls hugging the people that came with them, mums and dads and friends shouting advice as they head off for the doors to the theatre, cameras being shoved in people's noses right, left and centre. It's like a fucking riot, but that's not what's got me ready to practically puke. I turn to Ella.

Songs?

Yes, you know, she goes, this time you've got to go the whole way through a song. There's a band who're going to play it while you sing. Didn't you get the email? You were supposed to let them know in advance.

You're shitting me! I go, but I can tell from her face that she ain't.

I know what's happened. Me and Wend have the same email address, which we both gave on our forms, but I don't check it that often cos our connection's been down since they cut off our phone the other month after Mum didn't pay the bill. Can't believe Wend didn't tell me, the cunt. I'm gonna have her when I get back, simple as that.

Next to me Ella starts to go on about how nervous she is, like it's not fucking noticeable already from the way her knees are knocking together all the time. Meanwhile I'm panicking big time. What the fuck am I s'posed to do?

Just then I see the woman with the clipboard passing us and so I throw meself in her path shouting Excuse me, miss! She seems to not hear me, just looks at her clipboard like it's the only thing important round here and tries to go round me like I'm not stood there waving right in front of her nose.

EXCUSE ME, MISS! I scream in her face and grab her arm so she can't just ignore me. She gives me this glare like she can't believe it. A real angel, this one. It's sad to see someone so bitter, especially considering she's probably only a few years older than I am.

What is it? she goes, yanking her arm away.

I start telling her about not knowing about the song cos I didn't get the email. It comes out all desperate and I find meself trying to explain about Wend and how she didn't tell me about it cos she's jealous, but it just sounds stupid, like I'm making it up. The woman stares at me with this look like she's listening to a nut job. She shakes her head.

Well, it's too late to check your song with them now.

I stare at her with me mouth open. So that's it. Me whole chance is messed up, just like that. Suddenly these tears are coming out of me eyes. All this effort and now fucked just cos of a stupid email. It don't seem fair, like Jesus hates me or something. So much for being a pop star.

Oh, for goodness sake, goes the woman with this massive sigh like she can't believe what an idiot I'm being. Just wait and see what songs the other girls are doing, and pick one of them. This isn't Auschwitz!

I start whimpering thank yous at her. I'm practically ready to tongue the gorgeous miserable cow. She rolls her eyes like she's never seen such a tard and pushes past me.

But I don't care. I'm back in the game and that's all that matters. The song I was gonna do is 'Genie in a Bottle'. Been practising it all week. There'll definitely be some other girl who's picked it too.

My heart racing like a fucking rollercoaster, I turn back to Ella at the same time as this tall black girl with a hairdo like Tina Turner barges into her, nearly knocking the skinny scrap of nerves flat on her face. Ella lets out the sort of noise a kitten might make if you booted it across the room and starts groping around blindly at the air. I catch her arms and pull her back to her feet.

Oi slag, watch where you're going! I shout after the black bitch.

She turns to face me showing lots of straight white teeth. Got a smile like a light bulb, this one. But her eyes are all wide and glistening too and she's got these tiny little shakes, so small you'd think she was just bored if you didn't know the signs. Straight away I can see she's fucked on something. You can always tell from the eyes. Unbelievable. Me ex-manager from when I used to work at The Garter, back before they fired me for drinking on duty, was a right druggy – all he did was pull pints and sniff lines. Used to be a bit partial to them meself, before Baby come along. Since I had him I try to only do sniff and pills on special occasions. You got to act responsible once you're a mum.

Sorry, sister! laughs this girl and dives back into the crowd.

What was that? says Ella, like she's just woken up.

I take her hand, since she's looking around all confused like she don't know the difference between an arse and a tit, and pull her with me into the queue by the door. You got to wonder where she even got the idea of coming to a place like this. I look round for Mum but can't see her. Probably on her tenth fag by now and flirting with the security on the door. Well, good. Hopefully they'll lock her out of the theatre.

Listen, I says to Ella, what song you doing?

Ella frowns then gives me this little hopeful smile.

'Petrified' by Cindy Shaw.

Bollocks, I think, cos I've never even heard of it. But looking at Ella it seems like it's a pretty fitting song, since petrified is the only way to describe how she looks. I try to think of other songs I know in case no one's doing 'Genie in a Bottle'. That fucking Wend!

Oh my God, I'm so nervous, goes Ella for the millionth time, like maybe I'd forgot cos she hadn't reminded me for a whole ten seconds, I feel like . . . maybe I'm going to be sick!

Don't you dare, I snap at her. She shuts her mouth and her chin wobbles like she's just been slapped.

Look, I say, feeling a bit bad, just close your eyes and imagine someone who you want to see you on telly. Someone you want to feel proud of you. Or else someone you hate who you want to prove you're better than.

Ella's eyes grow all huge for a minute, like she can't believe what an amazing idea this is. Then she shuts them all tightly and scrunches up her face. Since there's still no sign of Mum I figure I may as well give it a go meself, and so I close me eyes and try to imagine Baby a bit older, seeing his mum singing in Purrfect on *T4* with this crowd screaming and cheering all around me. But instead I find meself imagining Gav, Baby's dad. I'm seeing him all poor and down to his last Mayfair in some crappy run-down shithole, turning on the telly and suddenly seeing me on it, all sexy and glamorous. I'm picturing his face as he realises what a stupid bastard he's been. There's this big close-up of me doing a solo looking like a supermodel, and these actual tears are sliding their way down Gav's cheeks, for being dumb enough to let me go. Course it's nothing but a nice fantasy. Pricks like Gav, they don't even know how to cry.

The fact is I've no idea where Gav is or what he's up to now. Could be dead for all I know, though that's some kind of wish. Bastard took off right before Baby was born. There I was, preggers like a fucking mountain and about to go pop with no one but me mum to stand there and listen to me screaming me head off as he come out. Don't talk about pain to me – I had me heart broken same time as I pushed a baby out me twat. Nothing Davy could ever do is ever gonna match Gav. Owes hundreds in child support as well. Meanwhile poor old Baby's just another kid on an estate with some heartless fuckwit that don't give a shit for a father. Somehow it don't seem fair how some kids get born into families that are together and well off, like this fragile thing stood here next to me, while some just get stuck with no dad and no money like Baby. Guess it's the fault of slappers like me, for opening our legs without protection. Still, I'm gonna change all that. This is me shot at making things better.

Excuse me! Do you mind? That's my daughter over there! shouts Mum. I open me eyes and see she's pushing towards us through the crowd, shoving girls out of her way like skittles. I look at Ella, who's still got her eyes squeezed shut. She's smiling this daft smile, looking a total tard. Like to know who she's thinking of.

What the fuck is this one on? goes Mum as she reaches us, stinking like she's been rolling in an ashtray. Looks like she's doing voodoo.

'I am so thrilled to be here. This truly is the most amazing opportunity and I'm so incredibly happy to be among those lucky few who were chosen. I cannot wait to get up there and perform and prove why I should be put into *The Purrfect Search*.'

As the drum slows its beat I hold the last note, flattening my tongue against the bottom of my mouth so that it comes out pure and clean, right until the final set of chords from the keyboard. Then I let it go and drop my head like I rehearsed with Mr Field, as though I am nothing but a vessel which, having unleashed the gift of song, is now spent and empty. A second of pure silence follows, during which I don't know anything; if I've given a brilliant performance or effed it up completely. In that second, with my head bowed and staring at the stage, I don't even know if there's anyone in existence out there in the darkness behind the light. Then comes the applause, thunderous, like God himself is clapping, and I look up and smile, seeing rows and rows of shining faces materialising one after the other as the main lights come up. The most wonderful feeling is building up inside. It's as if my body's been set on fire. Every nerve is alive and tingling. It's beautiful, better than any feeling I've ever had before, better than any prize I've ever won, more exciting than any award I've ever been up for. It's rather like how I've always imagined that drug Ecstasy must feel.

In the front row, just behind the judges, Dad and Mr Field are standing and cheering for all they are worth, and I see Mr Field's wig has fallen to one side and he's so excited he hasn't even noticed. Mr Field ended up coming instead of Mum. Of course she wanted to be here, but then the nursing home called to let us know Gramps had had a mild stroke in the night so she had to go visit him instead. All the way up from Appledore he was prepping me, reminding me of all the stuff we've worked on, not just the vocals but how to make it look as though the music is actually torturing the song out of you. Like you're channelling God is how I think of it, though I didn't say so to Mr Field since I know he's not religious. He's a funny little man. But he knows his stuff. He didn't need to worry of course, because God's been prepping me for this performance since I was born.

At the judges' table Emma and Joe are clapping and beaming away like crazy people. It's only then that I notice that Tess has her arms folded and her head cocked to one side, as though she's in two minds about the whole thing. Of course it's not possible that my performance was anything other than stellar, but even so I feel a tiny shiver running up my spine. That shiver is enough to change everything in the space of a heartbeat. Suddenly the wonderful sensation in my body recedes leaving me feeling small and frightened. The loose, sack-shaped dress the stylist said would give my body 'the illusion of curves' feels like a funeral shroud. I didn't know what they were going to put me in and so I didn't eat anything all day in case it was tight-fitting round the stomach. Tiny stars dance about the corners of my field of vision and for a horrible minute I think I might actually faint. Frantically I try to remember Dad's technique for when you get overwhelmed after a performance and feel like you're going to collapse. I give myself a resounding mental slap, thrusting out my chest, forcing myself upright and pushing my shoulders back, casually allowing the finger of one hand to slip unseen inside a fold of material and pressing the nail of my index finger hard into the skin of my hip. Instantly I am wide awake and in control once more. The crane on the left side of the stage that holds the camera comes rushing towards me as though it's going to attack. It slows to a halt a few seconds before impact, at which point Stina Ellis seems to magically appear beside me. She throws her arm around my shoulders and yells into her mic.

'Well I think I can safely say that was *A*-mazing!'

You'd think that with a band as big as Purrfect they could have got anybody they liked to host. A real name, like Tess Daly or Dermot O'Leary. Even the first time, before anyone knew who Purrfect was or if they were going to be a success they managed to get Adrianna Monk. But this time it's just some blonde nobody whose feeble claim to fame is hosting a late-night gambling contest, one of those shows Channel 4 sticks on in the early hours of the morning when they've run out of proper programmes for people to watch. When Stina Ellis came in earlier some of the girls clustered around her and actually asked her for her autograph, as though she's a real celebrity. Probably she doesn't even know how to spell celebrity, she's that dumb-looking.

'What a beautiful voice you have,' Stina Ellis shouts, flicking her great mane of extensions to one side so she can flash me her horrible bleached smile. 'Louise, is there *anything* you'd like to say about your performance?'

I resist the urge to wriggle out from the arm clamped round my neck as though we're the best of friends and raise my mic back to my lips, preparing myself to get emotional. It's always been easy for me to cry. Just like with regaining control when you think you're in danger of losing it, there's a technique, but this time it's one I discovered all by myself – with a little help from God, perhaps. All I have to do is remember this dream I once had. It's of Mum wearing her apron and humming away to herself as she scrubs out the oven in our kitchen like she does every Saturday morning. That's her routine. Only when Mum stands up to rinse out the cloth in her bucket I see it's not Mum but me. And I suddenly realise I'm this fifty-year-old suburban housewife. That I'm this dull, fat middle-aged woman stuck in some dreary marriage, with nothing to do but clean and scrub and pin her hopes on the futures of her own kids because she messed it up back in the days when she had a chance to be something herself. It's the worst dream I ever had and it's my foolproof method for bringing out the tears. It never fails.

'I just want to say that this song was for Gramps,' I say, feeling the reliable old stinging sensation welling up in my eyes. I let my voice tremble as I go on. 'He's very sick, and I was thinking about him when I sang it . . .'

At this point I trail off, as though I'm too overcome to say anymore, and Stina Ellis emits a great 'Ahhh!' sound, as though I'm just the sweetest thing she's ever stood next to in her whole life. There's another great round of applause, even louder than before. I steal a glance at the judges and see Joe's face is shiny with tears as well. Killed it. Then Stina Ellis distracts everyone by going on about how brave I am and how proud my gramps must be, and how she knows just how I feel because she's had sick relatives before and nobody knows how much strength it took for her to go on telly for her idiotic late-night gambling shows when they were in hospital heaving out their kidney stones. Some man with a card is signalling to her to stop but she hasn't noticed, or else doesn't care. The silly bimbo has a mouth like a runaway train.

'Judges,' she says, when she's finally run out of inappropriate things to tell us about herself, 'do you have anything you'd like to say to Louise?'

Tess reaches out. For a minute I think she's stretching out her hand to me, but then her fingers close claw-like around a glass of water. She raises it to her lips and takes a slow deliberate gulp. Emma leans towards the little mic set up before her.

'I thought that was gorgeously sung,' she says. 'It's a bold and original choice of song, and I thought you sounded just great. You're a fantastic singer, Louise—'

The applause of hundreds of parents drowns out whatever else Emma might have to say. Tess looks very irritated and glances round at the audience as if they're nothing but a pesky nuisance ruining the serious work she and the panel are trying to do.

'Joe?' says Stina.

'Well, as you can see, I'm a sucker for Lena Malone,' says Joe, pointing at his streaming eyes. Stina lets out a guttural noise that I suppose is her version of a titter. 'But seriously, that was just magic. You've obviously got talent. It's not a song I would have picked to showcase your voice, but you did a great job. Just be careful not to overdo those long notes, that's all I'd say. Otherwise, simply superb.'

More cheering. I am suddenly filled with hatred. I want to hurt this Joe for actually daring to criticise my performance, which was a perfect repeat of the one I've been rehearsing with Mr Field all week. In the audience I see Mr Field's face contorting too, and I feel a surge of anger towards him as well. He was the one who insisted I should do it, despite the fact that Malone's voice is a million times lower than mine. I fight to keep my smile. You can't let a bit of hatred get in the way of graciousness.

We all look at Tess, who clears her throat and leans towards her mic.

'Yes,' she says in her nasty toneless voice. 'Watch it on the long notes. My worry with you, Louise, is that I'm not convinced you're really enjoying what you do. Your performance was good, but there's something very processed about it. I'm sure your granddaddy is very proud of you, but what I'm looking for is a bit of animation. Spontaneity. Purrfect are a group with edge, which is something that right now you don't possess.'

I can hear vague mutterings and booing from the back of the auditorium. Tess shrugs and leans back against her chair like she couldn't care less what the plebs behind her think. The hatred I was feeling disappears completely. It is replaced by a dull sensation: the dread feeling of rejection. Hot tears form in my eyes, this time out of my control, and I have to blink like mad to keep them from spilling out.

'Well!' shouts stupid Stina Ellis. 'I thought she was just *brill* and wish her the very best of luck! Ladies and gentlemen – that was Louise!'

Everyone claps again and I force my mouth into a smile of thanks and wave before making my way off to the side of the stage, to the special seating area for the girls who have already performed, who're now all on tenterhooks waiting to find out who has made it into the intensive five-week programme. I hold my head high as I take my seat. I can't look across at Dad and Mr Field. If I do I know, despite everything, I will lose it. I'm the best, I tell myself, no matter what that bitch and the little queer might say for the sake of the camera. God was on my side and my performance was flawless. It's a fact.

'And now, ladies and gentlemen – let's hear it for Joni!'

The next girl in line who was behind me in the queue back at the first audition comes on stage. The one with the foul mouth who insulted Dad for no good reason. I'm stunned to see her. Obviously they've lowered the standard this year, but I suppose they also have to think of ratings and she might be good for comedy potential or something like that. She stands there grinning like an idiot and looking across at the band, who are all stood waiting for her to present them with her music. After a couple of minutes of her just doing nothing Tess leans forward and taps her mic.

'Are you planning on actually performing something?' she asks coldly.

'Ah,' says the girl in her ridiculous annoying accent. 'Thing is I didn't get the message about the songs, see. The woman said I could choose one that'd been done already.'

'Not a very promising start, is it?' Tess rightfully remarks.

'It weren't my fault—!'

'Not interested in that,' Tess snaps, cutting the girl off before she has a chance to explain. 'Which song were you going to do?'

'I was gonna do "Genie in a Bottle",' says the girl without flinching. What is rather impressive is that she doesn't even seem embarrassed by the way she's holding everyone up and making an absolute effing idiot out of herself in front of all these people. 'Only no one else has done it . . .'

'Well,' says Tess with a nasty smirk, 'since you haven't okayed it with the band, you'll just have to do it without. Off you go.'

For a couple of seconds the girl continues to stand there, prolonging her excruciating humiliation. Then she suddenly raises her mic and launches into the Christina Aguilera number. After the first two lines a pretty girl in pink sitting beside me suddenly starts to clap to the imaginary beat. I turn to look at her, astonished, since there's nothing in this for her. The muscles in her face are pulled taut, and she's shivering. I wasn't concentrating much during her performance but I do remember she was a nervous wreck, staring straight ahead throughout her own song and hardly even moving. For a few seconds she claps the beat alone, and then, amazingly, it is taken up by more and more people, and soon the whole audience are clapping while the slut on stage parades up and down, thrusting her chest out and waving one hand around like a gladiator. She sounds nothing like Christina – her voice is far too husky and dry – but in a weird way it sort of almost works, I suppose. It's almost a pity she's messed up her chances. Not that *I'm* sorry, of course. She finishes with a great flourish, dropping to her knees as she sings the last line, her hand on her chest as though clutching an imaginary bottle. It's quite an effective end, though far too much. But the applause breaks out nonetheless and people start to cheer, and I look down and realise I've been clapping along with everyone else.

When the applause has finally died down Stina Ellis strides on stage and congratulates the girl on her 'amazing solo' which is 'unlike anything she's ever heard before'. The girl starts grinning stupidly again, as though she really believes what Stina says might be true. After some more ridiculously over-the-top congratulations Stina turns to the panel.

'So Tess,' she says brightly. 'What did you think?'

Tess glares at Stina Ellis. It's obvious she hates the stupid untalented bee even more than I do. She turns her head slightly and addresses herself to the idiot standing next to her.

'Failing to provide the band with a song is pathetic,' she says. 'Ordinarily that would disqualify you right away in my opinion . . . However, after a performance like that, I'm willing to make an exception. I'll say this for you, Joni. You've got guts. And guts is what I'm looking for.'

The theatre explodes into applause again. It's the first time Tess has actually said anything even vaguely positive and everyone knows it. I can hardly believe it. The girl has been let off the hook and she doesn't even seem to realise how lucky she is. She accepts more praise from Emma and Joe and then saunters towards the seating area like she wasn't expecting anything less. I watch her sit down next to the blonde girl who started the clapping in the first place and as she does she gives her a wink and the blonde girl blushes. Stupid effing bloody cees – don't they know they're competing with one another? Still, it doesn't mean this girl is going through. Of course Tess might say something like that for the camera to put everyone off the scent, but when it comes to the big crunch she's not going to even consider putting a liability like that into *The Purrfect Search*. This is for winners only.

'And now, ladies and gentlemen, please put your hands together for . . . Riana!'

The next girl comes on. I've noticed her at the first audition too, because she's tall and has ebony skin like Alek Wek. She looks a bit mannish to me, especially with the way they've brushed her hair forward so that it sits around her face like she's wearing a carpet on her head. But she's got a pretty good way of moving, hips swaying from side to side as if she really is a model, plus she's got a massive bust, which must help when it comes to getting people's attention. When she gets to centre stage she drops her head and points at the band. The conductor immediately waves his baton and instantly they start up, no introduction or anything. It's an attention-grabbing way to begin, and I don't know how she managed to pull it off. People all around are sitting up straight and taking notice, which is annoying but not what's got me shivering with horror. It's the words coming out of the big-boobed show-off's mouth.

'*Well baby, the penny dropped, I'm sooo in love,*' sings the black girl, swinging those hips like a pendulum and staring dead on into Tess's face as if about to put a bullet between her eyes. '*Ain't never gonna get rid of me – don't ya knooow?*'

My song. The girl doing my effing song, the one specially chosen for *me*, to show off *my* diversity. And what's more she's good. She's better than good. Her voice is deep and raspy but also rich and strong, much more suited to a Lena Malone number than mine will ever be. Why did I listen to that quacking fairy with his big ideas of what the judges would be looking for? I knew God was telling me to do another LeAnn Rimes number, or even 'I Will

Always Love You', which sounds incredible when I do it because I can go right up into my highest register. I grip the underside of my chair to stop myself from flying up the stairs and attempting to scratch the black bee's eyes out. I will God to make her slip over and snap her ankle in those impossibly high-heeled boots they've put her in, but she simply bounces around the stage as though they were the latest Skechers. When she finishes, pointing at the crowd with her hand on one hip and smirking, the applause is simply deafening. I look over at the judges where Emma and Joe are clapping away like mad as usual, and I see that Tess has also got both hands raised. To my disbelief I watch as almost in slow motion she taps them together a couple of times, nodding as though she's finally seen something she reckons was worth actually sitting through. The black girl takes a deep bow and Stina appears beside her. They smile huge white twin smiles at one another. As the judges give their verdicts, tell the girl how flawless she was, waves of hot and cold spread through my body like I'm having a fever. My vision blurs and all I can hear is an odd buzzing sound, like the static that you get off the television when you switch on to a non-channel. My song. She took my song and did it better than me. Why, God – *why?*

It's only when the lights go down and girls around me start standing up and chattering amongst themselves that I come to my senses. I look up, confused, to see that the black girl is now standing nearby, still wearing that big fat smile, and being praised by a trio of other girls.

'Excuse me,' I hear myself say, not knowing exactly who I'm addressing and feeling my cheeks flush because I hate asking people I don't know for help. 'What did they say just now? I missed it.'

'There's a thirty-minute break before they get us all back in to let us know who they want.'

It's the black girl who answers. She towers over me with her enormous grin, her ridiculous chest and her pitying, penetrating eyes. For a second I imagine lunging at her, knocking her flying and throwing myself on top of her and pounding that smug face over and over until those perfect teeth are lying in jagged fragments all about the room. But even if I wanted to there's no way I could take her on. She seems impossibly grand and muscular, like a chesty marine. Instead I mutter thank you and turn to look for Dad and Mr Field.

'Hey, didn't we do the same song?' says the girl, reaching out and touching my shoulder. I turn back, flinching without meaning to, and the girl's smile widens even more. There's something about the tone of her voice that tells me not only does she know the answer to her question perfectly effing well, she is in no doubt as to who did it best.

'It's just tense now really. Very, very nervous and very, very excited. I don't know what I'll do if it turns out they've not picked me. Go back to stripping, I guess. Maybe go on the game – hear there's big bucks to be made there. *Joking!* You'll edit that bit out, won't ya? Anyway, point is at least I'll be able to say I tried. That's the main thing.'

When we get out into the entrance hall the cameras are waiting for us like a welcoming party. Right away they start lining up girls and doing the old vox pop stuff. I'm one of the first to get grabbed and I listen to myself going on about how tense and exciting it is. Can't concentrate on what I'm saying, so I just show them lots of teeth and hope I don't sound like some yakking twat. It's cos I'm on such a fucking high. I was the only one that Tess bint clapped for, I noticed – *and* this little scrap of a human being with a choir girl's voice had gone and sung my song already. Thought it was over when I heard her launching into it. I went up to her and congratulated her after and said how we'd both done really well, hadn't we? and she smiled and nodded but in her eyes I could see she was pissed off. Then she just walked off, not saying anything about my performance, probably cos I was ten times better and she knew it. Known lots of girls like that. Mean. At the club they're the ones who always try and get out there first, making right tits of themselves trying to bag the rich-looking punters before the other girls get on the scene, never figuring out that it's always the punters who choose the girl, no matter how much you smile or pout or wave your bits around under their noses.

The camera dude moves on to this ginger girl who fucked up her song big time by forgetting the second verse. Poor thing trembles in front of them like she's got pneumonia, trying not to cry while her mum and dad stand off to one side, watching like the sight of her so upset is breaking their hearts. It's definitely a good thing Eddy's not here. Not just cos she doesn't approve, but also cos I wouldn't want her to see me like that. All pathetic and snivelling. It's good that I'm here on my own, even if I do seem to be the only one not surrounded by people screaming, weeping or shouting. If I don't get through to the show there'll be no one round to see me fail, and that's just the way I want it.

As I stand there watching all these nervous girls hugging their friends and families and stuttering to the camera, at the back of my mind I get this tweaking feeling and I know something's not quite as peachy as it could be. Like there's a tiny muscle in my brain that's seizing up, a muscle that needs to be stretched so it can relax. I know this feeling. Very soon it'll develop into the jitters and then there'll be tiredness and then it'll be impossible to ignore. Don't want to go back on stage crashing. Time to visit the old powder room again, give myself a little congratulations hit. I start making my way through the lake of misty-eyed girls and parents towards the ladies'.

I've finally managed to fight my way to a cubicle, and I've just carefully emptied out enough for a couple of lines when my phone goes. Shit! I think, realising that the damn thing's been on all this time. Lucky it didn't go off during my song or that'd have fucked the whole thing up, no question, something Eddy, I'm sure, would have been glad of. I hid it in my boot along with the blow when they said we couldn't keep our bags with us. The security woman assured me our stuff would be quite safe but I've heard that one before. Once lost fifty quid I'd collected in a routine by just putting it down on the table and taking my eye off it cos the party was getting a little too crowded down in my G.

Hey, says Eddy in that no-fucking-about way she's got. Thought I'd see how it went.

It's not over yet, I tell her, I did my song, but we've got to go back in a bit and find out who got through. They're going to line us all up on stage and film us screaming and breaking down when they tell us the news.

I don't know if that's the plan really, but I play the whole thing up for Eddy, cos I know it'll piss her right off. Sure enough there's this sound of a long breath being sucked up at the other end of the line. Her disapproving noise – recognise it anywhere, I've heard it so often. Sometimes I wonder what she's doing with me when everything I say or do is always such a massive let-down for her. But I know she loves me really. Otherwise she wouldn't be calling, would she?

Don't say nothing, I warn her. We've had that chat, remember?

That chat ended in me going on a three-day vow of silence after she told me that while stripping could just about be confused with empowerment in this day and age, if I started gyrating around on a stage as a pop star and pretending I was doing anything other than titillating men she'd lose all respect for me whatsoever. Talk about overplaying the feminist card. What's wrong with a bit of softcore anyway? is what I said. Sometimes Eddy is so fucking up herself you have to wonder where it all comes from. Some deep trauma, no doubt, probably involving a dirty uncle with happy fingers. Like Eddy won't happily sit there and watch the Pussycat Dolls when they're on telly creaming herself just like everyone else. Sulking's the only way to get through to someone like her, cos she can't deal with silence. Sure enough, when she got that I wasn't letting it go, she was the one who caved.

Fine, she sighs, clearly meaning anything but. How'd your song go?

Like a treat, I say, not able to keep the glee out of my voice. Apart from the ethical shit, one of the arguments she used when she was trying to get me not to come was that I'd only end up chickening out at the last minute. But if that's what she really reckoned then Eddy doesn't know me as well as she thinks she does, cos when I want something, I go for it. She still thinks it was her who started things between us. I let her believe it cos I know she likes to feel she's in control, but in actual reality it was none other than this bitch right here. For touching me, wiggling her finger against my thigh the way she did when I sat on her lap and pushed my brand-new tits in her face, I could have got her thrown out the club. Reason I didn't was cos I didn't want to, plain and simple. Cos I knew the second I laid eyes on her that I was going home with her that night, no matter what club policy or Emily's stories about girls that end up as sushi for psychos. Tall as me, big strong lips, catlike eyes, sexy as fuck. You just got to ignore the skull on her neck, which she had done when she was seventeen and too young to know better.

Huh, Eddy says, not sounding the littlest bit pleased for me, I *suppose* I should say well done. Was anyone in the audience actually listening to you?

At this I can't help but feel annoyed, cos Eddy never can let it rest, even when she's promised to. But I figure let it go, seeing as I'm starting to get jittery here and anyway, it's not easy for her. I know the biggest reason she didn't want me to do this isn't cos of the political shit, it's cos I said she'd have to stay in the shadows. When I get famous I'll talk us up every chance I get, shout it out to the whole fucking world, but till then the closet door stays shut. Not taking any risks. Maybe once the ball is rolling, if all goes well, then I'll admit to being bisexual and see how that goes down. Didn't do Angelina Jolie's career no harm, did it?

You be nice, I tell her, and maybe there'll be a happy surprise in store for you when I get home.

I make a couple of lapping sounds with my tongue, case she didn't get it. Eddy can't help chuckling. She's always saying how she can't get over the way I'm always up for it, like a career in stripping is s'posed to make you yawn when it's time to get it on. Well, you try taking your clothes off and bringing other people to the brink of orgasm for a living and see if it don't make you sexually frustrated. I'll tell you something about strippers: we're the horniest bunch of bitches alive.

Got to go now, I say, I'll let you know what happens. Kisses.

I turn the phone off. Time's running out, so using my little finger I scoop up as much blow as I can fit on my nail and stuff it up my nose. As I do the second nostril, there's a knock on the door and I freeze.

Excuse me, but are you gonna be much longer? calls a voice. You been fucking ages!

I quickly slip the blow back into my sock. I open the door and find myself face to face with the same girl who had a go at me earlier. Some council-estate type with a mouth like Vicky Pollard. She's got this weaselly sly expression on her face, like she reckons she's got something on me.

I know what you been doing, she says meaningfully. Any chance of a favour?

Don't know what you're talking about.

I think you do, she says, and I don't think it'd go down well with them judges to know about it neither.

The little pikey folds her arms and grins at me. I have a quick look behind her at the crowd of girls checking their hair and faces in the mirror. None of them seems to be paying us any attention so I grab this girl by the hand and yank her into the cubicle, yelling All right, I'll fix your dress for you! as I shut the door behind her. The girl rubs her hands while I slip the blow out from my sock once more.

Cor! she breathes, you got enough there to do a fucking army!

Shhhh!

Sorry. How'm I gonna do it?

I roll my eyes and reach into the bag with my little finger, taking another smidge on the underside of the nail, then hold it up to her face. The girl flinches away for a second, like she thinks I'm going to stick it in her eyeball. Then she takes hold of my hand with hers and pushes the finger right up her nostril. She places her own finger on the other one and snorts it like a fucking elephant. I cringe at the noise.

Jesus. You want everyone to know?

Thanks! goes the girl, totally oblivious, dabbing her nose. Wow – that's the stuff!

I got to go now, I tell her, slipping the packet back into my sock. The girl lifts the toilet seat and starts merrily hiking her dress up.

Sure thing – see you out there! she shouts.

Outside the cubicle I fight my way towards the mirror and check myself for signs. I look fine so far as I can see – better than fine. That tensed-up muscle in my brain's starting to relax and I can feel myself picking right up. How the fuck did that little bitch know I had the blow? Still, she seemed cool. Or if not cool at least like she knows how to handle herself. I kind of like the way she just did that in fact, barging in on the action like she had every right to. Like a girl with guts, I do, even if she does sound like she never passed an exam in her life. I give myself a final once-over and start shoving my way to the door.

Back in the entrance hall there's so much noise it's like Stansted airport. But it's not just the sound of all these girls being given pep-talks by their mums and dads, there's some guy over by the main doors shouting at the top of his lungs. I do some more shoving and head over to see what all the fuss is about. Everyone's stood back and is watching this furious-looking dad, who's pointing his finger at this little blonde sweetheart in a pink dress crying like a dog just shat on her Manolos.

You listen to me! he's yelling. We expressly forbade this! And don't think by crying and trying to make me look like the bad guy you're getting away with it! Go and fetch your clothes this instant. We're going home!

The girl doesn't move. She just stands there shaking, her arms dangling at her sides, like she's slipped into an upright coma. The camera dude that filmed me doing my twirl outside the pop boutique pushes into the circle just in front of me and points his camera at the angry dad. Behind him the sound geezer appears and swings his boom over the heads of people around him. The dad stares at them like he can't believe his eyes.

You get that fucking camera out of my face! he shouts. There are several gasps from the parents at the word fucking, but this dad doesn't give a shit.

I'm not part of this travesty and you don't have my permission either!

He carries on shouting at the crew, who back away without a word but continue to shoot, as if he's some rare species of animal they're documenting for the Discovery Channel. I'm fucking warning you! he shouts, coming at them with his fists up. He's gone bright scarlet and there are veins bulging out at his temples. Spite of this he's quite cute. One of those metrosexual types that obviously believes in moisturising and taking care of his skin, since he don't look nearly old enough to be the girl's father. If only more of my clients at the club bothered with that sort of thing, the job'd almost be a pleasure. If metrosexual types is what did it for me, that is.

Please . . . says the girl, please . . . Jack!

This is your last chance to get that fucking thing away from me!

The camera crew calmly carry on shooting, and the man suddenly looks at his feet. Boringly it looks as though he's got a grip. Then he raises up his fists again and loses it completely. He lunges at the camera. Before he can reach it the sound geezer steps between them holding the boom out in front of him. Now listen . . . he starts to say, but he's cut off by the dad as he charges into him, sending them both flying into the crowd, which immediately moves out the way so that they land on the carpet on top of each other. The boom pole thumps down next to them.

Stop it . . . just stop it . . . the girl in pink is moaning.

Get the . . . off me! the sound guy is yelling as the dad twists his arm behind his back and then sits on him like a school bully, pushing his head into the ground with one knee.

I warned you! pants the dad.

For a minute everyone just stands around gawping at them and not lifting a finger to help. The camera guy is still filming as the dad grinds his buddy's face into the carpet. Disgusted cos of how pathetic everyone is, I leap into action-mode. I jump forward and tug at the crazy dad's shoulder, trying to get him away from the poor sound geezer who's now making these noises like he's gone into labour.

Get the fuck off him, you bullying bastard!

There are more gasps from all the parents. Now I'm no soft touch, but rage has made this guy strong as a fucking ox. The mother cunt shakes off my grip with a single shrug and then without even looking shoves me backwards with his arm. I land on the carpet flat on my arse. I'm about to go at him with teeth and nails when the miserable-faced woman with the clipboard arrives on the scene with two beefy security guards.

Excuse me! she screeches at a couple of gormless parents who are in her way filming the attack with their mobiles. Without waiting for them to move the security guards push them to the side and march forward like SS officers. They each take one of the crazy dad's arms and yank him off the poor spluttering sound geezer.

You can't do this! the man shouts. I've got rights! You've infringed them! Ella! Where's Ella?

Get him out of here! orders the woman. The security guards start tugging the dad through the crowd. Everyone's just talking in whispers like they're not s'posed to speak out loud. The camera dude follows the security guards, still shooting the angry dad as they take him out the doors of the entrance. The woman with the clipboard crouches next to the sound geezer. Apart from the purple colour he seems to be fine, and far more worried about his mangled equipment than maybe being concussed. Total fucking idiot, he mutters, flipping all these toggles on the box that connects to the boom. The woman stands up again and clears her throat. Everyone stops whispering and goes silent.

Right, everybody, show's over! she declares. I want friends and family back in the auditorium and girls to start lining up at this door. The judges will be delivering their verdict in ten minutes.

Instantly the room explodes into noise and movement.

'I feel . . . nervous. I never felt so nervous before! Not even the night before a test when I know I haven't revised enough. This means absolutely everything to me . . . If they don't pick me I don't know what I'll do!'

Jack's waiting in the car. His hands are resting on the wheel and his head is drooping over his lap like he's lost the will to live. I'm shaking with every step I take, but I keep on going and climb in beside him, leaving the door open. We sit there in silence for a while, during which I realise that he's shaking too. It suddenly seems funny, both of us quivering away like this, especially after what's just happened, and before I know it I'm giggling. Once I've started I can't stop, and the next thing Jack's giggling away like mad too. He lifts his head and I catch his eye and suddenly it's just like old times, the days when he'd pick me up after school and drive us to the common and we'd sit in the car looking out over the green and telling jokes about how rough our days had been. It's been so long since we laughed together, and it's so nice, I want to reach over and hug him. But I don't. I know that if I do he'll just draw back like he always does when I touch him, like I've got an infectious disease. Thinking about this makes me stop giggling, and gradually so does Jack. Then we're back to an awkward silence again.

'That was the absolute worst!' he says finally, giving me a weak and exhausted grin. 'I'm really sorry, Ella. I lost it big time back there. I . . . I don't know what came over me. I just completely saw red.'

'It's OK,' I say, wanting to sound strong and grown up but hearing my voice come out in the usual pipsqueak it turns into when I'm nervous. Jack seems satisfied though. He turns back to the wheel and starts the ignition.

'Close the door and put your seatbelt on,' he says.

I don't move. Down the street I notice a ticket inspector is checking the windscreens of parked cars. She's wearing one of those fluorescent jerkins which stands out like a streak of yellow fire against her dark skin. It's quite similar to an Armani one I saw in a recent issue of *Fascinate!*

'Come on, Ella, I haven't got time to mess around,' says Jack, putting on his pretend-grumpy voice, the one he uses when he's trying to get something done quickly with as little fuss as possible. He casts a hopeful look at me.

'But I've got to go back inside,' I say slowly, trying to enunciate each word so it sounds like I mean it.

'Forget about your clothes!' Jack cries. 'We can return that dress another time. Or else just keep it! I don't suppose they'll care, will they? You should keep it. It looks . . . it looks good on you.'

He gives me another grin, but I can see that it's desperate, that he knows perfectly well I wasn't talking about collecting my clothes.

'I have to go back inside to find out if I made it through,' I say. Even though my voice is still quivering, I think there's a hint of strength in it. A hint of Rita's no-shit-taking. The tiniest little bit, but there nonetheless.

Jack loses his grin. He turns back to look at the street. The female inspector is just a few metres away from us now, making notes on her pad about the blue car in front of us. Her expression is tired and bored, like she's been doing this job for years and years and is truly sick of it. I suppose it can't be much fun walking up and down streets, checking to see if people have paid to park and then writing out tickets if they haven't. I wonder how she gets up the energy to go to work every day? If that were my job I'd probably just end up at home, lying there all day depressed, staring at my fluorescent uniform and getting fat on Maltesers and yoghurt bars.

'I was good, Jack,' I say. 'I was really good!'

I can see he doesn't believe me. But the thing is, it's true. I was incredibly nervous when I went onstage, so much so that my knees kept hitting each other from all the shaking I was doing. I kept trying to think of myself as a character in a film, like Baby in *Dirty Dancing*, or Lauryn Hill in *Sister Act II*, doing what I had to despite what my family thought because song and dance was in my blood and one day the whole world would be changed by watching me perform. Then I got onstage and it was like nothing I'd ever experienced in my whole life. All these faces and bright lights, all aimed directly at me, watching and waiting. I thought I was going to have a seizure, that they'd have to get paramedics in to remove me from the stage. I could see Tess folding her arms impatiently at the judges' table, her mean old face unimpressed, and suddenly I thought to myself, You've got to try. Even if you fail, you've got to have a go. Otherwise there's nothing. As I began 'Petrified', which is a song I love because I know just how Cindy Shaw felt when she sang it, all frightened and alone, the nerves – they just vanished! It was amazing, like the audience suddenly ceased to even exist and I was on my own in my room, singing to the mirror the way I always do when no one else is home. And afterwards Emma said I was really good and Joe said that I made him really believe in what I was singing about. And Tess said I was stomachable. It felt just amazing.

'Look, Ella,' breathes Jack. His hands have tightened on the steering wheel and turned white around the knuckles. 'What is this about? Do you want to tell the world about us? Do you want me to get charged with statutory rape and go to prison? Are you trying to punish me? Is that it?'

I'm shocked. Shocked by the idea, shocked by the way he says this, shocked that he might actually believe it.

'That's not it at all!' I cry. 'I just want—'

I stop. I can't say what I want, because it'll only sound daft, and I know Jack doesn't want to hear it anyway. He's not interested in the real reason I'm doing this, only in how he can stop me. But what I want is for him to put his hands on me again, like he did back when we would sit side by side in the car at the edge of the common, on my shoulders, on my breasts, on my knees, before sliding them up to my pussy as he gently presses his lips to my lips, his face prickling ever so slightly against mine from a day's growth of stubble. I want him to grin when I act as though it hurts and for him to promise he'll shave if only I'll touch it, just quickly, just for a minute. I want to hear him groan as I take it out of his pants and hold it with both hands, revealing the dark red part that looks like a turnip. I want to feel him shudder as I put my tongue to it and run it over the little slit at the top, which always reminds me of a baby rosebud. I want to hear him whisper my name as his stuff shoots out, making me scream and then sit back giggling and telling him off for not holding it for longer. I want to see his eyes full of love for me as we sit in silence afterwards, not the awkward silence we have now, but the gentle, knowing silence we used to share, smoking forbidden cigarettes I'm not allowed to inhale while our hearts beat loud and hard because we know what the world doesn't, which is that we belong together.

'For God's sake, Ella!'

He suddenly turns to me again. He's got this horrible look of panic on his face, like he's a wanted man and I'm the reason he's going to get caught. I stare into his eyes. Jack's got eyes like no one else in the whole world. They're deep blue, almost violet, with massive black pupils no matter how light it is, and when he looks at you – and I mean properly looks – those pupils seem to draw you inside. I feel my heart begin to flutter.

'Don't you see that if you do this it'll all come out?'

'No!' I say. 'Nothing'll come out! I won't tell them anything!'

'You're not good with people, Ella – you're going to be under a lot of scrutiny. Don't you see what the consequences will be? For both of us? They'll say I took advantage of you! And that you . . . that you need help.'

I force my eyes to break away and look at the road. He's wrong. Poor Jack. He just doesn't get it. This is something I have to do. I take a slow breath of air, preparing myself. In front of us the inspector finishes her writing and leans over the windshield of the next car along to slide a ticket under its wiper.

'Do you love me?' I say.

'What?' cries Jack, obviously thrown by the question. 'Of course I do! How can you even ask a thing like that?'

I turn, hope flooding into my heart. But then I see his face and my hope dies like a puppy blown to smithereens by the shotgun of reality. He doesn't mean it. Not the kind of love I'm talking about. The kind of love we used to share. He just means he loves me as a person, that's all.

'I've got to go now,' I say.

'Absolutely not!' shouts Jack.

He puts his foot on the accelerator and turns the wheel sharply. The car lurches into the road then stops as it slams jarringly against the rear light of the car in front, sending my forehead walloping into the dashboard. Pain rushes into my temples and I let out a little scream. The traffic inspector jumps back, staring at us wide-eyed with surprise.

'Close that door!'

But I'm already climbing out. Jack suddenly reaches out and grabs me by the wrist, trying to yank me back into the car.

'Let go of me!' I scream. Immediately the ticket inspector leaps into action and starts to hurry towards us. Jack's grip loosens and I pull free. I leap out onto the pavement and start running, ignoring the inspector as she opens her mouth and asks if I'm all right, passing her and racing for all I'm worth towards the studio. I run through the entrance hall. At the far end the girls are all queued up outside the door that leads to the stage area, listening to the woman in the lemon Chanel two-piece, who's giving them instructions. Blocking my way are the men who were filming earlier, the ones that Jack attacked when he lost it.

'Hey,' says the guy with the microphone pole, 'where's your dad? He nearly bust my DAT!'

'I'm sorry!' I cry, not knowing what else to say, knowing that if I don't join the queue I'm going to miss it and then it'll all be over.

'Listen,' he says. 'Can we get a quick sound-bite?'

'A sound-bite?' I'm distracted and confused. 'What about?'

'Just about what happened. And how you're feeling.'

The man with the camera is already filming. My head hurts. I wonder if I've got a mark from where I hit the dashboard, and if they can see it. I start talking, apologising for Jack, telling them stuff about how I feel and not even knowing what is coming out of my mouth. Ahead the woman is opening the door and ushering the girls through it. I have to go. I give the camera a big smile, the sort of smile I imagine one of the girls from Purrfect might give in this situation, when everything has gone wrong but she still has to act like a professional and get the job done. The sound guy asks me another question but I don't answer and run to the back of the queue.

I scan the line for Joni as they file in, but there's no sign of her. She must have already gone inside. I slip into place at the back. Nobody pays me any attention, including the Chanel woman who's busy writing things down on her clipboard. My forehead throbs and I reach up and tug at my hair, loosening some strands so I've got something to cover it in case there's a bruise forming.

'Excuse me?' I whisper to the super-skinny girl wearing the Debbie Gee peasant dress in front of me. She turns round, looking annoyed. 'What's going on?'

She gives me a deeply scornful look, as if she's already decided I must be a lost cause. It's the sort of look I'm used to getting, that I get from all the teachers at school and from Rita at home whenever I make the mistake of trying to ask her a sensible question about the magazine.

'We're going onstage,' she says slowly, like she's talking to an idiot, 'to find out who's got through.'

The woman in the Chanel utters a harsh 'Shhh!' in our direction and the girl glares at me like I've made her look bad. I follow her, a couple of steps at a time, past the woman and through the door, into the room behind the stage where we're met by another camera crew. The woman enters behind us and splits us into two groups to enter from either side of the stage. I spy Joni on the opposite side, standing next to the tall black girl – the one who almost knocked me flying earlier – and chuckling about something with her. I try to catch her eye but she doesn't seem to notice me. She looks excited and confident, pleased with herself even, her eyes all bright and shining. I wish I could feel like that. I can barely admit it to myself, but I'm even more scared than I was when I did my song, which is ridiculous because that was the hard bit. All we have to do now is stand there and listen to what they say about us. But I keep thinking of Jack, of that desperate look on his face and about how I screamed at him to let go of me when he tried to stop me getting out the car. I've never screamed at him before.

A horrible feeling lurches through my stomach and I fold forward, crouching and dropping my head between my knees, wrapping my arms around my legs tightly.

'What's the matter with you?' says the skinny girl next to me, in this accusing voice, as if she thinks I'm doing it just to get attention. She sounds a lot like Mimi. I feel a pressure against my back which I realise must be her hand. In the background some pop music has started up and there's lots of movement as the girls start to file out onto the stage. From behind the wall comes the applause. It sounds like a hundred angry lions roaring for blood.

'Breathe deeply,' says the girl suddenly, in an unexpectedly kind voice. 'Long, slow and deep.'

I concentrate on doing what she says. I see Jack's deep blue eyes and those blacker-than-black pupils. For a minute I have the sensation of falling, and I realise I'm probably fainting and that's it, the competition is over for me, but then I open my eyes and find the girl has tugged me to my feet and is gently but firmly pulling me towards the stage entrance. Before we go on she puts her arms around me and gives me a quick hug. 'Come on,' she says, 'let's go out there and face the music!' As she pulls back I see the camera behind her filming us. The lens looks like a single massive unblinking eye. Reflected in its black pupil is a white face under blonde hair, with this expression of sheer terror. Petrified. It's only a few seconds later, as we're ascending the steps to the stage, that I realise it was me.

'Oh my God! Words don't go near telling what I feel right now! I'm like, so happy I can't even see straight. This is the most amazing and best thing that's ever happened to me! All I can say is ARGHHHH!'

All the train ride home I sit watching the fields pass by in this weird trance, like someone's slipped me a Val. I'm in a total daze because of the fact that a week today I'm gonna be travelling back up to London to stay in a posh house and take part in this programme. They picked me – out of all them girls, they reckoned I was one of the ones who got the potential to be in Purrfect.

Mum makes up for me being quiet by not shutting her trap the whole way back to Reading. When I got out of the theatre she was waiting for me in tears, and just threw herself at me like a mad person, all shrieking and crying. But for once I didn't give a shit about what an embarrassment she was being cos I was crying and shrieking too, and we stood there letting the cameras get a good shot of us acting like tards and not caring one bit. Even that face-ache in yellow had something that almost looked like a smile on her mug, and said congratulations when she handed me the contract.

When I get back to the flat it turns out Mum's texted everyone on our block and there're all these friends of mine waiting round our place. Fat Carol's in the living room already, holding party-poppers and vino. Some of them I ain't seen for ages. There's Mel T and her hubby Johnny, there's Tuff on her crutches from that accident she had falling down the stairs at Grouchy's the other night, and Mel G with her new short spiky hairdo that from behind makes her look like a bloke, there's Georgy and her boyfriend Ted, who's this big black fella I ain't met before with tatts all the way down his arms like he's wearing sleeves on his skin. There's even Irene who no one's seen since October, not since she got the job down at that posh bar on Evan Street and started working nights. They're all here cos of me, and as soon as I walk in the door they shout out Congratulations! altogether in this chorus and start lining up to take turns at hugging me.

Couldn't happen to a more deserving girl! shouts Fat Carol, handing me a glass. Come on everybody – hip hip hooray!

And off they all go. I've never thought of meself as much of a crier, but at this point my eyes start pouring with tears like I've sprung a fucking leak. I can't help it, and it just gets worse, especially when Mum fetches down Baby and everyone starts telling him how his mum's gonna be famous while he looks at all these people around him with them big innocent eyes of his, no clue what's going on at all.

There's only one thing that's missing, which is Wend. I'd sort of hoped she'd text me to wish me luck today, and that she'd do what she always does after we've had a bust-up and pretend like the last week didn't even happen. A right proud cow, she is. But I wouldn't of cared, even if she had of done. I'd of just acted like it didn't happen neither. Cept she ain't done that. It's like a cloud hanging over the party and I keep thinking about her and wishing she was here too. After a few glasses I get nostalgic, so I send her a text saying I hope she's all right and let's meet up for a last night out before I go to London. Don't get no reply.

Word spreads faster than an STD in this neighbourhood. The next day me phone don't stop bleeping with calls and texts from people I ain't spoke to for yonks, all wanting to congratulate me and tell me how excited they are about me being on TV. When I pop down the local everyone's all over me, buying me drinks and telling me how I'd better not fucking lose cos they're all placing bets on me. I feel like a proper celebrity. But I don't let it all go to me head. I know that just cos I'm into the house don't mean I'm in Purrfect yet. There's some serious competition out there and this is no time to be getting smug about things. I only have a couple and then I head right on home and do some singing in me room while Mum watches TV with Baby. And for the first time ever she don't bang on the ceiling and tell me to put a lid on it. Instead she brings me up a cup of tea and says I sound like an angel.

Monday afternoon I'm just heading down the shops for some milk and some of that apricot baby food Baby loves, and who should be there but Davy, leaning against the wall with a fag in his mouth and his hands in his pockets, all casual like him hanging out on my block is just a coincidence. When he sees me he spits out the fag and gives me this big shit-eating grin.

All right, Joni? he goes.

I just carry on walking but he jumps in front of me. When I try to go round him he shoots his arm out and leans it against the wall so he's completely blocking me way.

D'you mind?

Listen Joni, he goes, I'm really sorry about that thing with Shea.

Why's that then? I go. Give you the clap, did she?

I mean it! he goes. Look, Joni, I've been thinking about us over and over, and about what I did to you with that Shea. I know you can't forgive me. And I don't expect it neither. But if you'll give me the chance I just want to explain.

He's giving me this sort of look like a puppy might make what's drowning in a bucket of water. The sort of look he was always giving me when we was together, when he wanted me to spot him a fiver or cook him a fry-up. Always fell for it too. A right mug, I am.

I ain't interested, I tell him. Now can you get out of the way, please?

Davy does a sad slow nodding thing with his head and turns away from me. But watching him trudge away all dejected like that suddenly gives me this urge to know what he's got to say for himself. Back before I found out what a cheating bastard he was, I was having a good time with Davy. He's fun to be around. He don't ever lose his temper, and he makes you laugh, too. I've always had a bit of a soft spot for jokers, something about how vulnerable they is on the inside. He's got a decent-sized cock too.

All right, I go. Let's hear it. Should be good.

Davy turns and comes back with his eyes all shining. He starts telling me stuff about how he only went with that Shea a couple of times and they was only cos he was drunk and she was throwing herself at him – like he didn't have no choice in the matter. He tells me that he always loved me but he got frustrated cos I had Baby to take care of and couldn't always come out with him. He says that he knows it don't excuse his behaviour or nothing, but he's sorry for it and he just wants me to know that. It's dead weird, cos I've never heard Davy apologise before. It even sounds almost like he means it.

Okay then, I say after some considering.

Davy breathes out this great big gust of relief and gives me another big grin like I've just said yes to a blow job.

Oh Joni, he goes, I'm so glad! I never thought you'd—

I've heard you out, I butt in before he can say anything else, so see you round.

Davy's face goes all puppyish again, but he nods like he knows it's only what he deserves and starts to trudge off down the block. When he reaches the corner he turns like he's suddenly remembered something and shouts back, I heard you're going through in that contest – just wanted to say good luck! Then he disappears round the corner. I can't help thinking it was nice of him. To come here and say all that, especially what with me heading off to London next week. It don't mean he ain't a prick and a piss-taker, but at least he's man enough to come and say sorry. Even if it is a whole fucking month late. But it gives me a good feeling, like that's something I don't have to feel bitter about no more. Closure – that's what they call it, ain't it?

Thinking about this closure business, that's when I realise I gotta go see Wend before I leave. Don't want to go to London with this bad stuff hanging between us. I figure I'll go to the shops the long way round and stop off at her block.

When I get up the stairs to Wend's floor the door's open so I go right on in and find her mum Pam in the kitchen cooking noodles. Wend hates her mum cos of the way she looks. She reckons it's all Pam's fault for giving her short and tubby genes, but it could just have easily have been her dad's, since she's never met him and don't know what he looks like. Pam's a nice lady, but it's true she does like to eat. She used to be good friends with Mum back when me and Wend was growing up, till they had this stupid fall-out over who was meant to be paying for a round of drinks at some wedding bash a couple of years ago. It's sad really, but it turned out that was just one of hundreds of other moans Pam'd stored up against Mum over the years that she'd known her, like stuff Mum'd borrowed and never returned, times when Pam'd looked after us when we was kids so Mum could go out which Mum hadn't ever done for her, and these fat jokes Mum was always making about her. They never made it up, and now whenever they see each other in the shops or on the street they both make this big show of lifting their noses up and looking in the opposite direction like they've just smelled a ripe fart. It's a good thing Pam has a different local cos I'd hate to see what they'd be like if they saw each other after getting a few drinks down them, specially Mum, who gets a bit rowdy. Luckily Pam don't hold her moans about Mum against me, and when I come in she lets out a little scream and throws her little arms round me. Turns out even she knows about what's happened.

And to think, she goes when she's finished crushing me, I used to look after you when you was just a little one. You and my Wend, eh? You here to see her?

I nod and she smiles and tells me she's been miserable and sitting in her room all week. Too proud to say she's sorry, that one of mine, she goes, and gives me this meaningful look, like in case I don't know who it is she's really talking about. I shrug, since me and Wend have long since given up trying to get her and Mum to be friends again.

You go see her and I'll bring you in some tea, offers Pam.

I go through to the hall and knock on Wend's door. There's no answer so I just open it. She's on the bed against the wall, smoking and holding an ashtray so stuffed with fag butts she must've been chaining it all day to get it so full. The whole room's cloudy from the smoke too. I wave me hand in front of me face and say Cor, where's the fire? but Wend don't even look up at me. She just carries on staring straight ahead and chuffing out the smoke. After a pause like a century I go in and sit down on the end of her bed. Out of the speakers is coming 'Tied Up For You'. Our song. It's cos she's listening to that that I know that it's not just me and she really has been feeling shit about how things have got between us.

Heard you got through, Wend says finally, in this scratchy voice.

Yeah, I say.

Well done. You must be real happy.

She stubs out her fag on the mountain of butts and reaches down for her Mayfairs. She takes out another and after thinking about it offers me the packet.

Help yourself.

I'd better not, I say. Got to take care of me voice now, don't I?

Wend makes this frown and looks away. Right away I feel like a bitch for saying that, like I'm rubbing it in about me getting through and not her.

What the fuck? I go. I reach out and take out a fag. Wend lights it for me. More smoke wafting round the room. Suddenly I start coughing away like I'm choking on me own tongue, only it's not really coughing it's more like crying.

I'm sorry! I go.

No, I'm sorry! goes Wend. I've been a right fucking arsehole!

Next thing we're all over each other like a couple of lezzer grannies, clutching each other and stroking each other's hair and faces, saying stuff like how much we love each other and how we're never gonna fight again, which even being all emotional I know is pretty fucking wishful. But that nice feeling I got from when Davy apologised before is back. Suddenly everything is wonderful. I think of me life stretching out ahead of me and it seems so exciting and full of possibility. Right there and then on that bed is like the best moment ever, better even than hearing the judges say me name yesterday, or the first time I got shagged and found out it didn't just have to be the fellas who had a good time.

Hey, what you gonna do about Baby? says Wend finally, snapping me out of it, as she lights up another fag. D'they know you got a little boy?

I take a deep swallow cos I don't know what Wend's gonna think about this. What we decided, me and Mum, is that from now on Baby ain't gonna be my little boy anymore. He's gonna be hers. Those judges ain't gonna be interested in no teenage mum, she said, and the fact is she's got a point. When you're a parent you come with baggage. Can't just up and leave on tour to sing round the world, or go out and meet the right people, not when you've got a toddler waiting for you at home what needs feeding and cuddling and playing with and putting to bed. Course it's only temporary, just until the whole thing is over. And anyway, it's all for his sake in the end. Ain't like it's gonna change how I feel about him or nothing. It don't mean I'm not still his mum really.

Wend listens without interrupting while I explain it to her. I'm a bit worried cos of the way she's all silent that she's gonna start shaking her head and getting all moral about it, like she's some snow-white virgin who's never told a lie in her life. But when I've finished she gives this thoughtful nod and says if I want she don't mind looking after him for a bit while I'm away. I don't say yes, just give her another big hug.

The week passes in a blur. I'm so excited I can't seem to concentrate on anything proper, not even when I'm with Baby. I just keep thinking about what it's gonna be like in London, doing this competition. I end up doing loads of shit about the house to try and take me mind off it. I even clean out the oven, which is a real chemical job cos it ain't been touched since back before time began. Mum can't believe her eyes. When Baby's not asleep I get in a bit of singing practice, and when he is I plug in one earphone to the CD player and try and memorise lyrics. The information in the notes I got given by the face-ache says how each week all the girls have to sing a number and then the judges will vote one of them off. It don't say what numbers you're gonna get, but it's best to be prepared, I reckon.

Friday night I run into Davy again outside the toilets in Utopia. I'm out with Wend, Irene and Mel G to have a long-overdue get-down and a bit of a celebration. It's Wend's idea, since I'm gonna be pretty much cut off once I get to London, if what them notes say is anything to go by. Once you're in the house, phone calls and visits will be privileges that get decided on by the organisers and 'not subject to negotiation'. On Sunday this camera crew's coming to film me on me last day, saying goodbye to all me mates and getting sound-bites off of them about what I'm like. I've told everyone that if they don't say nice things about me I'll go round their houses and fix their noses for them.

So I'm just on me way out of the ladies' after taking the pill Mel G got me as a goodbye pressie, when I run right into Davy at the condom machine. He's giving it a right kicking and is swearing at it for not giving him his condoms and sucking up his change. He ain't seen me and I know I ought to probably just keep on going, but since we're friends now, sort of, I can't resist going up to say something.

Planning to get lucky? I says in his ear. He jumps about a foot in the air and whirls round, a real comedy-classic moment. I can't help grinning at the look on his face.

Hey! he goes, like he can't believe it's me.

It's all right, I say, I ain't gonna have a go. Nice to see you.

And I mean it. I ain't changed me mind about the apology. It's the nicest thing any man's ever done for me, to say sorry like that, which obviously don't say much about the men I been with, but still. It's something. Davy looks good too, well turned out, for a change. He'll pull tonight, no question, if that's what he's come out for.

I turn to go but Davy reaches out and stops me. When I look back at him he straight away drops his arm and gets all dappy.

It's nice to see you too, he goes. You look good.

Just good? I says. I can feel this flickering at the base of me spine. It's the pill kicking in. In a second I'm gonna need to get out there on the floor and dance like a maniac, but I can't resist teasing Davy just a bit. As a matter of fact, I've got a naughty little urge to give him a quick snog. He grins at me.

Like a fucking goddess.

That's better! I say. I give him a wink and head out to the bar. Irene's just shelled out on cocktails for us all, which is pretty enormous considering how tight she is. Must be the punters from that posh place rubbing off on her. We're about to do a toast when all of a sudden Purrfect's latest single comes on – 'Or Die Trying'. That's the best one to dance to, the one with the crazy deep bassline that makes you do sexy things no matter how bloated or spotty you're feeling. There's a special set of moves that go with it, too. Me and the girls all let out screams, down the cocktails and bundle onto the dance floor, really working it, pushing people out of our way and doing Purrfect's routine to each other. The whole time I'm thinking, one day I'm actually gonna be onstage singing this song with the real deal. One day this song's gonna be mine. And I start going for it like I've never gone for it before, imagining that Irene on me right is Fina and Wend on my left is Monique, and we're all in the band together, working it for the crowd. I'm properly giving it some, letting me hair flick around me face and weaving me hips in and out when this fit guy catches my hand and makes me do a twirl before yanking me in close. And it's only as he does, and the song comes to an end and he's leaning down towards me with this starry look in his eyes that I see it's Davy.

Joni, he's shouting in my ear, I want to get back with you! Say you'll think about it!

And right then the pill comes shooting up like a volcano inside me. I feel wave after wave of joy. But it's not just the pill cos I know somewhere deep inside what I've really wanted for a long time is to give it another shot, too. Maybe this contest'll be a good thing, like a test for us both. Davy's holding me looking at me waiting for me answer with these big eyes, almost as big as Baby's, and instead of saying yes or no I just reach up, pull his face towards me and start giving him a good hard snog. I feel his muscles around me tense and then he's kissing back with everything he's got. I'm all sweaty and me heart's beating super fast. It feels so good I practically fucking orgasm right there and then in his arms.

'. . . just totally absolutely thrilled. I hope I'm proof to others that you can come from nothing and still follow your dreams. I want girls like me to know that just cos they take their clothes off it doesn't mean they're not worth something. If I could make just one girl know that then I could go home happy!'

Friday night is my last shift at the club. Manager Dave offered to keep me on the payroll, just in case, but I said no thanks – this girl's done with a career of getting her tits out. At least in dives like this hole, that is.

When the place finally closes, the girls bring out some bottles of champers and have send-off drinks for me in the dressing room. After this long speech from Emily about how she thinks of me as a daughter and she just knows I'm going to be a star, they start on with the usual gossip about the punters – who was packing it in and who was minted and so on. Meanwhile I go to my chair in the corner and have a long look at myself in the mirror. I'm still wearing the diamanté bikini I always wear for my last set, and I think to myself: I'm never going to wear this number again, or sit here in this chair in front of this mirror. I'm not going to be this person anymore.

Here, says Emily, coming up behind. She's holding out a compact with a beautiful fat line on it. From me and the girls.

I look round at all the smiling faces, with their silver and gold eye shadow and dramatic red and pink lips, and suddenly I'm moved. Three years I been working in this joint. Feels like an eternity. But I'm going to miss these bitches, I can tell, even though they drive me half mad with their constant moaning on about money and relationships. I wipe away the tears that have sprung to my eyes and do the line. When I look up I see that Emily's blurry-eyed too, and it occurs to me that I'm going to miss the silly old bint more than any of them.

Ahem, coughs this male voice. We all look up and gasp when we see Dave standing in the doorway holding a huge bouquet of roses. Dave's a real sleaze. First warning you get from the girls when you start work here is to watch out for him and his wandering mitts, which are like ferrets with minds of their own. Thinks running the shop gives him a green card. But even so he never comes in the dressing room, since one of the house rules is that it's strictly off bounds to men – including all staff. Tonight though he walks forward all self-conscious till he's right in front of me and then hands me the roses.

Something to say goodbye, he says, to show how much you'll be missed. Spect you'll be getting plenty more of these in the future.

There's a big Ah sound from everyone. All the girls are suckers for flowers, including me. I'm surprised Eddy's never twigged that if she wants to get into my good books all she has to do is pick up a few half-price stems from Costcutter's and I'd be putty in her hands. But Eddy's never going to be one for romantic gestures like flowers and chocolates or jewellery. She thinks inviting me out to demonstrate's romantic.

I breathe in the sweet pong of the roses and say thank you to Dave. He grins awkwardly and says he'll let us get back to it and starts to back out of the room.

Aw, come on, Dave, have a glass of bubbly! calls Gem, who's still wearing just her nipple tassels up top. Dave hesitates, then shrugs and takes the glass she holds out to him. Then he lifts it up and proposes a toast.

I been manager here for five years and Riana is one of the best dancers I've ever seen, he declares. But let me tell you all something. I knew when I first saw that face one day she was going to be a star. Riana, you make us all proud, d'you hear?

Everyone cheers and we all clink our glasses together. The idea of Dave looking up from a girl's tits long enough to think about what future her face might have is pretty laughable, but it's sweet of him all the same. I never really thought of it this way before, but it's rather like a twisted version of a family we got here. Emily's my twisted surrogate mum and Dave's like a twisted surrogate father. Fucked up or what?

Pretty soon the girls start to get nostalgic and tell stories, like the time Mia had to go out onstage with a massive rash on her thighs from a botched Brazilian, or Connie's legendary fart midway through giving Ace Johnson a private. Dave even gets into the swing of things and tells us about punters who he's personally had to rough up. Then he looks round proudly like he expects this information to have impressed us all. After a line and another glass of champagne he grandly informs everyone we can stay as long as we like and have a good old party.

Thanks Dave, I say, but not for me. Gotta get home.

Aw, come on, yells Mia. Ya can't bail on us now! Things are just getting warmed up!

Here! says Gem. She hands me the mirror and a rolled-up fiver. Another doobie – for old time's sake.

The plan was to go home and see Eddy, seeing as how we don't have much time left together now. Tomorrow she's working a double at Candy Bar and the next day this camera crew is coming and I've told her she's got to either go out and stay out, or else pretend she's just my flatmate – her choice. Obviously she wasn't exactly thrilled about either option, and at first she said that if I wanted to lie about myself then fine but there was no way in hell she was getting thrown out of her own home or pretending to be my poxy co-sharer. Then I went down on her and that stopped her being difficult like a miracle cure. But I did say to her before I left there was a chance I'd be late back, and I figure I've been doing this job for way longer than I been going out with Eddy so I may as well see it through to the bitter end.

What the fuck, you only get one life, don't ya! I cry and take the fiver.

Three hours later I stumble up the steps up to our flat. I spend ages doing that thing where you fumble around in every pocket for your keys, only to drop them before you can get the mothers in the door. They ping off the second step and go flying into the road, where they magically disappear into a drain on the pavement. Luckily I'm too wrecked to give a shit, but it means I've got to ring and get Eddy to come down and let me in. Course I know she's not going to be thrilled at being woken up, but I'm still not expecting the death stare that welcomes me.

Hello Miss Grumpy! I sing, finishing with a big kissing noise. Eddy gives me this scowl like she's just opened the door to a Jehovah's Witness.

Aw, don't be like that!

I try to kiss her, but before I can even touch her she turns on her heel and stomps off up the stairs without a word, leaving me puckering up to thin air. I close the door behind me and follow her up. I've got this ominous feeling she's going to really let rip at me as soon as I get inside our flat.

Sure enough in the living room Eddy is stood with her arms folded facing the wall, just like Mum used to when I got in later than I said I would when I was a teen, waiting for me to explain myself. It's kind of uncanny actually. Cept that unlike Mum, Eddy doesn't wait. She turns round and starts giving me some.

Do you have any idea what time it is? You said you were gonna come straight home after you finished! I've been waiting up for you! Didn't you get my texts?

I know, baby, I say, but it was my last night and the girls wanted me to stay. I couldn't say no. Do you hate me?

I go up to her and put my arms round her. Eddy's always been a softy on the inside, and one of the quickest ways to melt her down is to give her a big cuddle. But this time it doesn't wash and she pushes me off.

Look at you! You're completely caned, aren't you? she snaps. If you don't mind me asking, Riana, exactly how are you planning to get through this stupid competition when you can't take even two steps before you need to shove another fucking heap of powder up your nose?

Eddy always starts on about me having a blow problem when she wants to pick a fight. She knows just how to needle me. It's pretty fucking rich, seeing as how Eddy loves blow just as much as me if not more, and is always sneaking off for little pick-me-ups in the toilets at Candy Bar whenever I pop in to see her.

Aw, stop being such a silly.

I'll stop being such a silly when you stop being such a fucking addict! snarls Eddy.

I'm not an addict!

That's what all addicts say!

She puts on this smug grin as if she's just come up with conclusive proof of me reaching rock bottom. There's obviously no talking to her right now. I s'pose what this really is about is me going away and how much Eddy's going to miss me, but it'd be nice if she could just tell me that kind of thing instead of acting like such a dick.

Fuck off, Eddy, I say tiredly, I'm going to bed.

I heave this deep long sigh just to let her know how stupid and immature I reckon her behaviour is and head off out of the room. It'd probably be more dignified if I didn't trip on one of my heels as I reach the door and twist my ankle. I let out a little scream of pain and fall against the wall.

Hey! says Eddy. I look up, expecting her to be offering me her arm. Stead she's kneeling down and excitedly examining the carpet like she's just spotted a twenty-quid note lying there. Then she looks up, holding something between her thumb and forefinger. It's a piece of fluff.

Look darling! she gushes in this mock beauty queen voice. Maybe you can wear this for your next performance!

I stare at her, totally gobsmacked. Here I am, fucking crippled, two days away from the most important thing I've ever done in my life, and my girlfriend is taking the piss. Time and time again I've made it clear to her that it doesn't make any difference what she thinks of what I'm doing cos I'm doing it anyway. I've explained how important this is to me, and how it's just a means to an end and it doesn't mean I'm ashamed of her or of what I am. And despite it all she still can't find it in herself to support me, not even just a tiny little bit. Inside something snaps. I pull myself up and kick off my heels. Ignoring this shooting pain that's going on in my ankle, I march up to her and poke her in the ribs.

What the fuck is your problem?

My problem? she yells, slapping my hand away. I'm not the one with the problem round here! It's you who's about to go and do something that's against everything we stand for!

At this I throw my head back and let out a big laugh. If there's one way to really piss Eddy off it's to laugh at her. Makes her fucking blood boil, it does.

Don't give me that shit, I go through my sniggers. This has nothing to do with that and you know it. This is about your insecurity. You can't handle the fact that I'm doing something amazing and you're not involved!

Eddy starts to shake, which is what she does when she gets crazy.

What you're planning to go and do amounts to nothing more than *prostitution*! she shouts in my face, probably waking up the whole street. Stripping's one thing, but I don't think I can cope with having a *prostitute* for a girlfriend!

Eyes flashing, she juts out her chin and folds her arms again. For a second, just one second, I'm so angry with her for being such a stubborn piece of fuck that I rack my brains for the most hurtful thing I can possibly say. Then, without thinking about whether it's a good idea or not, I spit it out at her.

Well, if you can't cope, then you should just leave, shouldn't you?

Even as the words come out my mouth I know I don't mean them. It's the blow talking – and exhaustion. I mean, fucking hell, I've been dancing since six o'clock yesterday. And I'm all nervous and stressed out about the competition. But as soon as they're said it's too late and I can't take them back. All I can do is watch Eddy's face as all the colour drains out of it.

Fine, she says coldly, I'll pick up my stuff tomorrow.

She walks past me and into the hall, where I hear her tearing her coat off the hook.

Eddy, wait! I scream after her. I didn't mean it!

But the only answer is the sound of the door slamming.

'I just want my family to know how much they mean to me, and I want God to know how grateful I am for this opportunity. I believe He's watching over this contest and looking out for me. I was chosen for a reason, and I'm sure as hell not going to let Him down.'

The camera crew were supposed to arrive at eight, but instead they arrive at twenty to nine. I've been waiting for them since seven, staring out my bedroom window, wearing my new zebra- and leopard-print pyjamas, my hair all brushed and then re-tousled so that it looks like I've only just got up – bedraggled but glamorous, like Jennifer Aniston had it back in March. My plan was that I'd open the door and then do a jokey scream and act all pretend-outraged at being caught on camera like this, but when the bell finally does go I'm on the toilet. I flush and hurl myself out on to the landing, but I'm too late and Mum's already got there first. I peep between the banisters and watch them filming her and asking her questions about what she thinks of me being a contestant. Like the doofus she is Mum just says stuff like 'Ummmm' and 'Wellllll' over and over, as though no one's ever asked her for her opinion before. Well, it doesn't happen often that's for sure – and there's a good reason for that. Finally she wonders out loud if anyone would like to try her brownies in this stupid hopeful voice, like the one Gramps puts on after he's regressed seventy years and wants to know if we can go and feed the ducks. The crew obviously don't want to hurt her feelings, or else maybe they're genuinely charmed by her total lack of a mind, because they follow her into the kitchen and a few seconds later I hear these disgusting chomping noises followed by 'How delicious!'

Since plan A is now officially sabotaged I hurry back to my room to finish getting up. If they've seen Mum up and about I don't want them to think I'm one of those teenage slobs who lazes around in her pyjamas all day long watching *TFM* and getting in her parents' way. I return to my bathroom which is en suite and quickly start going through my ritual. This is something I have to do every morning, no matter how important a day it is. I take off all my clothes, step onto the scales, close my eyes, take a deep gulp of air and then hold my breath for as long as I can. While I hold it I pray with all my might that the little digits which pop up in front of my toes will be more than they were the day before. If you could increase your body mass through the sheer force of will in the same way that you can turn around a bad performance onstage, I'd weigh exactly eight and four – the amount the doctor said a girl of my age and height could just about get away with weighing. But physics can't be worked like a crowd, and my weight never rises above seven and eight. Since this morning is the last time I'll be able to do this for a while, seeing as they might not even have scales in the house I'm going to, I hold my breath until I'm bursting. Finally, just when it feels like I'm about to pass out, I breathe in and look down. Seven and four. I haven't told Dad, but it's been sliding, steadily but surely, ounce by ounce, ever since that first audition two weeks ago.

Please God, don't let me lose any more.

To complete the ritual I turn and quickly study my body in the full-length mirror opposite. Because of my weight I always expect to see a super-thin girl staring back, but I never *look* that skinny. When I turn to the side there's even a slight protrusion where my gut is, in spite of all the sit-ups I do. It's effing disgusting. My new dance instructor, Edna, who started with me just a couple of months ago, promised I'd have the Britney belly by now. Okay, Edna, but have you even *seen* the pictures of the Britney belly lately?

I quickly clean my teeth and then go through to the bedroom to put on my clothes. I'm so excited now I can hardly contain myself. Today I am making history – at least, that's how I'm approaching it. The crew are going to be following me round all day in order to get a sense of who I am, and Dad and I have planned it right down to the last detail. First of all I'm going to take a walk about the village, so they can get some shots of me looking pensive and dreamy with some nice scenery as a backdrop. Then Dad's going to show them all my trophies, which he had a special cabinet built for in the garage. After that I'm having my last ever singing lesson with Mr Field, and then this evening we're having a goodbye meal before seven when the car is coming to take me to London. Then I'll go into the house and officially start the beginning of my career as the new Purrfect girl.

I straighten myself out and then pull out my make-up kit. I don't usually wear make-up around the house, unlike Mum who's in full foundation and lipstick before she's had her first cup of tea in the morning. Partly it's because there's no point, and partly it's because Dad doesn't like me wearing it when I'm not performing. He says cosmetics age you prematurely, and that once I'm twenty-one and have my first wrinkle that's the time to start slapping it on. But today there are the cameras so I brush some concealer over the two pimples that have ignored God's instructions not to come up, followed by a subtle dab of pink on my eyelids to bring out the hazel of my eyes. Then I pull my hair back into a ponytail and give myself a big smile. It's important to give yourself a smile before you go out and face the day. It preps you for whatever the Devil plans to throw at you.

When I get downstairs Dad has returned from his jog, which he does without fail every morning no matter what the weather is like. It's crucial to have a system in your life, is what he always says, and I know exactly what he means. Mercifully he's prised the hapless crew away from Mum's clutches and is with them in the living room telling them how talented and special I am. I pause just before the door, hearing him as he says that he knows I am his daughter and obviously he is biased because he loves me, but he also used to be in show business and knows a rising star when he sees one. For a second I actually think I might cry. I'm so incredibly lucky to have a father who understands me and believes in me.

'Louise, there you are!' says Mum brightly from behind, almost making me scream. I shoot her a glare because she knows how cranky it makes me when she does that. 'I was just bringing this up for you. Fresh from the oven!'

She's got her silly apron on, the one with the apples and oranges with smiley faces, and is holding a steaming cup of tea and a plate with a massive hunk of ugly fatty brownie – the sort of food that makes you put on weight if you even look at it for too long. She smiles at me, nervous and anxious to please, much like a spaniel. I don't say this to be mean, because she is my mother and I do love her and all that, but Mum really is one of those people nature designed to be walked over by others, and she's just lucky that Dad came along and saw whatever it was he saw in her and rescued her from herself. Sometimes I'm glad I'm an only child, because if I had a sister who was like Mum I don't know if I'd be able to cope. One idiot in the family is more than enough. I take the tea but wave the brownie away.

'But dear, you're sooo skinny!' she says, looking up and down at me fretfully.

'Mum,' I say, in this special stern voice which has become the code for letting her know to back off. She immediately bows her head and takes the plate back to the kitchen.

Another breath and then I enter the living room. Inside Dad immediately puts an arm around me and introduces me to Julian, who it turns out is the assistant director on the programme. Julian laughs bitterly at this, as though it is a horrible joke, and when he sees our expressions explains that there are about twenty people just like him and all he gets to do is direct the cutaway crews and set up interviews – like setting up interviews with potential *stars* is just a dull and boring job to have to do. Talk about a bad attitude, but of course I don't say anything since I don't want them to make me look bad. Next to Julian stands another man, his face hidden behind the camera. I'm surprised there are only two of them, since at the auditions there were people recording the sound as well, but then Julian produces special mini-microphones which clip on to your shirt, like the ones they use in *Big Brother*.

'Don't worry,' he tells me as he fastens mine on, 'before you know it you'll have forgotten it's there, just like the cameras.'

He stands back and asks me to do a twirl for him to make sure the mic doesn't fall out, and then suggests I sit down with Dad on the sofa so they can film us chatting about the competition. Unfortunately he also wants Mum, so Dad calls for her and right away in she trots, excruciatingly eager to please and trying far too hard. She sits down next to me and looks excitedly from my face to Dad's to Julian's. I take her hand, an action which she seems to interpret as a sign that I've decided she's the most wonderful mother in the world, because she instantly starts beaming and chattering away about completely dull things like how her hydrangeas have been doing, totally monopolising the conversation we're supposed to be having about me. Dad shifts on the sofa, but neither of us can exactly say anything to her, because there's simply no way of telling someone to shut the hell up and still look like a nice guy. Julian is the one to finally give up on politeness. He interrupts Mum midway through telling us all what a wonderful invention weed killer is to ask Dad about what it's like to have a performer in the family. Smoothly, like the pro he is, Dad takes over. He says that he knew the moment I was born that I was going to be a star. He tells them that it's in my blood, sure as the moon goes round the earth. Mum nods her head up and down in agreement and adds that I practise singing and dancing every day. I look down and try to seem demure about it.

'So, Louise,' says Julian, 'what do you do when you're *not* practising?'

The question takes me by surprise and for a minute I don't know what to answer, because the truth is, I'm *always* practising. I guess a lot of people would think my life was lonely, since I'm not the sort of girl who goes out to lots of parties or who is constantly surrounded by friends. Most of the girls I know at school are complete sluts, only interested in boys and clothes, no interest in actually making something out of their lives. They seem to find the fact that I actually have a dream and go after it impossible to understand. But I don't care. I'm an achiever, and achievers don't have time for all that stuff that ordinary people get up to. Performing is what I do. It's why I'm the best.

'Louise likes to hang out with friends when she's not working,' Dad answers for me. 'She's very popular.'

This is a lie of course, but only a tiny white one because when you think about it I really *ought* to be popular. I mean, what with all the competitions I've won and all the merits and awards and achievements I have, people ought to be falling over themselves to be my friend. Unfortunately it doesn't work like that in practice, because people are selfish and jealous, but you can see that's what God had in mind. Anyway, it's not like I don't have *any* friends at all. Becky and Tina who I know from drama club are coming over later today for my goodbye dinner, and they're my friends, even if they are both overweight and also act a bit like they belong in Special Needs, giggling and shouting all the time. This was Dad's idea, which at first I wasn't that keen on since they're hardly the kind of people a glamorous pop star would associate with. But I have to agree with him that it would be good to show me interacting with people my own age.

Julian nods enthusiastically to this and says he's looking forward to meeting some of them. Then he asks what else I've got planned for my last day. Dad leaves this for me to say, since he's done most of the talking, but before I can get so much as a sound out Mum interrupts.

'Why don't you come visit Gramps at hospital with me?' she says in her silly bright voice. 'It's been ages since you visited and he'd love to see you before you head off!'

I could kill her right then. Much as I love Gramps, he's neither photogenic nor what you might call reliable. In fact, he's an effing liability. He's even worse than she is, since he's always doing things that are horribly embarrassing like passing wind loudly halfway through a conversation or shouting out totally inappropriate things like how much he'd like to have it off with one of the nurses. But now that Mum's asked me I'll look like a heartless little brat if I don't agree to go with her, and I can't risk *that* on camera. I'll just have to pray that he still hasn't recovered enough from his stroke to speak.

'That was the idea!' I say, trying to sound genuine.

'Not a long visit, mind,' says Dad quickly, obviously having the same thought as me. 'You've got a singing lesson with Mr Field this afternoon, don't forget. And you don't want to tire Gramps out.'

'Righty ho,' trills Mum, completely oblivious that she's ruined my plans for the second time today. 'Well, let's all drink up our tea and get cracking!'

Just as I knew it would be, the visit to see Gramps is a total effing disaster. Not only does he fail to recognise either me or Dad but he shouts out 'Sod off and die, you Thatcherite scum!' as soon as he sees Julian. He spends most of the visit cowering behind Mum, who has to reassure him over and over again that we haven't come to take him to prison for tax evasion. Finally we manage to calm him down and Julian sets up a nice shot of me sitting beside Gramps and holding his hand. Gramps is smiling and for once I'm remembering how sweet he can be, when without warning he leans forward and coughs out a stream of yellowy sick all down the front of my top. And I have to smile and pretend this is darling and amusing, when really I'm thinking to myself why doesn't God just take him now and be done with it. That's not heartlessness, by the way. It's just that I don't think Gramps has anything more that he needs to do on this earth. He's fulfilled his destiny, and so God ought to reward him with Heaven. That's how it should work.

The last thing I wanted to do was go to my singing lesson covered in dried puke, but there's no time to go home and change so I scrape off what I can in the toilets and act as though it doesn't bother me. At least Mum's having a great time. She doesn't normally have company, since she doesn't have any friends and Dad and I are both motivated people with better things to do than stand around and talk to her while she does housework. She's in high spirits by the time we all get to Mr Field's and even threatens to sit in and watch while Julian and the camera guy do their filming. Fortunately Dad intervenes to remind her that there's shopping to be done for my last meal, which gets her even more excited since she's got a special casserole planned. Talk about a desperate housewife.

Mr Field is very serious when he answers the door, and completely ignores Julian and the camera guy apart from a curt hello and a quick scribble of his signature on the release form Julian asks him to sign. He lets them set up in the corner of his studio while he makes me do all the most difficult warm-up exercises. He's much stricter than usual, not saying a word of encouragement even when I get through a rendition of Dido's 'White Flag' lick perfect, something we've been working on for weeks. All he says is 'Uh huh' and nothing more, which is completely unlike him since he's usually brimming over with praise. Only at the end, when Julian positions him in front of his keyboard and the framed black-and-white photo of him when he met Shirley Bassey, does he offer some positivity.

'I've been teaching singing for twenty years and Louise is the best student I've ever had by a long shot,' he says, his many chins wobbling with sincerity. 'If those judges don't pick her to be in Purrfect then they don't know anything about what makes a real singer. That's all I have to say.'

When I hear this I'm so moved I forgive him for making me do 'The Penny Dropped' at the audition last week. After it was over he was so incensed by what Joe said about my voice not being suited to a Malone number he was almost ready to march on over and tell him what he thought. I didn't say anything about it, since I'd got through to the programme and that was what counted, but privately I was so mad. If they hadn't have picked me I wouldn't have been responsible for my actions. Even though I was way better than the other girls, for a few horrible seconds when I was called up to stand in front of the panel and receive the decision, I actually thought Tess was going to tell me no. That time three years ago when with two single awful words she ruined my life replayed in my head, sickeningly vivid. It took everything I had to hold it together. But God was watching, and this time He wasn't going to let me down. Because this time, He's taking me all the way to the finish line.

At four o'clock Becky and Tina arrive, looking like a pair of ugly sisters from a pantomime. I'm filmed opening the door and just like I knew they would the second they see the camera they both scream 'Oh my God!' in unison and start jumping up and down like psychotic rabbits. Then they jump on me and start trying to propel me upwards with them. I smile and play along, but really I wish they wouldn't make such idiots of themselves. I don't want people to think my only friends are mentally challenged.

'I can't believe it!' screams Becky. 'I'm so excited for you!'

'I know!' I say as enthusiastically as I can.

'Oh my God,' screams Tina.

It's not long before I'm completely regretting our decision to have them over. They literally cannot stop effing giggling and screaming. Somehow I manage to manoeuvre them inside and past the cameraman, who follows us up to my bedroom, where they throw themselves on my bed and mess up the duvet and then start bouncing around the room, knocking things over and not even bothering to pick them up.

'This is so insane!' screams Becky. 'You're going to be on TV!'

She bounces towards the camera and makes a face at it, then outdoes herself with an extraordinarily high-pitched giggle and grabs hold of Tina. Together they start waltzing about the room, followed back and forth by the camera. I try to join in without looking like I've lost the plot. Julian looks like he's wondering why I haven't just ditched Tina and Becky and been done with it, and I give him a special look to show him it's something I sometimes wonder myself. If only it were that easy. No one wants to spend their whole life alone. Not even those of us who have a calling. That's why celebrities are always surrounded by an entourage, no matter where they go. Everyone thinks these people trailing around after them are just toadying sycophants desperate to be close to the limelight, and wonders why the star even tolerates them. But a star needs to have those people, because a star requires lots of love and kindness in order to thrive. In order to do what they have to.

'So, guys,' says Julian in a conspiratorial tone. 'Tell us, does Louise have a boyfriend?'

Tina and Becky burst into another storm of shrillness, like they're trying to break the world record for idiotic giggling.

'Louise doesn't have time for boys!' Becky just about manages to shriek in between short fast breaths. She throws her arm around my shoulders and I suppress the urge to throw it off me. 'She's far too sensible!'

'Oh?' says Julian, obviously interested.

I feel myself going red. The truth is I've never even been out with a boy. The boys at school don't look twice at me. It's effing strange really, because I'm much prettier and slimmer than most of the other girls there. In fact, half those who do have boyfriends are complete dogs, to be honest. I guess it's because I don't constantly talk about sex all the time and make lurid jokes at every given opportunity, or wear ridiculously short skirts and low-cut tops. You'd think the girls at school were nymphomaniacs with the way they dress and flirt and what with the sheer dirt that comes out their mouths. It makes you wonder what happened to the good old-fashioned concept of dignity. It's not like it bothers me though. I mean, I'm not ashamed to be a virgin, especially since all the boys I know are completely immature and pathetic, and only interested in one thing. There's maybe one person who's actually worth considering, which is Felix, who's captain of the football and swimming teams, but he's been going out for the last year with Nathalie Holden, this absolute slut who comes to school caked in make-up and doesn't know the answer to even the simplest of questions. I've come to the conclusion that God is saving me for someone special. Probably I'll meet him once I'm in Purrfect.

'Let's just say I'm available,' I say, with a saucy smile.

'I'm available too!' screams Tina. 'I want *boys*! Where are they! I want them now! NOW!'

She starts looking for them under the bed and in the cupboards, flinging open drawers and rummaging in my pre-packed suitcase, rooting around in the clothes for some imaginary drop-dead gorgeous heart-throb – though knowing Tina any old male of the species would do. Becky shrieks with delight at this game and immediately joins in. I watch them turning my room and suitcase inside out and try to look like I love my wacky friends and their kooky behaviour, whereas actually they make me wonder why every person in my life is such a complete no-hoper. Apart from Dad, that is.

At this point there's a knock on the door and Mum pops her head in and surveys the scene with a fond smile before telling us that dinner is about to be served. Not a second too soon, I think.

The meal is tortuously long. Mum gives everyone massive portions of casserole and irritatingly points out to the camera how little I eat, as though she absolutely despairs of me. I'm so mad I'm tempted to point out that if I ate half the stuff that Mum cooks then the only reality TV show I'd be good for is *Can Fat Teens Hunt?* Luckily just then there's a toot from outside and Dad glances out the window and announces that the car has arrived to take me to London. Tina and Becky leap up and start doing their usual jumping on an imaginary trampoline thing. I pretend not to hear Mum's worried call for dessert and hurry upstairs to re-stuff my suitcase with the clothes my inane 'friends' threw about earlier. When I come out Dad's waiting on the landing, the camera crew nowhere in sight.

'Okay, Louise,' he says. 'This is it. From now on you're going to be on your own. Don't forget everything we talked about. Never get overconfident. Never get complacent. If you're worried or scared, at any time, just remember: failure is not an option.'

It feels like I'm going to war, and suddenly I'm afraid of how I'll cope without Dad there to prep me and believe in me and hold me up with his positivity. But then I look in his eyes and I see complete and absolute faith shining back. And I realise that this isn't just about me, it's about him too. Dad once dreamed of being a star, but his own dream never happened for him. He's always said he gave it up because he saw better opportunities in what he does now, but I know that's not the real reason. He tried and he didn't make it. Now I'm the closest he'll ever get, and I can't let him down.

'Kill it,' he says, and hands me my suitcase.

'Feeling quite nervous. So thrilled to be here. It's so exciting! I mean – how incredible *is this*? Out of all those girls who auditioned, we're the ones who got picked. It's like . . . we've been blessed!'

There are six others. We're all sitting in a half circle at the centre of the room, and everyone is chattering away excitedly as they wait for the judges to come and talk to us. The only one who's not speaking is me, because I don't know what to say to anyone here and because there's something strangely frightening about being trapped in a room with nothing but a bunch of pretty, confident performers. A few seats away from me is Joni, talking loudly to the girl on her left. When I said hello earlier, she just gave me the briefest of smiles and then turned away like she didn't want to know. It hurt, how she did it, but I'm not going to let it upset me. I can't, because at either end of the room cameramen are filming: enormous black pupils silently absorbing all the chatter and the darted looks girls are giving out as they size one another up. We were all fitted out with radio mics when we came in and I'm having trouble resisting the urge to play with it. I'm sitting on my hands to keep from fidgeting.

All last week was horrible. Jack made me feel like I was a murderer, the way he acted. He didn't say anything, but there was a dreadful coldness to his voice whenever he spoke to me, and he completely avoided being in the same room whenever he possibly could. When I got back that day with the news I was through he just nodded really slowly and then left the kitchen, like I'd just told him someone he knew had died. Rita was sitting at the table as usual, sorting through pictures of handbags. I waited for her to start shouting at me for being selfish and spoilt because I went to the call-back without permission. But instead she gave me a weird grin and then screwed up her whole face, making the pounds of foundation she wears crinkle up so much she looked a lot like The Grinch. Then she told me not to worry about Jack, that we'd work on him, in this conspiratorial voice like we were suddenly the best of friends, and that was when I realised with a shock that she wasn't screwing up her face – she was winking at me! It turned out she knew all this stuff about the competition because *Fascinate!* are going to be doing an article on it for the next edition. She's even said she wants me to give her my exclusive story after I get booted out, which is just typical of Rita, it not even occurring to her that maybe, just maybe, I might make it all the way through. But at least she's okay with me doing it. That's the main thing. Unlike Jack.

'So, what's your name then?' says the girl next to me in a thick Scouser accent, making me jump because I was completely lost in thought. She's got very pointed features, crimped brown hair and an expression that's quite scary because it looks so determined. Her skin is a blatant solarium job, which Rita despises because she says it gives you prematurely aged skin and looks like you've eaten nothing but carrots. You can see the first few lines around her eyes already I note, kind of like Geri Halliwell had back before she did the surgery.

'Ella,' I say, trying to sound relaxed and confident. I remind myself of a mouse, puffing itself out to seem big in front of a cat.

'Hi Ella, I'm Valerie. Nice to meet you!' says the girl loudly. 'Your song the other week was wicked! Loved it, loved it, *loved it*!'

'Thanks . . .' I say. 'Yours was good too. Really good.'

Her smile widens and she seems to be waiting for more. But I don't know what else there is to say, because the truth is I was so nervous I don't actually remember anyone else's song, apart from Joni's, which stood out because she didn't have any music. When it becomes clear to Valerie I'm not going to say anything else about how brilliant she was, she simply turns away and starts talking to the girl on her other side. Right away I feel stupid, because whenever I speak to people I don't know I always become all tongue-tied and start acting like I'm autistic. No wonder at school all the girls treat me like I'm a mutant and avoid me like they think it's catching.

I've been absolutely dreading what it's going to be like staying in a house with six other girls. We're all in a dormitory together and have to share this one big bathroom, and I'm just terrified of what'll happen once the lights are switched off. I've never even been to a slumber party before. When the camera crew came this morning they seemed surprised that I didn't have any friends there to cheer me on. Luckily I had Mimi instead, who made up for it by practically dying with pleasure at the chance to be in front of the camera. When they interviewed her she told them she was my biggest fan and she and her friends all think I have an amazing voice, which is complete BS since when I practise for choir she always complains of a headache. But she's U-turned since I got through, and for the last two weeks has acted like I'm a celebrity. It's weird to think that there's a possibility that one day very soon it might even be true. That there's a one in seven chance I'll actually win this and go on to become the new member of Purrfect. One thing's for sure: if that does happen I won't be ignored and avoided everywhere I go. But I can't think about it, because when I do it makes my head spin and my mouth go dry like I've just run a marathon.

The double doors to the studio burst open. The girls all immediately stop talking as Tess, Joe and Emma enter, all carrying big black folders and looking very, very serious, like they're attending an execution. A lurch of my bladder tells me I need the loo, but there's no way I can go now so I clamp my legs shut as tight as I can. Tess is dressed in a plain black suit with tapering sleeves, which I've seen in House of Fraser and which she bulges out of in all the wrong places like a fat rag doll that's leaking its stuffing. Emma's blonde hair is pulled back tightly into a bun, and she's wearing a brown pencil skirt topped with a sugar-pink silk shirt that's got to be Red Label. Joe is dressed in an Armani vest and combats topped with green shades, looking like a cross between a soldier and a tourist. With a grand sweeping gesture of hello, Tess lifts her folder and opens it up.

'Good evening, ladies!' she barks. We all chorus good evening back and she peers around the half circle like she's appraising the pathetic maggots she's got to train up.

'Congratulations to all of you for getting through,' she continues in a voice that couldn't sound less like she means it. 'We have selected you from hundreds of other wannabe singers, and that means you are all talented and all have the potential to become the new Purrfect girl.'

Next to me Valerie starts to clap and Joni lets out a whoop. Tess silences them immediately by raising a hand, rather like Hitler in one of those fuzzy black-and-white video clips we have to watch in History class.

'However,' she barks, 'only *one* of you will become that girl. The rest will return home and back to whoever they were before, be it studying for exams or stacking the shelves in Tesco's. This contest is not about losers. The stakes are high, girls, and the winner takes all.'

She swivels her head slowly round the semi-circle, giving each one of us a penetrating look, like she wants us to know from now on she's always going to be watching. When she looks at me I get a lump in my throat and can't stop myself from gulping. She's much scarier than any teacher, even more so close up than when she was sitting in the audience. Luckily at this point Joe steps forward with his folder and takes over.

'The next six weeks are going to be very exciting,' he reads. 'You will work with some of the best choreographers, singing coaches and image consultants in the industry. No expense has been spared on this chance to find the new member for one of the most successful girl bands ever to storm the UK charts. Those of you who make it through to the final round will be met and judged by none other than Purrfect themselves.'

There is an intake of breath from all around. I imagine myself shaking hands with Saffron, being so close to the lead vocalist of 'My Heart Is Not Your Toy' that I can smell her scent. I imagine this connection we will have as our eyes meet. How they will see me and know, just know, that I am one of them. It's a nice fantasy.

'Over the next six weeks you will face many obstacles and challenges. It will be hard work, the hardest you have ever done, and at the end of each week, those not up to scratch will be eliminated.'

Joe bows his head like a reverend at the end of a funeral, and Emma clears her throat and opens up her folder.

'Next Saturday night, you will face your first challenge,' she says. 'This will be a dance routine you will have been working on as a group with Patty Lion, our in-house choreographer. You will also be individually performing songs with expert vocal coach Edgar Hall. On Saturday the songs will be performed in front of an invited audience who will vote for their favourite. The girl with the most votes will get a free pass into the next round. Out of the remaining girls, the panel will then decide whose performance showed the least potential. At the end of this week, one of you will be going home.'

Her last words chill me to the bone. *One of you will be going home*. It sounds like a death sentence. Emma raises her head and stares straight out in front of her, like she cannot bear to look at us having conveyed this horrible news.

Tess slips her folder under her arm and sets her mouth in a big smile. Unfortunately she's got one of those mouths that can't really smile, that's obviously so used to pursing and sneering that it's no longer able to express things like love and joy. She looks like a shark opening its mouth in order to bite off a pair of dangling legs.

'Right everybody,' she says through her teeth. 'I expect you're all very tired and ready for bed. Tomorrow you'll be given your songs and then you will get straight to work on them. But before we let you go we've got a treat for you. A special preview of the first episode of *The Purrfect Search* before it's broadcast on Friday.'

Everyone gasps. But in the pit of my stomach there's another sudden sinking sensation. It's similar to how I felt when I first had to go into the room in front of the panel two weeks ago. The studio doors open and two men in black wheel a huge portable widescreen TV into the room. Tess nods to one of the men and he switches it on.

On screen up come all these shots of London, bright flashing lights and billboards with the girls from Purrfect on them, all pointing and a speech bubble coming out of their mouths saying 'Do you have what it takes to be a Purrfect girl?' Over the top is music. It's Purrfect's first number one, 'I Want to be Purrfect' – the one with the angry dance beat. The girls around me start cheering, but they quickly quieten down when a long shot of the music studio where we went for the first day of auditions appears. As the camera moves up the endless queue of girls lining up for the chance to sing before the panel, there are several shrieks as some of the girls recognise themselves. 'Hundreds of girls are here today to find out if they have what it takes to become part of one of the most successful girl bands the UK has produced,' announces a woman's voice, which I recognise right away as belonging to Stina Ellis. 'Only seven girls will be selected, to enter a house in which they will battle it out until just one is left standing, to become the new member of Purrfect!' Again everybody cheers, but this time it is more muted: all these sound-bites come up from girls of every size, shape and colour, all saying how much they want to be in the band, how it's the most exciting thing ever for them. It's disconcerting to see all these faces, all these eyes, all with the same thing written in them – the longing to be recognised as the next Purrfect girl. Then up come the auditions. I see Valerie singing a shrill but powerful version of Shania Twain's 'You're Still the One', followed by a tall girl with a bob who's sitting two seats away, who sings a slow version of 'Since You've Been Gone'. Several other girls who aren't in the room with us come next, all super-embarrassing to watch.

There's one which really gets to me. It's this dreadfully obese girl whose face is practically hidden by all the rolls of fat that surround it. First of all she's interviewed in the queue, standing there with her parents who're also super-fat, so much so they almost look like a different species altogether. The girl is really shy and won't say anything, just looks down at the tent-shaped dress she's wearing, which is pink and covered in little white flowers. Her blonde hair is all curly, and she looks like an inflated china doll. But her parents are both really raring and go on about how talented she is and how she's going to simply stun the judges when they see her. Already the other girls are giggling, but to me there's something really chilling about the way her parents' eyes are all shiny with hope, like they really believe there's a chance their chronically overweight daughter might make it. Then the camera cuts to the auditioning studio and the girl is standing in front of the panel, her little piggy eyes open wide with fear as Tess witheringly stares her up and down. Then she opens her mouth and in this ghostly thin voice she starts to sing 'The Power of Love'. It's just terrible, so bad it's not even laughable, and the panel are all making faces at one another like they can't believe this isn't a joke. But there's something about watching her sing, something about the mixture of hope and desperation in her face as she struggles through the song that's actually heartbreaking. She gets through the first verse and then trails off, noticing the expressions on the faces before her and obviously losing whatever nerve she had. Then, horribly, she just stands in silence looking at the ground like she wishes it would swallow her up. After a pause Tess leans forward and tells her she needs to lose half her bodyweight and that her mouth looks like the Dartford Tunnel. Everyone in the room laughs and I join in, but really I feel disgusted. The girl on screen nods slowly, like she's actually grateful to be told this, and suddenly it dawns on me that it's not just her dreams that have been stamped on, but her right to even have those dreams has been destroyed too. It's like Tess has only confirmed what she secretly knew already: that she'll never amount to anything. That she'll never be looked at or thought of as special, ever.

There are more auditions, and lots and lots of close-ups of Tess looking like she'd love to have the girl in front of her liquidated, and of Emma smiling sympathetically as some hopelessly off-key voice warbles out another wrong note, and also of Joe cringing or bobbing his head up and down to an imaginary beat. Joni is briefly in it, being told she's got good vibes by Joe and being given a dismissive 'Okay' from Tess, and I look over and see her eyes are wet and shining. All the girls in the room are shown on that first day, apart from me. I'm relieved but the sinking sensation in the pit of my stomach hasn't gone away yet.

'Join us after the break for the call-back,' says Stina Ellis, appearing in a red bustier and feather boa in front of a backdrop of London. She flicks her hair and gives us a dazzling smile and then there's a few seconds of black screen where we're told the adverts will be inserted. The programme starts again with the following week, showing the entrance hall to the studio in Shepherd's Bush, milling with girls and their families queuing up for the pop boutique. There are a few before and after shots, which include the tall black girl on the other side of the room, the one who almost bowled me over that day. In her before shot she's dressed like a trashy version of Julia Roberts in *Pretty Woman*, and in the after one she's all in black and looks like a conservative Kelly Rowland. It's quite a transformation, and I notice the girl is chuckling. Tonight she's back in her hooker clothes, wearing a fashion-disaster combo composed of a white PVC mini-skirt and a tight-fitting, low-cut green top that basically just spells out BOOBS in capital letters. I shift my attention back to the screen and that's when my heart stops. 'Unfortunately, some people aren't too thrilled by the opportunity these girls are getting,' says Stina Ellis's voice over the top. The crowd has formed a circle around a man who is pointing at the camera and clearly getting very angry. It's hard to tell what Jack's shouting exactly because there are so many bleeping noises. They've blurred his face, but you can see me perfectly, standing behind him in the pink Nancy Dee dress, looking like an albino rabbit frozen in the headlights as Jack lurches forward and attacks the sound guy. Everyone in the room turns to look at me, and I feel myself blush scarlet. 'Flippin' heck,' breathes Valerie. Onscreen two huge security guards arrive and prise Jack away, with lots more bleeps as he struggles and demands to know where I am. Oh my God, I think. Next week this is going to be broadcast all across the country. Everyone who knows us and sees me will figure out that Jack is the angry man who lost it, and even if they don't they'll be told by someone who has. Jack is going to be so miserable – he's never going to forgive me. I have to warn him, I realise. I have to get them to change it. I have to do something about this before it's too late. Otherwise there's no chance of him ever loving me again.

'Well . . . it's tough. You don't realise how much work there is goes into this professional [bleep]. Sorry. I just mean that I'm finding it real rough, that's all. I'm missing home. Me mum. Me . . . friends. Don't get me wrong. I'm still grateful to be here! Still one hundred per cent focused and all that.'

Raise your leg higher, Joni! goes Patty in my ear. The bitch then grabs hold of my ankle and gives it a yank. I scream at the pain.

Oh don't be such a wuss! she goes with this little laugh.

Get fucked! I want to shout at her, only I can't cos of the stupid cameras which film you every second of every day. They've seen me lose it several times this week already. The only time they leave you alone is when you go to take a crap, and even then they hang round outside the door to the toilet, waiting like they're checking that you've washed your hands properly.

Despite the fact I've got to share with six other girls I got to admit this house is a fucking luxury pad. There's hot water and fresh sheets every day, and someone even comes and makes your bed while you're doing the classes. There's all the soap and shampoo and stuff you could ask for in the bathroom, Oil of Olay, Tressemé, L'Oréal, Body Shop, you name it – even that new moisturising cream from Clinique which is so expensive they don't even give out samples. At breakfast there're these menus so you can just pick whatever sandwich you like and someone makes it up for you and has it ready for lunch. And in the evening after classes are finished there's this kitchen with cupboards full of any food you could wish for, so you can rustle up whatever you fancy. Makes you wonder if it ain't really some plan to fatten us all up. But there's not much weight being put on, that's for sure, not with all the stretching and exercising we're doing. And any fat I did have has fallen away faster than if it was dandruff.

Okay girls, turn over! shouts Patty. Now copy me and push up into Cobra!

She lies down on her belly and demonstrates this position. Looks simple enough, but as soon as I've got on to me tummy on the mat with me hands out it's like trying to lift a fucking lorry. Thought I was all right when it came to being fit till I got here. I walk everywhere all the time back in Reading. Sometimes the only thing that'll get Baby down is to put him in his stroller and take him for a good long wander, and I'm forever carrying that stupid contraption up and down the stairs to our place cos you can't leave it in the hall else it'd get pinched. I used to do aerobics classes too, Thursday mornings down at the Beverly Centre. But these classes of Patty's ain't nothing like aerobics. More like frigging torture.

God, this is all so *basic*, isn't it? whispers this toothy girl Anya next to me, really rubbing it in. Like half these bitches, she's all posh and annoying, one of them Paris Hilton types on a smaller scale. She's got a different coloured leotard for every day and walks round with this smug grin plastered over her mug cos she's already so bendy she could probably eat herself out if she wanted. I watch her stick out her tits and arse and push herself up into the air nose first like it's the easiest thing in the world. Meanwhile I can't even get halfway without collapsing.

Joni! If you can't do it with extended arms then try it on your elbows!

Five days in and me whole body's aching worse than it did after I had Baby. Seriously. Patty reckons that in three weeks all of us who can't already do the splits'll be able to slide into it no problem – smiling and all. Well, I've got news for her, which is that this fanny's done all the stretching nature intended it to do.

All right girls, enough. Let's go straight into a run-through of the routine. Only one more day and you've got to perform this, so let's all stay in focus and get it right!

Straight into the fucking routine without even a break. That's the kind of sadist this woman is. I'm panting away like a dog, whereas the rest of the girls all bounce into position with big smiles, like this is one of them beauty ads where women don't ever get zits or nipple hair or oozing pus in their privates. Cept for Ella that is. I couldn't sleep last night because of all the instructions racing through me head for this stupid routine, like when you've got to turn and twist and which foot goes where at what point in the stupid music. Again I thought this'd be all right, since me and Wend've been copying dances off MTV ever since her mum got Sky when we was eleven. But it turns out there are all these little details you got to be aware of, like keeping your shoulders back and your head up, and each tiny movement's got to be exactly right and in time too, which is a fuck of a lot harder than it sounds.

Feeling like a right twat, since I seem to be the only one here who actually sweats instead of glows (and when I say sweat I mean fucking buckets), I go to my position. The sadist has put me right at the front, with the others in this V-shape out to either side. These camera guys must have plenty of tapes of me acting like a spaz on speed while the rest of the girls do it all perfect behind me. Apart from Ella, that freak who somehow got through despite the fact that she needs to vomit practically every time someone even speaks to her.

Patty switches on the music and waves her finger in the air.

One, two, three, four!

We all turn our backs on the imaginary audience where she's standing and start wiggling our arses. Patty says this is called The Single Body Wave, but if you ask me The Classic Todger Tease would be closer to the mark. She's got all these silly names for every move you can think of. Even just turning round has to be called a pirouette, which makes it even harder to follow her when she talks us through the routine. I count the beats then flip round. Going out in pairs either side of me, the girls should be flipping round too, until we're facing the same way again. Now comes this jiggling dance which I actually quite like, cos it's like something from Destiny's Child where you all shake your bits from side to side and up and down. Twenty beats – or shit, was it thirty? Now's the hard part, where we all walk forward swaying our hips from side to side like models on a catwalk and then back and then around each other.

And everyone turn! yells Patty.

I turn and go face-splat into Louise. She's a real snake cos of the way she always gets this smile whenever someone has to ask a question, like the fact they might not know already is proof of how rubbish they are. She acts like she's too good to hang around with the rest of us, but she's a crafty one, cos whenever the camera comes close she switches right on like a light bulb, all sweet and friendly like she's your best friend. And she never gets it wrong, not once. Not even when we all went through it for the first fucking time.

Whoops! Louise goes and shoots me this lightning-fast look like I'm trailer trash before giving me this big smile as the camera guy moves towards us. Wish I'd accidentally nutted her while I was at it. Patty, she calls, Joni turned the wrong way again!

Patty turns off the music and heaves this long sigh.

Joni, how many more times? Right, *then* left. This is a very simple section and if you can't get it I don't know how you're ever going to handle more complex choreography.

Sorry, I go, meaning Die screaming.

And Ella, once again you're looking at the ground. Dancing has to look spontaneous, not rehearsed. If you're always looking to see where your feet go it doesn't work.

I'm sorry! cries Ella from my far left. I look over and see her eyes are all watery and she's this sickly shade of white, practically the same colour as the wall behind her.

Okay, sighs Patty, from the top – one, two, three, four!

I flip round and count. Wiggle arse. Flip back round for Destiny's Child bit. Hands down, step forward, step forward, step forward, walk back. Step forward, step forward, step forward, walk back – two, three, four. Okay. Now – right, *then* left.

I'm sorry! I'm so sorry! shrieks a voice.

We all stop and look at Ella, who's facing the wrong direction and is stood in Riana's way, shrieking. Tears stream down her cheeks. Riana's trying to tell her it's okay, but Ella's far too busy acting like she's just mown down a kitten to hear her. Suddenly she turns and runs out the room. Patty rolls her eyes in this way like she's trying to work out what she's ever done to deserve this.

Okay girls, she goes with another long sigh, five minutes.

She heads off out the room to go talk to Ella, followed by one of the camera guys. The girls all gang up in a corner apart from snake Louise, who goes to the bar on the other side and lifts her leg up over her shoulder like it's a perfectly normal thing to do while you're having a breather.

God, that Ella is such a fucking mess! goes Valerie, who always says what she thinks without giving a fuck about the cameras that are filming. She doesn't seem to get that this is a bad idea cos it means people watching are gonna end up thinking she's a bitch – which she is. Oh no – she's all proud of her fat gob. Reckons she's sassy cos she can't keep a lid on it. The camera guy comes up to her and she turns and poses for him.

I'm not being funny, she carries on, I mean, Ella's a nice girl. But she doesn't belong in this contest. She's all over the place. She wakes us all up in the middle of the night with her crying, and she always looks like death warmed up. She can't handle the pressure. And if you can't handle it, you shouldn't be doing it, simple as that!

She's just not tough enough, goes Rebecca, this tall girl who seems to get on real well with Valerie and always agrees with whatever she says. Five days and you can already tell who's who in the playground. If you ask me it's pretty rich for them to be complaining about being woken up by Ella's snivelling when they're making a right racket whispering bitchy shit to each other all night long.

The trouble with Ella, Valerie goes again, in love with her own voice, is that she's had everything handed to her on a plate. You can tell just by looking at her. I've had to work hard me whole life. I'm here because I'm good, and I'm good because I'm a worker!

She's too young, that's what I think, says Riana, whose gig is to act like she runs the shop just cos she's the oldest out of us and is a stripper, like this gives her some kind of deep well of experience to draw from. We haven't spoken about that time she gave me the coke at the audition, cos she always avoids being alone with me as much as she possibly can, which ain't hard when there're cameramen jumping out at you from every corner.

Everyone starts agreeing and then saying that it's a shame cos they do think Ella's such a *nice person*, but it just makes me feel sick. The reason I left school wasn't only cos of the bulge sticking out of me tummy, it was cos I never could stand all the backstabbing that went on. And this is just like that, only worse cos there ain't nowhere to hide.

I figure I may as well go check on Ella as hang out with this bunch of two-faces so I head off down the corridor to the toilet. Patty's standing in front of the door with a camera pointed at her, making a show of saying stuff to Ella like she's never going to make anything of herself if she don't toughen up and there's no point in crying about a silly dance routine, just come out and practise it. There's no answer from inside, and Patty sees me and throws her hands up in the air like she's saying, Take over if you can bear to cos I've had enough! She stomps off down the corridor and I go up to the door and knock. The guy brings his camera in close.

Ella? I say. It's me, Joni.

After a second the door opens a crack and Ella peeps out, eyes all swollen and red. I push my way in then close it quickly before the camera guy can get his foot in. To be sure I twist the lock. Ella sinks to the ground and starts sobbing away, pressing her face into her knees, skinny little body shaking away worse than a poodle in a lightning storm.

Come on, I go, it ain't that bad.

I want to go home! she whines.

I kneel down and put me hand on her shoulder. I do get what she's feeling, cos I'm missing home like mad as well. We all had our phones confiscated as soon as we arrived, so I ain't spoken to Mum since I left. Place is like a prison if you ask me. Never been away from Baby for this long before neither. It feels weird, and I'm worried cos I keep thinking how's he gonna get to sleep without his proper mum there to cuddle him and sing to him? I know it's stupid, cos Mum's taken care of him loads of times, but it still feels weird not having him there next to me in the room. And then there's the Davy thing. It was a bad idea getting back with him the day before I had to leave, cos now I'm horny as all hell and can't do nothing about it. Just before I got in the limo to go he gave me this real silver bracelet with good luck written on the inside in curly letters. Totally floored me cos one thing Davy ain't is loaded. Didn't even have time for a thank-you shag.

I don't know what to do, sobs Ella.

Just keep practising like that stupid cow tells you, I say. You'll get it in the end. At least you can *do* the steps.

Not about that! she wails, looking up at me with this face like the world's about to end.

Then what? I go.

At this Ella drops her head and starts crying twice as hard. Talk about a nut job. I pat her shoulder and try to think of comforting shit to say, like how whatever's bothering her can't be that bad, but all I can think is, What the fuck am I doing here? Me body's throbbing all over, I'm in pain and exhausted, I'm missing Baby like crazy, I got steps to learn, and here I am sitting in a toilet trying to help this girl who should blatantly just be carted off to hospital to get her brain fixed.

Ella raises her head and whispers something. I have to put my ear practically next to her mouth in order to catch it.

It's Jack, she goes. He's never going to forgive me.

Who's Jack? I say. Then I remember. That preview they showed us when we first got here, Ella standing there in front of the crowd and this man with his face blurred getting angry at the camera. Her behind him whimpering.

Rita's boyfriend, she goes, taking a massive sniff. She's my step-mum.

Right, I say. Then, What?

My father died when I was little you see, goes Ella. He was in a boating accident in Nepal. I've lived with Rita since then, and Mimi, who's her daughter.

Where's your mum then?

Oh, she died just after I was born, says Ella with this sigh. She had a weak heart. I was lucky to be born alive.

Oh, I say, totally stumped, that's real tough.

It's okay, goes Ella, all philosophical-sounding. It was a long time ago. I miss Daddy now and then, but I don't miss her because I never knew her. You can't miss someone you never knew, can you?

Jesus. I start to feel pretty bad right then, cos all this time I been imagining Ella as having this perfect family who've spoilt her rotten and given her anything she ever wanted. It would turn out she's a fucking orphan.

Well, I go after a bit, trying to be positive, I'm sure Jack'll come round. Maybe you'll win, eh? Then he'll change his tune, won't he? He'll be desperate for you to just look his way, I bet!

Ella stares at me, eyes all shining like this would be a dream come true. Course I don't add that I think her winning is about as likely as me getting bendy enough to drop into splits with a big smile plastered over me face.

Oh! she goes, all faraway-sounding. That's all I want!

And as she says that I realise something's not quite right with this situation. Like, why does she care about this Jack guy so bad? And suddenly I get this nasty suspicion, and like the twat I am I don't leave it alone like I obviously should and I go, Ella – why does it matter what he thinks anyway?

She smiles this totally daft smile, and once again I can't help but notice how annoyingly pretty she is even with no make-up and her whole face swollen up from tears. Least she didn't get fucked in that department.

I love him! she goes. That's the reason I entered this contest. To make him see me and love me back, the same as he used to!

And this is the part where I realise that it's true that Ella shouldn't be here, not cos she can't hack it or ain't tough enough, but cos she's been fucked up big time. You keep your distance, Joni, I think to meself. This is not someone you want to get involved with.

There's a bang at the door and Scouser Valerie shouts out, Oi, Patty says we're starting again so get your arses in gear, you two! I stand up and look down at Ella, who's all hunched up in this protective ball position, kind of like Baby does when he's sucking on his thumb. She looks so small and pathetic that I can't just leave and abandon her.

Come on you, I go, feeling like a right mug. I reach down and take her hand. We got dancing to do.

'All I can say is what a brilliant, brilliant time I'm having and how grateful I am to be given this opportunity. Loving every single last minute of it!'

I'm cold and sweating and itching all over. As we take our places for the final run-through it feels like I've got a ticking time bomb squished in amongst my brains. If I hear Ella whimper she's sorry one more time, or that Valerie's horsey laugh, or Anya with her posh fucking accent, telling us again why she became a vegetarian, I think I'm going to have to hurt someone. I always figured the girls at the club were irritating, but they're nothing on this bunch of dipshits. I'm even genuinely missing Eddy's political rants, just cos at least she's got a brain connected to her mouth. Earlier today in the bathroom Joni asked me what the bidet's for. When I told her she started having hysterics, like it's the funniest thing ever that someone might have gone and invented a facility for washing your privates. Still, least there's one good thing about being surrounded by twats, which is that if this is the competition, I'm starting to think I might have got a shot at winning after all. If I can make it through five whole weeks without murdering someone, that is.

Okay everybody – for the last time, shrieks Patty, a one, two, three, four – and GO!

We fall into step. As usual Joni turns the wrong way, but corrects herself right at the last minute and swivels round to face me just before disaster. She makes this stupid goofy face and grins like it's funny she's still getting it wrong even after five days non-stop practising. There's a camera pointed at us so I give her a supportive smile, though what really I'd like to do is ask her how she even manages to walk when she's so fucking inept.

It's not just the girls that are making this so hard. I thought the dance classes would be a piece of piss, but they're not at all. For one thing Patty keeps criticising me for dancing too sexy. You're not stripping anymore, she keeps on saying, you're entertaining! I mean, what the fuck is the difference? And all those naff names she gives the dance moves. It's like she's speaking another language. But the real killer so far has been the singing. We're being taught by this dick called Edgar, who insists on making us all do these weird warm-up exercises before we begin, like gurgling and singing la la la over and over until it makes your teeth itch. Spite of what they say, I've always thought it was a case of either you can sing or you can't, but Edgar, who went and threw a hissy fit when I called him Ed, says the voice is an instrument you have to *learn* to play. Well I like my instrument just fine the way it is thanks, but according to this prick I sound like a man that smokes too much. When I told him to fuck off, in a jokey way of course, he told me if I didn't sharpen up my attitude I'd be out of his class. Most of the week he's had me standing at the back with my finger pressed to my throat while everyone else gets on with it, singing in silence and trying to feel when my larynx bobs up towards my chin. Whenever he gets us to sing all together he gives the best bits to Louise, just cos she can go super high, which according to him means she's got perfect pitch. Well if that's perfect pitch, who wants it? You ask me she sounds like she's just sat down hard on something pointy.

Shit – it's the last bit. I spin my body round just in time and thrust one leg out, running my hands up and down my sides next to Valerie, trying to put on an entertaining pout without looking like a porn star. Can't tell what Patty's thinking. She'd make a great poker player. Six counts and then it's into the fanny thrusting.

The real reason I'm feeling so shitty is because I'm crashing. Like, big time. I didn't bring nearly enough blow in with me. What I did smuggle into the house was only s'posed to be for emergencies, only that went out the window after the second day. It's not like I can't handle the pressure, it's just that when you're getting up at seven in the morning and working through to ten at night, and surrounded by giggling brats that never shut up, you need the odd pick-me-up, take my word for it. Trouble is, I didn't think far enough ahead, and now the performance is tomorrow night and I'm definitely going to need a few lines to get me through. That's a few lines more than I got. It wouldn't be such a problem cept that this place is like Alcatraz, with no getting out unless you're ill or dead.

Okay girls, says Patty, as I stand behind the others in my final position trying not to shake cos of the stress, that's it. I suggest you all get an early night so you're fresh for the performance tomorrow.

Second she's gone everyone runs off to different corners of the house to practise on their songs, which means there's no escape. They're all power ballads and trust me the only thing worse than having to listen to someone covering a Celine Dion number over and over is having to cover it yourself. They've given me 'Falling Into You' and I want to puke every time I have to go into the chorus. If it wasn't bad enough that I hate the song, there's just no way I can compete with one of the best singers in the whole fucking world, so Jesus knows how I'm s'posed to make it happen onstage. I'll have to really work the crowd. Make them love me. It's lucky I've got three years' training to know how to do it.

Cept there's no way I can go out onstage tomorrow with a head like this. I got to get hold of some blow or else I'm up shit creek without a paddle. I need a master plan. Luckily, I got one.

The one place where no one's polluting the atmosphere with noise coming out their mouths is the bedroom, and since the crew are busy filming Ella whimpering her way through her Toni Braxton song and Joni ballsing up her dance steps, it's pretty easy for me to say in a loud voice, I'm off to bed, and then head off without them following. Once I'm upstairs I slide out my luggage bag from under the bed and slip it in under the duvet, patting it down till it looks like a body's under there. Then I plump up the pillows and voilà! – far as anyone can tell Riana is fast asleep and dead to the world.

Now for phase two. The house is a massive three-storey number, and the bedroom is on the second floor. But there's a fire escape off the bathroom with stairs leading down to the garden outside. So long as it doesn't set off some alarms this is what I am hoping will be my route to freedom. I push open the fire door and hold my breath. No alarms. Just like that I'm out.

Phase three. The garden is surrounded by this six-foot wall, which is half an inch taller than me. If I wasn't who I am I'd be pretty much trapped, but the good news is three years of twisting round poles and swinging up and down also turns out to be the perfect training for breaking and entering – or in my case exiting. I slip over the wall like Catwoman, landing on both feet on the pavement outside without so much as a scratch. They should build an army out of us strippers. We are fucking *hardcore*.

Only bad news is that residential wherever-the-fuck is not exactly jampacked with phone boxes, and it takes me a fucking eon to find one, by which point I'm sweating like a bastard and starting to wonder what I'm doing, jeopardising my shot at the big time with this crazy mission for blow. And please don't think I don't know it's crazy, it's just that I've got this image of tomorrow's performance, me standing in front of the panel, holding the mic, and this horrible headache pulsating up top. I see myself raising the mic to my lips and this shudder runs through me cos I know that if I open my mouth the only thing that's going to come out of it is puke. There's no turning back. It's a case of all or nothing.

Eddy answers after the eighth ring – just as I'm thinking her phone is about to screw me and go to voicemail. At the sound of her voice I suddenly realise how much I want her arms round me, holding me all tenderly in that way she does when she's pretending I'm just this naïve little girl that needs protecting from the big bad world outside. Right now I genuinely feel a bit like that and could really use a nice old cuddle. And a good long snog. As well as a decent snort.

Eddy, it's me – please don't hang up!

On the last day before I left the flat I kept expecting her to call, or else show up and make up. It upset me that she didn't. Maybe I should have called her, but I had that stupid crew following me around like a fucking entourage and then all the girls from the club dropping by one after the other to say goodbye and have a strut in front of the cameras, so I didn't get the opportunity. It's been bugging me all week the way we left things. Course we row all the time, and it often boils over and ends up in one or other of us threatening to move out or else leaving and staying with friends for a couple of nights. It's just that normally once those couple of nights are over and things have cooled down a bit I haven't moved halfway across London and been locked up in a houseful of girls and cameras and bastard coaches.

Well? goes Eddy after a long pause.

I'm sorry, Eddy. I was a total bitch.

I listen to her breathe, willing her not to make this difficult.

Yeah, she says, and I was a total cunt. I'm sorry too.

I let out a sigh of relief. We spend a bit longer saying sorry, and then I start to feel quite emotional and get all choked up. It's the strain, all that non-stop dancing and singing, and being constantly filmed and surrounded by gabbling wannabes. My voice cracks and I tell Eddy how hard it is and how much I just want to be curled up in bed with her. Eddy calls me her poor little baby and says she misses me like crazy.

I've taken a big risk sneaking out, I wail. I got to get back before anyone notices – maybe they already have! But I had to call you. I couldn't go another day without hearing your voice.

I wish I could see you! moans Eddy.

Well, listen, I say, trying to sound like it's just a spur-of-the-moment idea. Maybe that could be arranged . . .

Quickly I explain where I am, and say that if she wants she could come meet me in a few hours, this same spot, and that I'll sneak out again when everyone's asleep. They'll all be whacked out from today so there's no chance of anyone catching me, I figure. Eddy agrees straight away. I can tell she's quite excited by the idea of me taking this fuck-off big risk just to see her. Anarchy's in her blood, she's my little radical. I'm kind of turned-on myself. Breaking the rules is a sexy business.

Before I hang up I ask if she can score for me.

I'm desperate, I admit. I could really use some for the performance tomorrow. This environment is turning me into a nervous fucking wreck.

For a minute I think our connection's been broken, cos I can't hear anything from the end of the line, not even the sound of breathing.

Eddy?

You mean to say the only reason you called was to get me to ferry you over some coke? says Eddy coldly.

I should have known she'd choose to see it this way. Trust Eddy to turn something around so it seems like I'm nothing but a selfish shit who only cares about herself.

You know that's not the only reason! I say, struggling not to get narky. I just thought that if you're coming anyway—

Jesus! snaps Eddy again. I resist the temptation to say anything else cos I know it'll just make her madder. Instead I just wait. There's another long patch of silence and after a bit I start to worry maybe she's thrown the phone away in disgust.

Eddy . . . you there?

Yeah, I'm here.

I bite my lip.

Well?

What time do you want to meet?

I tell her four o'clock and say how much I love her. Then I start to get dirty and tell her how when I'm famous I'm going to make her drink champagne out of my pussy and then do things with the cork that'll make her blush. But before I've got on to this last bit she hangs up. Guess I'll just have to make it up to her when she gets here. We'll have our own little party, her, me and this here phone box.

Everyone's in bed when I get back. Valerie and Rebecca are doing their whispering thing under the bedclothes, like a couple of boarding school closet-cases, and there's the usual hog-snoring coming from Joni's bed. Nothing from Ella next to mine, so I s'pose she must have snivelled herself off to sleep already. It's completely dark and I stub my toe on the bedpost as I pull back the duvet. I can't help letting out a little gasp at the pain.

Who's that? calls a Scouser accent.

Me, I say to Valerie.

Thought you was asleep!

Was. Had to go to the toilet. Nighty night.

I slip into bed beside my luggage bag. It's only then that I realise I got no way of telling the time unless I get up again and go to the bathroom to check the clock there. I'm going to have to wing it. I close my eyes and let out a long breath. I need to relax. Another thing I miss about Eddy is the massage she sometimes gives me after I get off work. She's trained in Swedish and Thai from her days as a backpacker and it's like dying and going to heaven when she puts her hands on your body, specially after a night with it wrapped round a metal pole.

I don't mean to fall asleep, but once I'm lying there with my head on the pillow it's like this dark cloud just descends on me. Next thing I know the room's slowly filling with light and there's birds tweeting outside. It's the dawn-fucking-chorus. You don't really get to hear it in Hoxton, seeing as whatever birds there are get drowned out and probably run over by all the traffic. But all the way out here on the edge of London it's so loud it almost sounds like you've woken up in the middle of a forest. Sadly I'm not exactly in the right frame of mind to appreciate the wonder of nature. I feel like microwaved shit.

There's no other sound apart from the odd wheeze from sleeping girl-band wannabes, so I roll out of bed and tiptoe quickly into the bathroom. Fuck. It's four fucking thirty. I quickly push open the fire door. I'm only wearing my Mickey Mouse T-shirt and some panties but I decide not to bother with my shoes or putting on anything else, seeing as how Eddy'll already have been waiting for half an hour.

Course when I get on to the lawn this chill wind blows right up under the T-shirt and I wish I'd put more on. My head's thumping even worse than it was last night and I've got this nasty burning going on in my stomach, like there's acid eating away at my insides. My vision is cloudy and there's this synthetic ringing in my ears, kind of like all those birds are tweeting through a vocoder. I pull myself up and scramble over the wall, scraping my knee and coming away with a long bloody cut. So much for Catwoman.

The streets are still deserted so I chuck modesty out the window and race barefoot along the pavement without bothering to hold down the T-shirt, round the corner and up the road until the phone box is in sight. Then I come to a frozen halt. There's no sign of Eddy. I open the door and step inside, ready to start beating up the place out of frustration. Couldn't she have fucking waited? I'm only half a fucking hour late, aren't I?

Then I see it. There on top of the phone is a Boots bag and inside is a piece of carefully folded newspaper containing a little plastic bag of what looks like at least three good grams of blow. There's no note, no nothing. Just the bag, sitting there like one of those cakes in *Alice in Wonderland* with Eat Me written on it.

Oh Eddy, I breathe. You're a fucking lifesaver.

Even though it's a bad idea cos I'll be buzzing in bed, I can't resist a smidge, just to test that it really is the good stuff. It is. Straight away I feel better, and I can't stop myself from dabbing a tiny bit more on to my gums, to get a good taste of that wonderful numbness. I slip the packet into the back of my panties and take a moment to chill and get a grip. I'm kind of put out that Eddy just left it here like this. I mean, what if some tramp had come in and found it? I know she's probably still mad at me for making her get it and then for not showing up on time, but this stuff costs an absolute bomb. That's at least a hundred quid's worth she left sitting there for anyone to come along and nick off with.

I open the door and step back outside into the wind. As I hurry down the road a car slows down and honks at me. The driver's this middle-aged bloke, probably some repressed chartered accountant who lives round here. He leers and licks his lips in a totally pervy way. Normally I'd just give him the finger, but I'm too pleased with myself to give a shit about dirty old men, and instead I blow him a kiss and wiggle my arse for good measure as I run by.

Apart from missing Eddy the whole operation has gone so smoothly that I can't help congratulating myself as I make my way back up the fire escape. Turns out this is a lethal thing to do, seeing as I'm not quite in the clear yet. The fire door's closed and when I try to open it I find the safety lock on the inside's clicked into place. I turn and sink to my knees on the metal balcony, pressing my forehead against the railing, getting this sensation of falling into a great bottomless black hole. Suddenly everything seems hopeless. I've fucked it all up. They're gonna come here and find me and they'll twig that I sneaked out and throw me off the show. Then I'll be back to the club with my tail between my legs, and Dave'll give me this look like he never truly thought I'd amount to anything really, and Emily'll tell me it's all right cos I've still got her and I'll look at her and know that's me in ten years' time. I feel the tears begin to slide down my cheeks followed by a faint pitter-patter as they land on the metal platform below. I just want to die.

There's a sudden clanking noise from behind and I quickly turn, shielding the bulge on my butt as the fire door opens a crack and this thin suspicious face peeps out.

Riana?

It's Little Miss Perfect, Louise, who always gets the solos because of her pitch-perfect squeak of a voice. She stares at me like she was expecting to find a raving rapist.

What are you doing out here?

I just . . . I just needed some air, I lie. Louise's eyes travel down my body and I see she's looking at my muddy feet and taking in the bloody graze on my left knee. Got locked out so I went down to try the front door, only I tripped up, didn't I?

You know we're not allowed outside, says Miss Prissy, folding her arms. The tight-arsed little bitch is actually standing in the way of me getting back in. But in a weird, other-dimensional kind of a way, the whole situation is a bit hilarious and I have to stop this giggle that's rising up my throat.

It's the rules, she goes.

It was so hot in there I just wanted a breath of air! There's a bit of hysteria in my voice – funnily enough just what Edgar said I should be concentrating on trying to produce when I go for those high notes. It doesn't say anywhere in the contract that we have to deprive ourselves of oxygen, does it?

Louise continues to stare at me, her lower lip jutting out in a pout that actually kind of suits her. She's one of those girls who only look good when they don't smile, like Posh Spice. Then I realise she's not staring at my face. I follow her eyes down and see that they're focused on my chest. I inspect it quickly, but everything looks fine enough to me.

How do . . . they stay up like that? Louise murmurs, seeming to forget that I'm a tear- and mud-stained mess that she's stopping from getting inside. Even though it's the last thing I feel like doing, I force myself to give her this big sisterly smile.

They just do.

But . . .

She trails off and blushes. I realise I don't really know anything about her, cept for the fact she's been in training to be a pop star since birth or something. Next to Ella she's by far the quietest, just doing everything perfectly straight off and watching with this detached smirk while the rest of us all fuck up. It's nice to know she's got at least one insecurity. It makes her more human, something I might be more keen to appreciate if I wasn't freezing my arse off on a fire escape while she weighs up the finer points of having perky tits.

Got 'em after the first year of stripping, I tell her, putting my hands on my T-shirt and flattening it round them to show off their shape. Not bad, eh?

Louise stares at me, then looks down at my tits again, and then back up at me.

You mean to say they're *fake*? she gasps. I glance down at her own chest, nothing there at all hardly, apart from a pair of pointy little nipples poking through her silly heart-spotted vest. Still there's something promising about them, and even if this spoilt little madam's not my type, all skin and bone and flint, there's also something quite sexy about this situation. Me frozen and trying to protect a packet of coke strapped to my backside while Louise compares our bust sizes. I wave my hand in front of her face and she looks up. The red in her cheeks suits her too.

Sure, I say. Probably the most painful experience of my life, but definitely worth it. Suddenly everyone was fighting each other to slip their fivers between them. Wanna feel?

Louise looks shocked, as if I'd just suggested she have a suck on my tongue and see how she likes it. But she doesn't say no. I grab hold of her hand, pull her towards me, and then plant it firmly on my left tit. I'm already erect cos of the wind and her hand trembles as I push it down on the nipple, but when I let go she doesn't let it fall. Instead, ever so shyly, like she's worried my tit might come to life and bite her, she gives it a squeeze.

Three thousand quid for the pair and not one regret, I tell her. Got a discount for giving the surgeon a hand job.

If Louise gets that I'm joking she doesn't show it. Instead she flinches and steps back, lifting her head like she's suddenly come to her senses and can't believe what she's just been doing. She holds up her hand like she's been touching dog shit with it.

I have to get to bed, she declares. If you want to traipse around out here in the cold then that's your business, but some of us need our rest!

With these words Princess spins on her heel and marches back inside, the fire door swinging behind her. I catch it before it can close and lock me out again and then take a long, gorgeously satisfying breath of relief. I'm alive, safe and back in the game. And tonight, with a little help from the packet strapped to my arse, I'm gonna blow 'em away with my performance. This bitch is coming out on top.

'Oh, I'm not nervous. I don't actually get nervous, because I really believe in myself and in the music. I think some of the other girls are going to struggle to be honest, but not me. I can't wait to get out there and give it everything. It's what I was born to do!'

God – you have to get me through this.

I force my lips into a smile and turn my body round slowly to face the audience, trying to be sensual, refusing to acknowledge the cramp in my tummy. If only I'd eaten something at lunch. Just a few effing mouthfuls would have done it. But I was too psyched and I couldn't bring myself to swallow so much as a bite. I've always been like that in the hours before I go onstage – my performance is all I can think about. It just takes over everything, so that nothing else matters except for those precious moments when I'm under the spotlight with everyone's eyes upon me. I know I should have had something at breakfast at least, but I hate eating right after I get up because it makes me feel heavy and bloated for the rest of the morning, which is the last way you want to feel when you're practising dance moves.

Another shooting pain makes my tummy contract. I can't help but wince and so I hold the mic in front of my face to hide it.

'Don't let go of us!' I sing. 'Please – just – don't – let – go – of – us –!'

The three faces of the panel are completely blank, betraying not so much as a flicker of emotion. I don't know if they can tell my smile is forced and that I'm in agony or not. But they must be able to hear that something is wrong. My voice has lost that silky sheen that's supposed to go with this song, like in the Lindsay Star original. Instead I sound raspy and thin, a weak-voiced backing singer at best. How can this be happening to me? And with every breath there's another burning sensation inside, probably my stomach trying to digest its own tissue.

'I said just – don't – let – go –!'

I quaver horribly as I reach the crescendo, and for a second I'm not even sure if I'm going to make it. It's a live broadcast. I picture Dad, watching this on TV, seeing this pathetic performance and being let down by the mess his daughter is making of her shot at the big time. And of course Mr Field will be watching too, listening as my voice gets weaker and weaker and thinking, What the hell is she playing at after all our hard work? But even worse than the thought of Dad and Mr Field is knowing the girls are following my every move on the monitor in the waiting room out the back, sniggering to themselves and secretly thrilled to pieces because they all want me to fail. After just one week I can already tell that they all hate me, just because I'm so obviously better than they are. People are like that. They just want to see you screw up, each and every one of them, so they don't have to feel bad about being losers themselves. It's sad, but I suppose it's also human nature. Not that I give an eff about human nature, or about the other girls – because I'm not screwing this up! I'm the best. That's why I'm here and that's why I'm going to win!

Please, God, please, I pray silently as I sing, you have to help me. Don't let me lose it now. Don't let me fail.

I haven't weighed myself since I left home, but I know I'm down to seven. Yesterday, right in front of everyone, Edgar suddenly demanded to know if I'd ever had any issues with my weight. Of course I said no and acted all shocked, but I could tell he wasn't convinced from the way he looked me up and down and nodded with this wry expression, like he was an eating disorder expert and knew a victim when he saw one. I made a big deal of saying to the camera all about how I think girls who try to look like fashion models are messed-up victims of pop culture and that I've always been skinny and that I'm proud of my body shape. But all the while I was thinking 'too podgy'. Maybe if that witch hadn't called me that I wouldn't be having this hell going on in my tummy right now. Look at her, sitting there at the centre of the panel, all self-important like she's the queen. Jabba the Hutt more like. How can someone so completely unattractive be behind a phenomenon like Purrfect? It just doesn't make any sense.

With an effort that's like nothing I've ever known before I launch myself into the last chorus, even though my tummy now feels like it's being wrenched in two and I'm practically ready to faint from the agony. I try to make myself think of the music, of the meaning behind Lindsay Star's beautiful lyrics. I try to let the melody carry me upwards and onwards, towards the glory I know I deserve. Tiny sparkles are dancing about at the corners of my vision, like someone's sprinkled glitter across the stage.

'If you let go, you'll regret it. Please baby, just – don't – let – go –!'

I sink to one knee and reach out with the hand that isn't holding the mic, grasping at the air as if trying to grip on to that special someone Lindsay wrote this song for. I'm on the build-up to the last note and I know I can do it. I squeeze my eyes shut and concentrate hard. This is what you have to do when you're losing it. It's the last resort. You think of something that's so important that it makes everything else fade into insignificance – even unbearable pain. I read that Madonna once did a whole concert with a twisted ankle and a sprained knee. Cher was fifty-six when she did her farewell tour and she danced every single performance no matter how she was feeling. Even the Spice Girls managed to complete their American tour with two of them pregnant and vomiting into buckets in between set pieces. If they can do it then so can I.

I rack my brains for an image to hold on to, something that will carry me onwards and through to the end of the song. And as the music swells for the last time, a face suddenly pops into my head and I focus on it with all my energy and soul. Strangely it isn't Lindsay's face, or Dad's or even Mr Field's. For some reason it's the face of that black girl, Riana. She's got the same expression she had this morning, when I found her out on the fire escape doing who knows what, all splattered with mud and with a bloody knee, but shiny with relief because she thought she'd been locked out. Those boobs! I should have known that they were fake from the very beginning. No one has breasts like that, not naturally. Pathetic really, to feel that you have to have yourself cut open and then have these alien things stuffed inside behind each nipple – not to mention giving sexual favours in order to get a discount! What a slut . . . and yet they felt so real, or at least how I imagine real big breasts would feel. I've never touched anyone's apart from my own, which are hardly even existent anyway. I've never touched a black person before either. And no girl's ever done that, just invited me to feel her chest as if it was the most normal thing in the world.

There's applause from the studio. I open my eyes and realise that I've done it. I've performed without collapsing, and even though it was terrible at least I got through it. Surely that's got to count for something.

'Let's big it up for Louise!' shouts Stina Ellis, the enemy of all things dignified, tottering onstage in a pair of silly spikes that highlight what ugly plump calves she's got. The lights come up and flood the stage with yellow, so that for a few seconds I can't see a thing. Then Stina's nasty orange arm loops round my shoulder and helps me to stand, and the world starts to take shape again: row upon row of faces, the invited audience of Purrfect fans. I strain to hear what kind of applause they're giving me. You can always tell what the audience is feeling if you listen hard enough. It sounds muted, half-hearted, at best a sympathy clap. Nothing like the deafening noise that greeted all the others when they did their pieces. Even that snivelling twit Ella got a few standing ovations from this bunch of nobodies.

'Well, I thought that wasn't bad!' trills Stina. I hate her so much for this comment that I almost forget the pain in my tummy entirely. She's wearing a ridiculously tight red dress that compresses her breasts so they burst out at the top like half-deflated balloons. No doubt about the origin of those lumpy eyesores. 'But it doesn't matter what I think. Let's hear what the judges have to say!'

She propels me towards the three faces sat opposite, still blank as can be. Tess leans forward on her elbows and pushes her D&G glasses up her nose. Now she looks like a dark-skinned version of Jo Brand, po-faced and hair all frazzled as if she took one look in the mirror and decided there wasn't any point in bothering since it's not like anyone is ever going to think she's even okay-looking. Sometimes you can't help but wonder why God bothers creating unattractive people.

'I expected better,' she says in her horrible flat toneless voice, like she hardly even cares either way. 'I thought you were one of the stars of this operation, Louise. But I guess I was wrong.'

There is booing and hooting from the studio audience, but that's only because the man who does the placards is holding one up and waving it around. Really it sounds like everyone secretly agrees with her. My throat constricts like I've just swallowed my own tongue and I almost gag. The pain in my tummy is slowly diminishing now, being replaced with a dull throbbing. This must be what failure feels like.

'I agree with Tess,' says Joe in his stupid, camp, whiny gay voice. 'We expected better from you, Louise. I don't know what happened up there tonight, but that performance simply stank.'

God, how can you let this happen?

The placards man is now waving his card around madly and there's even more booing, only this time it's really loud. I take a deep gulp of oxygen and stand as still as I can. Only Emma's verdict is left. She's wearing a blue crop top and looks amazing with her long blonde hair all spread out on her shoulders. She makes Stina Ellis look like a toad. *Please God, let her be kind.*

'Louise, are you feeling all right?' she says, frowning and looking concerned. *Thank you, God.* I gulp again and shake my head.

'Oh no!' cries Stina like she's in a pantomime. 'What's the matter, Louise?'

'I'm sorry,' I say, offering a brave smile and shivering like I can't help it. 'I've not been feeling well. It's not nerves . . . it's a virus I think. But I didn't want to let anyone down!'

'Oh Louise!' cries Emma, sounding all motherly. 'The only person you let down if you come onstage like death warmed up is yourself!' She turns to the others triumphantly. 'I knew there was something the matter with her!' she exclaims. 'If you look at her progress over the last week she'd never perform like that under normal circumstances!'

'Well then, if she's ill why is she even performing at all?' says Joe, like he can't be bothered with sick people. 'And why didn't she say something earlier?'

He and Emma start bickering, much to the amusement of the audience, who begin to titter. Emma claims that I can't help being sick and Joe tells her that it's deeply unprofessional to tell a panel of judges you're unwell right after you've just performed. The smug-faced little queer is probably right, but it's the truth, near enough, and I can't help it, can I? Meanwhile Tess the troll just sits there rolling her ugly bug eyes. Finally she decides she's had enough.

'The fact is we're looking for the new Purrfect girl,' she declares, instantly silencing the other two. 'The Purrfect girls wouldn't let anything come between them and their audience, including a virus. Louise – you were capable of getting up there tonight and doing your song and that means you're still eligible to be voted off.'

For a minute I think a tidal wave has hit. Only a second later do I realise that it's just the sound of everyone in the audience booing and hissing; this time no encouragement from the man with the placards is needed. They're actually standing up in the front few rows and yelling for all they're worth. Tess looks surprised and even deigns to turn her head round and clock a look, as if she's only just noticed all these people are here in the studio with her. Then she turns back, her mouth set in a nasty grimace.

'I don't care how tough it seems,' she says firmly. 'That's show business for you. If you can't hack it, you shouldn't be part of it!'

More booing, like the roar of a thousand thunderclaps. Honestly, I've never heard anything like it. It feels . . . good.

'Well!' shrieks Stina, who I can only hear over the top because her mic is right next to my ear. She's clearly thrilled by what's going on and tightens her fat orange snake of an arm around my neck like she wants to show how much she's on my side. 'Sounds as though you've got some support out there, Louise! Let's hope they remember you at voting time!'

She suddenly releases me from her choke hold and turns to face a camera as it flies towards us, suspended over the stage by a long crane.

'Just to remind everybody how it works. Tonight's special audience will all have the chance to vote for their favourite performer, who will be given a safe pass into next week. From the remaining girls the judges will then select the one who shows the least potential, who will be going home. Tonight one of these girls is definitely *not* going to be the new member of Purrfect! Ladies and gentlemen – that was Louise!'

Everyone cheers as I walk off. I make sure to sway and make my walk seem as if I'm having difficulty remembering how to put one foot after the other. A real Amy Winehouse impression. It's not too hard to pull off since I'm genuinely feeling rather giddy. The cheering is at least as loud as any of the other girls got, and it continues for several seconds after I've left the stage. I hear Stina trying to calm them down without much success. I can hardly believe it as I stand there in the wings trying to pull myself together – I've never been so popular, not even with all the brilliant song and dance routines I've done. And all I did was say I hadn't been feeling well. It doesn't change my performance, or my voice, or what they saw. Yet it feels nice. In fact it feels wonderful. To be cheered on not because I was good but because I'm a human being who has problems just like the next person. It feels like people out there really care.

Michelle – the bee that was in charge at the auditions – appears and ushers me down the corridor past all these stage hands and technical crew, who all just seem to be hanging out doing nothing in particular except watching Stina's bottom in her spray-on dress and sniggering into their headsets.

'Right, someone'll be along with your costumes for the end,' she tells me as we reach the waiting room. 'Then you'll have ten minutes to change and get ready.'

'Could I have some aspirin?' I say coldly. This mean-faced bee is no one's friend and there's not even any point in trying to make her feel sorry for you. 'If that's not too much trouble,' I add. Michelle replies that she'll see what she can do in a voice that implies she couldn't care less and then stalks off up the corridor.

As soon as I enter the room all the other girls come rushing over to tell me how sorry they are and how much they hope I'm feeling better, apart from Ella, who's still sitting in the corner with a silly smile on her face dreaming away like she was before I went up. Like anyone would have even clapped for her if she weren't okay to look at. And Riana, who leans against the wall watching everyone with this smirk while Valerie announces all self-importantly that she could tell I wasn't well from the colour of my cheeks. Annoying giantess Rebecca informs me she thought I sounded fine except for that last part and not to worry because she's sure nobody noticed, which is the most ridiculously untrue thing I've ever heard. I glance over at Riana, who's wearing a long white dress with a strip missing down the middle, so half of her chest is on display. Even though I know they're fake, it's still difficult not to be a little impressed. She could deflect bullets with those things. No wonder she's smirking. She thinks I'm going tonight.

'Costumes!'

A young man opens the door and wheels in a clothing rack holding our outfits. They're all variations of the same thing: black, lacy, tight-fitting with lots of silver sequins. Behind the guy stands a cameraman, but no sign of Michelle with my aspirin. The girls immediately start tearing off their clothes and yanking costumes from the rack, searching through the nametags, ignoring the guy, who pauses, looking around at all the girls as if he can't believe his luck. Joni gives him a wink. You can tell she's a whore, that one, just from listening to the way she talks, she probably doesn't know the meaning of the word self-respect. Then Riana strides casually forward, plucks up her outfit, turns to the guy and says: 'Where I come from, a striptease costs *money*.' The guy, who's hardly any older than me, goes beetroot red and hurries out the room. The cameraman stays at the door, still filming, until Riana strides over and closes it on him. She shoots me a smile, and to my surprise I find myself smiling back. Weirdly, I actually have an impulse to hug her.

'Lord!' goes Riana to no one in particular. Instantly my nice feeling towards her vanishes. It really annoys me the way people take His name in vain all the time. I pick up my outfit and suddenly I'm filled with a horrible sense of foreboding. Maybe this is the last costume I'm going to wear. Maybe later tonight I'll arrive back home in the limo and Dad'll be standing there waiting for me with tears in his eyes, and he'll say it doesn't matter and that I'm still the best in the world, and although we'll go back to normal we'll both secretly know that it isn't true anymore. God, if you fail me now I'll stop believing in you, I mentally project, even though of course that isn't true because you can never turn your back on Him.

A few minutes later we're all lined up in the wings listening to Stina going on in her bubblegum voice about how insanely exciting this competition is and how the performances tonight make it impossible for anyone to predict what the outcome will be. My head feels light and fluttery, but at least my tummy has settled down. I almost wish it still hurt, so that at least I had something to concentrate on instead of the impending decision, which I just know is going to be me. I can see it perfectly, Tess saying my name and then the awful, awful, awful walk of shame while all the other girls put on relieved smiles and wave gleeful goodbyes.

I feel a tap on my shoulder. I turn to find Riana with a massive grin. Here in the dark the whites of her eyes shine like a zombie's.

'You feeling all right now?' she whispers.

I shrug, since I can't be bothered to talk to her right now. It's all very well for this bee – *she* doesn't have anything to worry about. Her voice was all wrong for her song and she looked like a total hooker up on stage, but you could see the audience liked her, and none of the judges had anything bad to say either. Probably she's in league with the Devil.

'Just remember to smile,' she says, as if I needed any advice from her. 'You'll be glad you did later, no matter what happens.'

I'm just about to say something really cutting back, like next time I want advice from a slab of singing silicone I'll ask for it, but just then the intro music starts and we're all walking out onstage in a line, holding hands like we've rehearsed with Patty. Ella's hand in front of me is ice cold and trembling so much it's annoying and makes me want to slap her. Meanwhile Riana's hand behind is almost red hot by comparison and completely still.

'So girls,' shouts Stina at our faces once we're all lined up in front of the judges. Opposite the light is blinding, and I can't help but think that it's like facing a firing squad. I've never felt such foreboding in my whole life. Oh God, please don't desert me. Not now, in my hour of need.

'Are you ready to hear the verdict?'

We all smile and nod. Effing Stina then takes out a card from the envelope she's holding and reads off it with heart-attack-inducing slowness.

'First of all I will reveal the name of the girl tonight's audience has chosen to go through into the competition next week,' she says. 'This girl will have a safe pass into next week and the judges will not be able to expel her.'

The band begins a drum roll. I shoot a quick glance at Riana, strong and confident beside me, and remember the way the crowd practically screamed after she finished her awful version of Celine Dion's lovely ballad. She's staring out into the audience, her smile so big and white it looks like a half moon stuck to her face. I'm smiling too, but next to hers it must look feeble and pathetic, the smile of a loser. I want to die.

'And the name of the girl through to next week is . . .' says Stina, and I want to kill her for pausing once again. I want to see her bludgeoned to death with her own stupid mic, her even stupider skin-tight dress all stained with oozing gore.

Strike her down, God. Strike her down this instant and I don't care what happens!

'. . . Louise!'

For a few seconds it's like my senses have shut down because I'm not even aware of what is going on. Then I realise the other girls are crowding round me and hugging me, screaming and clapping and pretending to be pleased that I got voted for instead of them. And Stina is giving my shoulder a nasty squeeze and congratulating me. I can't even hear what the stupid slag is saying. The tears are pouring out of my eyes and I just let them. I can't speak for happiness. God, I think, looking directly out into the light which seems the most likely place for him to be, I promise never ever to doubt you again!

'I'm so happy to have got through. So happy. But . . . it's strange . . . Like we're living our lives underwater or something. Nothing seems like it can be real!'

I'm woken up by the sound of screaming. At first I'm completely disoriented, and I think I'm in my own room back in Kensington and that Rita or Mimi are being murdered or something terrible like that. Then I sit up and see the dorm around me and the other girls, also shaking off sleep and peering up to see what the fuss is about. It's Valerie. She's standing at the door in her pyjamas holding a pile of newspapers, her mouth open as she reads from the one on the top. And then I remember: I'm here. I made it. I didn't get sent home.

The girls all spring out of bed and cluster around her. It's not long before everyone's emitting similar high-pitched shrieks of delight, snatching up papers from Valerie's arms and staring at them like they can't believe what they're seeing. I sit up and watch, wondering dimly what's going on. My head feels fuzzy from sleep and my stomach aches, which is a sure sign my period is coming on. I was having a weird dream about the contest, where we were performing on a ship that was sinking: everyone had to wear lifebelts while they did their songs, and we kept on going even though we knew we were all going to drown. I rub my eyes, trying to shake off that nasty hollow feeling of impending doom that's followed me into the real world. Valerie detaches herself from the group and marches over.

'Here you go, Ella,' she tells me, thrusting a paper into my lap. Her face glistens. It's funny how excitement really opens up your pores. 'Go on. Have a look!'

I look down at the paper. It's the *Telegraph*'s TV section with reviews of last night's telly, and there's an article about *The Purrfect Search*. What you immediately focus on is the picture above, which shows Valerie in her black all-in-one Dior jumpsuit with the rhinestones, her eyes closed and the mic raised to her lips midway through her performance of 'What a Girl Wants'.

'Oh my God,' I say.

For some reason it never occurred to me that the programme would be reviewed in all the papers, or that anyone would actually write articles about it, even though Rita told me *Fascinate!* were thinking of doing one. I was too busy being thankful for not being voted off. When Anya's name was read out and they showed the close-up of her face, all white and trembling, on the massive screen behind the stage, I thought I was going to die for her. She looked *so* upset. Like life for her was over. When we all went to say goodbye she clamped her arms around me in this vice-like hug, and it was like she was trying to hold on to the programme and not let it slip away. I felt like I was betraying her by letting go.

'Read what it says!' orders Valerie impatiently.

I read. It says that the programme is just another in a long line of reality TV shows, searching for the next big thing, this time for the super-successful girl band Purrfect. Then it goes on to say that no matter what you might think of this kind of programme, it makes for pretty addictive viewing, and mentions several of the girls by name. The last part is about Joni and me: 'Joni, sewer-mouthed chav, provides most of the laughs, while skinny blonde car-crash-waiting-to-happen Ella offers plenty of cringe-inducing moments that'll either have you rooting for her or else wishing she'd do us all a favour and get some therapy.' I'm stunned, scarcely able to hold the paper.

'Don't let it get to you,' advises Valerie in a worldly voice, as if she knows all about the pressures of being a celebrity. 'The important thing to remember is that you've got exposure. That's all that matters.'

I look over at Joni, who's poring over another paper with Rebecca. Both of them are laughing. 'Fucking mental!' she screeches, at which point she notices the cameraman who's edged his way into the room and is filming over their shoulders. Her hand flies up to her mouth since she's been told off for swearing lots of times and she giggles: 'Oops.' Behind them Riana is leaning against the wall, grinning. She looks up and catches my eye, turning her paper round to give me a glimpse of what she's reading. I'm amazed to see a massive picture of *her*, dressed in a white string bikini and smiling out like a page three girl. Next to her is the caption, THE SINGING STRIPPER! It's the *Sun*, and the article is entitled WHO'S GOING TO BE PURRFECT? There are little portraits of the rest of us, including me, but before I can see what's written there Riana shrugs and flips the paper back round. Over in the far corner the cameraman is now filming Louise, sitting up perfectly straight on the bed with her hair immaculately brushed and glossy as ever, turning the pages of a paper with a detached smile, like she gets written about all the time. 'I think it's important to stay grounded,' she's saying. I look back down at the *Telegraph* and my name in print and suddenly I'm overwhelmed because I've remembered the other reason I was so nervous about last night. Jack.

'Attention, girls!' barks a harsh, unmistakable voice. Everyone looks up, somewhat freaked out by the sight of Tess standing in the doorway of the dorm surveying us all in our night things.

He'll have seen it. Probably with Rita and Mimi beside him. Everyone we know will know that he went there and exploded in front of all those people and attacked the sound man. Everyone will have seen him making a fool of himself, and will wonder why he got so mad. I feel a lump rising in my throat, but Tess is talking and so I force it back down.

'I hope you're all enjoying your first brush with fame,' she says, gesturing dismissively at the papers. 'You can expect more of that from here on in. And if you're wise, you'll learn to ignore it and focus on the job at hand. Because we're looking for a performer, not some glamour model.'

She shows her teeth and lets her gaze drift round the room like she's probing for signs of weakness, looking each one of us squarely in the eyes. It's disconcerting, her way of doing this, almost as if she knows some incriminating information about you and wants you to understand she is only waiting for the right moment to screw you over with it. She reaches me last of all, and I look into her eyes, magnified by those horrid silver glasses that don't do a thing for her. I feel myself begin to tremble. Everything seems to go quiet and for a second. I wonder if she really does know something. Like about Jack, for instance. Maybe he's been in contact with the organisers to complain about the broadcast and she's put two and two together. Or else maybe she's just figured it out from reading my thoughts. It wouldn't surprise me in the slightest if it turned out she had some kind of evil superpower like telepathy. She's exactly the sort of person you'd expect to have it, and it would go a long way towards explaining how such a bitch got to be such a successful band manager.

Tess brings her hands together in a loud clap which makes me jump and breaks off her gaze.

'This week you will be working in pairs and performing duets with one another at next week's studio session. You'll be assessed individually, and as before, one of you will be voted off. No more free passes! Ten minutes to get dressed. We've got a treat for you downstairs. Remember, girls, this is no time to get complacent. You've got a lot of work ahead of you, and if you don't give it your all, you won't make it.'

With this she turns abruptly on her heel and stalks out the room. For a few seconds there is silence while we all absorb her words. Those feelings of relief and happiness at being chosen last night have been sucked out and replaced by a sense of urgency and fear. Immediately everyone is tense, and when I offer Valerie back the paper she merely looks at me like I'm a mutant and turns away to get dressed. I put it down on the bed and go through to the bathroom. I pause in front of the mirror and stare at my reflection, bleary-eyed, hair unkempt, skin red and still marked with pillow creases. Hardly the stuff of a future megastar. Hardly the stuff of anyone worthwhile at all. The lump in my throat is rising again, only this time there's nothing stopping it. I push open a cubicle door just in time to aim the pellet of puke that bursts out of my mouth into the toilet bowl. It's an ugly yellow colour, a bit like urine. I wipe my mouth with some toilet paper and drop my head over the bowl, waiting for the sick feeling to go away, trying not to think about Jack and how much he probably hates me right now. When I lift my head I notice what looks like a black snake on my thigh. I let out a little scream, before I realise that of course it's just a trickle of blood. Guess I've started. Shit, and my tampons are back in the drawer beside my bed. I pull out more toilet roll and make a wad out of it. As I do there's a pounding on the door behind me.

'Ella? You all right in there?'

It's Joni. I mumble back that I'm okay, only for her to shout 'WHAAAT?' forcing me to repeat myself and making me wish that I was more like her. Joni's so strong and confident. Nothing ever fazes her. Criticism, bad experiences, stupid mistakes – they all just bounce right off like they didn't even happen. Not like with me. Sometimes I still catch myself thinking about stuff that's happened to me ages ago and getting cold rushes from the memory of it. Even tiny things that don't matter, like nobody wanting to be my partner for a physics experiment at school and having to do it with the teacher at her desk up at the front of the classroom while everyone sniggered. Stuff like that – I still get shivers thinking about it. And big things too, like being told by Rita that Daddy wasn't coming back from Nepal. Or the last time Jack drove me out to the common and stared out at the woods for what seemed like an age before telling me it was time that we stopped seeing each other.

If only I knew he didn't blame me, then I wouldn't feel so bad.

'Come on Ella, everyone else has gone already!'

It's Joni again. Damn it.

'I'm coming!' I yell. I quickly wipe away the blood and push the wad up under my panties. Using the tank as a crutch I lever myself up to stand. It *isn't* my fault – that's what I need to remember. And maybe, just maybe, seeing himself as he can sometimes be is a lesson Jack needs to learn. I mean, maybe he's even grateful to me. He might even have seen my performance and realised that he made a mistake. He might even be thinking of me like I'm thinking of him, right at this very moment, wishing I was there in his arms and he was looking down into my eyes and getting lost in them.

'Ella!'

There's a scratching sound from the next cubicle and then a banging on the divide and I look up as Joni's head pops over it.

'Guessed as much,' she grins. 'Here.'

A miniature white torpedo flies past my face and plops onto the floor in front of me. I pick it up and give her a grateful smile, though I'm actually rather embarrassed.

'I'll see you downstairs, all right?'

Everyone's waiting for me in the studio room. Tess, Joe and Emma are standing against the wall and two cameramen with little headsets are set up in opposite corners. A semi-circle of chairs has been arranged facing the panel but only one of them is free since the other girls are all sitting ready and waiting. Everyone looks at me.

'Sorry . . .' I stutter.

'Ella, the music industry doesn't *do* lateness,' says Joe. He's wearing his usual combo of Armani T-shirt, combats and shades, only this time the shades are slanted upwards and have red lenses which make him look demonic. He taps the face of his gold Armani watch with a French-manicured nail. 'If you don't show up on time, people won't wait for you. They'll write you off as dead. It's as simple as that.'

'I'm really sorry,' I say again, feeling myself burning up.

'I told you, she got her period!' calls Joni from the corner, rolling her eyes like she can't believe how unreasonable Joe's being. I can't believe she's actually told them this is the reason I'm late. My cheeks now feel like they're on fire. Joe lets out this super-long sigh and shakes his head, looking at me like I've disappointed him deeply. Then, just as I'm about to combust with shame, to my amazement Tess comes to my rescue.

'Yes, *Joe*,' she says meaningfully, as though being a man he couldn't possibly understand – which is true when you think about it. 'There are certain times in a woman's life when she can't just drop everything to go compete in an industry dominated by *men*. For example when her vagina is *gushing with blood*!'

Riana, sitting right in the middle of the semi-circle, bursts out laughing, but everyone else just looks embarrassed. Joe wrinkles up his whole face like he's never heard anything so disgusting and holds up his hand with the palm turned towards Tess.

'I don't want to know!' he whines in a suddenly childlike voice. 'Let's just move on, okay?'

Emma shoots me a smile and motions for me to sit down. I slot myself into the last seat by the wall and duck my head, willing myself to stop blushing.

'Right,' says Tess. 'Now that we're done explaining the workings of the female body, we have a nice surprise in store for you girls. As a reward for passing into the second week, you are each to be allowed one fifteen-minute phone call to talk to your parents, spouses, siblings or whoever. You can make this call at any point over the coming week, it's up to you.'

My heart starts to beat faster. The burning in my cheeks is replaced by a burning of excitement. I can call Jack. I can speak to him and tell him that it wasn't my fault and that I love him and that the song I was singing last night was meant *for him*. When he hears that I know he'll forgive me.

'And now down to business,' says Tess, nodding to Emma. Emma clears her throat and steps forward, smiling at us. I wish the other two would smile like her – easy and genuine. It makes such a difference to the way you feel.

'Group work is a key component of being in a girl band,' she says. 'It requires strength, discipline, hard work and above all cooperation. At this week's final you will be performing duets with a partner. This exercise will test your abilities to form professional working relationships.'

Joe steps forward, puffing out his stomach as he raises his clipboard.

'The names of the duets and the songs you will be working on are as follows,' he says. 'Valerie and Rebecca – "Miracles".'

Valerie and Rebecca each let out little screams and grab each other's hands. They're lucky, since they get on so well already. I'm immediately scared, since no matter who I get put with they're bound to wish they hadn't got saddled with me. I don't think I've ever been in a team for anything where I wasn't one of the last people to be picked. *Let it be Joni*, I pray to the clipboard Joe is holding. At least she won't mind, since nothing bothers her.

'Joni and Ella – "Prayers for You".'

A wave of relief floods through me, so great that I almost pee myself. I turn to Joni with a big smile, only I'm shocked to see that she's not smiling back at me. In fact she looks horrified, like she's just been told she has to sing her duet with a performing monkey. When she catches me looking at her she quickly grins and shrugs, but it's too late and I've already seen how she really feels. I look away quickly, desperately pretending I'm not on the brink of tears. I guess her reaction is understandable. I wouldn't want to work with me either. Joe keeps reading, but I'm not listening anymore and I don't catch what song Riana and Louise are doing. Neither of them gives any indication of whether or not they are happy to have each other for a partner, they both just nod gravely like they've got a job to do and even though it may be grim nothing is going to stop them from doing it. Why can't I be like that? Why do I have to be so weak all the time?

'And now for the special news,' Emma declares. 'Working on your duets with you will be one of Britain's most respected vocal coaches, Billy Bickler. He's worked with the likes of Natalie Imbruglia, Rachel Stevens and Sophie Ellis Bexter. This week, he's going to be focusing all of his attention on you!'

She and Joe and Tess look at us expectantly. Everyone lets out little screams, including me this time, though it's obvious that none of us have ever heard of him.

'Right then, girls,' says Tess. 'Patty's expecting you all in the dance studio at eleven. Until then, you're free. I suggest you use the time to focus yourselves on your game plan this week. Last night we saw a talented girl leave the competition. You need to ask yourselves what she did wrong and what you can do to avoid the same fate.'

'As for the phones, use them wisely, because we're not giving out extra credit. Purrfect are often so busy they have to go for long periods of time without speaking to the people they love. You've got to be tough in this game. It's no place for sissies.'

She nods curtly at Joe, who picks up a box beside his feet which I didn't notice before. He and Emma then walk around the semi-circle distributing special white mobiles with gold stars and the word 'Purrfect' printed on them. Emma explains that they have exactly fifteen minutes' credit on them and do not accept inbound calls. She proudly adds that they're freebies from Vodafone, and we'll be allowed to keep them as mementos once the competition is over.

As soon as they're done and everyone's talking amongst themselves I hurry off back upstairs to the bedroom. I throw myself on my bed and type in our house number. My fingers keep getting it wrong because I'm shaking so much, but finally I get it. The phone starts to ring. Once, twice, three times. Pick up, pick up, pick up, I scream silently at it.

'Hello?' says a familiar voice.

'Mimi!'

'Oh my God!' screams Mimi. 'Ella!'

It takes about a year just to stop her yelling my name. I keep trying to tell her I haven't got much time but she can't stop screaming about how she's seen me on TV and everyone at school knows who I am and they all think I'm the best and are betting that I'll be the one who makes it through to Purrfect. It's very sweet of her, I guess. In fact it's more than sweet – it makes me feel wanted and special, like someone out there really does care about what happens to me. Tears come to my eyes. But I'm aware that precious seconds are slipping away.

'Thanks, Mimi,' I say, hoping she can hear how much I really mean it. 'Now can you put Jack on, please?'

'Put him on?' goes Mimi, like I've just asked her to do the weirdest thing in the world. 'Don't you know?'

This sense of foreboding hits me. I take a deep breath, and as I do I notice that a cameraman has stolen up behind me and there is a big black lens pointed at me from the other side of the bed.

'Know what?'

'He's not here,' says Mimi. 'I thought Mum would have got the message to you or something.'

'What are you talking about?' I say shrilly, fighting to keep the panic from taking over and feeling my hand with the phone against my ear begin to shake uncontrollably. 'Gone where? What are you talking about?'

'He's left us,' says Mimi. 'Since the night you went him and Mum have done nothing but argue. It's been like fucking bombs are going off. They even threw things at each other the other day. They broke that bowl I made in pottery class last term! You know, the one with the silver stars on it.'

'But . . . why were . . . they arguing?' I stumble over my words, almost choking with the effort of speaking.

'Oh, I don't know, adult stuff,' says Mimi, as if it hadn't even occurred to her to wonder. 'They don't love each other anymore, I s'pose. It's weird though because now I have to go home after school with Georgina and her mum. She makes microwave meals and they're disgusting! Rita says she's going to sort something better out once this week's issue is in but you know what she's like—'

'Mimi!' I shout, surprising the guy with the camera who is now holding it right in my face. He takes a small step backwards. 'Where did Jack go? How can I get in contact with him?'

'I don't know, he didn't leave a number. I don't think he wants to see any of us ever again. That's what he said, anyway. He was pretty cross.'

'But didn't he say *goodbye*? Don't you even *care* that he's gone?'

There's a pause at the other end and some talking followed by a rapid giggle. I hold the phone and tremble. I feel powerless, as though fate is coming towards me like the wide open mouth of a huge snake with poisonous fangs. I'm just this tiny paralysed mouse and there's nothing I can do to avoid being swallowed alive.

'Sorry,' Mimi comes back on the line. 'Listen Ella, you know that black girl – can you ask her how she gets her hair so big like that? My friend Alex is here and she's been desperate for a do like that since like, for ever, only nothing seems to work no matter how much Frizz-up she uses . . .'

'Mimi,' I say, trying not to weep. 'There's not much time. Can you get Rita?'

'Oh, she's not here. Can you call back later?'

'No,' I moan. 'This is the only phone call I get.'

'Oh,' says Mimi.

'Listen,' I tell her. 'I really don't have much time, but it's very important you get a message to Jack for me—'

'I told you, I don't know where he is!' goes Mimi stubbornly, doing her spoilt-little-brat thing. I feel my eyes stinging with tears and I quickly turn away from the cameraman, who merely glides round the bed to film me from the other side.

'Get Rita to tell you. I have to see him! There's something I need to say to him . . . Okay?'

There's no answer. 'Mimi! Will you do it?' I scream, wanting to murder her. But then I realise that the reason she's not responding is because the line has gone dead.

'I can't believe I'm in the bloody *Sun*! Right there in the middle of the page next to [bleep]ing Jordon! It's like being a proper celebrity! Me mum is going to totally [bleep]ing [bleep] herself when she sees it!'

I'm in the music studio in front of Billy at the piano, doing Edgar's singing posture thing (classic page-three pose more like – stomach in and tits out). We're waiting for Ella to get over herself so we can go again. Billy's this little old geezer with a crooked back and lots of ancient saggy skin. You'd never guess from looking at him that he was at the top of his game, working with all these famous singers and record producers and stuff. The only thing that's impressive about him is his ears, which are fucking massive, and which I s'pose must of been pretty useful, him being a musician and all. He sort of reminds me of the *BFG*, that Roald Dahl book which I was gonna start reading to Baby this month before I got on the programme. Makes me wonder how Mum's going with it. I been saving up me fifteen minutes for a time when it feels right, but the fact is I can hardly take it not knowing if Baby's missing his mum like she's missing him.

Sorry, sniffles Ella from the corner where she's gone to shiver and wipe her nose off.

Just take it easy, says Billy. Relax. Singing should always be an enjoyable experience. It should be what you love to do. Otherwise there's no point, is there?

He's a bit of a sweetheart, is this codger. He'd be a whole lot more of one if he didn't have a constant semi going on in his trousers, mind. Think you can guess what made him agree to this gig. Still, you can't help but like the old perv. Earlier on he told me stories about all the divas he's known, including this one whose name he won't say that leapt up on to the piano when she didn't get her way and started beating the shit out of it with a microphone stand.

No . . . says Ella, making this gross sound as she sniffs up all the snot in her nose, I guess not.

I know she can't help being a tool, but getting saddled with Ella is like being told you've got to breakdance with a fucking hump strapped to your arse. We've been at this for over an hour now and we ain't even got through the whole song yet. I'm starting to get the urge to give that pretty little face of hers a right good slapping. Every time the littlest thing goes wrong she starts weeping like it's the end of the fucking world. She hits a wrong note, off she goes. She misses her cue, boo hoo hoo. Even when she does something right she cries, like it's so unusual she can't handle it. She could teach old JT a thing or two about crying rivers and then some.

Okay, I'm ready, says Ella, I won't mess up this time, I promise.

She gives Billy this brave smile and glances at the camera all shy like she wishes it wasn't there. But it's always there, and it's always pointed at her no matter what's going on. I reckon them producers of this programme probably think she's a goldmine the way she can't stop blubbing, like Nikki in *Big Brother* cos of the way she always flew into a strop whenever she got asked to do anything. These basket cases always make good TV.

Great! goes Billy, like Ella ain't already promised this and then fucked up the last ten times we tried it. You ready, Joni?

Ready, I say, trying not to sound as snippy as I feel cos frankly I been ready for the last fucking half an hour.

On the count of three then. A one two three!

We get almost as far as the second chorus before Ella cracks. As per usual instead of just going on and finishing the job she just stops dead and starts apologising, forcing me to stop as well, since you can't very well harmonise on your own, can you?

I'm really sorry, she goes, sobbing away and starting to sound like one of them annoying ringtones you can't get out of your head. It's because of my period!

The bollocks it is. I watched her back the other day and told the judges it was why she was late cos I felt sorry for her. But the fact is she's been like this since she got to the house. Even when I first met her she was a mess. She's obviously totally ruined, what with this weird thing she's got going with her paedo of a step-dad. I mean, what the fuck is going on there? Not like it's any of my business, mind you. I don't want to know, even though she obviously wants to tell me. I got other things on me mind. Like winning this competition for instance.

Just take yoga breaths, goes Billy. In through your nose and out through your mouth, as slow as you can. It'll clear your system.

Ella takes another massive snotty breath and leaks a few more tears as she breathes out. Spite of all the crying her skin's still all pale and clear, like one of them zit-lotion models.

Okay, says Billy. Let's try it from the top.

He gives me a nod and a grin, and though he don't say nothing I know he must be thinking to himself, These girls are history! cos it's just what I'm thinking too. He plays the first few chords and off I go with my solo bit, trying not to lose control even though it's about the billionth time I done it.

I hear a whisper in the night, I sing, lowering me voice to make it sound husky and soulful like when Eternity did it, That is how I know you're still here beside me . . .

They're dead beautiful lyrics, really, and I can't help meself thinking a bit of Davy each time we do the song. Wonder how he's holding out. It's harder for a bloke than it is for a girl when it comes to not shagging, not cos we don't get the urge, just cos we're better at controlling it. But after what happened last time with that Shea it's difficult to believe he's not banging some tart right this very second. But maybe cos of the power of these words, or maybe cos I still ain't gotten over that good feeling I had in Utopia that night we got back together, or else maybe just cos the sense's been screwed out of me by all this fannying around waiting for Ella – whatever the reason, I *do* trust him. I do believe he's waiting for me. I gotta, cos I'm fucking gagging for it and the second I'm out of this gig I'm hunting that sexy bastard down and riding the life out of him. If only those sadistic cunts would give us more than fifteen fucking minutes of credit, and them cameras leave me to meself for five minutes, then I could give him a call and have a nice old wet chat. But course Baby comes first, so I'm making do with a text to tell him how much I love him and that he'd better not be sleazing on to no other bird or else I'll be stilettoing him in the eyeball.

I finish me bit of the song and hold me breath as Ella starts off. Her voice is all shaky still but at least she's singing. Billy's wrinkly face gets even more wrinkly as he scrunches it up, obviously on the edge like me to see if she's gonna fuck up. Again.

Prayers for you before I shut my eyes, she goes, wavering all over the place like she's got a creepy crawly stuffed down her bra, Prayers for you before I lay me down . . .

And we're off, into the chorus. We go right through it and into the next two bits of solo, and she don't fuck up once. As we finish Billy turns to us both with a massive smile of congratulations, the sort of look you'd give a couple of tards who've just figured out how to chew by themselves. Ella starts sniffling and looking all proud like she's just won a fucking marathon. Suddenly I'm screeching at her like I'm off me head. All this stuff I can't control is coming out of me trap, like word diarrhoea.

Listen up, you silly bitch! I'm going. Pull yourself together and stop acting like a fucking *tool*! We gotta rehearse this song and have it perfect for the end of the week and at this rate we'll be lucky if we don't just go onstage looking like a pair of fucking *morons*! You might not be serious about this gig but I fucking *am*. I've made *sacrifices* for this and I ain't having it screwed up by the likes of you, *get it*?

Ella looks at me, eyes so big it's like they're gonna pop out of her face. She gets it. And sure enough here come the tears, only this time she don't stick around to do her bawling. Before anyone can say another word she pushes past the camera guy and races out of the studio.

Fuck. Forgot all about the camera. Now they'll have footage of me looking like a right bitch, and you can bet your arsehole that's going out on telly at the end of the week. I look at Billy and he gives me this look like he reckons it was totally mean and unnecessary what I just said, which maybe it was, but frankly I'm so pissed off I don't even give a toss. The camera guy recovers and pauses for a sec like he don't know whether to go after Ella or to keep on filming here. Then he takes off, probably figuring she's always good for it.

Maybe you should take five, says Billy in this pointed way, closing the lid of the piano all firm and taking out a pen and notebook like it ain't really a suggestion.

I don't say nothing, just walk out the studio and into the corridor outside, trying to stop meself from shaking. If you can believe it I've actually got tears coming out me own eyes now. Can't seem to stop them streaming down me face, totally blinding me so I don't see where I'm going and run splat into a mound of green, knocking her into the wall.

Sorry, I go.

I wipe away the tears and see that it's that face-ache, the one with all the attitude who looks like she'd just as soon watch all of us girls drown in our own piss as make anything of ourselves. Michelle's her name, ain't it? Just the bitch I don't fancy seeing right now.

Can't you watch where you're going? she snaps, reaching down to fiddle with the strap of her shoe and giving me a proper death glare.

Go fuck yourself, I tell her.

I mean to just walk off and leave her looking all shocked and outraged, but the words don't come out as smooth as I mean them to, more like a request than an insult. I hold up me head and try to go past her, only I catch my foot on the bitch's stupid strappy shoe and end up tumbling face first into the wall meself, mashing up me nose right next to a framed photo of Purrfect doing their famous controversial performance of 'I Want To Be Purrfect' at the Brit Awards, the one where they all dressed up in those black letter-box outfits that Muslim women wear and then threw them off all dramatic, showing they had nothing but bikinis on underneath. Lucy was still in the band then, and she's at the centre in an orange string. I look at the photo for a second and then sort of slide down the wall like I've just been shot, and end up in this heap of snot and tears.

Are you okay? goes the face-ache.

She takes a look around like she don't want anyone to see her doing this and then quickly crouches down next to me and presses a tissue to me nose. I'm off sobbing badder than fucking Ella, only now I'm not mad at her anymore, just at meself for being such a shit. I've got in plenty of fights in my time, but I ain't never picked on someone what didn't deserve it, and no matter how much of a dead weight that girl is Ella ain't a bad person. It's this house, this programme, and all this tension. It's turning me into a psycho. I take the tissue off this bitch and have a good blow.

Did you hurt yourself? Michelle goes. That was a nasty crunch.

I tell her I'm fine, but she's looking at me in this funny way, like she's really worried. I try to push her off and get back on me feet, but before I know what's going on I'm cracking up all over again, and this time I've even gone and thrown me arms around her and I'm boo-hooing away on her shoulder like she's the big sister I never had.

There there, she goes, it'll be all right.

Huh, I say.

She don't seem to hear me. I feel her hand on me back, patting me and her arms squeezing me too, and it sort of feels pretty good, even though I know I'm making a right tit out of meself. But I don't care about that right now. I close me eyes and just let it all out. Finally when there's nothing left I open them again and take me arms off her.

You know, it really isn't worth it, goes this Michelle.

She smiles at me in this sort of sad way, a bit like how Mum smiles after she's just watched Barbara Hershey dying in *Beaches*, which is her favourite film. I feel pretty fucking bad about all the mean thoughts I've had about Michelle though. She's obviously a nice person deep down.

What would you know? I says, still managing to sound like a bitch without even meaning to.

More than you think, says Michelle. I've been working in PR for years. I've seen plenty of girls just like you, all wishing they were special. And they all make exactly the same mistake. They forget they're special already.

I stare at her. Can't help meself. She's the last person I'd of expected to come out with this sort of thing.

Everybody's special, she carries on. Everybody's worthwhile and you shouldn't need a camera or an audience to tell you that.

She stops and looks at me like she's waiting for me to start crying all over again. I give her a smile, since I am grateful for the hug and all that. But I ain't that far gone. I mean, sure we're all special and supposed to be equal and so on, but everybody knows life don't work that way in reality. Everyone knows life is all about competition in the end, don't they? I sort of want to ask her what she's even doing working in TV or PR if she's really so dead against it all, but before I can get the words out her face suddenly changes into this big frown. I look up and see she's looking at that photo of Purrfect, and when I look back she's gone and changed back to being miserable again.

I don't have time for this, she goes, like she suddenly don't know what she was thinking, wasting them precious minutes of her life being nice to me. I've got to get on!

With this she takes off down the corridor like she's just been whipped with a wet towel. I pull meself up and go the other way, till I reach the loo. I lock the door behind me and then stand in front of the mirror. Then I start to do something a shrink at the hospital once told me to do when I was depressed after Baby was born. What with Gav having left me and me not having no job or nothing I was feeling pretty low in them days. This shrink said the thing to do was to find a mirror and repeat to meself that I was not a waste of space. That just cos me baby's father ain't bothered to stick around don't mean we both didn't have a chance of being happy ever. Course it sounded like bollocks, but it turned out that she was dead right, that shrink, cos whenever I did it I always felt amazing afterwards. But I'd sort of forgotten about doing it until now.

You ain't a bad person, I say loudly, feeling a bit of a tit but better all the same cos it's true, and there's nothing like saying out loud something you know deep down about yourself but thought you'd forgot.

I say it again, just to make sure, and then I have a look at me face, which is all red and swollen up from the crying. Me mascara's run to buggery. I cup me hands and splash on some cold water. Right. Time to find Ella and say sorry before she goes and tops herself.

I go out the loo and through the hall looking for her. She ain't in the kitchen – there's Riana and Louise in there, holding their song sheets and staring daggers at each other. I ask them if they've seen Ella but they both just shrug and carry on looking all murderous. It's pretty funny, since Riana's big enough that she could probably just step on Louise if she wanted to.

I'm just about to go up the stairs, since I figure the most likely place I'll find her is the bedroom, when there's this noise like somebody's screaming their head off.

I go around behind the stairs and over to the furthest door, which is supposed to be forbidden to us at all times cos that's where the panel do their decision making and compare their notes on us and shit like that. But it's where the screaming came from and I can't just stand here when someone's obviously being killed or raped or whatever in there. I pick up the fire extinguisher off the wall so I've got a weapon just in case and then without stopping I kick the door open and barge right on in.

Emma's crouched in the corner with her mouth open, letting out little sobbing sounds. Her hair, which is usually so perfect, has all fallen in front of her eyes like she's been doing a spot of head banging, and she's staring out in front of her with the sort of look people get on soaps when they've just walked in on their sister doing their boyfriend.

Emma? I go, half thinking this is a test and she's gonna snap out of it any second and tell me I've lost marks for entering into the forbidden room.

Joni, she goes in this weak voice, I need you to go and get someone quickly . . .

She trails off and I turn around, trying to see what's got her acting like something's coming to get her. Nothing looks out of order to me, not that I know how it's supposed to look, but it's a smart room with lots of nice comfy-looking chairs with proper leather on them and a big shiny wooden table that no way come from IKEA. Then I notice there's this little streak of red coming out from one of the folders on it. I reach out and open it up.

Don't! goes Emma, but it's too late, I've done it.

There's a pigeon laying there, just a normal one, and at first I reckon it must of just flown in somehow and bashed its head on a wall and died, and that Emma's overdoing it like a right twat. But then I realise that this bird ain't got no head. It's been cut off, and pretty neatly by the look of things. And what's more there's a little piece of paper folded next to one of its feet with TESS written on it. Even though I know I shouldn't, cos it's obviously nothing to do with me, and I oughta just go get someone like Emma wants me to, I reach down and pick it up. I'm a right nosy parker and always will be, just like Mum. The paper's got a message written on it. In this weird writing it says:

If YoU dOn'T sToP yOu'Ll WiNd Up
AnOtHeR DeAd BiRd.

Shit, I go, totally forgetting about not swearing in front of the judges.

'It's shocking, just shocking. I can't believe somebody could be capable of something so awful. It's just so cruel and evil . . . I'm just going to keep on doing what I do and not let it get to me. I can't, not now that I know I've got the public behind me.'

We sit in a semi-circle, just like we usually do when the judges have got something in store for us, only this time it's different because everyone's silent and sneaking secret glances at each other while the first policeman takes Joni out into the corridor with Joe to interview them about what happened. The other two policemen stand side by side at the door with awkward smiles, obviously trying to set everyone at ease but instead managing to do the complete opposite. Everyone looks nervous and mistrustful, apart from Ella who's sitting with her head between her legs, and the atmosphere is charged with tension. It's a really damaging atmosphere to be exposed to when you're working as hard as I am; my nerves are already frazzled from trying to create something that sounds vaguely like a song with that egotistical slut Riana. Honestly – as well as being fake and a stripper the loud-mouthed bee has no training whatsoever, and the concept of harmonising or getting something down lick for lick is completely foreign to her. Every single time we practise she starts making it up, or breaking away halfway through the refrain to sing extra 'Ahs' and 'Babys' and 'Oohs' – like she's the star and I'm just her backing singer! All that advice Billy gave us about toning it down because we've got such strong voices (which I'm sure he only said about both of us to be diplomatic) she insists on ignoring. And whenever I ask her to please stick to the script she replies that this is the way she always sings – as if the fact that she's always been clueless about singing is some kind of justification. I'm ready to strangle the stupid effing bee. The only good thing about it all is that it's so obvious she'll never make it into Purrfect I really don't have to worry about her anymore. She's unprofessional, and in the end there's no way they're going to want someone like *that* for the band.

I shoot Riana a quick sideways look. She's got her arms folded over that massive bust and is biting her lip. It makes a nice change to see her actually perturbed by something at long last.

'Won't be long now, everyone,' says one of the policemen cheerfully, startling everyone. It's the one with the ginger hair and the face that looks like he's been hit by a meteor shower. I don't get pimples, but that doesn't mean I want to go near someone who does, and I wish people like that would do something about their skin if they're going to take jobs that involve dealing with the public. No one knows if he means before they figure out who did it or before they let us get back to working on our songs. It's ridiculous to think it might have been one of *us*, though I wouldn't put it past that Valerie. She gets a crazy look in her eyes sometimes when she's onstage, and it wouldn't surprise me that much if she turned out to be a terrorist. But it's not very likely really, since we've all got alibis because we've been working in our pairs all day, and even if we hadn't it's not as though any of us would have had time to go outside and catch and murder a pigeon. If it's someone connected to the programme it must be one of the crew. If you ask me they should replace the lot of them, just to be on the safe side.

I do think it's completely disgusting what's happened. When they first got us in here and told us about it I could hardly believe it, but everyone was acting so serious there was no way it could have been a joke or another trial in the competition. The policeman was very mysterious at first, just wanting to know if any of us had seen anything but refusing to tell us what he was hoping that might be. Then Joni butted in and told us what she'd found, and then he couldn't shut her up about it. I hope they don't forget to punish her for going in the panel's room, which we were told right from the first day is forbidden to us – *under any circumstances*. If you ask me it's gross and I'd rather not have known, thank you very much, but of course Joni had to go into graphic detail about how the stupid bird's head had been sliced off and the blood was *oozing* out of it, which right away made Ella go green and say she felt sick. That little drama queen is getting too much attention, if you ask me. I mean, it's totally awful and creepy what's happened, but it's just a dead bird. My money is on her to go this week, although right now I'd rather it was that slutty Riana. But probably they won't get rid of her till near the end because she's black and they won't want to upset any minorities who might be watching the show.

Tess lets out a long sigh. She sits in front of us all with her arms folded, staring at us one after another with a weird smirk, like in a way she thinks this is all rather funny. She's the only one who isn't in the slightest bit ruffled by the whole thing, despite the fact that from what Joni said she's the one the note and bird were for. Apparently poor Emma freaked out big time when she saw it and her husband's taken her home. It's just typical that the nicest person would find it. It's just a shame she didn't realise it was meant for Tess and not her.

I glance at Tess and get a little shock because she's looking right at me with those horrible bug eyes of hers. I quickly look away. It reminds me of one of those detentions where the teacher detains the whole class just because one idiot has done something wrong, and refuses to let them go until the idiot owns up. Tess looked really sour on Saturday when the audience voted for me to have the free pass, and even went ahead and said she wasn't sure I deserved it because it was obviously just a sympathy vote, which is the worst kind of vote to have. It would serve the ugly fat-faced bee right if she does get her head hacked off by a psycho if you ask me, and I can't help but think there's maybe something a little bit divine going on here, and that maybe, just maybe, this is God's way of warning her she's got the wrong attitude. It would have been better if He'd chosen a dove rather than a dirty old pigeon, but I suppose they're not as easy to get hold of.

Oh, hurry the eff up, I think, seeing as Joni and the first policeman have been gone for well over twenty minutes now. How long does it take to answer a few stupid questions? No doubt she's giving him all the gory details bit by bit and loving every second of it. Meanwhile, some of us need to get back to work on our songs. It has to be perfect this time, especially after Saturday. I'm not letting that happen again no matter what. I've been making sure I eat at least a whole bowl of muesli every morning, even if it does make me feel heavy and bloated an hour later. But there are people out there rooting for me, Saturday proved it, and I mustn't let them down. One way or another I need to get back to what I do best and in the process somehow find a way to put that silicon-enhanced hooker in her place.

Just as I think I'm about to die from waiting the door opens and Joe and the first policeman enter, with Joni trailing behind. She's got this silly grin on her face – not that she has any other sort of smile. You can tell that Joe just loves all this, too, from the way he's holding his head up as if he thinks he's playing the starring role in a major exciting drama.

'Right,' says the policeman. 'Thank you everyone for your patience. We're done here now and I don't think there's any further cause for concern.'

He goes on to say that as far as they can tell it was probably someone who slipped in from outside and that if any of us see or hear anything suspicious in future we're to contact the police immediately. In the meantime they're going to ask around the neighbourhood to see if anyone saw anything, and Joe assures us he's going to be talking to the television station about getting in some proper security. At this Riana sits up like she's going to raise her hand and object, but then she seems to think better of it. I really should have reported her that time I caught her outside, but I wasn't thinking straight, and of course I can't do it now because they'll want to know why I waited for so long. The policeman smiles at us and nods to the other two. There's an audible sound as we collectively let out a sigh of relief and start to stand up. But before anyone can so much as move Joe clears his throat.

'Okay, girls,' he says loudly. (I notice that one of the cameramen has appeared at the door and has started filming so I quickly adjust my posture. You have to be constantly aware of these things, and not let your guard down. Once I'm famous I'll probably have paparazzi following my every step so it's good practice for me.)

'I know it's very scary and challenging, but I want you to look for the value in this experience. Being a celebrity means exposing yourself to some twisted individuals, and you need to be strong and not let it affect you . . .'

On and on he goes, telling us how he wants us all to know that we can come to him and talk to him if we need to 'express our feelings' about what's happened, as if anyone would ever want to confide in *him*. You've got to feel sorry for the idiot really, he's just so tragic, standing there in his silly sunglasses and fake army vest. He never misses an opportunity to lecture us, and it's starting to get on my nerves, to be honest. You can tell that he desperately wants to be a personality, like Simon Cowell. I mean, God obviously gave the man *some* talent, since he is the stylist behind Purrfect, but he's just never going to be an actual *name*. Probably his fantasy is that he could be up there onstage like us, but because he's a he – and also short and not very good-looking – he's had to settle for being behind the scenes.

Just as he's launching into a story about the dangers of not expressing your feelings Tess interrupts him. For once I'm glad that she's such a rude old bee, because otherwise we'd be here till doomsday.

'Okay, girls, time to get back to work!'

Instantly we all spring to life. Rebecca and Valerie gallop to the door, thick as thieves, while Joni goes over to Ella and starts whispering stuff to her while she listens and nods stupidly. It's like *Dumb and Dumber*, watching that pair of nincompoops. Joe looks extremely put out at being interrupted, but it really just serves him right for being so gay and pompous. I turn to Riana, steeling myself not to let her get to me. 'Are you ready?' I say coldly, but she's not even listening. Instead she strides up to Joe with her hands on her hips, really working that ghetto-attitude thing she does, which is such an act it's hard not to cringe when you watch her.

'Do we really need security guards?' I hear her ask. 'I mean, this weirdo isn't likely to try it on again, is he?'

'How do you know it's a "he"?' cuts in Tess. She cocks her head to one side and gives Riana a sly look. Riana opens her mouth and then shuts it. Even she can't help flinching under Tess's lizard gaze. She shrugs and smiles brightly then steps back over to me.

'Well, Louise, shall we get back to work then?' she says, as though *I'm* the one who's been holding us up. The camera is on us I see, so I nod, trying not to look like I want her to melt. But as we go to leave the room the ginger policeman with all the acne steps up and clears his throat. I make sure to put Riana between myself and his face. Make him arrest her, I pray.

'Can I have your autograph, miss?' he says shyly, holding out his pad and a pen. 'For me and me daughter? We reckon you're just fab!'

Riana gives the simpering idiot one of her ridiculously proportioned smiles that makes you wonder how God managed to cram so many teeth into one mouth. It wouldn't surprise me in the least if it turned out they were dentures, fake like everything else about her. *No one* has teeth as white and big as that – apart from Kylie, of course, but she's an exception.

'Absolutely,' she purrs.

Sickened by how stupid human beings can be sometimes I go out into the corridor and then stand there feeling like a fool while behind me Riana asks the spotty ginger idiot to spell his daughter's name. I hook my thumbs into my holsters and discover a big lump in one pocket, which freaks me out at first, before I remember what it is. I've been saving my phone call up for Saturday, for when I get through a proper performance, so I can phone home and listen to Dad being all proud and telling me not to worry about the previous week because it happens to everyone once in their lives, even megastars. But suddenly I find myself thinking, Why wait? Anything could happen on Saturday, and I could really use some good advice right now after all that I've been through.

I take out the phone and put in our number. Mum answers right away, no doubt because she's got nothing better to do than sit around in the kitchen, waiting for me to call. With a small sigh I prepare myself for her to start crying and tell me how much she misses me.

'Mum? It's Louise.'

'Oh, Louise!' She sounds faraway, like I've called her on the moon. I simply must teach her how to project – it's really not that hard and something she could easily practise while she's doing the cleaning. 'I thought you were the church.'

I wait for her to get tearful and tell me how beautiful I looked on TV last week, since it would be typical of her not to have even noticed how weak my performance was. But oddly there's just silence at the other end.

'Well, I'm not!' I snap finally, thinking she could at least make an effort. I am her only daughter and after all I haven't seen her for over a week, which might not seem a very long time but it's still the longest I've ever been away from home. Plus I am potentially about to become a member of one of the *biggest bands* in *history*. She could allow herself to get just a little bit excited, if only for my sake.

'Darling . . .' says Mum and then there's a bit of static down the line, followed by the totally disgusting sound of her blowing her nose. 'Oh Louise . . . it's so good to hear your voice!'

Here we go, I think. Obviously she was just trying to be strong, thinking that I didn't want to hear her getting upset, when really I suppose I was rather looking forward to it. It's sweet of her to actually try and make an effort to stay composed. Mum's so daft that I sometimes forget that one of her good qualities is that she's really quite a kind-hearted person.

'It's all right, Mum,' I say, trying to sound daughterly. 'I'm absolutely fine, you don't need to worry about me. Is Dad there?'

There's no answer, just more static and sniffing.

'Mum?' I say. I turn and see that one of the cameramen and Riana are standing behind in the doorway to the studio, watching me. Riana's got her arms folded and her massive mouthful of teeth are hidden behind a smirk. I quickly check my posture and roll my eyes at the camera in a knowing way, smiling as I do it, as if to say, aren't parents just adorably difficult?

'Mum, there's no need to get upset!'

'It's Gramps,' she sniffles. 'He passed away last night.'

She says something more but I'm so surprised I completely miss it. My shock obviously shows in my face because both Riana and the cameraman react. The cameraman quickly steps forward and brings the camera closer, panning around my face, while behind him Riana loses her smirk and unfolds her arms, putting on a concerned face.

'But . . .'

I can't think of what to say. I suppose I ought to start crying, and get really upset, but for some reason I don't feel particularly sad. Weirdly, I don't feel anything much at all.

At the other end Mum's sobbing again. Really deep, gut-wrenching sobs are transmitted into my ear, sending vibrations right through my skull. I hold the phone a fraction of a centimetre away, since I can't afford to get a headache, not at this stage. Then there's a scuffling sound and I hear Dad in the background saying 'I told you not to say anything!' in an angry voice. A second later he comes on the line.

'Louise?'

'Dad!'

The cameraman is filming me dead on now, and I imagine how I will look onscreen, receiving the terrible news that a family member has died while away from home. I let out a sob and then choke it back, as though I am trying with superhuman effort to be strong and not fall apart.

'Listen, Louise, you mustn't think about it!' says Dad. He sounds determined, how he always sounds at competitions right before I'm about to go on. It's so reassuring to hear his voice that I almost drop the phone.

'I don't have much credit,' I say. 'They only gave us fifteen minutes . . . Dad, is it true? Is Gramps really gone?'

Now that I've said it they won't need to use a voice-over, but can simply edit the scene so that it begins with me saying that, so the audience will know what's going on. I let out another sob, and do the stifling thing again.

I'll start crying properly in a minute no doubt, as soon as the news actually sets in. Right now I can't absorb it though, not with the camera there pointed at me. It may seem cold, but I have to consider how I'm going to come across. I can't help it. I'm a performer, a star, and this is what we do. It's not that I'm callous, it's just how God made me.

'Is Mum all right?'

'She's sad, but he was very old and it was his time,' Dad tells me. 'Look Louise, you don't have the option to dwell on it. So don't, all right? You've got a competition to win.'

'Dad . . .' I wail, making myself sound small and lost, as if on the brink of despair. I make a shiver run through my body, as if to show that on top of all this my fever from Saturday is coming back. Riana is still giving me that concerned look, which is obviously just for the sake of the camera, even though for once it's not even pointed at her, the conniving bee.

'Sweetheart,' says Dad. 'Your grandfather loved you and somewhere up above he's looking down and rooting for you. You've got to make him proud. You've got to use this to make you stronger!'

'Okay,' I say in a tiny voice.

'Louise, you're a star. Use what happened to Gramps as ammunition. Let it fuel your performances! That's all I can say, darling. You and I both know I'm right. There'll be time for you to grieve later!'

He says some more things, about how I'm a fighter and this is what I was born to do and never to forget that, but for some reason his words don't have their usual effect. Maybe it's because I'm listening to them down a phone when I really need him to be here with me so I can absorb the positive vibes he always gives off. Instead a strange feeling is settling over me, like I've got this huge burden that weighs as much as the whole world. It's a bit like that feeling I got when Jemma, this total drop-out from school with short punky hair that makes her look like a boy, did a presentation in RS class on why God didn't exist, and actually made me wonder for a few minutes if maybe she had a point. I remember this terrible emptiness as I considered it, because the idea of a universe without God was so horrific. It was as though all the goodness and beauty of the world had just been sucked out of it and replaced with nothing but endless, awful meaninglessness. Fortunately I remembered that faith is what God requires, and that people who don't believe in Him lack that and therefore can't feel His presence, which is why they're always so bitter and unhappy.

'Dad, I'm going to run out of time!'

'Well, Louise, I've only got one piece of advice for you about Saturday night,' he says. I wait. 'Kill it, darling. You know you can.'

We say goodbye and I press the button to end the call. Then I stand there stupidly, holding the phone like I don't know what to do now. I'm not performing anymore: I'm really at a loss. I should be crying, I know that, so that it doesn't look as if I'm just a mean heartless bee who cares more about winning some competition than she does about her own family. But the tears just aren't coming, which is doubly weird because usually I find it so easy to cry. It ought to be especially easy with Gramps dead, but for some reason I just can't. I try to pray to God, but that terrible empty feeling is all over me, and I have the odd sense that He can't hear me right now. Almost as if He isn't listening, even though I know He must be because He always is. Something's blocking Him, some kind of negative energy getting in the way of me feeling Him.

'Louise?' says Riana, the stupid two-faced self-serving bitch. 'Are you all right, honey?'

Is it because I'm in shock? I wonder. People don't cry when they're in shock, do they? I look at the camera and make another shiver run through my body. I wonder if people watching at home will know about shock and how it works.

Riana reaches out and touches my shoulder. Her big hand with its stupid long pink nails turns me towards her, and suddenly I want nothing more than for her to hug me. Even though I've spent the whole day hating her, I'm so grateful as I feel those strong arms wrapping around my body and pulling me in towards her that another shiver runs through me without my having to create it. I put my arms around her too, pressing myself into those silly big boobs, and, instead of worrying about them bursting or what God will think of me for hugging a stripper, I bury my face in her shoulder where the camera can't see it, close my eyes and feel more shivers running through me, until my body is shaking in a way that feels like it's never going to stop.

I should have killed the pigeon first. That would have made it easier. Instead like an idiot I held it against the table while it was still alive. It was horrible the way it thrashed around, as if it knew what was coming. For a minute I didn't think I was going to be able to do it after all, and I thought about letting it go and finding some other way. For a minute I almost showed mercy.

But then I thought of her. She's never showed mercy once in her whole life. And I remembered that because of her I'm empty inside, dead, no longer capable of sympathy, not even for a harmless bird.

I brought the knife down hard as I could and cut off its head. There was a splash of red against the grey feathers and that was all. It didn't bleed nearly as much as I thought it would. Its wings continued to flap for several seconds though – that was grisly. But then, just like that, the body went limp. I held it in my hands for a while, feeling the warmth of it and watching until the blood stopped dripping from the hole in its neck. There was something very moving about it. Life suddenly seemed so fragile it almost made me want to cry.

But I didn't cry – because of her. She's the one who should cry. I took the bird and I left it on her table with my message – a message I know she has paid no attention to. It's like asking a snake never to strike. But I had to give it to her, this last chance to change, in order to prove to myself once and for all she is beyond redemption.

I won't hesitate when it's her who's struggling in place of the bird. I'll bring the knife down without a second thought, cutting her out of her life just like she cut me out of mine.

'These girls are great, they've become like family to me and I love them like sisters. But at the end of the day they're the competition and I can't forget that.'

The crowd before us looks like it goes on for ever. You can't see anybody's face cos of all the light shining in our eyes and their applause sounds out like a percussion grenade. I swear that each time you hear it, it sounds louder and louder. It's an awesome feeling, a trillion times better than the leering grunts of appreciation you get at the club. And each time I hear it I think how I don't want to leave. How I just want to stay here on stage listening to that applause for the rest of my life.

Thank you so much, girls! I'll see you back here in ten to find out who's through and who's going home!

I catch Louise's eye as Stina waves us offstage. Her face is glowing and she looks really happy. She smiles back at me and it's the first time I've ever seen her smile in a way that looks halfway towards something genuine. She does look good tonight too, in her tight black dress with her hair long and straight down her back. She's got beautiful hair – a sort of reddish brown with these streaks of dark yellow, kind of like maple syrup. Her lips look good too now that she's got some lippy on them, fuller and kissable. Not that I'd do her, mind. She's still way too thin, like one of those lollipop women that everyone wanted to look like back when I was a teen.

Remember, everybody – we've lost the audience vote this week. It's all in the hands of our panel. They've got to decide who's got the Purrfect potential and who's just another desperate dreamer!

We step into the wings and witch Michelle gives us this curt nod and then gestures for us to go back to the changing room. But once we're in the corridor this giggle explodes out my throat and I clutch Louise and pull her against the wall. For once she doesn't resist me, or act like I'm trying to molest her. Instead she starts giggling too.

We were awesome! I tell her. Even that old troll liked us!

A funny expression passes over Louise's face, like she's experiencing two different feelings at the same time. But she's obviously caught up by it all, still on a high from all that love and adoration from the crowd.

Course, I know it's not real adoration and love you're getting out there. It's just as fake and misplaced as the emotions of those men at the club that start crying and saying they're in love the second you've finished wiggling your tits in their faces. Sad truth about human beings is that they need stuff like that. Whether it's a god, a queen, a prime minister or a pop star, it doesn't matter. They just have to have something to believe in, to distract them from how boring and shit their lives are. People really want to believe that not just anyone could get up onstage and give a performance – that you have to be special, like there has to be some magical shift in the universe and the planets properly aligned or something in order for a true star to be born. It's kind of ironic, because when you think about it, what they're really watching and cheering for is some bunch of competitive bitches who all just want to *feel* special. Girls so hungry for love and adoration they'll do whatever it takes to get it, even if it means dancing around onstage singing silly songs and being made puppets for some stupid TV show. It's one of those vicious circles, and I can kind of see why Eddy's so cynical about it. But whatever Eddy says, the high it gives you has got to be better than anything else in the world. Even blow. And I'll tell you something else – it's a fuck of a lot more satisfying than wiggling your tits in some crevicey old face too.

It was a good performance, goes Louise quietly when we've stopped giggling and are gasping for air side by side against the wall. She's looking at me when she says it but it's like she's really talking to herself. We killed it.

Same old Louise, I think. You can tell how badly she wants to win by the way she doesn't seem to be able to relax – ever. It was pretty fucking hellish working on this duet, since she just wanted to sing it like a couple of robots and kept on saying I was doing it wrong – like a bit of expressing yourself can ever be wrong! Then her grandpa went and died, which you might have thought would have made her a bit less up her own arse, but oh no, if anything the opposite. Made it even more of a strain cos she kept looking away and sobbing whenever I tried to sing it my way. But I don't back down without a fight, and after a lot of patience I managed to find a compromise. And it paid off because we totally nailed it up there. Or killed it, as Louise says.

We did indeed, Missy, I say, doing a Sharon Osbourne impression. We killed it dead as a dodo and they fucking loved us!

Louise peers at me all suspiciously like she can't tell if I'm taking the piss. Her face sets me off giggling again. She's so serious all the time and serious people always make me laugh. Without even thinking about it I lean forward and give her a quick wet kiss on the mouth. Under my lips I feel her freeze, every muscle in her scrawny little body seizing up tight like she's turned to a block of ice.

Urghhh, get off! she cries, pushing me away with her little toothpick arms.

You love it!

For a second I think she's going to make this into a big deal and start accusing me of sexually assaulting me, but then she breaks into a grin too. She shakes her head like she can't believe my nerve and wipes her mouth off with the back of her hand.

Yuck!

Ladies and gentlemen, I give you Joni and Ella! Stina's voice echoes down the corridor. There's lots of cheering and whooping. Louise's face changes and she bolts down the corridor and through the door to the changing room. I follow her. The euphoria's starting to wear off and it's getting replaced by this throbbing, which sadly can only mean one thing.

Inside the changing room Valerie and Rebecca're on the sofa against the far wall watching the telly. On the screen Joni is standing in one spotlight doing her solo while Ella stands in another, looking like a small furry animal about to get dissected.

Oh my Lord, says Valerie. Look at her face!

Behind them the camera dude lets out a snigger. Rebecca glances back at him and sniggers too. Louise frowns at the screen and shakes her head.

Those two are never going to make it, she says.

Seeing as everyone's clearly enjoying themselves I grab the opportunity to nip to the toilet. Quickly and carefully, doing this at warp speed like the pro I am getting to be, I take out my stash and slip my little finger into the bag. It's pathetically small what I've got left, even though I've been frugal as an old bitch with it this week – which has taken some fucking effort, let me tell you. As I bring it to my nose I lift my leg (best thing about being flexible) and use my heel to push down the lever. While it flushes I do the snort. Straight away I feel better, and I almost have to pinch myself in order to stop myself from just hoovering up the rest. But it's all I've got and I need to save it for emergencies. Next week is going to be hell. There's no way of me getting hold of more, not now that stupid troll Tess has gone and got herself a stalker and had the house all trussed up so it's more like a prison than ever, with security guards and everything. Chances of me sneaking out again without getting caught by some burly bastard and put in a body lock are zero times zero. That means I'm going to be cold-turkeying it. And *that* means headaches, jitters, fever and mood swings like the PMT from hell. *The Purrfect Search*'s not exactly the kind of environment you want to go teetotal in.

Outside I can hear Ella doing her solo. She sounds weak, like she's almost not even there. It's a joke, the poor thing. I don't make bets, but it's pretty clear Louise's right and she's not going to survive this. Just hope it doesn't scar her for life.

Jesus Christ, guffaws Valerie as Ella and Joni launch into the second chorus. They're completely off key! My God!

Do you think you could stop being profane, please? goes Louise.

Fact is I've been giving the matter some serious thought and I reckon I got a much better chance of being in Purrfect than anyone else. This is for one totally fucking obvious yet totally fucking unPC reason. Purrfect is a white girl group. Even the one who left – that Lucy – she was white. In this day and age too much whitewashing and you're limiting your appeal. Don't believe me? Look at other mega girl bands: Pussycat Dolls, Sugababes, All Saints, Spice Girls. Girls Aloud're just a fluke. You got to have some kind of diversity going on. It's like Eddy's always saying to me – it's a multicultural world out there. And after all, Tess is a black woman herself – just about. Somewhere in that empty old soul of hers she must feel some kind of a sense of duty towards her sisters.

I quickly slip what's left of my stash back into my boot and pull out my phone from the other one. There's just time to send a lightning-fast text to Eddy, telling her how much I miss her. Wonder if she watched me tonight. I've lost count of the number of texts I've sent her, and seeing as the phone won't take incoming messages or calls I don't know if she's tried to reply. I did call her on it the other day when there was no one around, but she didn't answer, which was just as well cos I turned round to find one of the camera dudes had snuck up behind and had his camera trained on me. They're cunning fuckers, those dudes, always trying to get the drop on you. I flip open the lid of the mobile but before I can key in a single word there's some kind of commotion outside.

Oh my *God*! screeches Valerie. Oh my *God*! What is she *doing*?

I slot the phone back in my boot and unlock the door. On the telly Ella is gaping at Joni with this totally helpless look. Her chin trembles and her eyes glisten with tears. She's obviously forgotten the words, but she's not even bothering to mimic Joni or pretend. All you can do is cringe as Joni stumbles on through the rest of the duet alone, her voice wavering all over the place under the pressure of trying to carry the tune on her own. When she finishes there's applause, but it's a weird kind of applause, polite and kind of muted, like someone's turned the volume down. I hope no one ever applauds like that for me – I'd rather be booed off. It's a car crash. A total fucking pile-up.

Tears are dripping down Ella's cheeks and you can actually see her shaking. It's heartbreaking to watch. Arse red from all the effort, Joni grabs Ella's hand and bows, pulling her down too as Stina Ellis prances onstage and starts asking what went wrong. Goodbye, Ella, I think sadly.

Girls, two minutes, says Michelle from the door, tapping her clipboard and staring at us as if she can't understand why we aren't all standing to attention.

There's no costume change this week, just straight out back onstage to get the judges' decision. Everyone turns away from the telly, which now shows this big unflattering close-up of Tess, who simply rolls her eyes and averts her face, saying, I don't know where to begin so I won't even bother. As the audience starts to boo we all rush over to the mirror at the same time and start frantically checking our make-up.

I put on my best endearing woman-to-woman smile as we take our places in a line before the panel, so's they don't think I'm complacent about tonight. Next to me Valerie totters on the ridiculous tall spikes she's wearing, that make her even taller than me. The judges all look like they're at a funeral. It's standard for Tess, of course, but Emma and Joe are normally a bit more relaxed. Oh well. Who gives a shit? I'm feeling great, untouchable, like I'm protected from anything they can do to me by some kind of magic shield. I feel strong and alive – so good I could quite happily do our song all over again if they asked.

Okay girls, roars Stina. Funny how she still doesn't seem to have figured out having a mic means you don't have to shout. Are you ready for the judges' decisions because here we go! One of you *will* be leaving the programme tonight!

At the centre of the line-up stand Joni and Ella, cacking themselves. It's almost as if their fuck-up has gone and produced all this extra heat up onstage, cos even I'm sweating and I've just put on a coat of Sure.

Riana, says Emma, please step forward.

I step forward, smiling.

Riana, says Emma, you are a strong and confident performer. But Joe, Tess and I all agree that you sometimes give it too much. Sometimes watching you we feel like we're watching someone doing a send-up.

Suddenly I get a quivering feeling in the legs and I have this realisation that maybe I'm not so safe after all. That nobody is in this game. Eddy was right – the competition is about nothing but raping the egos of young women, getting them to prance around half naked in a spotlight in front of millions of people, all for the faint chance of maybe getting to keep on doing it indefinitely. Why don't I ever listen to her? Why did I never go along to one of her SCUM meetings? Why did I tell myself that they were just her thing and nothing to do with me? Maybe if I'd gone along to one I wouldn't be in this fucking position, waiting to get judged by three twats who think the sun shines out of their A-holes.

Riana, Purrfect are a band of professionals, says the troll beside Emma. They are not village idiots. They make stars of themselves on stage, not fools. That's why they are as big as they are.

The thing is, says Joe, you have to tone it down. Your challenge is to find the balance and control it takes to be a true Purrfect girl. However, we agree that you also show a lot of potential. And that is why tonight you will *not* be leaving the programme.

Cheers as a thousand hands come together. Feeling like a total dick for getting scared, I step backwards as the spotlight on me goes down. Suddenly I am able to see all the faces in the audience, each one all tense and tight as Tess tells Louise to step forward. I'm almost directly behind her and from this viewpoint she looks so small and defenceless. It's hard to believe she was able to make me so frustrated this last week.

Louise, goes Joe, last week was catastrophic and had you not been saved by the audience vote, you would have left the programme. This week you had a lot to prove. We all know it was a hard week for you, because of your grandfather, and we want to offer our condolences and congratulate you for holding it together.

Louise lifts her head. Unexpectedly I get this ripple of affection for her. There's something a bit sweet about this spoilt, determined little girl with her head held all high and proud like Cleopatra about to shove an asp on her tit. Bless, I find myself thinking.

This week you showed everyone what you can really do, says Emma. You showed that you have amazing vocal range and extraordinary control. However, the Purrfect girls are more than just machines. They are, above all else, artists.

I almost burst out laughing at that. I wait with everyone else while Tess shuffles her fat arse forward in her seat as she gets ready to give her own verdict. Don't let her be going home, I think, totally surprising myself. I look past Louise's scrawny figure at the mass of faces and as I do I catch this glimpse of a pair of eyes I know and love. At first I think it's just a hallucination, and I almost lose my cool, wondering if that blow was cut with something else and I've gone and rocketed off the deep end. But when I blink she's still there, watching with her chin set forward in that adorably stubborn way when she's seeing something she doesn't approve of.

Louise, says Tess, this week you showed us that you do actually have an identity and you realised that you don't have to sing a song exactly as it's already been done for it to be good. And that's why tonight you will *not* be leaving the programme.

Eddy's face gets lost as the crowd start clapping and cheering. Desperately I look again, but I can't find her. It's like she's been sucked up into all the other faces out there. Wasn't a mirage though. I *know* it was her. Question is, how the fuck did she manage to get in?

I go into this daze as Joe tells Valerie to step forward. I think about all the times I've taken the piss out of Eddy for being so serious and angry. Like when she tries to tell me about her SCUM meetings and I just yawn really loudly and point between my legs. Or when I come in late from a shift at the club and she's watching a rerun of *Newsnight* or *Question Time*, which if you ask me are the most boring programmes on earth, with lots of people spouting opinions and you never knowing which one to believe because they're all just as crooked as each other – but Eddy's face will be all scrunched up with concentration and she'll be really following it, nodding along or else shaking her head and muttering under her breath at some official defending some new scheme or policy. And I'll put my hands over her eyes and say Guess who? and she'll say, Not now cos I'm watching, but I'll just pester her till finally she gives up and pays me attention, like I'm far more important than anything else that goes on in her life. I'm such a selfish shit, and the fact that Eddy's crossed London and found a way to sit in the audience for a telly programme she's religiously fucking opposed to shows that as per usual I'm making her do what I want her to do without even trying, pulling her strings just like I'm having my strings pulled by this show. Guess it's just another vicious kind of circle.

Valerie, you are *not* leaving us tonight.

As she gets the all-clear the light fades on Valerie and Rebecca gets told to step forward. Emma starts to list the good things and bad things about her performance. Meanwhile Joni and Ella have taken each other's hands, I notice, and are holding on so tight Ella's shaking is passed on to Joni, a bit like one of those physics experiments you see on the Geography Channel that shows how the vibrations of one building as it falls down can bring down another.

I keep scanning the crowd for Eddy, but now I can't even remember where I saw her. All the faces just look the same, like everyone out there has got the exact same dumb, freaky expression, desperate to know who's going tonight, as if it'll make a shred of difference to their own lives. It's enough to make you fucking despair, and that fantastic feeling I had before when the applause rained down on us is gone completely. Now all that's left is this feeling of sadness at the way human beings have evolved. The one saving grace about it all though is that somewhere in that sea of puppets is Eddy – and she's here cos she loves me.

Rebecca, you will *not* be leaving tonight.

The light goes down on Rebecca and Joni and Ella are told to step forward. Stina roars into her mic that this is the final pair and one of them *will* be leaving tonight, and there's a burst of the fast chorus to Purrfect's single 'Or Die Trying'. From the wings miserable old Michelle is making signals for the rest of us to leave the stage so we all troop towards her while behind us Tess tells Joni and Ella what she thought of their song.

It made me want to cover my eyes and ears and curl up into a little ball, she says. Nobody points out that with all that bulk she carries round curling up into a *little* ball's not exactly an option. I honestly can't recall the last time I watched something so devastating. A total and complete mess.

There's booing from the crowd, but it sounds muted again, a bit like everyone secretly agrees. *I* agree. Even so I can't help feeling sorry for them, for having to stand there and take it from that troll. And for letting themselves be humiliated in front of these people.

Cos I've got my head craned round so I can watch Joni and Ella as they quiver away like two frightened poppets while the panel tears them to pieces, I don't see how it happens. I hear this muffled cry and turn my head back just in time to see Valerie as she goes over headfirst, like she's doing a penguin dive. She twists in the air, the heel of one of her spikes getting caught in the long swirly skirt of the dress she's wearing. There's this sick crunching sound as she lands and then a shriek like you've never heard before. She lies there in a heap for a second with everyone just staring at her like we've all been struck dumb. Then she starts to groan and sob, and we all rush down the steps and crowd round her, asking if she's okay. She's not. Her face is this unnatural ghostly white and her eyes are open wide but not seeing, like a veteran soldier in one of those films that's been traumatised from all the war he's seen. Get back, everybody! snaps Michelle, kneeling beside her and having a feel of her back. She lowers her voice and says something very fast into her headset about calling for an ambulance. Behind us one of the security guards appears and motions for us all to get back while Michelle lifts Valerie's skirt up.

Joni, you sang this song without the slightest shred of feeling, Emma is telling the girls onstage. It felt as though you were just trying to get through it, like that was all you were concerned about . . .

Oh my God . . . breathes Michelle. Rebecca makes a gagging sound and turns away.

Valerie's ankle is bent at what looks like a ninety-degree angle. There's something red and white protruding from it which at first I think must be the strap of her spike, but then I realise it's a bit of bone. It's one of the grossest things I ever saw. Next to me Louise gives this shudder of horror.

Michelle steps back and the security guard squats down in her place and starts to talk in this gentle voice to Valerie, who's still sobbing and looking wildly around like she can't focus on anything. Now missus, says the security guard, I need you to help me by staying focused and talking to me, okay? You're gonna be right as rain, but you've had a very nasty fall. So why don't you tell me about yourself?

Valerie moans and turns her unseeing eyes in his direction. Her mouth is all slack but the lips are forming shapes. It's like she's been robbed of her voice.

I need control, says Michelle into her headset. Get Stina to stop the panel. There's been an accident in the wings and we're going to have to get an ambulance in. Yes, that means clearing the stage . . . well, they'll just have to go to ads while we sort this out.

A stab of pain jerks through my head. The blow's wearing off. I look back behind me over towards the other side of the stage, where I can see Stina talking into the little radio thing that wires into her ear. Her pointy orange face is frowning. She peers across the stage in my direction and for a nanosecond our eyes meet. Then she looks away, nods and says something to the radio. I watch as she gathers up her mic and puts on a big bright smile.

Ella, Tess is going, you are the weakest link in this competition. Not only did you give a feeble performance, but you also committed the cardinal sin of not performing. For this reason you—

She stops as Stina strides out onstage. I look back at Valerie, who's now gone this nasty yellow colour. Next to me Louise shudders again, and I put my arm around her and pull her close. Again I think about Eddy, somewhere out there in the audience, watching. I badly want to escape from this corner of the theatre and run up the aisle calling her name. I want to feel her arms round me and her lips on mine. I so want to stop all this endless fucking smiling and pretending. But I can't. Not now I've come all this way.

Okay girls, orders Michelle, I need you all to clear the area so back to the changing room, please.

**'Everything's changed. I can't explain it exactly, but it's
like the whole world has come crashing down . . . I don't
know what to think. I'm just so confused about everything
. . . I don't know what I'm doing here anymore!'**

Last night I dreamed of Jack. It was one of those brilliant,
ridiculous dreams, the sort you only get to have about
once a year, and that's if you're lucky. I was onstage
singing a ballad all about how true love has the power to
devastate your life, and everyone out in the audience was
waving lighters, like they do at discos when the DJ plays
Robbie Williams's 'Angels'. I was wearing a long Versace
silver and white dress, a bit like a wedding dress really,
and my hair was falling all the way down to my waist in
those huge twisted waves I've never been able to get right
with Rita's GHDs. When I came to the end of the song
everyone stayed completely silent, not because they were
all horrified by how bad it was, but because they were
all so moved by its beauty. Then one by one the crowd
parted to make this passageway down the centre, and a
man appeared at the far end. At first I couldn't see who
it was because of all the spotlights, but I knew because
of the way my heart was fluttering as he approached.
When he reached the stage two security guards helped
him climb up and he stood there in front of me with his
beautiful dark violet eyes shining with emotion. I could
see that he was even more moved than everyone else.
'Jack?' I said, but he didn't reply. Instead he dropped to
one knee and took out a tiny little box, then popped the
lid open. Choked up, I nodded to him and he reached out
and slipped the ring on my finger. Then everyone in the
audience finally started to applaud, but it wasn't just like

any old clapping, it was like there were angels singing all around us. Jack drew me close to him and it was so real I could practically feel his breath. That faintest prickle of stubble he always has. The solid warmth that always emanates from his body. It was him, and he wanted me and loved me and it felt like the truth. That's how good this dream was. Impossibly good.

Of course I had to wake up, and the trouble with those amazing, fantastic, stupid dreams is that when you wake up everything seems twice as shit as it did before you fell asleep. Now here I am staring back at myself in the bathroom mirror, a blotchy-faced girl with wispy hair she can't do a thing with, who looks more like a frightened blonde rabbit than ever, feeling like I've been through this incredible ordeal and now I have to make a decision that will change the course of my whole life. I don't know what to do.

'Oi, Ella?' shouts Joni, bursting in with just her bra and panties on, holding up one of today's papers. 'Have you fucking seen this?!'

All today's papers had pictures of Valerie singing her duet with Rebecca, apart from the *Sun* which had a shot of her being stretchered into the ambulance, a close-up of her face with her mouth all twisted from pain. There've been a few articles about the death threat to Tess and how we're all living in a state of fear about being stalked by a crazy girl-band hater, and a lot of the papers had pieces going on about how I didn't deserve to stay and should have been voted off on Saturday. It was pretty horrible to read, but weirdly it didn't affect me like I'd have expected it to. I suppose it's because I know it's the truth.

I look at the paper Joni is holding, expecting to see another scathing article about me saying how I should have been the one to go if there had been any justice in the world, but there's no mention of my name. Instead there's a picture of Joni, a really ugly shot of her in mid-song with her nostrils flared and her mouth open, looking quite a lot like a pig, which isn't at all how she looks in reality. She taps the photo with her finger and shakes her head murderously. I'm rather surprised since it isn't like Joni to let a bad photograph upset her, but I suppose it's just the strain of the competition showing. It's doing funny things to everyone.

'It's not that bad,' I say to her gently. 'It's just an unflattering light.'

'Not the picture!' snaps Joni. 'For fuck's sake! *Look!*'

I look again and this time I read the headline above, which says, VIOLENCE OF POTENTIAL PURRFECT GIRL. Also under the headline is another, smaller shot of another girl with frazzled brown bangs staring sourly at the camera with her arms folded.

'Can you believe that little slag?' Joni is saying. 'I'm gonna fucking *have* her when I get back. I'm gonna grind her head on the pavement till it's *fucking flat!*'

I take the paper from her. The article has an interview with the girl in the photo, who claims Joni attacked her because of 'a romantic dispute', pushing her into a wall and giving her a black eye. Of course it can't be true. Despite her big attitude and her constant swearing I've never met anyone as kind and gentle as Joni. Last night after the disaster, right there onstage, she took my hand and whispered to me that it didn't matter, that I wasn't to feel bad about it. She's so sensitive, she could almost be a mother. And I'll never forget that day at the first audition, when I was so nervous I thought I was going to hurl and couldn't even bring myself to come out of the ladies'. I'd never have even made it into the audition room if I hadn't met her.

'Fucking shit,' mutters Joni.

I think about what happened to Jack that day he came to the auditions and exploded, and how awful they made him look in the programme.

'It's probably just a mistake . . . she probably just said something she didn't mean and they just took it out of context.'

'I'll fucking take her out of context,' snarls Joni, glaring at me in this way that's actually rather frightening. I've never seen her so angry, not even when she exploded at me last week. 'What the fuck's *context*?'

I start to explain but she cuts me off and starts ranting about the girl again, whose name is Shea and who according to Joni is a two-faced bitch and a whore who puts out for a cigarette. It's pretty weird to hear her talking about someone like that. I try to concentrate and say helpful things, but every sentence that comes out of my mouth just seems to annoy her even more. I can't concentrate properly on what she's saying. I know that it's selfish of me, especially after how kind she was to me last night, but my own problems just seem so much worse that I can't focus on anything else right now. Finally, looking like she's disgusted with both me and the paper, she screws it up into a ball and tosses it into a toilet bowl before stomping out of the bathroom.

Feeling like I've let her down I turn back to the sink and my blotchy reflection. Looking at that weak girl in front of me I'm suddenly stricken with hatred, and in a frenzy I start to splash icy cold water in my face. Each cupful feels like the slap of a tidal wave, and when I look back up my skin has turned a raw reddish colour. But I look tougher, I think. More ready for what life has to throw at me.

At breakfast everyone is quiet. Now that there's just five of us the room seems weirdly empty and desolate, especially since Valerie was the loudest and you could hear her talking pretty much anywhere in the house. Rebecca sits in the corner turning the pages of a paper and looking totally miserable. I suppose she must be the most upset, since she was Valerie's best friend. Opposite Riana chomps noisily on her cereal and Louise nibbles daintily on a piece of unbuttered toast. They seem to be friends now, those two, which is quite strange considering how different they are. But it's nice too, since it proves opposites can get on. Like me and Joni. I take the seat next to her and give her an apologetic smile, but she just turns her head away and looks through the window at the beefy black security guard who's patrolling the lawn. I pour myself a bowl of Alpen, but just as I'm reaching for the milk jug Emma bursts into the room followed by a camera and looking completely amazing in a red satin shirt, a bit like the ones in the new Toya Roy Allis collection. She must have her own private make-up artist, there's no other way to explain how anyone could look that gorgeous at this time in the morning.

'Good morning, girls!' she announces. 'I hope you're ready for a big day ahead of you!'

We all chorus good morning back, but it sounds forced, like we're greeting our own deaths or something.

'Girls, I know you're all very upset about what happened to Valerie,' Emma says in a quieter voice. 'And I wanted to assure everyone that she's getting the best care. We've sent some flowers on your behalf, and she wanted me to relay that she misses and loves you all.'

We all go 'Ahhh', as if this is the sweetest thing we've ever heard, even me, though actually I doubt it's true since I overheard Valerie whispering with Rebecca one night that she couldn't believe I was even in the competition and she hoped I'd be the first to go because I held everyone back.

'Unfortunately,' continues Emma, 'she does have a broken ankle, and after some discussion we've reached the unfortunate decision she won't be returning.'

She waits a moment for this to sink in, as though we didn't know it already. Just the memory of Rebecca's description of Valerie's joint snapped in two makes me feel queasy. I push my Alpen away from me.

'However, the show must go on! Purrfect girls do not let anything stop them from doing what they have to do, and today is extremely important. There's a car waiting for you outside and I want you ready to leave in five minutes. So let's eat up, folks!'

Five minutes later we're all standing outside in front of this enormous limousine. It's much bigger than a normal limo, almost the size of a tank, and so highly waxed you can see your reflection in it as clear as if it was a mirror. The driver, a tall thin man in black who reminds me of Count Dracula, slides open the door to reveal a whole miniature room inside, complete with a table, TV, mini-bar and even a little crystal chandelier. Rebecca and Joni both let out little gasps.

'In you get, everyone!' calls Emma, who's now wearing a figure-hugging eggshell-coloured coat. We all pile inside. Joni deliberately takes a seat by the window away from me, and I end up sandwiched between Riana and Rebecca. A cameraman who I didn't see before is already sitting at the back with his camera pointed at us. It's funny how I've almost come to stop seeing them, as if it's completely normal to be followed around all the time by someone recording your every move. Emma gathers up the folds of her coat and gets in with us, taking the seat next to the TV. The doorman slides the door shut and a minute later the engine starts.

'Okay, girls,' commands Emma. 'Here's what today is all about. We're on our way to Lockwood Studios, where you're going to be doing a short shoot to provide cutaways for Purrfect's upcoming single "Adam and Eve", due to be released in August. That's right, girls, you are all going to be in a music video!'

Everybody gasps this time.

'Now, I have here a little message from some very important people. As you know they're on tour right now, but these girls still want you to know they've been watching the programme religiously and are absolutely rooting for you guys!'

She produces a remote and points it at the screen. Instantly it lights up and four familiar faces appear, sitting in an exact replica of our limo and looking at us with bright clear eyes, their skin flawless, their smiles perfectly white. My heart practically stops. It's hard to believe so much beauty and grace can be contained within a single moving vehicle.

'Hi girls!' they cry in unison.

We can hardly contain ourselves. Rebecca and Joni let out screams and even Louise is practically panting with excitement. A private message from the greatest girl band in the world – just for us.

Monique, who's wearing a powder blue halter neck that sets off her blue eyes, leans forward towards the camera. 'Girls, we just wanted you all to know that we've been watching and we all think you're stellar, each and every last one of you.'

'We can't wait to get to work on a new album with the winner,' agrees Kharris beside her, brushing her golden blonde fringe to the side. 'We've been missing a little something for some time now and that something is you!'

'But first of all, you've got to win,' says Saffron, frowning like she wishes this doesn't have to be the case. She's wearing a black tank top with a red, white and black Union Jack on it. 'There's only room for one more girl in this band and that girl has got to be special.'

'Riana, Louise, Rebecca, Joni and Ella,' says Fina. A little thrill passes through me at the sound of my name on her lips. 'You all have the potential and we're rooting for each one of you. And just to show you how into you girls we are, we've prepared a little something for you to have a think about!'

The girls all look at one another and do little nods, and then, still flashing those stunning pearly smiles, they launch into a harmony: 'We can't wait to meet you, we can't wait to greet you, oh, we can't wait to make you one of us, so hurry up and win the contest!' They shout the last line and then, cackling, Kharris raises the controller and points it at us. The screen goes black. The instant it does it's like a massive light in the sky that made everything okay has been switched off. The reality that Jack has gone enters my heart again with a thud, and I realise guiltily that for thirty seconds I'd forgotten all about him.

'Okay girls, here we are,' says Emma.

We climb out of the limo one by one. We're outside the back of a rundown-looking warehouse, in a part of London I don't recognise. It's quite eerie, and I have a weird sense that maybe they're going to take us all inside and slaughter us, like they do with cattle. Emma leads us over to the door and says something into a little radio box beside it. There's an electric buzzing noise and the door opens. We follow her in.

'Darling!'

It's so different inside the warehouse it's like we've walked into another country. Massive bright lights with sheets of white paper over them stand all around the studio, which is covered in exotic plants and flowers. There's a rock face on one side of the room, rather like the climbing wall we have at school, only there's a stream running down this one and a little waterfall over a tiny pool full of floating lilies. It's almost as though we've just stepped into paradise, except for all the people rushing around adjusting the set and rearranging the plants under the supervision of a plump man with a tiny moustache who's wearing a bruise-purple silk shirt. He turns as we reach the centre of the room, sees Emma and lets out a little shriek. He rushes forward with both arms out. He and Emma air kiss each other on both cheeks in that same way they do on *Ab Fab*. It's obviously a joke between them because they then start to giggle and chatter away excitedly even worse than Valerie ever did. Emma calls him Bradford and he insists that a passing photographer take a snap of him and her wrapped in each other's arms and pouting in front of an enormous cactus next to the rock pool. The rest of us all stand there watching and starting to feel uncomfortable just doing nothing, until Bradford finally turns and looks down his nose at us like he's never been so unimpressed before in his life.

'So these are the victims, are they?' he says. 'How do you do, sweet things? My name is Bradford and I'm directing. Now, I don't want to know your names, thank you very much, I'll only forget them, anyway – I want for you all to go straight over there and get into costume, okay?'

We all stand there for another minute like we've been sprayed with cold water. Riana takes a step forward like she's about to let rip at Bradford for being so rude, but he turns away before she can get a word out and tells Emma he'll give her an exclusive tour of the set. Feeling like idiots we trudge over in the direction he pointed, where a plump woman with curly orange hair is waiting beside a set of costume rails.

'Oh my God!'

Joni nudges me. She's obviously incredibly excited about today and seems to have forgiven me for earlier, or else forgotten about it. I look over where she's pointing and that's when I get the fright of my life. A man is standing under a palm tree holding the hugest snake I've ever seen, cooing over it like it's a baby, while it curls itself around his arms and slithers up his shoulder. Behind him are four glass tanks, and in each one you can see another mottled collection of slithering, slowly moving loops. I feel sick.

'Do you think we're going to have to touch them?' whispers Joni.

'Come on, girls,' says the woman with the orange hair. 'I've got half an hour to get you decked out and over to make-up so let's step on it, shall we?'

The costumes we have to wear turn out to be little more than rags that wrap around your private areas and put everything else on display. At first I feel very shy about this, since it's almost like walking around in your underwear,

212

but it's funny how fast you get used to being practically naked. It reminds me of the time when Rita let Mimi and me hang out at the back of a charity catwalk show she was a guest designer in. It's another world behind those divides, with models throwing off clothes and rushing around topless while everybody else fights over each other to put more clothes and make-up on them. Today is just like that, and nobody cares the slightest bit what you look like because they're all too busy applying body paint to your thighs and weaving flowers in your hair to bother to really look at you. I'm the first person to be finished and I stand next to a clump of lilies, trying not to move and smudge the make-up on my skin. It's funny to watch the other girls being made up. I notice how Louise is obviously hating the whole process, since she looks like she's sucking on a lemon and has her arms folded across her chest the whole time as if she's completely ashamed. Riana, on the other hand, is obviously in her element, and thrusts her chest out for the photographer like modelling rags is what she's always secretly wanted to do with her life.

'Okay,' says a voice in my ear and I jump and turn round to find Bradford looking me up and down critically while a nervous-looking woman with a clipboard waits behind him. 'I *suppose* she'll do. Let's have her by the fountain for the first take, then.'

His assistant leads me over to the rock pool. There waiting for me is the man with the snake. I stop dead.

'Basically all we want is for you to stand still while our snake handler Gunther wraps it around your shoulders,' explains the assistant. 'Then just follow Bradford's instructions.'

She looks up with a little smile and sees my expression.

'It'll be fine, don't worry. It's perfectly tame, and Gunther will be right on hand to take it off you the instant we stop shooting. Isn't that right, Gunther?'

'It's a *she* not an *it*,' says the snake handler, stepping forward. 'And *her* name is Sweetie.'

Sweetie raises her head from Gunther's shoulder and peers at me with tiny slit eyes. A sharp forked tongue slips out and licks the air before disappearing inside the freakish elongated head again. Despite all the hot light that makes this place feel like a sauna, I'm suddenly very cold. A familiar lump rises in my throat and I gulp it down as the cameraman who's followed me over steps in for a close-up.

'Come along, people!' shouts Bradford. 'We're wasting precious life here!'

You can do this, I think to myself. After what happened on Saturday, surely holding a tame reptile for a few minutes can't be that bad. Except that for as long as I can remember I've been terrified of snakes. Even worse than spiders. The only snake I've ever been able to come close to is Snakey, who's made of yellow felt and looks nothing like a real one.

I step closer to Gunther. He grins and unloops the snake from around his shoulder. The guy who's filming the shoot points at a white X on the ground and tells me to stand there. One of the make-up artists appears from behind the rock fountain and quickly touches up my forehead and cheeks while Bradford starts explaining that he wants me to stand as still as I possibly can, as if I were a statue that happened to have a snake crawling on it. It's not as though I'm going to be able to bring myself to move anyway, I want to tell him.

'Okay, are we ready?'

A young guy with greasy skin who doesn't look any older than me arrives with a clapper. Bradford tells him to get in place and he comes and stands right in front of me with the clapperboard. I want to tell him to move away because I'm sure he can see down the slit between the rags over my boobs. But even if I wanted to I couldn't because my mouth is paralysed with fear. Gunther is holding the snake right next to me, preparing to drape it over my shoulders. 'Now, be gentle with her because she's a fragile little thing,' he's saying, and I don't know if he's talking to me or to the snake.

Suddenly I realise that I cannot have that thing on me under any circumstances. If it so much as touches me with its slimy scaly skin I am going to have an aneurysm. Desperately I try to think about Jack, about how bad I feel and how much I want him – anything to take my mind off the long thick dangling body Gunther is holding out for me to take. And as the snake's body gets closer I have a blinding revelation: the reason Jack stopped wanting me isn't because he doesn't love me. It's because I've never stood up like a real woman should and said out loud what I really want. When he told me it was over I just accepted it, when what he really needed me to do was to refuse, to tell him that what we had was special and make him understand that I wasn't letting go of it. I've always been so frightened and pathetic – even in entering this competition. I thought he would see the real me, but of course it just took me away from him and made him think I didn't want him anymore! I'm *so* stupid.

The snake's head is pointed downwards. Steeling myself, ever so slowly I reach out and let Gunther place my hand over the meaty centre of its body. Stars twinkle at the corners of my eyes, but I'm surprised to find the snake doesn't feel like I expected it to. It's not slimy, but solid and heavy. Real. Maybe I actually *can* do this, I think. Maybe I actually can take the snake – and if I can, then maybe I can do other things as well.

Gunther transfers the rest of the snake's weight into my arms. Just then the snake raises its head. It's just inches away from my face. Little black beads look right into my eyes as if it's seeing everything there is to see inside me. Then it opens its mouth to reveal two long fangs, devilishly pointed and sharp. It gapes at me. Behind the fangs is an endless red tunnel. I can't move. I'm hypnotised. Everything starts to glitter. Then it all goes black.

I open my eyes to see all these faces looking down at me. At first I think I've travelled back in time, slipped through some hole in reality and ended up back in the Tube station that first day after I auditioned when I blacked out and Jack carried me out of the train onto the platform. I wish I *had* gone back in time, because then Jack would still be here, reachable and touchable, and somehow I'd think of a way to make him stay. But I'm still in the present, still in the studio, and the faces looking down at me are the make-up artist's and the guy with the bad skin.

'She's okay!' I hear Bradford snapping huffily to someone in the background. 'Just give her some water and get the next one in, would you? We've only got this space till five.'

The clapper helps me to sit up. A few feet away Gunther is cradling the snake in his arms, rocking it gently back and forth. 'Aw,' he's cooing. 'Did Sweetie get a nasty knock from that silly girlie when she yawned?'

'Cor,' breathes the guy. 'You went down like a brick!'

He grins and gives me a pat on the back, like he's congratulating me for fainting so successfully. I smile weakly at him and a bubble of laughter escapes me. I feel dizzy and sick, but also strangely in control. Like suddenly I understand what the score is. I don't know what I'm doing here on this video shoot, taking part in a contest and driving myself crazy to be in some band when it's not what I want. What I want isn't in this competition, it's somewhere out there, moving further and further away from me the longer I remain. Maybe I did slip through some kind of hole in reality after all, because suddenly I know what I have to do. It's clear as day. Jack: I have to find him.

'I can't believe I'm still here. That I'm still in the running and I really got a chance at being the next Purrfect girl. But I tell you something – I ain't come this far for nothing. There's gonna be no more pussying around from this bitch cos from now on she's in this to win.'

Basically what we want to know is if there is any truth to it, goes Emma. She's got her arms folded and has this teachery face on like she's disappointed in me, as if I've cheated in a test or something. Back when I was at school that was the only look you ever got off teachers. Ain't no wonder most of me class all left or else got knocked up stead of hanging around to be disapproved of for another two years.

A yes or no answer, agrees Joe, giving the camera this quick look like he wants to make sure this is totally clear. Whatever you say we'll believe you, but either way we have to know.

I'm in the special panel room again, this time cos they've been getting letters complaining how I shouldn't be on the programme no more cos I set a bad example to girls across the country and stuff like that. The letters are all laid out across the table between them and me. I can read a few and they ain't pretty. There's this one near me elbow which says I oughta be slapped silly for what I done, which is pretty fucking ironic when you think about it. All this cos of that fucking tart going to some paper and telling it I kicked the shit out of her. She'd better take cover if she ever sees me coming, cos next time I see her I'm gonna show her what it means to have the shit kicked out of you and that's a fact.

There ain't no truth to any of it, I say clear as I can.

Tess is doing her thing of not saying a word, just staring at me through her flashy glasses like I'm a smelly piece of shit with arms and legs. The other two I reckon I could talk round, tell them the whole story about Shea and how she fucked Davy behind me back and get some sympathy off them about it. But not this Tess. Asking for sympathy off her would be like asking them to throw in a foot massage while they does your smear. And cos she's here being all official and shit, the other two reckon they've got to take it just as serious so they don't look like they don't care. Those cameras make prossies out of everyone – that's something I've really come to notice.

Okay, says Joe, if that's your story, then that's what we'll go with.

I grit me teeth. So much for just believing whatever I say.

It ain't me story, I say, trying not to get angry cos this is obviously one of those situations where that ain't gonna help. It's the truth, and I ain't gotta justify it.

Well, that's good enough for me, declares Emma, giving me a big smile and shrugging like that's all there is to it. But there's this look in her eyes which says to me that really it ain't.

Great, says Joe, not sounding like he thinks it's great at all. Thanks for talking to us, Joni. You understand why we had to take this seriously. No matter who it's from, an allegation is an allegation, and we can't have somebody who uses violence in the band.

If that cunt Shea's gone and ruined me chances of getting into Purrfect I'm gonna hunt her down like a fucking dog. Joe nods his head like that's all he wants off me so I start to stand up. Of course now that bitch Tess clears her throat and decides to do some cross-interrogation.

Just one thing, Joni, she goes in this superior voice, like she's so smart sometimes she just makes herself cum. Why do you think this girl *made* the allegation? What would be in it for her?

She's nothing but a slag who wants attention! I say before I can stop meself. I don't even know her hardly!

But living on a council estate you must see plenty of roughness, continues the rhino-faced bitch. You must see fights all the time. It's a way of life, isn't it? I bet everyone gets drawn in now and then?

Could you try just *a little* not to stereotype? goes Joe, making this wincing face at the camera.

I grew up on an estate, too! Tess snarls, making Joe and Emma jump almost a whole foot in the air. I know just what it's like and that's why I'm trying to give her the opportunity to explain herself in case there're anymore little stories hidden away! This is one of our Purrfect potentials! If we put her in the band then we don't want to have anymore nasty surprises, *do we*?

She heaves this sigh like she's passing real bad wind through her lips, then sticks her hand over her eyes like the effort of trying to talk with all us idiots has given her a migraine. There's a bit of silence while everyone just looks uncomfortable and don't know what to say.

It ain't true, I say. That Shea is just jealous of me, that's all.

Nobody says anything for a minute, then finally Tess drops her hand and gives off another deep mouth-fart.

I hope for your sake that's all it is, she goes.

In the corridor outside I find I'm totally shaking from what just happened. I take a minute to try and compose meself, taking a long deep breath and holding it in. I ain't gonna let it spoil me mood, I tell meself, cos today is the day I'm getting to see Baby and I could hardly sleep last night for thinking about it. I've missed him so much it's like I've been carrying around this bleeding wound inside. When I called up Mum and told her she could come and visit she burst into tears and started going on about how proud she was of me, and before you knew it I was in fucking fountains too. But I gotta be careful. She's bringing him as me little brother and I got to make sure that's what everyone thinks he is.

I let out me breath and turn to go and do some practising of me song for this week. I'm doing 'Confide in Me' by Kylie, which is a good one except it goes way too high and I have to practically fucking scream to hit the last notes.

I look up and see Ella standing there, all pale and washed out, but still looking pretty as anything, of course. On Sunday I could of sworn she was going after she fucked up our duet. Couldn't have done it worse if she'd tried, and made me look like a twat in the process. Afterwards, when we had to face the judges, I took hold of her hand and gave it a good hard squeeze, which was meant to be my way of saying goodbye. Didn't think I'd be seeing her again. But somehow the silly bag of nerves just keeps clinging on, even when it looks like a sure thing she's out. I'd swear it's almost like somebody up there is watching out for her and jinxing it for the rest of us.

Hello Joni, she goes. Her voice is all high, even more than it usually is, and her eyes are bloodshot like she ain't slept for a week. On anyone else of course this'd look freaky, but on her it just seems like the latest look from some magazine.

All right? I go. Shouldn't you be rehearsing your song?

No, she says simply. There's no more rehearsing for me.

She gives me this smile and I tell you it's like the sweetest smile you've ever seen, the sort of smile Jesus on the cross probably gave them Romans right before they stuck a spear in his scrotum.

I've decided to drop out. I was on my way to tell them.

What're you talking about? I say, though something inside clicks and I get this sudden suspicion I might know.

I've got to find him, Joni, she goes, suddenly sounding all desperate. I've got to find Jack and talk to him. I only entered this competition so he'd be able to see me. But now he's left and no one knows where he is!

Okay, let's just think about this, I say slowly, trying to buy some time while I figure out a way to talk her out of it. I might of known it would be about that fucking perv of a step-dad. I'm about to start on about how this is a chance of a lifetime and it don't come knocking twice, but then I take another look at her face and I think, Why bother? This girl is a fruit loop. Since day one I been doing me best to take care of her, like she was me little sister or something, but at the end of the day what she is really is competition – just competition all trussed up like a blonde Bambi who faints a lot. But we're getting closer and closer to the finish line and even though it don't seem like she should have a shot in hell of getting it, the way things have been going you can't never be too sure. So why not let the dappy bitch go right ahead and dig her own grave if that's what she wants to do? It ain't like I ain't tried with her.

There's nothing to think about, she goes, still smiling like a fucking saint. I've made up my mind. I'm not meant to be in Purrfect, Joni. Someone like you is. Someone stronger and better. I should just be happy that I got this far.

Well, I go, if that's really how you feel . . .

Suddenly Ella lurches at me. For a second I think she's attacking me, like maybe she's flipped out and gone psycho. But then she spreads out her arms and wraps them round me in this choke hold of a hug. I put me arms around her too and wait for a big wet patch to spread down me back. But she don't start bawling. Instead she pulls away and gives me a last nod, like she's blessing me, then turns and knocks on the door to the panel's room. There's a pause and then Tess's voice goes Yes? like the voice of death, and Ella pushes it open and goes inside.

I feel sort of weird about it, but it's too late to do anything now so I go to the studio to practise. I don't see Ella again all morning and I feel bad about not trying to talk her out of it. But I can't dwell on that, not when I'm almost ready to pop a blood vessel at the prospect of seeing Mum and Baby again. I can't believe it's been nearly three weeks since I left home. Feels like a fucking lifetime. I keep going to the front door to check and see if any cars have pulled up, but all there ever is out there is that stupid security blockhead, marching around with his massive fat tummy. Finally I give up and decide to stay in the studio and either get the song down or else die till they get here.

I'm in the middle of screeching 'Confide in Me' at the top of me lungs when I hear a voice say me name all quietly from behind. I turn round and see Mum standing at the door with Baby in a pushchair. She's wearing her smart jeans and a new lacy pink top with ribbon over the cleavage, and Baby's in his blue dungarees and has got a red balloon in his little hand with Good Luck written in a heart on it. I stop singing and stare at them. It's funny how people look different when you don't see them for a bit. You suddenly notice all these little things about them that make up what they look like. I notice Mum's long neck and her cheekbones, which she's always been so proud of cos she reckons they're why stars pay to have silicone implants in their faces, but which sure as hell don't look so pretty first thing in the morning after a night on the razz. I notice her brown eyes, which I've always thought would suit her better if they was blue like mine, only now I'm glad they're brown and I can't believe I ever wished they was anything different. And as for Baby, I look at him and it's like the first time I saw him after they snipped the cord and asked me if I wanted to hold him. I was practically half-dead from all the pushing and said did I look like I was in the mood for holding a fucking baby? But of course when they put him in your arms that all goes out of your head and it seems like it was worth it after all. I look at him now with his tiny little fist all wrapped round the string to the balloon and I suddenly get this flash that what I'm doing is for him. It's funny though, cos I'd almost forgot.

Mum, I say, feeling weak all of a sudden.

With a little scream we rush towards each other, and I hug her and then reach down to lift Baby up. He does a gurgle and these little bubbles of spit appear out his mouth. Mum tries to say something but ends up starting to cry instead.

Oh Mum, I say, you wouldn't believe how good it is to see you!

You make me so proud! Mum manages through her fountains. Watching you on TV with all the girls round at ours and knowing you're me daughter . . .

I give her a kiss on the cheek and start dancing about with Baby, doing the aeroplane with him, making him giggle. It's always been one of his favourite games. I sweep him around holding on to just one leg and arm. Mum's always telling me off for doing it cos she says it'll make him longer on one side than the other when he grows up, but Baby fucking loves it. Sure enough he starts to giggle away, and it's the cutest thing ever.

How's my little one been? I go. How's my Baby waby—

Suddenly I stop dead, cos I've just remembered about the camera. It's there, of course, in the doorway, always pointed at you, always recording. Can't have anyone twig Baby's me own kid, not after what the panel said to me cos of that fucking Shea. Ain't gonna ruin this, not now I'm so close.

Yuck! I go, letting out a little scream. He just *drooled* on me!

I shove Baby into Mum's arms with a disgusted face and start patting meself down. Mum looks a bit surprised but she takes him. I try not to look at Baby's face, cos I know if I do them big brown eyes of his'll break me heart.

This is for you, Baby, I try to tell him in me head. One day you'll understand.

We have a seat over in the corner and while she bounces Baby up and down on her knees Mum fills me in on the gossip back home. People've been making lots of bets about me getting into Purrfect down at the local, she says. The highest one is five hundred pounds, if you can believe it. No pressure there! Meanwhile Fat Carol's been told she's morbidly obese, which is hardly newsworthy, only they've said that if she don't shift some of that lard her heart could be in danger. I ask about Wend and about Davy, but Mum says she ain't seen them and changes the subject real quick, telling me about this Italian fella she's got her eye on who just started working at Domino's. I tell her not to bother with him cos he's sure to be a bastard, since all the men Mum ever fancies are. Mum laughs and says it's true, which ain't like her since she's usually right touchy when it comes to the subject of men. I get the feeling she's keeping something back. In between bouncing Baby she keeps glancing at the camera and doing this flickering thing with her left eye. At first I thought it was just nicotine cravings, since if Mum goes for more than twenty minutes without a fag she starts twitching away like a weirdo. But then I remember it's also what she does when she's nervous cos of something.

Here, I go after a bit, looks like Baby needs changing!

Mum holds Baby up all confused and sniffs him, but before she can say something I grab her arm and start guiding her over to the door.

I'll show you where the loo is, I say, and drag her out into the corridor. I pull her up the stairs, trailed all the way by the camera. When we get to the bathroom I close the door on it, going in this jokey way, Oi you can't come in here, this is ladies only! Then I turn round to face Mum with me arms folded.

Well? I go.

He don't need changing, she says.

Never mind that, I hiss. What the fuck is going on?

I dunno what you're talking about, she goes, all innocent. But the thing about Mum is that when she tries to lie she just makes it more obvious than ever she ain't telling the truth. She'd make a rubbish crim. I cock me head to one side and give her this look. She gets it.

Oh Joni . . . I wasn't gonna tell you. There ain't nothing you can do about it in here, and I've been going round telling everyone it's a pack of lies so you shouldn't worry!

What *is* it? I practically roar at her.

It's that Wend, goes Mum, holding Baby out in front of her like a shield as if she reckons I'm gonna run at her. She's been spreading some awful nasty gossip about you.

What gossip? I say, all dumbfounded. Wend wouldn't do that!

Stuff like how you ripped her dress at the auditions so they'd pick you instead of her. And that you've always been a bully. It was her who first started saying you smacked that Shea round when she was doing your Davy.

I never smacked her round! I go, almost dying from the effort of not screaming. This is bollocks! Wend's me best fucking mate!

She's a right little missy, goes Mum darkly, setting Baby down on the floor. She holds up two crossed fingers. Shea and Wend is like that! They been going round together just like you used to. But don't you worry – I saw them at the Co-op the other day and I had a right go at her in front of everyone! Should of known, I said to her. Like mother like daughter! A family of bitches, that's what you Sturges are!

She starts to get carried away.

Shhh! I snap at her. I look down at Baby trying to toddle towards me feet and try to let go of the anger. There's nothing you can do, I tell meself. But it don't work. I go over to the far wall and give it a kick, hard as I can.

Fucking hurts me toes, but even that makes me feel a little better. How could she do it? We been friends since we was tots – we're practically fucking sisters. I guess it shows you just what an ugly thing jealousy is. Turns people into fucking monsters. Probably I ought to be feeling sorry for her, since after all, here I am in this house with the opportunity of a lifetime and she's stuck there back in some estate going round saying nasty shit cos that's all she's got to do. It's pathetic. I turn back to Mum, who's looking at me all scared, like she's worried I'm gonna start trashing the place.

Is that all?

Mum shrugs and squats down next to Baby, like she suddenly wants to play with him. Phew! Think he really might need a change you know, she says, all casual.

What else!

Davy, goes Mum quietly. He's with Wend now. I seen them going round together, all over each other like they're a pair of school kids or something.

I feel weird, choked up, like I got someone's hands around me throat. I'm both hot and cold too, as if I'm gonna explode or melt or maybe even do both at the same time. The world looks funny, and for a second I wonder if I'm about to do an Ella and black out like she did on the day of the video shoot.

He wouldn't! I yell suddenly, surprising Mum, Baby and even meself. I don't even give a shit about the stupid camera on the other side of the door anymore. He fucking wouldn't! Not after everything! He wouldn't fucking *dare*!

I could of gone on shouting like a maniac till I was blue, but then Baby starts to cry and that brings me back to me senses. Mum picks him up and starts rocking him back and forwards, going Shhhh! and making faces at him and shooting me these worried looks. I hold out me arms and she puts Baby into them, and I look down at his big old eyes and feel all the anger slowly leave me. Fuck Wend. Fuck Davy. Let them fuck each other if that's what they want to do.

You okay? says Mum, all jittery and tapping her foot up and down. You want me to go and find you an aspirin or something?

I'm okay, I go, trying me best to make meself believe it, I'm all right. I'm going places. I don't need them. I don't need no one.

That's the spirit! Mum grins. She glances back at the door. Here – what do you say to a quick fag?

Sometimes I just stare at her. I can't help it. She's so hideously ugly in everything she says and does. So much so that she's almost beautiful. Beautiful like a cobra is – the sort of hideous beauty you only find in a creature so naturally ruthless it takes your breath away. I can marvel at the way she manipulates everyone around her. It's like it's instinctive for her and she can't help herself. I watch that big round face as it sizes up those girls onstage, those great bulging eyes, that fat lipstick-stained mouth, those great holes for nostrils and those rolls of flab under her chin, and it's like I'm hypnotised. She's a monster that sees others only as products with which she can add to her own success, or else as obstacles to it that must be snuffed out as quickly as possible. I wonder if she even still has emotions. Is there sadness there, buried deep down under all that fat and bitterness where no one can ever get at it? I can't believe she was always this way. Not to begin with. Once she must have been one of those girls too, perhaps not pretty or talented but full of dreams and hope just like everyone else. Just like me. Time's been cruel to her though, cruel as only time can be, and in such a way as can never be undone. Only finished. That's what I believe.

Sometimes I feel like we're the same person, like the inside of her is the same as the inside of me. Like behind that empty round face with its cold dead eyes the soul inside is exactly like my own. After all, in the whole wide world I'm probably the only one who actually understands her, and that must give us a connection. I think that somewhere deep down she knows I'm coming for her. I think that maybe she even welcomes it.

Sometimes I almost wonder if it's hate I feel for her and not love.

'God's seen me this far and He's going to see me all the way to the end. Every last bit of me is focused on the prize now. It's what I was born to do and it's what I am *going* to do. Nothing's going to stop me now.'

I'm upstairs at the top of the house rehearsing by the window in the relaxation room when I see Dad's BMW pulling up in the drive below. My heart skips a beat, but because I'm a professional I don't move until I've reached the end of my refrain. Then I hurl myself at the door, not even pausing for the cameraman, who turns his camera too fast and smashes it into the wall. I hear him cursing behind me as I rocket down the stairs. It's funny how people always resort to profanity whenever something goes wrong.

As I turn the corner at the bottom I run right into that whining Ella, who's holding a suitcase and dithering in the middle of the landing. I just about manage to throw myself to the side before I collide with her, stumbling against the wall instead and twisting my foot.

'Sorry, Louise!' cries Ella.

'Can't you watch it?' I snap, picking myself up and rubbing my ankle. It had better not be sprained, or else she's going straight to hell. I flex and point it quickly a few times to get the blood going, while Ella puts down her suitcase and hovers about, patting the air around me as if this is going to help.

'I'm okay,' I say, mostly to get her off me, though luckily for her it turns out to be true. I wave her away and notice she's wearing that soft white coat of hers with the big lacy collar – the lucky little minx always has nice clothes. I look over at her suitcase. 'What are you doing?'

'Oh,' says Ella, looking back like she's only just noticed it herself. 'It's my things . . . I'm leaving, you see.'

I'm speechless. Ella gives me a little smile. My first thought is that she's been ejected from the competition. It wouldn't be that surprising, since she's by far the weakest link. She deserved to go on Saturday, no question about it, and it's only her good fortune that Valerie had that accident and they decided to call it off. Maybe they've changed their minds again. But then it occurs to me they wouldn't just do that, not unless Valerie is back, and I remember the sight of Valerie's ankle, which was just sick and makes you wonder how God can be so cruel, though obviously He does work in mysterious ways. There's no way she could be returning.

'Why?' I finally manage. Ella looks down.

'I've decided I want to leave,' she tells me in a voice so quiet I can barely hear her. 'I didn't want to cause a fuss, that's why I didn't come up to say goodbye.'

I gape at her. You don't just *walk* out of a competition like this, even if you are destined to fail. This is the chance of a lifetime, and only a crazy person would leave now that we're so close – only an idiot, only one of life's ultimate losers, someone destined to be trodden on for the rest of their life.

Just then a blonde head of hair with caramel streaks appears on the stairs below. It belongs to a woman with lots of make-up who glances coolly at me and then at Ella.

'Ella?' she says tersely, like she's intolerably busy. 'If we're leaving we're *leaving*. I'm not going to try and argue you out of it, I don't care what Mimi says. But we have to go *now*.'

Ella's mother looks nothing like her. Annoying as she is, Ella's reasonably good-looking, I suppose, not that it's much of a distraction from her incessant snivelling. But this woman's got a very heavy face, big cheeks, a long chin and lots of frown lines, like she spends a lot of time being frustrated with the world. She's not good-looking at all really, but she's definitely stylish. The complete opposite of Ella, since no matter how many designer clothes she wears Ella just doesn't carry herself well enough to be properly chic. She's never had that star quality, and they obviously only put her in the competition for entertainment value.

'I'm just coming,' says Ella quickly, turning to pick up her suitcase. As she does the cameraman appears on the stairs above with the camera, which obviously hasn't suffered much damage, pointed at us. I think fast.

'I can't believe you're going!' I cry, throwing my arms around Ella so that she drops the suitcase again. Over her shoulder I see her mother rolling her eyes impatiently. What a bee – no wonder Ella's such a wreck. It almost makes me grateful for who God chose to be *my* mother.

I tell Ella that I'll miss her and that she's really talented and I know she's going to make it one day, which is a massive lie but one I think God will forgive me for, especially since she starts crying and telling me what a wonderful time she's had. Then her mum emits a sound like a growl in the back of her throat and Ella pulls free. With a last pat of my shoulder she wipes away her tears, picks her suitcase up again, and then follows her mum down the stairs. I wait for a minute, letting the camera see me struggling to control my mixed emotions at her leaving and also to give her time to get to the bottom floor, since I don't want to catch up with her again. Then I slowly nod like it was obviously meant to be and start to make my own way down.

Dad is waiting in the hall with his arms wide open. I throw myself into his hug and feel a great surge of relief flooding through me at the warmth of his body against mine. It feels like a century since I climbed into that limo and watched him and Mum and those idiots Tina and Becky wave me off. I've got so much to tell him I don't even know where to begin.

'We talked about it and decided your mother wouldn't come,' says Dad, gently stroking my hair. 'She's still very upset about Gramps. She'd only cause a scene and you can't afford to lose your focus. But she sends all her love – and cookies, of course.'

He lets go of me and reaches down to his bag to take out a tin, which he gives to me. Inside are a dozen chocolaty, fatty skin-nightmares with little messages saying Good Luck! in icing sugar on top of each one. Dad and I grin at each other knowingly. Suddenly I feel a pang of regret that Mum hasn't come, and even though I know I'll pay for it later, I open the tin, pluck one of the cookies up and start to nibble on the end of it. I notice Dad's grin gets even bigger, since he always likes it when I eat. Then he loses his grin and squints at something past my shoulder on the stairs. I remember the camera.

'So where can a doting father get a nice cup of tea in this joint?'

I take him into the kitchen, where Rebecca was rehearsing earlier. Fortunately she's not here anymore since her family, which is absolutely huge, arrived half an hour ago. I saw her from upstairs meeting them in the driveway. They all piled out of the car one after another, like it was generating them or something, each family member screaming as if they were in the presence of the ultimate diva the second they got out and saw her. I'm glad Dad and I don't need to make such exhibitions of ourselves. He sits down next to the radiator while I put the kettle on. The cameraman films from the opposite corner, presumably so he can get us both in.

'My little girl really has grown up,' says Dad fondly. 'That duet you did on Saturday was stellar, sweetheart. You completely killed it.'

I turn and see he is grinning again, full of pride. He starts to list all the little details he noticed that made it so good. Sometimes I think I'm the luckiest girl in the whole world to have such a caring, clued-up dad. The kettle clicks and I pour out hot water over two teabags.

'But what the hell happened the week before? Honey, this is your big chance and you can't afford to pull a stunt like that! And so unlike you – why, I could hardly believe that was my girl up there onstage!'

A sudden spasm of hatred explodes inside me. It is so unexpected that I spill the hot water all over the sideboard and almost drop the kettle. I grab a J-cloth and start mopping it up. The feeling dissolves as quickly as it appeared, leaving me only to worry where it came from. Dad's only ever been on my side, behind me one hundred per cent. He's the last person in the world I should ever feel angry with. I suppose it's the stress. I really must try not to let it get to me.

'I mean, that wasn't the Louise I know and love,' Dad is saying. 'I don't know who that person was. All our hard work and effort . . . I really thought you were going to let me down.'

'Me too,' I tell him. 'I wasn't well and I shouldn't have gone out. But it's not going to happen again.'

'That's my girl. My future superstar.'

I smile and take our tea over. Dad raises his mug and clinks it against mine. The cameraman comes closer and takes a seat at the other side of the table, putting his elbows on it so he has a base to rest his camera. As he fiddles with a toggle on the side I catch a glimpse of his face. He's probably around the same age as Dad, only balder and with lots of blackheads and frown lines – most men Dad's age don't understand about the importance of cleansing and moisturising. But it's funny, because you really forget that there are actual people behind these contraptions. When you do see them it's quite a shock.

'Louise, is something the matter?'

'No!' I exclaim, far too brightly. 'Why would something be the matter?'

'I don't know,' says Dad. 'You just looked distracted, that's all.'

I laugh as if this was ridiculous. But the truth is something is very much the matter. Only I can't say anything about it. Ever since I heard about Gramps passing away my relationship with God has been oddly stilted. Almost like we've been taking a break from each other. I still pray to Him of course, and I know he's still there watching and listening. I mean, He must be, because He watches and listens to everything, it's just that it doesn't *seem* like He is. In fact, what's worrying me is that it *seems* like He isn't there at all. And this last feeling scares me more than anything else I've ever been afraid of in my whole life, because if He isn't there, then *who* is? Who've I been talking to all my life? Who is out there onstage with me, watching over me and making sure I kill it each time I go out? The idea of standing onstage in front of a crowd of people, all alone, without the presence of something divine looking out for me is unbearable. It's unthinkable. And yet for some reason I keep finding myself thinking it. It's that Riana's fault. She's done something to me, I know it. Hanging out with her last week was a bad idea because it made me complacent and lazy. I even found myself swearing the other night when I dropped my toothbrush on the floor, taking the Lord's name in vain, which is something I never do. It's the worst timing ever for a crisis of faith. If only there was someone I could talk to, a reverend or a fellow believer. But none of the other girls care about God. Dad has never been much into Him either, which is why I've never told him just how much I depend on Him. It's the one thing Dad wouldn't understand, because he's always said that a man makes his own luck and that religion is for losers. He has issues with the idea of a higher state of authority, I think.

I realise that Dad's peering at me questioningly so I shake my head and give him my perkiest smile. Even if I could talk to him about it I wouldn't, not with the stupid effing camera there. It'd make me look like a moron.

'I'm just so happy to see you,' I say.

'Well, then,' he replies, grinning back at me and relaxing into his seat. 'Let's not waste this time we have together, eh? Let's do some strategising!'

He asks which song I'm performing this week and I tell him and then we go through it slowly, picking out the high parts and the low parts and figuring out at which bit I should really let the song take over and at which bit I should sink to my knees like I'm overcome with emotion. It's amazing to have Dad sitting here, giving me all the benefit of his wisdom and advice. In a way it's hard to believe I've managed to survive this long without him. But all the same, a tiny shred of me still sort of regrets that Mum isn't here too, even if she would have just got in the way. She would have been constantly asking if I was eating enough and getting enough fresh air, and that would have driven me crazy, of course. But maybe because she isn't here to ask those things, I find myself really wishing she was.

We agree that I will do a slow rotation on the final 'Ooh baby', so that I face all directions and make every member of the audience understand I am singing for them and them alone. It's a brilliant ploy. Dad beams and tells me he can't wait to see it. Just then Riana enters the kitchen looking like death warmed up and wearing nothing but her bed things, which consists of just panties and white T-shirt. Dad immediately goes stiff and studies the tablecloth. Riana completely ignores us and crosses to the fridge.

'Why aren't you dressed?' I call over as she opens it. She shrugs as if to say, Who cares? and starts rummaging inside. Over the last couple of days she's been behaving very oddly. Definitely not the way a potential Purrfect girl ought to act. She's been snapping at everyone, no matter what you say to her, and at meal times she doesn't talk at all, just stirs her food around and glares at it like it's her worst enemy. Yesterday morning when Patty said she was singing like a drag queen she actually answered back 'At least I don't look like one', as a result of which Patty stormed out shrieking that it didn't say anywhere in her contract that she had to put up with *that* sort of thing, and that was the whole morning gone, us waiting while they persuaded her to come back. She still hates Riana though, and just tells her what to do in a disdainful voice as if she's the lowest form of scum alive. But Riana doesn't seem to care. She's been acting like somebody died, which they obviously did, only it happened to *me* not her, and if anything *I'm* the one who should be acting weird.

We watch her select a Diet Coke and shove the door shut. The way she does it is as though she's bitter at the whole world. Maybe it's because I'm feeling happy because of Dad's visit and can't stand the sight of someone else miserable, but for some reason I hear myself blurt out: 'Where's *your* visitor? Aren't they here yet?'

Riana gets to the door and turns back. The cameraman is obviously struggling trying to figure out which one of us to stay focused on. He ends up opting for her, and it's a good decision, since she replies 'I don't have any visitors' in a low and throaty, bitter voice, dramatic as anything, before exiting.

'Probably no one else is cheap enough,' says Dad, snatching an opportunity while the cameraman is changing tapes to say what he really thinks. He winks at me, but all of a sudden I feel strangely protective of Riana, even though I thought she was nothing but a cheap whore when I first met her, too. Without really thinking about what I'm doing I set my mug down and stand up.

'I'm just off to the bathroom, be right back – maybe you can do some vox pop for the camera!' I say. I skip quickly out of the kitchen. The cameraman doesn't follow, so I guess he's decided to take me up on my suggestion. I head up the stairs to the dorm. Sure enough, there's Riana, lying on the bed taking sips from her Diet Coke and staring at the ceiling. Her chest heaves, and those huge boobs of hers look like mountains during an earthquake.

'Riana?'

'What?' she mutters, snapping her eyes in my direction as if I'm nothing but a hassle to have to deal with. It's rather insulting, especially considering how hard I worked with her last week. I can't help bristling a bit.

'Actually I just came to see if you're okay,' I say coldly. Riana doesn't reply to this, just rolls her eyes back to the ceiling. I feel myself starting to get mad at her. Here I am being perfectly considerate and charitable and having it shoved right back in my face.

'Well?' I say.

'Well what?' says Riana.

'Well, *are you?*'

A slow smile snakes its way across her cheeks. It's one of those mean-spirited smiles that I used to see on girls in the corridor at school when I passed them on the way to class. The sort of smile you get from slackers and sluts, from the ones who whisper behind your back and give you rude nicknames that stick around for ever. I just remind myself they're jealous of me because they don't have the same passion and drive that I have.

'Let's not pretend you care, shall we?' says Riana, sounding bored. It's an absolutely maddening thing for her to say and I have to struggle like crazy not to lose my temper. But that's clearly what she wants me to do and I'm going to be the better person. Because no matter what she says, that's what I am.

'I care,' I say as calmly as I can. 'I'm a nice person.'

I expected to sound cool and dignified, but it comes out sounding just stupid. What's worse is that it comes out sounding like it isn't really true. Like I'm trying to convince myself that it is.

'I've got to go now. My dad is waiting.'

But I don't move. It's almost as though I'm under a spell, watching that huge bosom as it rises and falls.

'That's right, run off back to daddykins,' trills Riana. 'Give him my love, won't you?'

In a flash I'm so furious I can't think straight. I've never known anything like it. I want to slap the arrogant fucking bitch silly – *the fake-chested nigger whore from hell*! I step forward, feeling my face burning up with anger. But I mustn't attack her – that's probably what she's hoping for. Probably she's got it all planned, how she'll say I'm violent and get me kicked out of the contest even though she goaded me into it. Instead I rack my brains for the most cutting thing I can possibly say back. The trouble is I've never been much good at retorts, which is why those girls at school always seem to get the better of me. But suddenly I have a flash of inspiration, so brilliant I know for sure it's come from God.

'It's no wonder *you* don't have any visitors!'

It comes out sounding amazing, a million times as nasty as all the things I've ever had said to me at school. I say it with a sneer and turn and begin to swagger away, just like a femme fatale from one of those black and white movies. But then the great feeling is interrupted by a jarring screech of pain, which comes out of my own mouth. Riana is up and on her feet and she's taken hold of my hair and is yanking my head backwards.

'What the *fuck* would you know?' she hisses right in my ear. 'You're nothing but a spoilt little daddy's girl who's never had to work a day in her *whole fucking life*!'

She drags me towards the bed. I fight her all the way,

before it occurs to me to just throw myself backwards into her. I use all my strength and knock her off balance so that she lands hard on her bottom on the carpet with me on top of her.

'You're for it now!' I shriek. 'After I tell them about this, that's it! You'll be out! Out like you deserve!'

I wrestle with her, kicking and clawing. She's still holding my hair, practically tearing it out at the roots, and hot tears of pain are forming in my eyes, but somehow I manage to break free and leap to my feet. I head for the door, turning round at the last minute in case I need to shield myself from a blow to the back of the head.

Riana is standing, too, only she hasn't moved forward and her head is bowed and her eyes are closed. It looks like she might actually be crying. It also looks like she's off guard, and snatching the opportunity I leap quickly forward and give her a resounding slap that sends her face whipping towards her left shoulder. My hand tingles from the sensation. It feels wonderful. Riana's head stays in the place I've knocked it to for a few seconds, frozen like in a cartoon where the character suddenly discovers the ground has disappeared and remains stock still while the realisation they're about to fall sets in. Then, as Riana slowly turns her head back towards me I lift my other hand and prepare to give the other cheek a good hard slap. She catches my wrist before I can strike, so I lift the other one again, but then she catches that too. I try to twist away, but she won't let go, and all I end up doing is twisting myself closer to her, so that I end up pressed right up close against those ridiculous great tits and that smug knowing face. I struggle and squirm against her but she holds me rigidly, and I'm suddenly aware that I'm laughing manically, just like the Wicked Witch of the West in *The Wizard of Oz*. I can taste blood in my mouth, and there's adrenalin rushing through my veins like crazy, as if I'm onstage giving a performance. Being so close to the hateful black bitch turns everything upside down. I can't think straight. All I can see is her mouth. Those massive negro lips just a centimetre or two from mine.

For a second I think she's going to kiss me. Not like she did last time in the corridor after our duet, but properly, like a real kiss. I stop laughing, stop moving, stop struggling, stop trying to attack her, and hold my breath.

Then I feel the pressure of her hands loosening on my wrists and then I'm pulling away, staring at her and trying to think of something to say. But nothing comes. Riana's looking back at me with this ghost of a smile, like she's just found out something deeply personal and secret about me, and I'm burning up with anger and shame. I realise I'm still holding my breath and take a great gasp of air.

'Louise—' says Riana, but I'm already leaving. I hurry out the door, stumbling and catching my sweater on the handle. There's a tearing sound but I don't stop. I keep on going until I'm down the first set of stairs and on the first-floor landing. Only then do I pause to breathe some more and wait for my stupid heart to stop its ridiculous incessant pounding.

'Victory's so close I can practically taste it. There's four of us left and we all want to be here for the final. Everyone's really bringing it now. But I'm not scared, cos I've come to realise something over the last week – that I'm here to win!'

Right, announces Emma, it's time to get this party on the road!

Everyone starts rushing round, running brushes through their hair and checking their faces for spots that might have sprung up since they last gawked at themselves in the mirror five minutes ago. While Rebecca wrestles with a tangle and Joni screams that her left earstud's fallen out, I shove all the shit on my bedside table, the lippy, compact, comb, hair pins, security pass and other junk, in my handbag. Then I slump down on my bed and lie back, fucking exhausted already.

That means now! yells Emma, who's got a whole lot more bossy over the last week. Being a judge's obviously gone to her head. It's pretty funny in a way, seeing as when you think about it we're basically in the same place she once was when she was a few years younger, only difference being the band we're trying to be part of is a thousand times better than Kissy Piss Piss or whatever it was called. Can't help but wonder if it doesn't make her the smallest bit bitter.

Come on Riana, she orders. This isn't like you! I don't know what's got into you this week, but you'd better snap out of it. If you don't perform tonight – *you're out*!

The camera dude trotting along behind her stops for a quick shot of me. For his benefit I mouth the words Blonde Bitch to her back and then haul myself to my feet.

I'm hit by this head rush so bad I have to sit right back down again. Thing is, that blonde bitch has a point. It's the first time since the beginning of this competition I've genuinely felt nervous about going out on stage, and I've got good reason cos tonight there's nothing stuffed down my boot to give me that extra bit of umph I need to get me through. Not even the chance of some Dutch courage – seeing as how alcohol was forbidden on day one by our bastard joy-hating judges. Jesus, what I wouldn't give to be able to knock back a couple of JDs. All week long I've been battling the headache from hell, not to mention hot and cold flushes. You'd think I was up the duff or menopausal the way I've been off and on. Guess maybe Eddy had a smidge of a point yelling at me all those times that I had a problem, cos by Wednesday I honestly thought I was going to have to jack it all in and haul ass like Ella, just so's I could get hold of a pinch and shut up those fucking squeaks and groans scrambling up my brains. It was only the knowledge that my place in Purrfect is within licking distance that stopped me. That's why I can't afford not to get through tonight. Not after all the shit I've gone through. No matter what it takes, I've got to go out there and dazzle them, give it one million per cent and bring home the bacon. And I can do it too, I know I can. Funny, but I guess there's some truth in what Edgar said earlier this week after all – that true stars've got the ability to stand up and perform no matter what kind of crap is going down behind the curtains. Cos if this competition has made one thing clear to me, it's this – I'm going to be a star. A fucking supernova. Just wait and see.

Right – we're leaving! declares Emma. I snatch up my bag and fall into line behind her. We all troop down to the front drive where the limo is waiting to take us to the studio. Louise waits until Joni and Rebecca have got in behind me before climbing in herself. As she does I catch her eye and give her my saucy welcome-comrade smile. Silly little madam instantly jerks her head away like she'd just been flashed. For the past two days she's been avoiding me like she thinks if she comes too close I'll turn her into a raving lesbian. Yesterday when Patty paired us up for stretches she even faked a muscle strain that neatly lasted just up until the end of the class, when she suddenly magically got better for singing with Edgar. It's pretty hilarious. I probably ought to explain to her that our little tiff the other day was only cos my temperature was out of this world, and cos I was at an all-time low and missing my girlfriend like chronic – only leaving out the girlfriend part, obviously. But seeing as she won't let me within five feet of her I've not exactly had the chance. It was obviously a major deal for her, probably the closest she's ever come to experiencing pent-up sexual tension. Guess I shouldn't be surprised seeing as she carries herself round like she's never so much as copped a feel. Tragic, really. It'd be kind of delicious to give her a tour of what the other side has to offer, force it down her throat till she surrenders, and under normal circumstances I'd probably have a ball playing with her. I remember the first time I nearly kissed a girl and all the mixed emotions that went on in my head. The fear of what other people would say versus this incredible need I had to touch her. Realising I might actually be gay – or bisexual, since that's how you always start off – was the ultimate head-fuck. Sometimes I wonder what Mum'd say if she'd lived long enough for me to come out to her. I like to think she'd be supportive, even if every other decision I ever made disappointed the hell out of her.

Here we go! cries Rebecca, biting her lower lip as we draw up outside the studio. There's this weird humming sound coming from outside. As we pass through the gates I realise it's a small crowd of people making woos outside the main doors. Some of them are holding banners and when I look closer I'm amazed cos that's when I see the people are here for us. The banners say things like BRING BACK ELLA! and I FANCY RIANA! and BECCA 4EVER!!! People I don't even know have taken their evenings out to come and stand round in the cold, just for my sake, so's they can cheer me on.

I straighten up in my seat and prepare a big smile. Fact is, I never got a chance to tell Mum about being gay. It's sad, but there you go. And as for this thing with Louise, well these're not normal circumstances. Mum's dead, and Louise is competition. Just got to get over it and on with it, doncha?

Girls, says Emma, because tonight is special you'll be thrilled to hear there's a treat in store. World-renowned make-up artist Shelly Summers and her team are on their way to the studio. That's right, everyone – the make-up artist of the stars is going to be working on you. No blaming hair and make-up if it all goes wrong!

I laugh along with everyone else, but I can't help noticing no one's laughter sounds quite like they mean it. Looks like I'm not the only one that's nervous about tonight. Good – cos that means everybody else's vulnerable too.

We get out the limo and the woos of the crowd turn into cheering. For a small group of people they make enough of a din to fill a fucking stadium. As we're led down this path with barriers along either side of it to keep them out, I have this sudden feeling like I'm a gladiator going into battle. Flashes are going off left right and centre. For the benefit of the crowd I push my chest out and try to wiggle my arse a bit as I move. As I do I hear this young voice calling my name, and I turn and see this little girl with her mum. The girl's got skin dark as coal and a large squat nose. She's totally dwarfed by the massive pink bomber jacket she's wearing, which makes her look cute as a button, like one of those old-fashioned trolls everybody was raving about back when I was her age. I go over and crouch down.

Hello there, I say. What's your name, then?

Her name is Rose, says the girl's mum in a deep Caribbean accent. She your biggest fan, ent you Rose? She watch you on TV and want to be just like you!

Rose, I say, giving her a big smile. What a beautiful name. You *really* my biggest fan, Rose?

The little girl gazes up at me, mouth open and eyes all big and starry. I want to pick her up and cuddle her to death. I imagine how I must seem to her, and for the first time I have this realisation that as the only black girl in the show I really *do* have a responsibility. Who else are little 'uns like this Rose going to look up to when they watch telly? Ha, goes Eddy's voice in my head. Responsibility to what? To be a role model so she grows up with the ambition to jiggle her bits around onstage? But I force Eddy's voice to shut up. She's not here, and she doesn't get it. She never has. That's why I couldn't invite her to come and visit me like all the other families last week. Couldn't risk her going off on one and ruining this for me.

Mummy, Riana's nose is dripping, pipsqueaks Rose.

I look down and see a dark spot has appeared on my jeans, like a tiny black button. Another one appears. From behind the girl comes the flash of a camera, blinding me. Quickly I dig out a tissue from my back pocket and shove it over my nose to catch the blood. As I get my sight back I see Rose's staring at me open-mouthed. I pat her head and step back. Some role model.

I look round and see the other girls are all signing autographs and Emma is watching us at the entrance to the studio. Her face is all hard and serious, like she's seen all this before and knows it'll only end in tears.

Come on, come on, she calls. We haven't got all night!

We all follow her in, waving to the crowd, blinking away cos of the strobe effect of all the flashing cameras. A security guard shuts the doors behind us. In the entrance hall Michelle is waiting, clipboard held in front of her chest like a piece of body armour. Tonight she's dressed head to toe in dark purple, and with her pale white skin and red lips bears more than a passing resemblance to the Joker. You can't help but wonder where she gets *her* style tips from. She peers at us down her nose, as if she was hoping that, like Ella, we'd all have quit by now, sighs like she can't believe what she has to work with and tells us to follow her. Emma just has time to wish us good luck and say she'll see us onstage before we take off with Michelle.

The make-up team will be here in ten, says Michelle briskly as we power walk up some stairs. While you're waiting get yourselves into costume. The clothes have already been selected. They're labelled and on the rail.

She makes a couple of ticks on her pad and turns a sharp corner. The camera dude, who's stopped to fiddle with his camera, gets lost behind us. We turn another corner and Michelle comes to a screeching halt in front of a large red door with a gold star on it. She turns the handle and throws it open.

Remember, we're on an incredibly tight schedule tonight so no faffing, please. And also please, please, please, no more accidents. *Watch* where you step, and take *extra* care if you're wearing heels!

We troop in and she starts to close the door on us. Just then Rebecca lets out this scream like she's just been fingered. I almost do as well, cos at first it looks like someone's smeared blood all the way across the mirror. This glistening wet trail of gore has been shaped into words that say:

gEt OuT wHiLe YoU sTiLl CaN

Then I see that it's lipstick, some of that new shiny crimson colour from Starzy, and that the leftover Starzy lippy has been squished onto the surface of the mirror at the end of the writing to hang there in a neat 3D full stop. But what's really shocking's not the words. It's all the torn-up bits of material all over the room. They were obviously once our costumes, seeing as the rail by the far wall's got nothing but hangers with shreds on them. Looks like Edward Scissorhands has been having a fit in here – ragged triangles of gold, pink, white and silver lie across every square inch.

Oh fuck, mutters Michelle, pushing her way in and seeing what the fuss is about. She taps the mic of her headset and starts talking in a low urgent-sounding voice. I need security in the second-floor dressing-room area *immediately*, I catch her saying. She turns back to us. Right everybody – out we go!

We stand around in the corridor waiting for security. Oh my God, Rebecca keeps saying, over and over till I want to turn and yell at her to shut up. Louise is quiet and her little face is all screwed up in a frown. Meanwhile Joni's all excited and wonders out loud if we're being stalked by a psycho.

In between bursts of whispering into her headset Michelle decides we can't possibly go back till after the police have arrived. They might want to dust for fingerprints, she explains. A few seconds later this whole platoon of security guards appear. After some words with Michelle half of them cram into the room and the other half race off up the corridor, I guess in case maybe the psycho's still hanging round looking for more innocent costumes to party with. Michelle okays something to her headset and turns to us.

Right. New plan. Follow me.

She leads us back up the corridor where we came and down some stairs to a bunch of green doors and tells us to each pick one. Behind each one are little cupboards, each containing a mirror, a chair and a shelf, just enough room to squeeze a human being into. Michelle tells us these are the reserves, normally used for back-up dancers.

Look on the bright side, she suggests. At least now you get your own rooms.

She smiles kind of cruelly, and it's probably the first time I've seen her look amused about something. Then there's the sound of static and someone talking to her through the headset and she says Yes, yes, impatiently, looks at us and goes serious again. Security are just round the corner, so you're all completely safe, okay? So just hang tight until I return, she says.

But what about our costumes? cries Rebecca after her. They've been completely ruined! We don't have anything to go onstage in!

I'll sort something out, snaps Michelle, and marches off up the corridor again. We stand there facing each other for a minute. It's the first time in as long as I can remember we've all been together without a camera or anyone from the show there too. Last night they even set up a camera in the dorm to record us at night – for our protection they said, but really it was obviously just so they could catch any secret bitching or juicy after-dark cat-fights. Course *we* got no say, seeing as we all signed away our dignity right back at the beginning of all this.

Alrighty, says Joni, first one to make the best of a bad deal. See you girls out in the ring, eh? Check it.

She goes into one of the dressing rooms, shutting the door behind her. Snorting like she can't believe how unprofessional all this is Rebecca goes into hers too, which leaves just me and Louise. We stare at each other. Louise's eyes are narrowed, as if she thinks I'm going to jump her or something. But I can't be dealing with her hang-ups right now, so I just give her a curt little nod and go into my own cupboard, shutting the door firmly behind me.

Inside I stand in front of the mirror and take a slow lungful of air. A cold tingle runs through my body, right from the tips of my toes up to the back of my neck. There's something about that lipstick warning on the mirror that chills me. It's the style of it – that mix of the capitals and small letters. Loads of times Eddy's proudly shown me photos on her mobile of the little messages she's scrawled on the walls and floors of department stores and cosmetic surgery clinics targeted by SCUM for being regressive or anti-feminist or whatever. They're always written exactly the same.

For a second it's like my brain's flipped into overdrive. I shut my eyes and open them again, trying to will myself to stop it. But you can only will yourself to stop doing something if you got willpower, and I don't. Stead I find myself thinking back to last week when I caught sight of Eddy in the audience. It wasn't my mind playing tricks on me, it was definitely her. Of course I thought she was there for me. But what if, just maybe . . .

God, who I wouldn't fuck for a line right now.

I take myself in hand and give myself a good shake. Eddy's capable of some pretty cunning stunts, but she's no mastermind, able to break into the studio of a major network. She's not got the know-how. And even if she did, she just *wouldn't*. She knows how much this means to me. That's why she was there last week. Cos she loves me and cos secretly on the inside she wants me to win and show these other bitches who's best.

So quit being all Nancy Drew, I say out loud to my reflection. Focus on the bigger picture, girl. You got a show to ace.

Soon as the words are out my mouth the door behind me opens and this angular shape slides into the remaining space in the room, shutting the door quickly behind itself.

Riana?

Louise is pale and her eyes are huge. There's a look on her face I recognise, that I seen on the telly watching her doing her performances, and also when we did our duet together, and sometimes in class when Edgar gets her to sing a solo as an example to the rest of us of how it's s'posed to be done. This look of total determination.

What's up? I say.

She doesn't reply, just stares at me. Two hazel orbs with big dots of black inside them, unmoving and unblinking. You'd think she was a soldier about to leap off the boat and head into enemy ground. She takes another step into the tiny dressing room, so she's right up close. I can hear her breath, which is short and noisy, like she's extremely nervous or excited. It must have been the scene in the dressing room that's got her all worked up. I grin to try to set her at ease, but Louise doesn't react. Stead, still staring at me like she's daring me to resist her, she reaches out and without warning sticks her hand on my right tit.

Look, Louise, I don't think . . . I start to say, but then I stop. Cos it feels good. I've missed being touched so badly, and it's not like there's anywhere you can go to have a good old wank in that house, what with cameras or girls popping out from round every corner. I reach out and put my own hand on Louise's chest. I feel the little swelling that's all she's got – those tiny buds of tits which are probably still growing. Then, without thinking about just what I'm doing here, I take my other hand and put it on her waist. The hand touching my own tit suddenly starts to move round, exploring, gently at first and then firmer and almost rough. I feel my nipples going erect. The whole time Louise keeps looking at me with those big funny determined eyes, like the snake in that Disney film hypnotising its prey. Suddenly I'm so turned on it's like I've been infected by a sex virus.

I reach down, grab the sides of my top, yank the thing off and chuck it on the floor. Louise immediately puts her hand back on my tit, squeezing and kneading it even harder under my bra. Breathless I take her other hand and guide it down to between my legs, pressing it against my clit. For a fraction of a sec there's shock on the face before me, those two determined eyes opening a little wider as it occurs to them just what they're touching. But then Louise swallows and pushes out her lips in her Victoria Beckham pout. This jolt of excitement runs through my body as I feel her take over, fingers taking on a life of their own, frigging me harder and deeper. She's clumsy and hasn't got a clue, but I'm so on the edge I feel myself getting wet anyway. I start to gasp, I can't help it.

The doorknob turns with a squeak. We just have time to leap apart before Michelle sticks her head in.

Good news, girls. Come heaven or hell the show's going ahead. And Shelly's team has just arrived too. They'll be down in just a minute, as soon as they've sorted out who's doing who.

She peers down at my top on the floor and then eyes us both suspiciously. I glance round at Louise and see she now has the kind of expression you might see on someone that's just been caught in the middle of committing an axe murder. Luckily she's facing away from the door so Michelle can't see.

Louise was just helping me fix my bra, I explain, reaching up to fiddle with it. Stupid catch at the back just kept digging into my spine . . . think it's okay now, Louise. *Thanks*.

Louise stares at me, gobsmacked. I give her a wink.

Good, she manages to say finally, about half an hour too late, I'll go and wait for Shelly in my dressing room, then.

She takes a step towards the door, staggering a bit and grabbing at the wall to keep her balance. Michelle stands to one side to let her go past, but then, stead of leaving, Louise suddenly turns back round to look at me. Her face has changed again. This time it's panicked, desperate, torn in two. Suddenly I'm aware of so much soul being bared in that pointy little face it almost breaks my heart.

Good luck, Riana, she says quietly.

'It ain't me fault . . . I had to do it! And it ain't like I was hurting no one! All this [BLEEP] what's been written, it ain't like that! I just wanted the best for me little boy, that's all. I thought if they knew I was a mum they'd never have me in Purrfect . . . It ain't like I *wanted* to lie about it!'

The picture of Rebecca being voted off is one of those fucking horror snaps you usually get right after a massive night out, of you looking rough as vag with your face, tits and everything else all going south and only your eyebrows going upwards. Her mascara's run too, never mind what Shelly and that lot swore to us about it being cry, sweat and blood proof, and her lippy's all smudged from Stina practically trying to tongue her when the judges all said her name. It ain't a photograph you'd want to be remembered for, that's for sure.

But Rebecca's photo ain't the problem. That ain't what's making me blood run hot as I sit here on the loo trying to pull it together so I can have a piss. Rebecca's gone, out of the competition, history. It's me what's got to worry, cos I'm the one what's been made to look like a total heartless shit by all the papers.

'Selfish single mother abandons baby to pursue own dreams in Purrfect' goes the beginning of the article in the *Daily Mail*. Can't bear to read the rest of it. Just one glance tells me it's all about what a fucking irresponsible slag I am, letting me own ambitions stop me from being a good mum. Piece in the *Telegraph* ain't no better, calling me 'crazed with fantasies of grandeur', whatever the fuck that's s'posed to mean. Who the fuck writes this guff? But it's the one in the *Star* that's the worst. It's got a picture of me onstage last night, waving at the audience right after

I'd done me song and they was clapping me, smiling and looking all pleased with meself. Over the top is written in big thick letters: PURRFECT BITCH!

Shit. Me thigh muscles are starting to seize up. I'm that furious I can't even piss. Furious and worried. Cos this is bad. This is really, really, really fucking bad.

It's Wend who done it. Who else could it of been? After what Mum told me about her I tried to think there must have been some mistake, like that Mum'd got her wires crossed. She's dappy enough, and it wouldn't be the first time it's happened neither. Tried to tell meself I'd better give Wend the benefit of the doubt. Or at least the chance to tell her version of what'd happened and how the papers got wind of that thing with Shea, before I tore her eyes out. Even let meself imagine that maybe her and Davy was just Mum jumping to conclusions like she always does, and that maybe they was just being friendly or out buying me a present together or something. After all, we're best mates, me and Wend, and we've grown up together too. That oughta count for something. But from the papers this morning there's no doubting anymore that this girl I thought I knew is really one mean twisted bitter cunt. In one of the articles there's a quote from her, telling the world how I never took no care of Baby and how I'm such a bad parent I couldn't even be bothered to give him a proper name. There's another one where Wend is saying *she's* always been more like a real mum to him cos of all the times she's took care of him. Makes me want to choke on me own puke. She'd better move to fucking China cos I'm gonna hunt her down and fucking *eat* her.

I breathe and finally it starts to come out, a tiny trickle all tinkly as it splatters against the bowl. Been bursting ever since I got out of bed. Saw the papers by the door on me way to the lav and couldn't resist a quick squiz. Big fucking mistake. I manage to get out hardly anything at all before me bladder seizes up again.

There's only one thing to do. I gotta go find the judges and explain me own side of things. Maybe they'll kick me out and maybe they won't. But I gotta try.

I pull up me jimjams and go to put some clothes on. Louise and Riana are still asleep, both of them snoring away. It's weird now that there's just the three of us in here, like we're the last survivors after the world has ended or something. I s'pose in a way we are, since getting chucked out the contest now would be like the end of the world. It'd be like a fucking apocalypse having got this far.

I throw on me jeans and a T-shirt and head on out of the dorm. Outside on the landing is a camera guy, who's probably been up since the crack of dawn waiting for one of us to come out. He's dozing on the armchair by the window and wakes up with a yelp. I walk right on past him while he scurries around getting his camera shit together. One thing I ain't gonna miss after all this is having me every fucking blink recorded by one of them things.

I go downstairs to the hall and pick up the house phone. The only way to get hold of the judges when they're not around is to call Michelle and tell her you need to speak to them. The phone's been rigged so that you can only dial her, or security or 999. Just as I'm about to press the number for her I see someone sitting slumped over in the kitchen and realise it's none other than the mistress of bitches herself, Tess. I stick the phone back down and go on in.

Tess? I say.

She don't give no sign of having heard me. She's obviously fucking furious, so mad she can't even bring herself to look up. I hover at the door for a second, wondering if I should just call it quits and leave. But that ain't really an option, not when you've made it all this way, so instead I go in and draw up a chair opposite her. I half expect her to start screaming at me but she still don't move.

Tess?

Finally she looks up. Her eyes are all bloodshot, like she's been doing pills all night. With what you wouldn't exactly call model good looks, the overall result ain't pretty.

Joni, she goes, like she's just waking up. Where's everyone else?

Asleep, I go. Listen Tess, you gotta understand my situation. It ain't easy for me. We ain't got money or second chances where I come from, we've just got our heads. You know what it's like, cos you grew up on an estate too. You said so . . .

Tess frowns and I stop and wait for it.

What in God's name are you on about? she says, all slowly.

What the papers are saying. All that nasty stuff.

Joni, Tess says in this ultra-controlled way like she's having trouble not cracking up, I haven't got the faintest clue what you're talking about. But in case you hadn't noticed, I've been on the receiving end of some very serious *death threats* which are taking up most of my concentration right now.

She looks past me suddenly and lets out this hissing noise.

Get out of here! she snaps.

At first I think she's talking to me, but then she leaps up and rushes over to the door, slamming it closed on the cameraman. A second later he knocks and says, Excuse me but can I come in, it's my job? But she don't open it. Instead the old dragon turns back to me.

There was another message this morning. A letter in the post, addressed to me. It came to my house.

What did it say? I go, trying to sound sympathetic, like Tess getting death threats is awful when really it's all the old bitch deserves.

I'm not divulging that information, snaps Tess. Now, what I want from you is to get Louise and Riana and meet me in the studio right away. I've got something I want to ask you all before the others arrive and turn this into another fucking circus like they have with everything else.

But listen, I go, about the papers—

Now please!

I start to rise, moving sort of slow cos I'm still trying to get me head around what she's told me. Tess claps her hands loudly in me face.

Move it! she goes.

She glares at me for a bit, before it occurs to her she's standing in the way of me getting out the kitchen. With this sigh like she's just sick of the whole world being against her she shifts her blubber back over to the table and I go out, almost bashing tit first into the cameraman who's still there with the camera pointed right at the door. He follows me upstairs where I'm surprised to find Riana and Louise are now awake and sat on Riana's bed, chuckling away over the papers. Their arms and legs are touching like they ain't never been nothing but the best of mates. A bit like what me and Wend used to be like. It's a dead funny sight though, since Riana looks like she could floss her teeth with Louise if she wanted to. It ain't half weird the way they seem to get on one day and then hate each other the next, but this time it's obviously all these bitchy articles about me that've buried the hatchet for them. No doubt they reckon I'm over, just like Rebecca and all the others. It just goes to show how one person's misfortune is another's stroke of good luck. Cruel, but true.

All right? I say, making both pairs of eyes snap up to me.

Morning, Joni, goes Riana in this knowing voice that makes me want to put me foot into her face. Louise just smiles all smug like always and looks down. I decide to just get it fucking over with.

Yes, I say, I'm a mum, all right? I have a little boy and he's a year and a half old. His name's Baby and he's the most important thing in me life, no matter what those fucking rags say. Got any questions?

Riana puts on this offended look, as if she'd never even dream of asking me about it or thinking anything bad about me, while Louise carries on looking down like she's just fascinated by Riana's ankle. They look a bit like a couple of dykes, all wrapped up there with each other, and I'm tempted to say so, but I don't since the camera's right behind me and the last thing I need is to get meself into even more hot water.

Right then, I go, like that is that. Tess wants us downstairs in the studio pronto. It's important.

I don't say nothing more, just walk back out the room with me head up like I've made me point. I go down to the studio where Tess is already waiting, like a queen in the seat at the front of the room where Patty usually sits so she can slag us off while we do our routines. She don't say nothing as I come in. I take a seat on the floor and we sit there in silence for what feels like a century but is probably only a couple of minutes, till Louise and Riana arrive, both of them grinning away like they've just had it off. The cameraman slides quickly in too and goes to stand at the back of the room. Tess stares at him like she's thinking what a lovely sound his bones breaking would make. She slowly gets up and then goes towards him. It's only when she's practically on him that the cameraman takes fright and actually peers out from behind the camera like he can't believe she's really coming for him. He's quite young, not bad, in fact, if you like them barely legal. Tess reaches out and wrenches the camera off him like he's made of matchsticks. Hey, you can't do that! he goes in this whiny way, following her and waving his arms around all pathetically as she marches to the door with it. Oh yes I can! goes Tess and tosses the camera outside in the hall. The guy cringes at the crashing sound it makes as it connects with the opposite wall. No sooner has he raced out to get it than Tess slams the door behind him and turns the key. She pants for a few seconds then goes back to her seat all casual like nothing just happened.

Okay girls, she goes, I've called you here because of a very serious matter. As you already know, the show has been targeted, either by a single person or a group, and we've been subjected to a series of incidents.

At this Riana sits bolt upright like she's just been tasered. It ain't really bothered me up until last night when they got into our dressing room and left that weird message with the lippy. That was when it got scary, cos it meant whoever it was had gone and given security the slip. Like they actually got to be pretty smart.

I wanted to talk to you in private about it before we embark upon the final week of the programme. As the person at the centre of all this I want to assure you that the police, security and myself are taking the issue very, very seriously.

As she says this last bit Tess's voice cracks a little and she looks quickly away and makes this long gulping noise like she's about to dive into a swimming pool. That's when I realise something that ain't occurred to me before, what with being so busy rehearsing and dancing and shit. The mean old shrew is fucking shitting herself.

The police will be coming in to question you later on today, but I wanted to conduct my own little investigation first, just for my peace of mind. This morning I . . . I received another message. I'm not going to repeat its contents verbatim, but the . . . the author of it mentions a life they seem to believe was destroyed by . . . what we are trying to do here.

She pauses like she's trying very hard to keep it together.

I wanted to ask if any of you can think of anyone who might have a vendetta against Purrfect, or else against me personally. Perhaps because of how they feel about you taking part in the show. I won't be angry. I simply want to know, woman to woman, if you have any information ...

The idea of having this woman-to-woman bond with Tess ain't an attractive one, and you can see Louise and Riana are both thinking the same thing. Then Riana opens her mouth like she's got something to say, only to close it again when Tess looks at her all expectant with her single hairy eyebrow up on one side of her face. Riana smiles and shakes her head, like she's just realised that no, actually she don't know who's been making these threats after all. Then there's this long silence, broken every now and then by Tess making snorting sounds like an angry bull. It's like she's not going to let us go without getting something out of us, and the longer it goes on the more determined she's becoming. I'm about to say something before it gets out of hand, like, Sorry Tess, but none of us knows anyone all right?, when I get this crazy idea. What if it was Wend?

I have a rapid think about it. At first it seems just stupid, like there's no way she'd be capable of doing stuff like that. But then I'd never of thought in a million years she'd be able to double-cross me the way she has, running to the papers with them stories about Shea and about me being a bad mum, or getting with Davy behind me back. I mean, when you get down to it, she ain't gone about it in no half measures trying to fuck this all up for me, has she? So how far would she be prepared to go?

Louise clears her throat.

Tess, she goes, I'm really sorry, but I don't think any of us can tell you anything.

Tess turns her stare on Louise, who gives this unconvincing smile like she ain't terrified of Tess just like the rest of us. Then Tess's expression softens. Well, not exactly softens, since her features ain't really capable of that, but they relax a tiny bit, like she's realised how totally unhinged this little get-together of hers is.

No, she goes all quietly, evidently none of you can.

And as she says it I realise that it's also totally unhinged of me to be suspecting Wend. Not cos the two-faced little tramp ain't messed up enough to send a death threat or even to bash the brains out of a pigeon, but simply cos there ain't no way Wend'd waste a perfectly good lippy scrawling out a message on some mirror. She might be totally different to who I thought she was, but there are certain things you *do* know about someone.

Well, girls, says Tess, we're stepping up security, and the police are thoroughly investigating the matter, and it's important that you know you're absolutely safe. Remember, you're in the running to be Purrfect girls, and Purrfect girls don't let anything stand in their way. The show must go on . . .

She don't sound too convinced, but she gives us one of her nasty smiles which look more like grimaces and pushes back up her big glasses which have slipped down to the tip of her nose. Just as I'm wondering if now ain't a good time to try and have another go at explaining what's going on with me in the papers while she's all distracted and shit, there's all this hammering at the door and Joe's voice yelling for Tess to open up. Acting all slow like she wants us to know she don't have to do it if she don't want to, Tess goes over and turns the key. Into the room bursts Joe, followed by Emma and the cameraman and then Michelle.

What's going on? goes Joe angrily. You can't just lock yourself in here with the girls and no camera without okaying it first!

Joe's right, agrees Emma, with her hands on her tiny waist. It's not professional.

It's downright arrogant, that's what it is! fumes Joe, who's pretty much panting cos he's so worked up. I don't care how many silly letters you get sent.

Everyone gasps after he says that, like they can't believe he could be so mean, and then there's this long pause. Tess cocks her head to one side like she's considering how to reply. You kind of have the sense of two cowboys facing each other off in a showdown to see who can be the biggest bitch.

I'll do whatever I like, she goes finally, because I'm the one who's under threat. No matter how much you *wish it was you.*

She follows up with this laugh. She ain't laughed once during the whole time I've been in this programme, and it's freaky as fuck to hear, all scratchy and croaky, almost like a cough. Joe's whole face goes the same shade of pink as the sunnies he's wearing.

Oh don't deny it, carries on Tess, suddenly all cool again. Don't pretend you're not jealous. You'd give your right arm to have someone stalking you and we all know it. That's how desperate *you* are.

For a minute it looks like Joe's gonna throw himself on her, and in me head I cheer him on, even though Tess'd be able to bat him off with one hand, no probs, given her stats against his. Behind Joe Michelle's got this smirk on her face like she's thinking the same thing, and of course the cameraman can't get enough. But then Emma steps in between them before Joe can start anything.

All right, she goes. Never mind who's the most stalked round here. There's another issue that needs to be dealt with right now and that's got nothing to do with either of you.

She makes sure she's got both their attention and then turns her head right around the room. Everyone follows her eyes until they're all looking at me. Oh shit, I think.

Well, what's she gone and done? goes Tess, all impatient.

Haven't you *heard*? goes Joe in this super-sarcastic voice like he can't believe anyone could be that thick. Haven't you *noticed* what's going on outside?

I've had my mind on other things, says Tess, all icy.

Joni, says Emma slowly in this dramatic voice that makes you think she's about to reveal the most shocking thing ever, is a mother!

Tess don't even blink.

So what? she goes.

So she lied about it! carries on Joe like he's explaining it to an idiot. And now the press are shitting all over her! They're outside the front of the house right now baying for her blood!

I get this picture in me head of a whole army of reporters all camped outside waiting for me so they can boo and hiss and take nasty photos and write even nastier pieces in their horrible papers. I panic and have a quick peep out the window, but all you can see is the wall round the garden, all grey and reassuring. But what if right behind it there's all these paps? I catch Louise and Riana giving each other these satisfied looks, like they're just fucking loving all this. Then Louise catches me eye and quickly turns her face away, and I have this chronic urge to give her a good kicking and have to clench me bum cheeks and remind meself I'm saving it all up for Wend.

I mean, what are we going to *do*? Joe is going.

I can explain – I start to say, but no one's interested. They're too busy all yakking at once about how they're going to be another girl down and what a disaster this is for the contest and how their contracts'll never get renewed for another series and so on. Real selfless stuff.

Well, Tess says suddenly like she's been hit by a brainwave, there's only one thing to do, isn't there?

Everyone stops talking and looks at her like she's the Second Coming.

We've got to take her outside and make a statement right away.

Are you serious? shouts Joe all super-high like he's just done one of them gas balloons you used to be able to do at clubs. They'll eat her alive! She hasn't even had the most basic training in how to handle the press!

They start arguing about it again, Joe insisting that I'll only make it all worse and if they're really going to do it then they've got to go through the right channels and do a proper conference. Tess snaps at him there's no time for that cos it'll take ages and the longer the press are kept waiting the more difficult they'll be. Michelle puts in her opinion even though no one asks her for it and tells them that it's not fair on me cos I'm only a girl, to which Tess goes I must know something about being a woman if I've managed to *give birth*. Emma agrees with her and says it's the logical course of action, at which point Joe throws up his hands and shouts Fine – but I want nothing to do with it! and storms out of the room. Emma turns to me.

Okay Joni, says Emma, this is your last shot. We've got to go out there and turn this nightmare around. Let's go over what you're going to say, shall we? Riana and Louise, why don't you go and get yourselves some breakfast?

Riana and Louise head off out the room, practically floating on their own smugness. I'll show them, I think to meself. I'll turn this around and come Saturday they'll be laughing out their arses when they see how I've sneaked up behind them and got into Purrfect in spite of it all.

Soon as they've gone Tess and Emma get me to draw up a chair while they go through what I'm gonna say. Michelle watches from behind with this look on her face like she totally disapproves while they sit there firing off questions like Am I a lazy mother? and Don't I worry about what my little boy will think of me when he grows up? The questions make me all flustered and upset, cos they're all really negative and cunty, but I do me best to answer them without getting pissed off cos I know that's how it works. If you get pissed off then they shit all over you. I saw that Heather Mills interview like everyone else. What's interesting is that at no time do either Tess or Emma actually bother to ask about the real story why I lied about Baby being mine, although at one point Emma does roll her eyes and say what a shame it is when it comes out how old I was when I had him.

The truth is that you're young and inexperienced, she goes. That's what's going to turn this around for you. The fact that you're doing the best you can.

I *am* doing the best I can, I want to say, but her and Tess look so serious I don't risk it. They hit me with another barrage of mean-arsed questions, only this time I'm tougher and make me answers short and simple. It's pretty easy once you get the hang of it. Soon Emma and Tess are nodding and saying I'm ready.

It'll be a trial by fire, Joni, says Emma like I'm going to fucking war. You'll just have to think of it as part of your training should you get into the band. Celebrity means having to face off the media every other day. It's a gruesome battle of wills but that's how it works.

And let's not forget that you did bring it on yourself, adds Tess, like the old witch she is that can't resist an opportunity to stick the knife in. She raises her voice like she always does when the camera's rolling and you know she wants them to catch it and use it for the programme. I don't know why you'd think that having a child would change your chances of getting into Purrfect. I think it's one of the most wonderful and natural things in the world!

Evil fucking troll. I hold me breath for ten. All the effort to keep from getting angry is making it harder and harder to keep a lid on, and I'm worried that any second I'll just lose it and go on a full-on rampage. This Tess knows as well as I do that it ain't true I'd have the same chance if

I'd told them about Baby. Like the fact that I'd have to lug around a little boy from gig to gig and always put his needs first wouldn't make no difference.

Are you ready? goes Emma.

She takes me hand and leads me out of the room. The camera guy follows us. In the hall I have a quick glance back and through the door I see Tess is still sat there staring into space. She looks a bit sad, kind of reminding me of Fat Carol at the last Christmas bash down the local when everyone was up and dancing except for her cos she was too hefty and none of us could be bothered to try and cheer her up. Lonely – that's what I mean.

Okay Joni – deep breath, goes Emma, stopping me at the front door and brushing me hair away from me face. It'll be over in five minutes and then you can relax.

I have a big gulp like she says, cos suddenly I'm panicking off me fucking head. But before I can say nothing or chicken out she's opened the door and is pushing me out in front of her. Up past the end of the driveway you can see them, all these men in leather jackets holding cameras and bits of equipment. As Emma and me make our way towards them they catch sight of us and this excited murmur runs through them, like they can't believe their luck. They start to aim all the equipment at our faces. There're so many flashes going off it's like the fucking Blitz.

It's now or fucking never.

I remember it like it was yesterday. How excited I felt when the woman handed me my ticket. How full of hope I was as I took my seat with all the other girls. How behind those double doors it seemed like wonderful things awaited me.

I was nervous, too. So nervous I went into a trance and didn't hear when they first called my number. They had to repeat it several times, and it was only because the girl beside me leaned over and touched my shoulder I snapped out of it in time. I can't help but wonder whether if she hadn't – if I'd missed my slot and been sent away unseen – I'd still be the same girl today. But there's not much point in thinking about that. I didn't miss my slot. I stood up, walked over and handed over my ticket. Then I was shown through the doors and into that room.

Just like now there were two other judges – an ageing Barbie doll and a smug idiot with carrot-coloured hair. I can still see their faces perfectly. Her broad pitying smile and his self-assured grin. But neither of them spoke during my audition. They didn't need to. She was the one who ran the show – it was obvious the second I entered the room and was caught within the glare of those bulging, dead eyes.

She asked me for my name and the reason why I deserved the chance they were offering. I opened my mouth and a tiny wavering sound came out, like the squeak of a vole. As best I could I tried to explain. I told them about my dissatisfaction with my situation and how I knew this was the opportunity for me to turn everything around. I explained how it was what I had always secretly dreamed of doing but never until now been brave enough to go for. Despite my nervousness there was something about her stare that made me go deeper and reveal things I would never have revealed in any other situation. I told her about the little girl who had always been ignored and second best, and about the woman she'd become, still haunted by the need to be noticed. And I told her about the love that had been missing in my life since Andrew left, which I knew I could find again onstage under the spotlight. Bit by bit I told her everything there was to know, and all the while she sat and listened, her face betraying not a flicker.

Let's hear you then, she said when I finally ran out of things to say. So I began the song I'd prepared. I had to stop and start again three times because my voice was so shaky from nerves that I couldn't hit the right note. But finally I found it. I didn't get beyond the first verse before she stopped me. I almost started crying then, but I told myself that maybe she'd already heard enough to know I had something. That maybe with just a few bars I'd already guaranteed my place in the show.

Then she dismissed me. She said I was too old, and not suitable for the band. Goodbye, she said, and looked away. It was like my throat had been cut. I stood there, speechless, just staring at her. One side of that fat mouth was tilted up – that half smile I've come to know so well. It was the worst moment I have ever had to live through. The moment that makes me go cold and start sweating whenever I think of it, which is all the time because I can't get it out of my head, not even when I'm asleep.

It wasn't rage I felt as I left the room. Just an overwhelming numbness, as if nothing mattered anymore. Outside I stood like a zombie while I was ticked off the list and then told to move along. I watched as the next girl went into the room, her face shiny with hope and excitement. I looked about at all those other girls with their families and friends, some of them singing, some of them laughing, some of them crying, and I realised I'd never be like them again. That because of her it was over. The future that stretched out ahead of me was bleak and endless, and I knew I couldn't face it.

I went home. When I got there I stood in front of pictures on the mantelpiece – of my father and me when I was a little girl. Of me in my graduation gown, fresh-faced and triumphant. And of Andrew and me a few years later, he looking sheepish for the camera and me flushed and laughing. That last one was taken just a few days before he called things off. It seemed a lifetime ago. But I didn't care anyway. I only knew I was tired of having them around, so I picked them up, took them out to the front of the house, and dumped them next to the bins. Then I went upstairs and ran a hot bath. While I was waiting I lit some candles and turned off all the lights. I took my shaver out of the cabinet and sat down with it in the steaming water. Trembling, I prised the blade out of the plastic. As I did it slipped and bit into my thumb. Droplets appeared in the water, floating red clouds that faded into pink and then dissolved altogether. But it wasn't the pain that made me hesitate, it was the knowledge of what they would think when they found me and examined the reasons. Of what they would say when they saw the empty house, the empty rooms – my empty life. I knew I'd leave behind nothing, not so much as a murmur for the world to remember me by. That I'd be forgotten in a heartbeat, fading from people's minds as fast as those droplets of blood had merged with the bathwater.

I couldn't do it so I threw the razor aside and shut my eyes. And I saw her face again, the face I've come to know better than my own. I saw her lips move as she dismissed me and then that awful half smile.

When I finally opened them again the candles had gone out, and it felt as though a century had passed. The water was cold and I was shivering, but it didn't matter because it had come to me what I was supposed to do. I didn't know how I would do it then, only that I'd find a way. Because I had to. Because there was nothing left for me to lose.

'When I first got into the house I was worried that maybe there'd been some mistake. I couldn't believe they were actually going to give me the chance to be a member of Purrfect. I'll never forget what this competition has done for me. It's given me the confidence to finally be myself!'

I'm sitting on my bed surrounded by snotty tissues because of the horrible cold I came down with on Sunday, watching TV and trying not to let myself be crushed by these overpowering feelings of dejection. I don't think I've ever felt so completely and utterly wretched in my whole life. Not even when I found out Daddy was dead.

I was supposed to find Jack. That was the plan. I had this stupid vision of me tracking him down wherever he was and of what his face would look like when he saw me again after all these weeks apart. I wouldn't even have to say anything, I thought: he'd just suddenly have this revelation about how much he'd missed me and needed me, like I was the piece that had been missing all this time in order to make his life complete. Then he'd take me in his arms and whisper my name and stroke my hair like he couldn't believe I was really there, and I'd tell him how I'd quit the show to find him and he'd be so moved by my sacrifice he'd kiss me more deeply than ever before. Then we'd go to his room and undress, like genuine couples who aren't ashamed of what they are, not merely snatching a stolen hour every other afternoon while parked at the common, but taking the time to properly touch and feel one another's bodies, to rediscover our love. And then, ever so gently, he'd put it in me and make love to me and I'd know from the way he groaned that we would never ever be apart again.

But driving home with Rita and Mimi that vision quickly faded. At first I felt almost sick with relief that I wasn't ever going to have to go onstage again. I had my mission to find Jack and it felt like I was a brave young girl in one of those films about finding true love against impossible odds – maybe starring Anne Hathaway or Kirsten Dunst. But as we drove through London and the real world seeped back in through the darkened windows of Rita's 406, my excitement soon got replaced by feelings of anxiety. In the driver's seat Rita was already on her hands free, laying into somebody at work while she cut people up on the road, and beside her I could hear Mimi sighing into her own phone, telling her best friend Amy how lame I was because I'd just quit the programme. And gradually in the course of a simple journey back to Kensington all that confidence and determination just bled right out of me. In its place all that was left was the old, insignificant, weak Ella who'd been there hiding away all along, and try as I might I couldn't seem to recapture any of that resolve I'd felt when I walked out the door of that house. I desperately wanted to ask Rita to turn the car around and drive me back, except that I knew there was no point because it was too late. I was never going to be a Purrfect girl. And when I got home and tried Jack's number, and there was the message saying it wasn't recognised, that was when I knew I was never going to be with Jack either.

The commercials are almost over so I reach for the remote to turn up the volume. Rita's banned us from watching *The Purrfect Search*, but of course me and Mimi still do, though not together since she's not spoken to me since I quit, and doesn't even say hello when we pass each other in school. Nor does anyone else, actually. I had this secret hope that maybe I'd suddenly be really popular when I got back to class, and that everyone would surround me asking to know what it was like. But it's the complete opposite. People even seem to go out of their way to avoid me. The only recognition I've had from anyone about being on the programme was from Miss Simmons, our gym teacher, who told me not to expect any special treatment just because I'd been on TV when I asked her if I could skip Lacrosse because of my cold.

The screen goes bright pink and is filled with flying silver stars, which gradually come together to form the words *The Purrfect Search*. A snatch of 'Or Die Trying' plays over the top and I get a familiar feeling in my stomach, like my insides are tying themselves up into multiple knots. It's how I felt on Saturday, lying in this exact same position on my bed watching the others onstage as they competed in front of Tess, Joe and Emma. I couldn't believe that just the week before I'd been performing in front of them myself. It seemed like a hundred years ago. And I couldn't believe that I'd actually given it all up. They didn't even bother with showing me telling the judges I was leaving or saying goodbye to anyone. All they had was a brief bit at the start where Emma explained that due to personal issues and ill health I'd been taken out of the running, followed by a few quick interviews with the other girls on how they felt about it. Of course they all said what a terrible shame it was because I was such a nice person and that they already really missed me, which was nice but probably untrue. Except for Joni maybe.

'Welcome to *The Purrfect Search*!' says Stina excitedly, materialising in front of the title wearing one of those bright checked boob tubes that were on all the catwalks three months ago. 'In tonight's one-off special we're going to really get to know Joni, Louise and Riana. Things are so tense now, because as you know this is the last week before we discover who is the next Purrfect girl!'

The screen changes to a clip of Riana making a wrong move in front of Patty, over which Stina's voice continues: 'Coming up – Riana struggles to convince Patty she's got what it takes!' Patty closes her eyes, puts her face in her hands and groans. This is followed by a cutaway of her being interviewed, telling the camera: 'I have never in my life worked with someone who so wilfully refuses to listen.' Then there's a clip of Louise performing her dance routine and slipping over. 'Louise takes a tumble!' exclaims Stina's voice as if she can't believe such a thing is humanly possible. There's a shot of Edgar being interviewed, saying 'She is the strongest contestant . . . if only she can learn to be more natural with her voice, I truly believe that she has the potential to win.' Finally there's a shot of Joni dabbing her eyes in front of a massive group of photographers. I pull myself up, surprised. 'And the big secret about Joni finally gets out!' Big secret?

The programme continues. I watch impatiently, waiting for Louise to take her silly tumble and for Riana to finish messing up her routine so I can find out what's going on with Joni. Instead of the girls this episode seems to be devoted to interviews with the judges and teachers, all saying what they think about each one's chances of winning. They seem to agree that Louise is the best singer, Riana the best performer and Joni the strongest character. Finally there's a repeat of that quick shot of Joni sobbing in front of the press, and then a shot of her looking weak and ashen-faced as she sits in front of Emma, Joe and Tess who are all arguing. 'Haven't you *heard*?' says Joe to Tess. 'Joni is a . . .' says Emma and then Stina pops up smiling and almost bursting out of her top to assure viewers that we'll find out right after the break. I almost throw the remote at her.

Just then there's the sound of heels down the corridor. I quickly hit the mute button as Rita does her usual pointless tap at the door before opening it and coming right on in.

'Ella? I need you to take Mimi to her music lesson tomorrow after school,' she says without so much as a hello, even though it's the first time I've actually seen her today since she had to leave early this morning to deal with a crisis at *Fascinate!* and has had her door shut all afternoon.

'Okay,' I say.

For some reason Rita decides I'm being difficult and lets out a long sigh as if I'd just flat-out refused. With no Jack around to take care of us, I've suddenly become the one who's expected to do everything, and if I forget it just doesn't get done. We wouldn't have had clean shirts for school today if I hadn't suddenly remembered to wash them last night and put them on the radiator to dry.

'I don't like her travelling across town on her own,' Rita says sourly, like she's sick of explaining this to me. 'At her age the city is a dangerous place to be.'

I nod, but apparently this still isn't good enough. Obviously what Rita really wants is someone to take her bad day out on.

'Look at me, when I talk to you, can't you?' she snaps.

I look at her, focusing on the big frown line that goes down the centre of her forehead which she's always complaining about because not even Botox can iron it out. She looks old and ugly, and I suddenly feel this great revulsion towards her. When I asked her where Jack had gone she refused to say. She told me that all she knew was that it was another city, and that even if she did know which one it was she wouldn't tell me and we were well shot of him. Actually she said more than that – she said that he was nothing but a lazy free-loader with no talent or qualifications, and that he was probably shacked up with some wealthy ex-debutante sucking dry her bank account and fucking the help. It's just as well that Rita has no heart, because if she did I swear she would have realised about Jack and me from the sound of my heart breaking. Of course she's wrong, though. She's never understood Jack like I have.

'What are you watching anyway?'

Rita peers over at the screen suspiciously. With perfect timing the programme begins again, silver stars on a pink screen spelling out the title. Rita purses her lips.

'So that's why you're so sullen. Well, you can't blame anyone but yourself, Ella. You're the one who wanted to quit. I never gave you anything but unconditional support!'

I look at the bed, willing her to go away. Thankfully she gives up and goes out, though she slams the door behind her. I listen to the crisp click of her heels going back up the corridor, and just for a second my heart forms this powerful wish that she would die. Maybe in a freak car accident or even just falling down the stairs and breaking her neck. I know it's wrong of me, but it's not as though a single person in the world would miss her, or even as if it'd deprive Mimi of this wonderful mother. Maybe Jack would even seek us out when he heard the news . . .

My attention flicks back to the screen and I realise I've missed the scene where the judges were arguing in front of Joni, and Emma was about to reveal something crucial. The screen now shows a cluster of photographers standing around the front of the house. Joni stands at the centre with Emma beside her. She looks small from this angle. I never really noticed that she was so short. Next to Emma she looks almost like a child, which is strange since when I was in the house she seemed so old and wise all the time.

I quickly turn off the mute button so I can hear her. She's saying that she's sorry, and that she never meant to hurt anyone and that she's nothing but proud of what she is. It takes me a good moment to process what she's talking about, and then when I do I almost fall off the bed, completely dumbstruck. Joni is a mother?

One of the men is asking her why she lied about it and if it's because she's ashamed, and I crane my head forward and whack up the volume, even though it's risking Rita thumping the wall. Joni takes a few seconds to answer, like she's collecting herself because she's been made so upset by the question.

'No,' says Joni. 'I am not nor ever will be ashamed of my little boy.'

Her voice is firm and hard, like she's daring the press to argue with her, but two silver streaks down both cheeks show how she really feels. Even though she's not wearing a scrap of make-up or even very nice clothes, I think she looks more beautiful than any of those times I've seen her onstage performing. I'm almost crying with her.

'I want to be a member of Purrfect because I love my boy and I want him to have the best life possible – and if that meant seeming like I was selfish to all the papers then it was a risk I had to take!'

I still can't get over it. Joni's my age – maybe a year older! The very idea of having a baby makes me feel queasy. To have something come out of you down there – the pain must be unbearable. But Joni's done it. And it makes sense too. That's the reason she's always so confident and together: because she can't afford not to be. Not when she already has this great responsibility. She's a risk taker. She's taken a chance and had a baby, and she was there in the house taking another chance, just like she said. All for his sake.

The screen changes to Stina interviewing Emma about Joni's chances after the revelation. Emma says that she thinks Joni still has a shot because she's shown herself to be a strong character and a good singer, and that even though she lied at least she had the guts to confront her lie, and that's a brave thing to do. After a couple more questions about the other girls and their reaction, Stina turns to the camera and warns it that it had better join her on Saturday for the grand finale – or else. The programme finishes, and 'Goodbye Forever', the beautiful hidden ballad you get if you wait thirty seconds at the end of the album *Count On It,* starts playing as the credits come up.

I switch off the TV and sit there feeling small and stupid, more like an insignificant nobody than ever. Even though there's no one else here I can feel my face colouring with shame because my own problems, which seemed so impossible just seconds ago, seem like nothing beside what Joni's been up against. I mean, she's got another human life to worry about. Even now, with all those reporters hounding her, she's still trying, still standing there giving it her best. She doesn't give up, no matter what. Not like me.

It's enough to make you want to just curl up and lose the will to live. I turn off the light and pull the bedcovers up over my head without bothering to go and clean my teeth or wash or put on any face cream, since after all, now that Jack's never going to look at me again, what's the point? Better to just lie here and wait for sleep or preferably death to take me.

But as I lie there, clenching my eyes shut and thinking about how if I were Joni I'd never be in this position, something twigs. It's like when you suddenly see something that's been right under your nose the whole time you were looking for it. I almost leap out of bed and start dancing around the room. It's an idea about how to find Jack and it's so obvious I can't believe I haven't thought of it before. I start to chuckle, surprising myself with how manic it sounds. I haven't given up, Jack, I think. Not yet.

And that's how I find myself at Fit For Life early the next morning when I'm supposed to be on my way to first period. The gym is only a ten-minute walk from school so it's easy for me to get the bus with Mimi and then double back as soon as she's inside the building. Sometimes Jack would come here to work out while he waited for me to finish in the afternoon, and then he'd pick me up and I'd joke that he smelled all sweaty and it was disgusting, even though secretly I always liked it and would breathe in the smell and try to memorise it so I could recall it for when we were apart the next day. I remember reading in *Cosmo* that when you like the smell of a man's sweat it means you're genetically compatible, which is one more reason why we belong together. But the reason I'm here is that Jack had quite a few friends at Fit For Life. Someone is bound to know where he is now or how to find him.

I push through the big glass door and walk into the reception room, which is all clean white walls and full of bright plasticky-looking tropical plants, like they've uprooted a whole rainforest and dumped it here in this modern little room. Sitting at the desk is a pert woman with a silvery blonde ponytail wearing an ugly mauve tracksuit. She's probably about forty, but her body is so small and compact that at a glance she looks more like a seven-year-old.

'Hello, young lady,' she says in an Australian accent, peering over at me like she's already assessing my body weight and thinking I could use a few bicep curls. 'Can I help you with something?'

I clear my throat. I'm going to have to make this good.

'It's really important,' I say. 'I need to find out someone's address. He used to come here to work out and I was wondering if maybe anyone knows it . . . it might even be on your system.'

The woman frowns.

'His name is Jack Gibbons.'

'Oh Jack!' she exclaims. 'But I thought he moved to Edinburgh.'

Edinburgh! My heart skips a beat and I clap my hand over it, worried I'm going to have a cardiac arrest right there and then in front of her. How can he possibly be that far away? I think fast.

'I know he did,' I say, trying to keep the panic out of my voice. 'But I've lost the address, you see.'

'Who are you, hon?' asks the woman. She's smiling but there's a hint of suspicion there, I can sense it. 'What do you want to know for?'

'I'm his . . . younger sister,' I invent, hoping she didn't notice the tiny pause I made. The Australian frowns like she's trying to work something out.

'He never told me he had a younger sister! And how come he didn't tell you his address, anyway? Can't you just call him?'

'His phone is off, and . . . well, I wanted it to be a surprise.'

The woman stares at me. I stare back, smiling, feeling myself melting under my network of lies. I'm such an idiot. What was I thinking, coming here and imagining I would actually be able to somehow get someone to tell me where he is now? My instinct is screaming at me to just turn around and run. But that's not what Joni would do, is it? She wouldn't give up until there was no other option.

'It's his birthday soon, you see,' I say quickly, praying to some higher power the woman is believing any of this. 'I've got to send his present by the end of today or else he won't receive it in time, and I spent such a long time choosing it. It's a belt by his favourite designer. It cost me an absolute packet! He's going to love it, I just know he will. But it has to arrive by Thursday!'

For a second I think it's all over. The woman stares at me as if she's never heard anything so preposterous in her whole life. But then she suddenly grins and gives me a wink.

'Well, we can't have that happen, can we? Let's have a lookie here. Maybe his details are on the computer. We've got a couple of branches in Edinburgh and we often get clients' new addresses when they move, so that if they want to carry on they don't have to go through the whole induction again . . . ah yes, we may be in luck.'

I hold my breath as the woman looks at the screen and clicks a couple of times with the mouse. Adrenalin is running through my veins and I'm full of nervous excitement every bit as intense as I ever felt when I was onstage. It's funny because I never used to be able to lie, and I can't help but feel proud of myself. It must be the effect of love. It makes you capable of anything.

'Hang on a sec,' says the woman. 'It says here Jack's birthday is in January.'

My heart takes a running leap and ends up in my throat. Think, you idiot. *Think*.

'Oh, but we've always celebrated his birthday this month, on account of January being so soon after Christmas . . .'

The woman turns her head slowly back to look at me. This time she isn't smiling and so I smile at her instead. But it's the smile of a desperado and I can tell she's on to me. My chance of finding out where Jack lives is disappearing before my very eyes down a dark tunnel, getting swallowed up for ever.

'I'm sorry,' says the woman, now sounding bitchy and not remotely sorry at all. 'We can't disclose that sort of information. I'm sure Jack'll understand if the present is a day or two late.'

'But he won't!' I wail.

It's no good. The woman starts to look around and I have the impression that any second she's going to call for security to come and frogmarch me out. I spin on my heel and race out of the gym, venting my frustration on the door by giving it a good shove as I go out and hearing it slam loudly behind me. Outside I squat down against the wall, hot tears of anger and disappointment streaking down my cheeks.

In a flash I have another idea. It's so crazy and stupid I hardly dare even to let myself think it, and I'm about to just forget about it when I remember Joni and her words on the TV last night. I think about those times when I went up onstage, and how I performed in front of all those people and how they cheered for me. I tell myself that I'm strong, I must be. That I can do it. The next thing I know I've stood up and gone back into the reception. The woman peers up at me.

'Forget something?'

'Sorry, but could I use your toilet? I've got a bit of a . . . ladies' problem,' I say, trying to look small and vulnerable. Luckily that's something I *can* do well. She's still suspicious, but I give her a pleading stare, trying to appeal to a sense of feminine duty, which seems to work because the woman sighs and nods.

'Through that barrier there, round the corner and on the left.'

The corridor leads up to a glass door, behind which is a gym where a few wrinkly old men are sitting at those scary machines that look like they could crush you, lifting weights that exercise tiny hidden muscles in obscure parts of the body. As soon as I'm out of sight of the reception I start searching along the wall. It's not long before I find what I need. Screwing up all my courage, partly because I can't believe I'm really doing this and partly because I'm scared that the glass will cut me – even though I know from fire training at school that it's supposed to be safe – I make a fist and send it into the alarm.

I don't even notice the glass breaking because I'm too busy being deafened. Instantly bells start ringing, so loud the noise practically paralyses me. But I have to act. I race back to the reception and almost collide with the Australian.

'Sorry!' I cry.

She ignores me and hurries past towards the gym. Luckily she doesn't seem to notice the shattered glass from the fire point on the floor.

I turn the corner and push through the barrier. That

perfume ad for One Time Only races through my head, the one with the gypsy woman who tells the model in it that she's only got one chance and that she must grab it with both hands before it gets away. Of course her chance turns out to be the scent One Time Only, but for me it's Jack's address. I hop round the desk and sit down in front of the computer. My heart is hammering in my chest like a techno beat. But to my amazement and delight, the computer screen still displays the page with Jack's details. I put my shaking hand on the mouse and scroll down. At the bottom of the screen is:

9 Fenland Avenue
Edinburgh

Two lines, so simple and yet the key to being with Jack once more. I repeat them again and again until it's taken up by this mental voice in my mind which chants it like a mantra. As I stand up, my head swimming because of my success, the woman reappears, herding all the wrinkly men who were working out in the gym along in front of her. She catches sight of me and stops dead for a second. Her mouth opens and she starts to shout something, but whatever it is it is lost on me because I'm already hurtling out of the building.

'It's been a rollercoaster. I've met so many wonderful people and done so many exciting things. But in the end, all that matters is tomorrow night. That's my time, and I'm going to show everyone that I'm a star. You're looking at a future Purrfect girl.'

I don't know how to describe the way I'm feeling. It's like I'm floating a hundred miles up in the sky and surrounded by stars and rainbows. But it's also like I'm sinking into this lagoon full of thick dark sludge that's going to suck me down for ever and leave no trace.

I enter the bathroom and quickly go into the furthest cubicle over by the fire escape. I can hear the sound of my own breath, short but heavy. I'm panting like an actual dog and I can feel sweat building up under my armpits. It's gross but I can't help it. I push the door shut and stand there looking down at the toilet bowl, watching tiny ripples cross the pool of yellowy water. The whole thing is disgusting really, coming here like this, and I don't know why I'm doing it, taking such a risk. Except that when I think of her my skin tingles all over and the beat of my heart quickens, just like in *Wuthering Heights* or *Hollyoaks*.

It's only a crush, of course. It doesn't mean I'm a lesbian or one of those bisexuals or anything like that. It's totally normal for teenage girls to get crushes on girls who are older and more experienced than them. I remember old Mrs Hingle, our form mistress back when I was a fifth telling us about same-sex crushes when we had our sex education. At the time I thought it was just her projecting, since everyone knew she was secretly a lesbian because she only ever put girls in detention. But obviously Mrs Hingle wasn't just projecting, she was telling the truth, because here I am experiencing it. It's a relief really, to know that, since I don't think I could handle life as an actual gay. I'm not sure what God would have to say about it either. He's been very quiet of late, but I'm sure He's watching over me and blessing my actions as a necessary character-building experience. It's okay to experiment. So long as it doesn't get out of hand.

There's a creak nearby, which almost makes me jump right out of my skin. I listen carefully for the lazy tread of Riana's feet. She saunters everywhere, like no matter where she is she owns the place. It's ridiculous, really. She ought to take some body language classes, since there is such a thing as being *too* confident. I make a mental note to tell her this. But after the creaking there's only silence – and the annoying sound of me panting. Where the hell is she anyway?

These meetings started by accident. The first time was because we both ended up in here while everyone was concentrating on Joni that day, trying to figure out how to make the fact that she'd abandoned her baby to try and be a pop star look like an act of sacrifice. I don't know why they bother with her. If you ask me it serves the stupid foul-mouthed bee completely right that the media are all over her, calling for her to drop out and be investigated by social services. What a waste of time and resources! But while they were all busy with her Riana and I were up here, away from the cameras and the microphones and the judges. Maybe it was because of missing home, but suddenly I just had to kiss her. So I did. It was easy, and for a few minutes it felt like we were the only people in the whole world. The next day I found myself here again at the same time, and there was Riana again too, and somehow meeting here has become what we do.

It's strange. If God Himself had told me when I first entered this house that I'd end up kissing Riana I'd have thought He was the Devil playing tricks on me. I'd never have believed in a thousand years that my first experience would be with another woman. But I genuinely think it's a good thing, because women always know how to do it right, especially Riana who's obviously got tons of experience as an ex-stripper. Obviously God wanted me to meet her for this reason, so that when I do eventually come to do it with a man I'll be really good and he'll have nothing to complain about.

There it is again, that creaking noise. This time it's unmistakably the sound of the door sliding open. There's definitely someone else in here too. A shiver of panic runs through me. What if it's one of the cameramen sneaking in for a naughty exclusive?

'Hello?' I call out. 'Is there someone there?'

There's no answer, but I'm sure there is. Suddenly I'm afraid. Why aren't they answering?

'Riana? Is that you?'

Silence, but it's the sort of silence where you know you're not alone. It feels like one of those scenes in those unbearable late-night films I'm not supposed to watch, where the heroine's being chased by a stalker and there's a close-up of her quivering in terror while he slowly homes in on her hiding place. A sick sense of dread is building up inside me. What if it's that psycho who's been sending the death threats and breaking in? The blood in my veins runs cold. What if they've somehow sneaked in and are now working their way through the house, butchering people one by one? Trying not to whimper I slowly back into the corner of the cubicle and wedge myself in beside the tank. I look down at the light under the divide and almost die as a shadow passes by.

Then the cubicle door bursts wide open. I let out a pathetic squeak of a scream which catches in my throat. For a few seconds all I can hear is the sound of my heart thumping. A familiar hourglass figure stands there with an infuriatingly disproportionate smile plastered all across her infuriatingly smug face.

'Gotcha!'

I throw myself at her, fists clenched, furious beyond anything I've ever felt before and ready to beat the life out of the arrogant piece of trailer trash. But as soon as my body meets hers it's like I melt into it, just like a slice of cheese on a grill, and instead of thumping her I'm kissing those big lips of hers and putting my hands over those silly perfect breasts.

Each night this week I've closed my eyes and tried as hard as I can to hear God's voice telling me what I ought to do about this. Should I ignore the way I'm feeling or let myself be led by it? The thing is, I still don't hear Him. It's worrying, because without His guidance I have to make the answer up for myself. I know He's planned this, because He plans everything, which means that Riana's meant to have something to show me. But what if this isn't what it is? This is a tense time, and a crush is the last thing I need to distract me. Tomorrow is the last night, the one when we sing in front of not only the judges but in front of Purrfect themselves. Tomorrow night the new Purrfect girl is going to be chosen out of one of us three. It's not that I'm unfocused, because I'm still one hundred per cent in this. I'm still rehearsing my piece every spare second and gearing myself up to give the performance of a lifetime. But the trouble is that instead of my impending moment of glory, I keep thinking about what I'm going to do the day after it, and the day after that – once I'm in Purrfect and my new life has started. What I'm going to do when I can't see Riana ever again.

Riana lets out a gasp, far louder than she should, and I clamp my hand over her big mouth in case there's a cameraman skulking around outside in the bedroom, waiting like they often do to catch one of us the second we come out.

'Shhhh!'

Her lips close over my fingers, wet and warm. She's got such amazing lips. Sensual, I suppose is the word. I daren't even think about what other kinds of things might have gone in between them, though.

'Oh Eddy,' Riana sighs. I don't know if this is a word for darling in another language but I don't want to make myself look stupid by asking. Riana lets out another gasp and I feel her hot breath all over my hand. Then I feel her fingers digging into my crotch, into that place that's supposed to be sacred to a woman. I don't mind touching *her* there if it's what she wants, but it always frightens me a bit when she tries to touch me and so I always draw her hands away from the area. Technically I'm still a virgin, and I don't intend for that to change until my wedding day.

Riana pulls back. She gives me her smug smile, which these days produces these impulses both to slap her and to kiss her and I don't know which one is stronger, and then goes out of the cubicle. She doesn't turn back, and a second later I hear the door creaking again as she leaves. I look down at myself and start straightening my clothes. Somehow Riana always comes away looking just like she did when she came in, whereas I look like I've been mauled by a caveman. I go over to the mirror and check my face for redness. I can't help feeling that these days I look different. A tiny bit wiser maybe. Hopefully even a tiny bit more womanly.

Sure enough, outside in the bedroom stands a cameraman. It makes me feel a little light-headed to think that he's been out here all this time while Riana and I were in there . . . doing what we were doing. I give him a bright smile as I pass, hoping it doesn't look guilty.

'I think you've got a phonecall,' he says.

I hurry downstairs to the kitchen, careful not to go too fast so that the cameraman can keep up. The phone is off the hook on the table.

'Louise?' says Dad the second I pick it up.

'Dad!'

I'd almost forgotten that we were allowed to speak to people again today. They only told us this two nights ago and it's almost for certain they only decided it because of Joni, so that they could get a shot of her making goo-goo noises to her brat down the phone. I watched her doing it earlier, golfball-sized crocodile tears sliding down her face, the common little phoney. When the original band was being put together they weren't allowed to talk to their families or friends until after the final performance when they got selected and I was totally prepared to be on my own for the last week too, to show them all just how strong I could be.

'How's my baby star?'

It's weird to hear his voice. When I saw him the other week things weren't the same between us and now I know why. It's because I've grown and he hasn't. Being here at the centre of it all I've learned things he doesn't know about and can't begin to appreciate a million miles from sleepy little Appledore. The trouble is Dad never made it in showbiz, and he can only understand what it's like by remembering his dreams of making it. He doesn't have the reality to draw on, because he never got this far. I always used to see him as this big protective figure who's there for me no matter what, but suddenly I'm seeing him a different way. As needy.

'You're almost there, darling,' he says and I realise I've never noticed before how old he sounds. His voice is raspy, like it's been slightly ruined from always speaking a shade too loudly to get heard above everyone else.

'I know,' I say.

'Tomorrow you'll go out and you'll perform like a superstar, better than you've ever performed before. And you'll make me the proudest father in history.'

I imagine him as an old man. Really old, like Gramps. Mum'll be dead by then, of course. She'll definitely be the first to go since she's never been much good at taking care of herself and has already got varicose veins and high cholesterol. I always thought it would be nice when it was just Dad and me together. I used to have visions of taking him to concerts, of him being my manager, the most loyal and loving roadie in the world. But there's another possibility which I haven't wanted to face up to, which is that it won't be nice at all. That he'll become this presence I can't get away from, who always thinks he knows best and always tries to control me and convince me that what he wants is what I want too. Dad didn't make it, but I'm going to, and what happens to the people who don't? They latch on to the people who do. The tragic thing about this competition is that I'm starting to see how truly lonely it is at the top. Even your own family ends up on the outside.

'Louise?' says Dad. 'Are you with me?'

There's real nervousness in his voice behind the urgency. As if he can sense what I'm thinking. As if he's already wondering how he's going to fit into the equation once I've made it into Purrfect.

'Yes,' I say firmly.

'This is the most important night of your life. You cannot afford to lose focus. If you do then you'll never forget. You'll regret it always.'

When he says that I almost choke up. Here I am betraying my own father with these horrible thoughts when all he wants is for me to succeed. And he *does* know what he's talking about, because what he says is *true*. This is what I've been working towards since I was fifteen. Since that first audition when they were putting Purrfect together and I stood in front of Tess and the other judges, willing them to give me a chance, and had that chance torn away from me by two hateful words. Dad didn't make it in the industry, and that makes him an expert in the field of needing to make it. He loves me and I can't afford not to listen to him.

'Okay,' says Dad. 'We're all going to be there. Me, your mum, Mr Field, everyone you know. I've arranged a special trip for your whole class at school, my expense.

They're all coming, Louise. They're coming to see you win. So don't let us down!'

'I won't,' I whisper, trying to imagine my whole class in the audience, all those girls who've laughed at me and called me rude nicknames in the school corridor. I bet they all want to be my friend now.

After a few more words of encouragement Dad says goodbye without putting Mum on, since he says he doesn't want me distracted by her at this stage in the game. Trembling, I set the phone down. Opposite me is the camera. Its dark lens looks like a black hole and I'm suddenly struck by how obsessed we all are with these little machines – especially when you consider that's all that they are. When you think about it we treat them a bit like God, because like Him they see our every move. They catch our every word and record our every last blink. But the way they differ from God is that unlike Him they can't see what's going on on the inside. They can't read minds, they can only read faces and actions. They don't see your soul.

Just then the guy behind the camera shifts in his seat, making the dark circle before me wobble and bringing me back to my senses. I must have fazed out for a moment. I'm tired and drained. And hungry. I need to practise, eat and then get a good night's rest. As Dad said, tomorrow night is the most important night of my life, and if I mess it up I'll regret it for ever.

But instead of getting up and going to the studio to rehearse I continue to sit there at the table, not moving, almost like I've turned into a statue. I'll move in just a moment of course, it's just right this second I can't seem to motivate myself. It's the strangest feeling. I suppose this is what fat people and the drop-outs at school must feel like all the time. I ought to be getting panicked and focusing myself on the prize. But all I can think is that for what I've been doing with Riana I'm probably going to go to hell, and yet what's really amazing is that I just don't seem to care.

'I made a mistake! I was given this amazing opportunity and I blew it! But Purrfect are so fantastic and brilliant – if you'll please give me one more shot I just know I've got what it takes!'

I buy the ticket with Rita's card, which she gave me to pay for Mimi's music lessons. I ask for a single since I don't plan on ever coming back again. The woman in the ticket office, this fat redhead with piercing blue eyes, gives me a funny look across the counter and I find myself getting instantly paranoid that maybe Rita's already twigged somehow and alerted the authorities that I'm missing, and they're keeping a look-out for me at all the stations. But then she leans forward and says in a quick whisper: 'You were ace on that show, love.'

The journey takes for ever. I listen to the radio on my iPhone and they keep playing Purrfect's new single, 'Adam and Eve', which makes me feel nostalgic. It's like the further away from London I get, the further away I'm getting from this amazing opportunity I gave up. I keep remembering them talking to us from the television set when we were in the limo, and how great it felt to hear my name coming out of Fina's mouth, like she actually knew and cared about who I was.

Eventually I doze off in my seat. I wake up with a start to find we're drawing into a station. I think surely we must be there by now, but then I catch sight of a sign and realise it's only York, which means there's still half of England to cross yet. I lean back against the seat and drift off again. This time I start to dream. I'm walking down a red carpet towards the studio and I'm dressed in this amazing backless black gown that flows out behind me, like the dress Nicole Kidman wore in that Chanel advert. All around me photographers are taking pictures and fans are screaming my name. I pass them and walk through the entrance. A big security guard stands before me with Tess at his side. They both have their arms folded and are staring at me like I have no right to be here, and that's when I remember that it's true, I don't, because I've quit. 'Please,' I say, 'please just give me a second chance!' Tess looks at the security guard and I know she's about to tell him to throw me out. I start to beg, telling Tess that I realise I was a fool and I won't let them down again, but I know it's hopeless. I'm going to have to turn around and walk back out through those doors and down that carpet, and this time the fans will be jeering and laughing, and the cameras will be taking pictures of my shame. Tears slide down my cheeks. Then, to my astonishment, Tess extends her hand. Ever so softly she strokes my face and as she does she smiles. It's an amazing smile – warm and genuine. With that smile all the fat and the ugliness falls away from her face. Underneath she's beautiful. Not in the way a model's beautiful, but in the way that Mary in one of those stained-glass windows you get in cathedrals is beautiful, like she's all surrounded by light. Her eyes shine with so much love and kindness I almost start crying again. 'Of course you can have another chance,' says Tess gently. 'You always were my favourite, you know.' She takes my hand and leads me past the security guard and up the stairs. Just then another voice, a loud female computerised monotone, informs us that 'The next stop will be Edinburgh where this train terminates.'

I open my eyes. Instead of Tess there's a creepy-looking man in a grey raincoat sitting opposite, staring hard at my legs. I quickly scramble up from my seat and join the others getting off the train.

Still feeling a little woozy from the journey, I follow the tide of people along the platform until we're through the barriers and inside the station. Here everything is loud and confusing. There seem to be glass partitions in every direction, and people are jostling me right, left and centre as they make their way across the main floor. As I stand there trying to get my bearings and not be swept away, I catch sight of something that makes me gasp. It's a huge billboard, the size of a whole wall, hanging above a Costa Coffee. In massive curly golden letters is written *The Purrfect Search*, and next to it is a picture of all the girls in the competition back from when we first entered the house. I remember them taking that photo, how the photographer had us all cluster around and pout at the camera wearing these little sparkly corsets and feather boas that looked like they were from the same wardrobe as the one Mya, Pink, Christina and Lil' Kim had for their 'Lady Marmalade' video. Seven faces stare moodily out of the poster. Anya, Riana, Valerie, Rebecca, Joni, Louise. And me. I'm there too, right at the centre with my hands on my hips, giving it attitude I've never really felt in my whole life. My hair is all wavy and exploding out about my face, and the other girls are spread out around me in sexual, decorative stances. I look strong, confident and determined – powerful even. Nothing like how I really look. It's the most extraordinary picture and it completely stumps me. For a few seconds all I can do is stare at this huge Amazon version of me standing in the centre of this billboard and think to myself: that's who you were, that's who you could have been, that's what you gave up.

But I gave it up for love. Love is the reason why I'm here in this unfamiliar city, and I mustn't forget. Behind the billboard, almost hidden by some steps, I make out the words Tourist Information and I start to fight my way over.

'Excuse me, can you help me get to this address?' I ask the gaunt man behind the glass, and show him the piece of paper I've written it down on. He looks at it blankly and then at me like he's wondering if maybe I'm a runaway. Finally he reaches down and posts a little pamphlet under the glass. There's a map of Edinburgh on it.

'It'll be somewhere in the north,' he says, his cheeks getting even gaunter as he speaks. 'You can get the bus to that district from Waverley Bridge. It'll take you about an hour.'

'Thank you,' I say, though he's already turned away. I hurry across the station to where there's a sign that says TAXIS. I'm so close to Jack now I can practically feel him breathing, and there's no way I'm prolonging our separation by messing about with buses.

I get into the first taxi I come to, even though the driver's this ugly bald guy who gives me a leering look I don't like when I ask him if he'll take me north. But it turns out he actually knows the street, and in a Scottish accent that takes me a minute to decipher he promises to have me there in just fifteen minutes – unless I want to stop for a quick drink, that is. I'm a bit freaked out by this but I suppose maybe this is the way they do things up here, so I tell him no thank you as politely as I can and he grunts and starts up the ignition.

Of course I'm far too distracted by thoughts of Jack to appreciate Edinburgh properly, but I can't help noticing how pretty it is. There's this huge, beautiful castle on a hill right outside the station, just like the ones you get in fairy tales. I imagine Jack and me walking through it, me wearing a beautiful brocade ball gown and Jack in breeches and a long flowing cloak, a bit like the outfits in the Prada campaign for autumn, holding each other's hands while white rose petals rain down upon us. The driver notices me looking at it and turns midway through steering round a bend to tell me they used to tie nooses round convicts' necks and then throw them off the battlements. It's horrible how someone can just completely annihilate your lovely perception of something, even if they are telling you something cultural. I pretend not to have heard him and start fiddling with my mobile, like I'm typing in a really important text.

There's some traffic so it takes us much longer than the driver said it would to get to Fenland Avenue. It's starting to get dark by the time we arrive, which is annoying because I had this really strong image of me walking down the street and Jack coming in the other direction and us seeing each other at exactly the same time, and sunshine pouring down on us as we run open-armed to meet each other.

'Well, here we are, m'dear,' says the driver, turning to wink at me. I look at the street we've turned into. It's ugly and shabby, lined with buildings that look like they're one gasp away from falling down completely. Not at all the sort of place I'd have expected to find Jack. No doubt it's only temporary though, while he looks for somewhere better to live. And anyway, I think, what does it matter? I don't care if he and I have to stay in a dump with no hot water and no electricity, with dogs that bark all night and screaming babies in the next room, just so long as we can be together.

It's absolutely freezing outside. I'm wearing my Fornarina coat, which is my favourite because it's such a lovely slinky material, only it's also very thin and I stupidly didn't think to bring a scarf with me. I quickly pay the driver. It occurs to me that maybe I ought to ask him to stay until I'm inside Jack's flat, but as soon as I've shut the door he drives off, honking his horn as he turns the corner. I take out the piece of paper again, even though I've had the address memorised since I got it off that woman's computer. Number 9, like the love potion in that song. Slowly I walk up the street until I reach a set of crumbling stone steps leading up to a faded brown door that was probably once red, with a nine scratched crudely above the eyehole. This is it. I climb the uneven steps and press the button by the door. There's a jarring sound of rusted bells.

No answer. I ring again and again, but still nothing. He's out, probably flat hunting. Shivering, I turn to look up the street. It's completely deserted, eerily illuminated by pools of yellow light from the street lamps. I slip my earphones in and press play, then huddle myself up into a ball against the door to wait for the love of my life. Weirdly, I actually feel good about doing this, even though I'm probably risking pneumonia and frostbite. But it's like a trial I have to go through, the final one before Jack and I can be reunited. If I can just do this, then everything will work out. I'll wait here for days if I have to.

After a few minutes all the exposed skin of my face and neck starts to go numb. It's a horrible feeling when that happens, because it's like you've lost control of your own body. My face could actually be coming off and I wouldn't know it. I try to shift around and bury my cheeks in the folds of the large Fornarina collar, but that just means exposing more of my neck. I screw my eyes shut and attempt to lose myself in Monique's beautiful lead vocals to 'Kiss Me Before The End Of The Night' while the other girls Ooh and Ahh soulfully in the background.

I'm shaken awake by a tall figure standing over me. I'm so cold I can hardly think, and it takes me a while to remember where I am and why I can't feel any sensation in my arms and legs.

'Ella?' a voice I recognise is saying with alarm.

Jack is looking down at me, his cheeks red and puffy from the cold, his jaw slightly slack in this adorable expression of complete bewilderment. He looks like an astonished little boy. I try to get up but my entire body is so devoid of feeling I simply tilt forward, almost tumbling head first down the steps. Jack catches me by the shoulders and pulls me up. I stand unsteadily, leaning against the door for support.

'Ella . . . what are you doing here?'

I try to smile, but even my lips are frozen solid. I concentrate, channelling all my joy at seeing him into my eyes. Jack stares back at me, as if he's unable to comprehend what he's seeing. I know he must be wrestling with the mixed feelings in his heart, but I also know that buried somewhere amongst them he must also be deeply glad to see me.

'Jack, who *is* she?' whines a nasal voice. At the bottom of the steps there's a tall thin woman wearing that amazing long black coat with the tassels on the sleeves that Giselle was photographed in during Paris Fashion Week. She's in her forties at least, with blonde hair and highlights quite a lot like Rita's, only shorter and sleeker. She's also caked in bronze make-up, like she's just dived into a swimming pool of foundation. The streetlight doesn't do her any favours and even from here I can see that it's practically standing out an inch off her face. Out the corner of her mouth dangles a long white cigarette, which she drags away on without having to remove it, puffing out great tufts of toxic cloud.

'Nobody,' replies Jack over his shoulder. 'Just a girl I know.'

He's obviously ashamed of being with her, and I would be too. Rita's words come back to me, about how he would be with some rich woman, spending all her money. It doesn't matter to me though, and I try to convey this to him through my eyes. That all that matters is I've found him and we can be together.

'Well, what does she want?' moans the bronze woman. 'I thought we were going to spend the evening just you and me. She's not going to be hanging around, is she?'

'Ella,' whispers Jack. 'You can't be here. Not now. You have to go.'

He doesn't mean it, I can tell. He's just saying it because he thinks he has to. He's obviously made some silly promise to this woman and feels like he has to keep it. A touch of feeling comes back into my lips and I force them into a smile. I wish I had the strength to kiss him. That'd get the message across loud and clear to that old prune down there.

'Ella, *please*!'

'Jack, what's going on? Who *is* she?'

My vision starts to blur and their voices suddenly begin to sound faint. It occurs to me that all that time sitting on Jack's front doorstep waiting for him may really have damaged me. But I don't mind. Even if I die now, it'll be a good way to go, because at least I'll have been reunited with Jack.

I'm only dimly aware of being helped inside the flat, being led into a tiny living room with peeling wallpaper and no furniture apart from a single moth-eaten settee. Despite how shabby it is it's deliciously warm in here and when I sink down on the cushions it's like heaven. The woman doesn't come in, and I hear Jack saying something to her at the door and her huffily saying 'Fine!' in this voice that makes it totally clear it's anything but. She sounds so much like Rita that in my haze I almost think she *is* Rita. Then Jack comes back in and kneels down in front of me. Slowly the feeling returns to my limbs and fingers, and my vision starts to become clear again. I look into the most beautiful blue eyes in the world and it's like I've finally come home.

'Oh my God,' Jack keeps repeating. 'How can this be happening?'

It's obvious he's not saying it to me. Groggily I sit up.

'Jack.'

My voice is all over the place, but at least I can speak again.

'Jack, I came to find you ... Has she gone, that woman?'

'She's waiting for me at a pub round the corner,' says Jack. He sounds stressed out. I suppose he's still getting over the surprise. It's obviously knocked him for six.

'Jesus Christ, Ella! I mean . . . what the hell do you think you're doing showing up here? And how did you get my address?'

'I went to your old gym,' I explain. 'They've got it on their system. I had to distract the receptionist there by setting off a fire alarm – it was crazy! But I did it! Jack – I left the contest. I left it for you!'

I can't help smiling as I tell him. Jack stares at me, his beautiful violet eyes the size of planets. He mouths the word 'Jesus' but no sound comes out.

'Does Rita know where you are?' he says suddenly. 'Oh God, she'll be going mad with worry!'

I start giggling. The idea of Rita even noticing that I'm not there is pretty funny. The idea of her going mad with worry doesn't even register.

'She won't care!'

Jack suddenly leaps up and starts pacing around the room. Since it's only tiny he can only take about three steps before he has to turn and go the other way. It's quite disconcerting and I wish he'd stop doing it. I notice there's more than a trace of stubble on his chin, which is funny because he's always been so meticulous about shaving.

'Are you growing a beard?'

He doesn't reply, just continues pacing, frown lines creasing his forehead and growing deeper and deeper with every step. It's clearly up to me to take charge of the situation, to show him how much I've grown up and learned in the time we've been apart.

'Jack,' I say gently. 'It doesn't matter. Jack, don't you see?'

I smile at him. Abruptly Jack stops and faces me.

'There's nothing to stop us being together now.'

'What the fuck are you talking about!' he screams at me. 'What the fuck is the matter with you? I mean . . . are you completely and utterly *out of your fucking mind*? *You spoilt worthless little idiot!*'

It's like he's just punched me in the face. All I can do is gape at him. Jack bites down on his lip so hard that it turns white, and drops his head, staring hard at the carpet. His shoulders rise and fall heavily, like he's having difficulty breathing.

'Listen, Ella,' he says in a very tight, controlled voice. 'I'm going to put you in a taxi to take you back to the station. Trains go to London all the time. Do you have money?'

'No!' I scream at the top of my lungs. Over the past few weeks I've built up quite a bit of lung power with all those classes of Edgar's. I use his technique of focusing on one single note – the O sound – in order to really achieve some volume. The result is spectacular and surprises even me. Jack takes a step back, his face transforming with horror. He raises both hands and waves them at me desperately. I stop screaming and take another deep breath.

'Ella . . . don't scream like that again, okay?'

I don't have the energy to, anyway. Tears are coursing down my cheeks. I can feel them sliding off my chin and practically hear them as they splatter like a miniature waterfall on to the lacy collar of the Fornarina coat. Jack smiles at me. But it's the sort of smile you get from someone who's terrified of you.

'It's okay,' he says, suddenly super nice. 'Ella, it's okay. We'll work it out. I'm sorry. I was hasty before. It was the shock of seeing you. But I really appreciate you coming all this way. I really, really do. No one's ever done that for me before.'

'Really?' I say. My voice is small, hopeful and desperate. Desperate because I know he's lying. He doesn't love me. He doesn't love me. My heart hurts so much from the realisation it's like I've been stabbed there. It actually feels like it's been cut open and is bleeding, just like in that Leona Lewis song.

Jack's smile quivers, like he's having trouble maintaining it.

'Just wait here while I go and . . . call Freda and cancel our plans tonight, huh? Then we'll have the whole evening together, just you and me. How does that sound?'

I nod, unable to speak, this time not because of the cold but because of my heart. Still smiling manically, Jack goes out of the room, carefully shutting the door behind him. After a few seconds I stagger over and put my ear against it. In the next room I hear him talking on the phone in a hasty, urgent voice. He's not talking to Freda.

'Mimi! It's Jack . . . never mind all that. Never mind! Look, I need you to put Rita on. It's about Ella and it's important . . . Then you'll just have to interrupt her, won't you?!'

He doesn't want me and he's never going to. Never.

I realise that I have to get out of here – right away, before he comes back. I go to the front door and fumble idiotically with the latch. I can still hear the low murmur of him talking in the next room, and suddenly I can't bear the sound of his voice. Suddenly I don't want anything more to do with him. I don't know where I'm going to go and I don't even care. I just need to get out of here, away from this terrible, awful, impossible pain. With a little cry I fling the door open. An icy breeze welcomes me to the outside world, and I'm actually glad that it's freezing because maybe it'll numb that shuddering agony in my heart, which right now feels like it's going to be there for the rest of my life.

I pull my coat tightly around me and hurry out into the cold.

It's still early when I get up, but I just can't sleep anymore. After all this waiting and waiting and waiting, the day has finally come. This is it. This is really it.

In the bathroom I run a shower with very hot water, as hot as I can stand. Each droplet seems to sizzle as it hits my skin. It feels like I'm being cleaned on the inside as well as on the outside – like I'm being made pure for the task ahead. Only when the water starts to run cold do I throw a towel around my glowing pink body and head back into the bedroom.

Outside over the city a red sun has burst through the grey cloud, and it paints the room with orange light, making the gun on the chest of drawers sparkle like a metal jewel. I pick it up and balance it in my palm. It's old, this weapon – an antique, in fact. It was a souvenir of my granddad's from the war, and it's so large and heavy it feels as if it would do more damage if you threw it. But it still works. On my day off I drove out to the country, to an abandoned farm where I used to go for walks when I was a teenager, when things got too much at home or when school had been particularly crushing. Carefully I loaded it, following instructions I found on the Internet. My hands were shaking from excitement as I took aim at a tree and fired. It sounded like the world had split open, and for a few seconds I wasn't sure what had happened. But when I inspected the tree there was a tiny hole where the bullet had embedded itself deep in the trunk.

I bring the gun to my lips and kiss it, tasting the cold metal with my tongue and imagining suddenly what she will feel when the bullet embeds itself in her. Perhaps it's stupid but I don't think it will hurt. I don't want it to, either. I want it to be quick and painless. I want her to pass out of this life easily, because the honest truth is that I don't hate her anymore. She can't help being what she is. It's the only thing she knows how to be.

The alarm by my bed starts to beep, startling me out of my thoughts. Ever so gently I set the gun back down and go over and switch it off. I put on the outfit I laid out last night and then carefully comb my hair before pulling it back tight from my scalp, enjoying the pain as follicle after follicle is stretched taut. Then I put on my make-up – or my disguise, as I like to think of it.

I remember when I first came before her after getting the job. I was terrified she would recognise me, and had applied so many layers of foundation and blusher it felt like I was wearing a second skin. I needn't have worried though. The faces of those hundreds and hundreds of girls whose dreams she's destroyed are all the same to her. All those moments that changed all those lives have had no effect on her own. She looked through me as if I didn't even exist. Yet strangely I've come to need this face. It's my warpaint, and without it I'd feel open and exposed. It seems to me that all women have two faces – the one they're born with and the one they create. You can't help wondering which is the truest.

When I'm done I put away the make-up case and pick up my handbag. I take it over to the chest of drawers and put the gun inside. Then I clip it shut and check the mirror one last time. Soon, I whisper to the sad, thin woman before me. It feels as if my whole life has been leading up to this day. I can't afford to fail.

'I'm on the blimmin' edge. I mean, it's all about tonight, ain't it? Everything we've been working for. All that struggle and all that blimmin' heartache. It all comes down to this one single night. So yeah – just totally blimmin' nervous!!!'

I breathe in like never before, like me lungs are the size of airships, then release the last note. I been trying to hit this bitch all week in the studio, and every time Edgar sighs and goes No that ain't right. Finally he said to just forget it and go low cos the way it could go wrong didn't bear even thinking about. But I swore to meself I'd do it. Even if it fucking kills me. After last week I gotta turn this competition around, cos otherwise I ain't got no chance whatsoever, not against old mega boobs with her plastic stuck-on smile or that horsey little bone bag with her perfect fucking pitch.

It nearly does kill me. The air comes rushing out through me mouth at a million miles a second, almost making me gag as me throat contracts into a little tiny hole. It's like someone's reached out and clamped a fist round me windpipe. But I hit it. I hit it and then some. This sound, right on key, like something that could of come out of the gob of an angel or out of Barbra Streisand even, fills the whole auditorium. It's rich and pure and loud and all them things a voice is s'posed to be. Somewhere out there I know Edgar is eating his fucking words.

– looove me!

Them's the last words. I hold them for what seems like an eternity and then it's over. The lights fade down on me and I slump forward, like I'm so exhausted I'm ready to drop dead. I ain't never sung like that before. I don't care what them judges say. They can swivel cos that was as good as it gets.

Here comes the applause. It's funny cos the first time you hear them clapping for you it's like the sky itself has gone and opened up and it's raining down fire like in one of them biblical scenes the religious crazies are always going on about. But a few times and you get used to it, and then you start measuring inside your head how long it goes on for and thinking Is it as loud as what thingummy got? Well, I'm glad to say that tonight it sure as fucking hell feels like it. Practically does me ears in.

The biggest whoops and cheers are coming from the back of course, where Mum and her mates are. They've got up on their seats and are jumping up and down like they're all having fits or something. They've gone and got these T-shirts made up too that have a black and white photo of me face printed on them, which is a bit weird – y'know, seeing your mug jiggling around on all these forty-something women's tits. This usher is standing next to them trying to make them all get down, but she's got Fat Carol in the way who's four times the size of her so I don't much fancy her chances.

I sneak a look over at the judges. Emma, Joe and Tess are all clapping. Even Tess. She clapped for Louise and Riana when they did their bits too, so maybe for just this one night she's dislodged the broomstick. Or else maybe we was all just plain good. Maybe it's a bit of both, who knows? I reckon she must be relieved that it's nearly over, since those letters and stunts almost made her fucking lose it last week. Every time she came in to watch us practise and give us her advice she bit your head off, going on about how we was never gonna be as good as Purrfect and how they never had any of the problems we got. But now there she is nodding up and down and looking almost pleased, probably about as close to it as she's able to get, a bit like she's just been proven right about something.

Left of the judges is Purrfect. The band themselves, here in the flesh to see us and give us their own verdicts on whether or not we should join them. They're all clapping away and cheering too. Fina is even standing and wailing her head off with everyone else. Right away she becomes me favourite, even though it was always Saffron before. All these feelings are rushing into me head all of a sudden. I'm getting all choked up with the emotion. I can't believe that was it, that there ain't nothing more for me to do, that all there is left is to wait and see what they all says. It's out of me hands. But I gave it me best, I really did, and that's all a girl can do.

Wow . . . shrieks this scratchy voice over all the applause. It's Stina, course, coming on to the stage in this tiny little purple scrap of a dress which is even more revealing than the red mini what I've got on.

That really was the business, wasn't it? yells Stina at the audience. Ladies and gentlemen – the character that is Joni!

She sweeps her arm out in this motion towards me, almost slapping me in the face, the silly cow. I give the audience a wave. Fuck it, cos I done it, I think to meself. I let out this big whoop and before Stina can say nothing more I raise me mic.

That was for me little boy! I yell.

There's more cheering at that, even louder than before, I reckon. It almost sounds like the roof's being blown off. Over at the back Mum's so excited it looks like she's being electrocuted and even Fat Carol's jumping up and down. The usher's standing well back now. The only one who's not still clapping is Tess, who folds her arms like she's used up quite enough effort already thank you very fucking much, miserable old arse-face.

Okay folks, goes Stina in a low dramatic voice, raising her hands to quieten everyone down. It takes a while, since Mum and her mates are out of control, but eventually they realise they're the only ones still going and can it. Can I get Riana and Louise back onstage please?

There's a slow drum roll, real ominous, and the other two come on. They're holding hands and both smiling their big phony smiles. Riana's is so fucking massive tonight it could practically be used for a satellite. When they get to me Louise reaches over and takes me hand too. I'm tempted to snatch it back, since there's no way this little witch would ever do it if it weren't for us being onstage in front of all these people and cameras, but instead I find meself clasping it real tight. Suddenly I ain't concentrating on her or Riana no more. I'm concentrating on the judges and on those girls from Purrfect. Cos this is what it all comes down to. This is what it's all about. This moment, right here, right now. One of them moments that defines the course of the rest of your life.

Riana, Louise and Joni, says Stina in that voice like we're all doomed as fuck, you are the last three girls and in just a moment, one of you will be going home. The remaining two will perform their songs one last time in a knock-out round, before the new Purrfect girl is crowned. It's time to hear from our judges, Emma, Joe and Tess, and of course from Purrfect themselves. Let's hear it for Saffron, Kharris, Monique and Fina!

There's another big burst of applause, only it don't last very long. Everyone wants to know who's it gonna be. Me fingers tighten around Louise's little hand and I feel hers tightening back. Funny how in moments like these all that matters is that you're human beings together and none of that stuff that's gone before is important.

Girls, goes Emma, super serious, you all have great potential but the girl I'm voting off tonight hasn't shown enough of herself over the week for me to really feel that I know who she is. A pop star has to be true. She's got to be honest about her emotions and let that come across. That's why tonight I'm choosing Louise to go home.

A big ooh-ing sound comes out of the audience, like half of them is disagreeing. The fingers around mine weaken slightly, then come back even stronger like they're clinging on for dear life. And even though I know Louise is the kind of person who'd sell her own parents if she thought it'd get her somewhere, I feel sorry for her. But there's more coming, and I ain't in the clear yet.

Joe? says Stina.

Joe makes this show of clearing his throat.

I feel that over the past five weeks you've all come such a long way, goes the old poof like he's trying to be all original. You're all brilliant, all truly fantastic, and all have great potential. However, while I think you each have your own style, for me there are two that particularly stand out and have done right from day one. A Purrfect girl has to be *vocally* perfect. And because of that . . . I'm sorry, but it's Riana.

Riana gasps. You can tell she didn't see that coming. Neither did I. Me legs are trembling so much I'm probably burning off any last cells of flab I've got left on them after all them hardcore dance sessions with Patty. Everything's unreal, a bit twisted, like anything could happen. It's a bit like being on acid, only there's all this adrenalin pumping through me too, like maybe at any second a bomb is gonna explode.

Tess? goes Stina.

Tess lets out this long breath and cocks her head to one side. She don't say anything at first, and I realise that she's loving this. The audience are fucking hating her and so am I, but she's milking it and in a way we're all enjoying that she is. Enjoying wanting to kick her fat face in. Cos being hated is what she's really good at.

I have to push you, please Tess, goes Stina.

Tess ignores her and carries on looking at each of us, all slow like she's still making up her mind.

Well, you've all done your best, she goes suddenly, and I can see problems with all of you.

There's booing like you never heard before. One corner of Tess's big gob goes up in this smart-alecky smirk, like this is just the reaction she was hoping for.

But I can also see the plus sides and you should probably know that you're all good. To have got this far you've got to be good.

This gets lots of clapping and cheering. The thing about people like Tess is no matter how much you hate them, you really end up believing what they say in a way you don't with people who are just nice all the time. So it seems like the smallest positive thing they tell you is the best compliment you could possibly ever get.

Tess's paused again, like this is all she's got to say. Next to her you can tell Joe's fuming, totally jealous cos of the way she's working it and getting away with it.

Tess? goes Stina, now all whiny. Could you pick someone?

Tess leans forward.

The girl I'm choosing is purely because she hasn't conducted herself as properly as the other two, and one of the most important lessons I've ever learned in this business is that you have to conduct yourself professionally. Otherwise, it'll all come down around you in tatters. So, Joni, I'm afraid it's you.

It's like I've been stabbed or something. She was looking at Louise when she said that last part and I really thought I was in the clear. Me hand in Louise's is like a vice, and I know that her hand on Riana's must be the same way too. It's almost too much and I could do with a bucket so I can have a good old puke. There's a lot of woo-ing and ahh-ing and whispering going on out in front of us, like no one can believe how tense it is.

Wow, goes Stina, looks like each one of our finalists has a vote, everybody! That means it's all down to our guest judges, Purrfect. Girls, thanks for coming on the show—

She gets drowned out by cheers. When we met them briefly before the show I nearly wet meself. Being kissed on the cheek by the girls in one of the biggest bands in the UK, the one we're trying to be a part of and have dreamed of getting into for the last few weeks, it was like something magical. And to have them sit there listening to us – it's like something out of a fantasy. But then it just brings home what we're doing here, cos at the end of this one of us is really gonna be in Purrfect. Pretty soon, this ain't gonna be some fantasy no more.

Stina laughs and waves at the audience like they're all cheering for her. They quieten down and she carries on. Could you now confer among yourselves and give me the name of the girl you would like to send home?

Saffron, Monique, Fina and Kharris all huddle up together in this kind of formation I seen them do in the docu of their success which was on TV the other month. It's what they always do right before they go out onstage, all cluster together and have a quick group rally. You can tell they really understand and support one another, these girls. To be in this band, to have these other girls who really are your best friends and who ain't just bitches that only care about their sodding selves, that'd be the best thing ever.

Girls, goes Stina, I need an answer from you, please.

The girls stop whispering with each other and sit back. They all look fab tonight, but totally different and individual. Fina's in this white suit with a black tie that makes her red hair look punky and cool. Monique and Saffron are both wearing proper evening dresses all the way down to their ankles. Monique's is fiery red and off her shoulders whereas Saffron's is dark green with a slit down the middle that cuts right between her tits and has silver stars at the waist. And Kharris is wearing this genie-style number, all blue and silvery, with lots of sequins and a strip missing around the hips that shows off her super-flat tummy. Course their make-up is flawless, defined and all subtle too so you can only tell they're wearing it by looking real close. Over the last few weeks I've learned a lot from all the make-up people, and it makes me fucking cringe when I think about the slop I used to go out in. As for Mum, first thing I got to do with her is chuck out all that shit from the market and treat ourselves to some proper products, like that miracle concealer from Glossy X that makes even warts disappear. It's true that the good stuff is pricey. But it's like the difference between chocolate and shit, and like that Shelly said to me, beauty's one of them things you only get to play with once.

Monique's nodding at the other girls, who all nod back at her and look down like this whole process is killing them. She often ends up doing the talking for the girls, which don't seem fair on her really, specially when it comes to hard stuff like this. When I'm a Purrfect girl I'll be sure to pipe up whenever I get the chance.

We've reached a decision, goes Monique, and it was the hardest decision any of us has ever had to make. You've all been just great and we would feel privileged to have any one of you in the band.

There's more cheering and Monique looks at us each in turn. It ain't like when Tess looked at us, which was this pitying stare like she was looking at deformed children in Africa or something. Monique's look is full of emotion. You can tell she really understands how much this means, that she's probably remembering when she had to go through it herself two years ago. There're actual tears in her eyes, and I've got tears in me own eyes too just from looking back at her.

However, she goes, we had to choose someone, and we all feel that although this girl is a fabulous performer and a real character, she's wrong for Purrfect. Coming into this competition, this girl made a bad decision early on. Although we all know how much she regrets it, we feel that lying about your family isn't something to be taken lightly.

I realise she's looking at me and me only. Me heart stops.

Joni, you sang that last song for your little boy and I thought it was really moving. But it's a shame you didn't want the world to know he was yours in the first place.

There's noise and stuff going on, but this numb feeling comes over me and I can't seem to get a grip on any of it. I know Mum's standing on her chair again and shouting out that if Monique had ever had to squeeze out a fucking baby and then look after it she'd know it ain't that fucking easy, and that Stina's announcing to the world that I ain't gonna be in Purrfect. But I don't feel nothing about it. Not angry or sad. Just numb. Even the clapping sounds like it's coming from far away.

Next thing I'm being hugged by Louise and then by Riana. For some reason I don't want to claw their faces off or nothing like that. Instead I hear meself wailing at them Good luck! and I hug them back like they're me best mates in the world. It's only when I get to Stina and have to hug her too and she tells me God bless that I realise I'm crying away. It's like this automatic thing I'm doing without having any control over it. And before I've even got me head around it, Stina's pointing me off the stage and off I'm going, out of the spotlight, down the steps and into the darkness. Behind me I hear her telling the audience what a great contestant I've been, and it's only then, as I go down the steps, that it hits me. It's over. I ain't never going back on this stage again.

Okay, everyone, Stina's going all excitedly, we're sooo close to finding out who our winner is! We're going for a quick ad break now, but don't anyone dare go away! In just a few minutes the judges will reveal who is the most perfect potential Purrfect girl!

I stand like a dummy on the bottom step, staring off into space all gormless. These two techies are both concentrating super-hard on their headsets like they're receiving very important instructions, but you can tell it's only cos they can't bring themselves to catch me eye. There's a cameraman opposite who's filming me, and I know I must look like the biggest loser on the planet just standing and staring off like this, but I can't seem to snap out of it.

Come on, says Michelle gently, stepping forward from the corner. She takes me arm and leads me over to the door. Let's take you back to the dressing room.

I let her guide me down the corridor like a fucking mental patient. As we go I notice that for once the cameraman ain't bothering to follow, and I realise it's cos he ain't got no reason to anymore. Cos I ain't worth wasting the tape on, not now that I'm officially out of the running.

Here, goes Michelle.

She opens the door and stands back to let me go in. Like a zombie I enter and stop in the middle, looking right at meself in the big mirror there. What I see there is this stupid tarted-up wannabe with no job and no prospects or nothing. Makes me want to fucking smash that mirror into pieces.

After a minute I realise Michelle's still there at the door, watching.

It's for the best you know, she goes.

Fuck off, I say.

You should count yourself lucky, she carries on like I ain't just swore at her. This show, this business, it can wreck your life. It can even kill you.

Then she gives me that same dappy smile what she had on when I mashed into her the other week after I lost me cool with Ella in the studio. She's wearing all black tonight, head to foot, like she's going to a posh person's funeral. Cos of how thin and white she is she looks sort of frightening, a bit like a dead person and not at all trendy like she's s'posed to. And with that freaky smile of hers she don't look right in the head neither. One person I ain't gonna miss.

Could I be on me own? I say, trying me best not to fucking snap.

She nods, still smiling like she's this fucking clairvoyant that knows all this mystical shit about what a good thing this is for me, and then closes the door.

I'm about to sit down and have a good cry, or maybe even just drop down dead from how shit I feel, when there's this rustling from the clothes rack in the corner. Before I can stop meself I let out a scream. It's the psycho, I think. He's been here all along and now he's gonna knife me while the others do their songs, right under everybody's stupid noses.

Then two of the dresses slide apart and this little face I know all too well appears between them.

Hi Joni, goes Ella, all bright and cheerful. How's it going?

For a minute I ain't got a clue what to say. I just stand there gawping at her. Seeing her here, randomly like this, is just plain fucking off, like I've somehow slipped into another dimension or something. She's wearing this dress from off the rack, only she ain't got it on properly, and it's too big for her, too, and the straps are hanging off her dainty little shoulders. She's had a go at putting on some make-up, only it looks like she's done it with her eyes shut cos it's all over the place. Her hair is tangled and it looks like she's used the tongs and has gone and fried a whole chunk of it. It's the first time I've ever seen her looking rough.

I came back, Ella goes, like everything's just completely fucking normal. I realised I was stupid to have left. Do you think they'll let me still do my song? I've been thinking I could sing 'My Heart Is Not Your Toy'. I know I haven't practised, but I know it off by heart anyway and I'm really good. I don't even need the music!

She gives me this hopeful look, and if ever there was an expression of somebody what'd lost it, Ella's got it down. If you thought that Michelle looked daft in the head, well she ain't got nothing on Ella. I mean, the girl looks positively raving.

How'd you get in the building? I go, calm as I can.

Oh, it was easy. I still had my security pass so I just showed the men at the desk and they let me right on in. I don't think they realised I was supposed to have left.

She giggles, like this is too funny.

Ella, I go, slowly but firmly too cos that's the only way to deal with someone who's lost it big time, they ain't gonna let you perform. You left the show. They're down to Riana and Louise now and any minute they're gonna decide which one of them's in the band.

Ella looks at me smiling, still totally not getting it.

I've just been voted off! I go.

From the TV over on the side you can see they've started up again on stage, and Stina is introducing Louise. Ella shakes her head like I'm just messing with her and she's not having any of it.

My plan is that I'll surprise them, she goes. I'll go onstage and sing and they'll just be so blown away they'll forget about everything that's happened and want me for the band. I'm good, Joni, I really am. I'm really good enough!

But her voice is cracking, and next thing you know those famous old tears are pouring out of her like a fucking flash flood. I'm good enough! she keeps wailing, and even though it's me who ought to be all upset and miserable cos of not getting the gig, I find meself going over to her and giving her a squeeze, and telling her I know she is.

314

I didn't mean to give up! she keeps on wailing, I'm not a quitter, Joni! And I'm not worthless either!

Shhhh, I go, pushing her head into me shoulder and letting her start soaking the sleeve of the minidress. All gentle I explain to her how she don't need to cry cos it don't matter, of course she ain't worthless, she's got her whole life ahead of her and anyway, it's just a silly fucking singing contest. On the TV Louise is starting her song and is singing out the words It's been so long and I feel so old, but still got hope inside me, and there's this big fucking close-up of her looking all sincere and ridiculous as she stares out into space. And suddenly I find meself figuring out that it's true what I'm saying, and it's true what that Michelle was saying as well, and out of nowhere I get this amazing revelation, like everything's just become lit up by a bright light. Who I am at the end of the day is Joni, and all I need to be happy is me little boy. I just want to hold Baby in me arms again. Nothing else matters in the whole world, not this contest, not its stupid cameras, not any of these crazy fucking girls, none of them people out there and not even them bitch judges. Not even those cunts Wendy and Davy. Nothing matters, cept for me and him.

'So psyched now . . . never known anything like it! All I can say is how much I've loved doing this, the whole thing, and how much I'm going to miss it all. I'm not the same person as I was when I started. I really have the competition to thank for that!'

Up ahead's Louise, standing at the centre of the stage bathed in rose-coloured light. Little stars of white appear and swirl about her before fading away again. Her long silver gown with the slit all the way almost to her fanny makes her look curvier than she really is, and the way it folds out loose over her tits makes her look almost a whole cup size bigger.

It's been so long and I feel so old, she sings softly with her eyes shut, lots of tiny purple specks glittering on her eyelids, But still got hope inside me . . .

Listening to the beautiful lyrics to Martha Sole's song, that Louise didn't even know when they first chose it for her, I can't help thinking how much she looks like a woman. Grown up and independent, almost like a real diva. She's going to be properly devastated if she doesn't get this – I wonder if she'll ever be able to get over it. The other day after we touched each other up in the toilet right under the nose of that stupid camera dude, I whispered to her what would she do if she didn't get picked? She looked at me with these eyes all narrowed and suspicious like she thought it was a trick question. Then she whispered back that she *was* going to get picked, and before I could say anything else she broke away and stalked off out the bathroom, which was a surprise seeing as up till then I'd always been the one to leave first. I couldn't help laughing. Let's just wait and see, shall we, little madam? I thought, since I was just as positive it was going to be me. But now, for the first time, I realise Louise is good. Real good. She's just not my style, that's all, but I can see how she's worked really hard for this and that she wants it so bad it hurts. What's more, I can see that maybe, just maybe, she might even get it.

Gotta take a moment . . . never thought I'd feel this way . . .

So I guess I should be hating her. I should be willing her to trip up, to do a Valerie, or have a coughing fit, or suddenly have to puke, or something else that'll swing this my way. But for some reason, watching her from here in the wings, I don't feel jealous or spiteful at all, just sad. Not quite sure why.

I peer over to where Purrfect're sat. Four pretty white faces with designer-plucked eyebrows all creased up in concentration. Was wrong to think that it's just like stripping, what they do. Sure, there's an element of sexuality in performing, but it's so much more. That's what I've come to understand. It's about properly engaging the audience, getting on the same wavelength as them and then leading them through the emotions of a song, whether it's slow and sad or fast and sexy. It's about connecting with people. And it's not something just anyone can do either.

Life's been so full of heartache, can't handle it no more, sings out Louise, suddenly all loud and wavering. As normal she's faultless, perfectly in tune and not a note out of place. Only her voice sounds the same as how it's always sounded to me. Empty. Like maybe she doesn't really feel what she's singing about – probably cos she doesn't.

I look past Purrfect at the judges, sat in a line at the table right in front of Louise. Joe looks serious and is nodding along as if he's discovering for the very first time how much he agrees with the lyrics, while Emma's got this big smile like she's watching a baby bird she's nurtured all through the winter finally find its wings and fly. Only Tess's face is blank and unreadable. But there's something about the total lack of anything in those fat features that makes me think this troll's really felt what Louise is singing about – that she really understands how much love can fucking hurt. After all, how else does a woman get to be so cold and bitter? Jesus, man, I don't ever wanna be like that. Rather be a lost cause, like Emily from the club, who cries for all the babies she never had and tries to act like everyone's mum while they all snigger behind her back and think of her as a loser. Least her heart's still there.

I want to feel loved! croons Louise, raising a hand and pointing at the audience like she's singling out someone that she just knows is going to demonstrate to her what it's all about, Need to feel loved!

I follow the direction of her finger, pointing out towards the back row, thinking that I'll never be able to just sit and listen to someone performing ever again without wishing it was me. There at the back I see a face that makes Louise's song disappear as if someone had suddenly flicked an off button. For a few seconds all I can hear is the sound of blood pumping in my ears, and all I can see is her. Eddy. She's got a black scarf wound round her neck and is wearing one of those military berets that I hate, which hides her whole forehead. But I'd know her face anywhere. Those cat's eyes are staring towards the stage, all slitted with hate. And just like that I know for sure it was her that sent the threats, her that broke in and wrote on the mirror and shredded the costume and murdered that poor pigeon. What everyone's been frightened of all along is nothing but Eddy and her stupid SCUM group. And tonight she's got something new planned, something to really bring the house down.

Louise is going down the steps from the stage into the space right before the audience, still singing the chorus, reaching out to touch some of the waving hands in the front row. She's smiling sweetly in this way that's all wrong considering what she's singing about. But I can't focus on that right now cos suddenly Eddy is upsetting everyone in her row by pushing her way down it towards the aisle. In her arms she's holding a yellow rucksack, the one she always takes on her little terrorist adventures, which I recognise cos it's tatty and hideous and I've tried hundreds of times to throw it out. My heart pounds like it's doing The Locomotive. As she reaches the aisle her right hand dips into the rucksack, yanking it open, and I catch a flash of something metallic inside. Behind her at the door there's a security guard, but he's off watching Louise along with everyone else, trying to work out what he thinks and totally oblivious to what's about to happen right under his fucking nose. Eddy makes her way down the aisle, striding like nothing's gonna stop her towards the stage and Louise. Still no one fucking notices. They're all too busy going soppy over Louise's naff performance. I watch as Eddy picks up pace. The hand in the rucksack comes out and it's clutching a shiny blue cylinder, and suddenly I know exactly what Eddy is up to.

For a second I'm tempted to let her go through with it. After all, it's not like she's going to kill someone. Louise'll scream and probably cry when the paint blast hits her, and it'll bring the whole competition to a standstill for a while and cause a right sensation, but that's all. One way or another Eddy'll be caught and get carted off by security or the police or whatever in front of a whole army of snapping cameras, which is no doubt what she wants. Then there'll be lots of publicity for her silly old SCUM group and she can go back to them feeling all proud of herself and that'll be the end of it. No big deal.

I want to feel loved! Need to feel loved!

Cept that it'll be a big deal for Louise. This is her last shot, her crowning moment, and even if she is the competition I can't just stand by and let Eddy piss all over her dreams, not after feeling up her skinny body and making her frig me over and over in the upstairs toilets of the house while right outside some dumb camera dude waits for us with no idea about what we're up to. Only a total irredeemable cunt would just watch and do nothing.

I turn to Michelle beside me.

Someone's about to spray paint all over Louise! I cry.

Michelle nods slowly. I don't have time to grab the useless bitch's shoulders and shake her about while I spell it out for her. Eddy's halfway down the aisle and rapidly getting closer. She's shaking the spray paint canister up and down as she gets ready to take her shot. People are finally looking up at her as she passes them but no one's making any move to stop her. Meanwhile Louise has closed her eyes again and is launching into the final lines of the song. She opens her arms and holds them out in the exact direction of Eddy. It almost looks like she's planning to give her a welcome hug. No time to think about what I'm doing, I just hurl myself up the steps and onto the stage. Straight away I'm blinded by rose-coloured light. Behind me I hear Michelle yelling at me to get back but I don't listen. I run in the direction of where I know Louise is standing.

Stop her! Somebody stop her! I shriek, loud as I can. I don't have a mic, but all these weeks of being made to stand in a corner humming Ah while I play with my throat have done their job. I almost break the fucking sound barrier. As my eyes adjust I see the auditorium, hundreds of faces staring at me in amazement, the panel and Purrfect themselves all open-mouthed at the front in this one line of O shapes.

Louise's voice fades as she turns to see what the commotion's about. Her eyes crease up with rage when she realises it's me and that I'm messing up her song. There's someone onstage behind me now too, one of the techies shouting at me to get off. But I don't stop. I stumble forward, pointing and shouting, focusing on that figure behind Louise.

It's her, she's the one who's been sending the threats! I'm screaming, sounding like a maniac that needs to be sedated. She reckons it's up to her to reshape the *whole fucking world*!

I feel these hands closing around my arms and shoulders, trying to pull me back and force down the hand that's pointing at Eddy. I throw them off, only for them to come back again twice as strong. Everyone in the place seems to be on their feet shouting, but I can't hear anything cept my own voice as I carry on shrieking for someone to do something.

Eddy's eyes meet mine. I will her not to do it, but what I see there makes me realise there's no going back. Suddenly, maybe for the first time, I have this feeling that I truly understand Eddy. It's what I should have understood from the moment we met, when she first came to the club with her SCUM flyers trying to convert us all, insisting that what we did meant we were letting men rule our lives. Thought I'd got something on her when I managed to get her to sit down while I gave her a private, right in front of all those jeering dicks at the bar. Figured I'd proved she was just like the rest of us really, no matter what she might like to think. And all along I've believed it – that behind all the talk she's the same, another hopeless human with dirty thoughts and desires, someone that'd watch a show just like this one and secretly enjoy it no matter what it stood for. What a twat I am! Cos what I've never got is that Eddy won't ever come to terms with it. Here's someone that hates the world for not living up to her expectations. Someone that'll do anything to get revenge on it for not being as perfect as she wants it to be. Noble or pathetic, it doesn't make a blind bit of difference, cos that's who she is and she's never going to change, not for me, not for anyone. And that's why I know it's over between us for good.

Still holding my eyes she smiles a nasty, bitter kind of smile, then breaks her gaze away and strides the remaining distance between her and Louise. She raises the spray can to Louise's eye level. As she does Louise turns back round to look at her, offering up her face to the gleaming cylinder of doom.

Don't— I shout, but it's useless. My wonderful loud voice dissolves into nothing but this pathetic wail and I shut my eyes cos I can't bear it. I feel those hands that were pulling me back fall off as the people they belong to finally cotton on to what's happening, but it's too late, I know it's too late, and I wait for the sound of Louise screaming. With my eyes closed I suddenly notice that all along the music to the Martha Sole song has still been playing, just as it cuts out midway through the last chord. Then all I can hear is roaring as everyone shouts at once, till suddenly this familiar voice starts up, closer and louder than all the others.

You mean nothing to me, Riana! *Nothing!* You're just a sad bimbo with no *fucking* self-respect and I should have known you'd end up *whoring* yourself out like this! You'll get everything that's coming to you, just you wait! You'll be sorry when your pink and *fluffy fucking world collapses*—!

I open my eyes. Eddy is covered by so many security guards it's like she's wearing them as a human ball gown. Somehow she's still putting up a fight but all her breath is now being used up from the effort. The can of spray paint rolls forward and backward on the carpet where she dropped it. One of the guards that's struggling with her accidentally kicks it and sends it spinning off towards a member of the audience, this skinny guy with glasses who picks it up and cradles it in his arms as if it's a holy relic or something. Louise is sobbing but looks okay and is being comforted by her dad, who's appeared from nowhere and is hugging her like he's protecting her from the rest of the world. Over at the judges' table Joe and Emma are actually holding on to each other as if they've been driven into each other's arms out of fright. Meanwhile Purrfect have been surrounded by another blanket of security guards, who've walled themselves around the girls, facing outwards, like any second now they're expecting this follow-up army of activists to rush them. But there're no more SCUM members with spray cans. They got her. It's over.

You'll never be happy, you stupid brainless fucking bitch!

Eddy's last words. She spits them out for all she's worth, somehow still managing to be heard over all the noise. Then she's dragged through the double doors at the back and out of the room. The doors swing shut behind her. Still being comforted by her dad, Louise is led back up onstage and over to the wings by a security guard. She's got her hand held to her face. I try to catch her eye as she goes past, but she looks away.

The audience is nothing but this one gigantic fucking body with hundreds and hundreds of arms and mouths, all waving and shouting. People struggle to get past each other, either back to their seats or out to the aisle. Everything is in chaos, and it's the kind of chaos that looks like it'll go on for ever and ever.

Then, to everyone's amazement, Tess takes charge. She stands up and brings her hands together in a single clap right in front of the mic that's pinned to the sheer silk shirt she's draped over her massive wobbly chest. It creates a sound like a gunshot. Everyone instantly falls silent and stops moving.

Well, says Tess, totally calm, that was an unexpected little piece of drama!

There are chuckles from all over. Voices begin again,

but this time it's just a hum, nothing like the din it was before. Row after row of seats groan as people plant their butts back down again. Saffron and Monique from Purrfect push through the security guards that're still walled up around them and wave at them to leave, like their presence is nothing but a big hassle they're sick of having to put up with.

We all owe a big thank you to Riana for diverting that little catastrophe, Tess continues smoothly. I think we should give her a hand to show our appreciation.

You'd think I'd gone and saved someone's life the way the room goes off. I swear it's like fucking something else. Emma and Joe are clapping away as if they're trying to make fire and the girls from Purrfect are all giving me standing ovations and showing off these brilliant white teeth. Even the bunch of security guards, now back in their places at the sides of the stage, are putting their hands together.

My skin turns to goose-flesh. I'm trembling like I've never trembled before. I look out over the rows of cheering faces and once again all I can see is one single expression, only this time it's totally blank, like everyone's wearing a mask, the same mask, one that spookily has nothing behind it. Freaked out, I force myself to put on a smile. Always been proud of the way I can deal with anything life throws at me by smiling, overcoming all fear and doubt just by parting my lips. It's my secret weapon. But for once it's not having the effect on me it's s'posed to. The trembling in my arms and legs won't stop, and neither will the weird sense that I've just done something that crosses a line, taking me into a place I can never come back from. Eddy's last words echo in my head. *You'll never be happy.* Sounds like a curse.

I let my eyes travel round the room until they come to rest on Tess. With a bit of a shock I realise she's smiling too, this big grin you'd never have believed her able to make. But there's something chilling about her grin. Something that lets me know she knows perfectly well I'm no hero in this situation, but that it doesn't matter, cos what she also knows is that me and her are the same. Didn't I just prove it by rushing out onstage like that? It's written in her nasty fat face plain as fucking day. I'm gonna win this, I suddenly realise. I'm really gonna win it. It's not some dream or fantasy no more. I'm the new Purrfect girl.

Take a bow, Riana! screams Joe, beside himself with excitement.

As I bow and the applause gets even crazier, I glance back into the wings. I can see Louise stood there watching me, her face pale and her eyes huge and full of emotion. It's so sad, that look on her face, cos I know she's seen it too – that she's not going to get this. She knows that it'll be me, and suddenly I find myself wondering what I'm doing here. If I really want this so badly? Enough to fuck the dreams of that silly spoilt fucked-up little madam over there? Enough to kiss that troll's spotty fat arse, just so I can sing songs in a bikini about love to thousands of people? Badly enough to become empty and fake and heartless?

The noise finally starts to die down and I straighten up. As I do there's this sound of crying from the other side of the stage. I turn to look. To my surprise I see that miserable old Michelle, her head held high and her eyes blazing like a demon's. Her arm's locked around Stina Ellis's neck and pressed up against Stina's throat she's got a handgun.

'Even before Purrfect existed, I was meant to be in the band. I've never felt this way about anything. I don't just want to win, I *need* to. It's the only thing that matters to me in the whole world.'

It happens so fast. One minute all I can focus on is Riana and how much I hate her. There she is at the centre of the stage, stupid boobs exploding out of her obscenely low-cut gold top as she does this grand bow in front of everyone, like she actually deserves their applause for doing nothing. Then she shoots a look my way. Her smile has never looked so big and fake, like it's nothing but a jagged piece of plastic glued on above her chin. It seems like the only reason for that smile to be there is to taunt me, because she's ruined my performance and ruined it in such a way that even if I get to perform it again no one will be interested because it's beyond obvious that she's going to be the new Purrfect girl. I've never wanted anyone to die so much. If only a bolt of lightning could strike her down, turning her into nothing but a heap of ash and a smoking pair of heels, I'd laugh out loud and not even care who heard.

Then there's the most terrific bang that makes me and the technical crew all jump. It's followed by the sound of tinkling glass and of someone screaming. I look up and see that one of the lights has exploded, and a cloud of tiny glass particles is gently drifting down over the stage, catching the other lights and sparkling like fairy dust. At first I think it's just blown because it got too hot, like our garage lights at home sometimes do, but then I see Michelle and Stina and I know it has something to do with them. Oddly, they seem to be hugging. Stina is hardly standing and Michelle has got one arm tightly around her neck which Stina is clutching at like she needs it for support. Then I realise that Michelle and Stina aren't hugging but that Michelle has got Stina in a choke hold, and only then do I notice she's got something which looks an awful lot like a gun pushed up under Stina's chin.

What is going on here?

'Good evening,' says Michelle in a loud sarcastic-sounding voice. 'How's everyone doing tonight?'

She's holding Stina's microphone in her other hand and she sounds surprisingly clear given that she's half doubled up dragging the weight of Stina's body. She'd make a far better presenter, that's for sure.

Over at their table at the front of the audience the judges are all panicking. Security guards from either side of the stage are starting up the steps, but Michelle just digs the gun a little deeper in under Stina's throat, producing a little whimper from her. The guards stop dead.

'No, thank you,' Michelle says to them with mock politeness. Then her face turns grim. 'However, you don't need to worry, this isn't going to take long.'

Stina whimpers again and I notice she's got a patch of red on her forehead. Michelle must have smacked her before she dragged her out onstage. Despite all the times I've looked at the silly orange-skinned bee and imagined something horrible happening to her, I actually feel sorry for her as her eyes roll helplessly back and forth. Her make-up is smeared across her face as if someone just scraped half of it off, and her cheeks are bright red, rather like the cheeks of one of those homeless alcoholics who are always sitting outside banks begging for change. Of course this is all being caught on camera, and a choke hold is possibly the least attractive position in which to be filmed. Tomorrow, her bloated red features are going to be on the front page of every paper.

'Well,' says Michelle, not loosening her hold on Stina. 'Isn't tonight just the *perfect* occasion?'

She looks meaningfully over at Purrfect. Even in this situation it's hard for me to look at them and stay calm, because no matter how terrified they are they still all manage to look sexy, glamorous and self-assured, as if they'd just stepped out of the stylist's when in actual fact they've been sitting there in a hot auditorium watching the show all evening. They shoot each other lightning-fast looks, and I can tell they're transmitting messages with these looks, like a special language that only girls who have bonded over and over and gone through trial after trial and triumphed again and again can share.

There's a long silence, during which no one dares to say anything. Amazingly the entire audience sits watching, like they think this is just another performance. It's not though. That look on Michelle's face, it's not the look of a performer. It's the look of a crazy person.

As ever, it's Monique who speaks. She leans forward, her expression fierce and brave. She looks like a warrior princess, ready to defend her girls to the death, as she takes a deep breath and says: 'Look, miss, don't hurt anyone. Just tell us what you want.'

Michelle licks her lips, really slowly, as if savouring the fear in Monique's voice. It's only as she does so that I put two and two together and realise it must have been her who sent the threats and chopped up the pigeon and ripped up our costumes, not that punk with the spray paint. All along it was misery-guts Michelle. The realisation that all this time we've been herded back and forth from the house to the studio and looked after by a psychopath sends a shiver down my spine. I'm glad I'm safely over here out of the light in the darkened wing, where there's no way she's going to take a shot at me.

Is she going to shoot at Purrfect?

I notice that the camera guy on the crane has been drifting closer and closer to her since she's been standing there. He's almost as close as Riana is. Michelle suddenly turns to face him for a second and the guy stops moving abruptly. But he doesn't stop filming. I suppose so long as she doesn't shoot him this must be great for his career. Then, to my surprise, Michelle nods at him, jerking Stina up and down with the movement. Then she turns back to Purrfect.

'I'm not interested in you,' she says abruptly. Monique jumps backwards in her seat like she's just been bitten. 'My issue is with the dog at the top.'

At first I don't know what she's talking about, but then I figure it out. Everyone in the place is turning to look at one person. On either side of Tess Joe and Emma draw back, like they're trying to disassociate themselves from her. You can't blame them, really. But incredibly Tess doesn't even seem surprised. Instead she calmly returns Michelle's gaze and pushes her glasses back up to the bridge of her nose.

'Okay,' she says. 'In that case let me repeat: what is this about, Michelle?'

She sounds completely unfazed, as if this kind of thing happens to her all the time. No matter how much I hate her, I can't help but admire the woman. She's got nerves of steel.

'It's about you,' replies Michelle, in a voice just as calm. 'It's about the sins you've committed. The lives you've damaged. The dreams you've killed. It's about ridding the world of evil in order to make it a better place. Does that answer your question?'

A murmur ripples out across the audience and the first flicker of alarm shows on Tess's face, only for an instant but I spy it because I'm practically an expert at interpreting her looks by now. Her furry caterpillar monobrow twitches and one side of her mouth droops slightly, like she's just tasted something sour.

'Well, Christ,' she says, taking His name in vain just like people always do in high-pressure situations. 'But I'm very sorry because I don't have a clue what you're talking about. You must have the wrong person, *darling*. I'm not evil. Tasteless, I've certainly been accused of that – but *evil*!'

A couple of people in the audience titter. At her use of the word 'darling' I half expect Michelle to simply blow her away. The words 'Too podgy' race through my head and I realise that somewhere beyond the pounding of my heart I might actually want her to do it a tiny little bit.

But she doesn't. She just nods very slowly.

'You don't remember ruining my life, do you?'

At this everyone in the entire auditorium lets out a gasp, myself included. Even Tess is thrown. Her bug eyes widen to circles and her lips move dramatically up and down with no sound coming out as she repeats what Michelle just said to herself.

'That's right,' says Michelle, this time with a dark smile, as if she's deeply gratified by everybody's reaction. 'I was once one of these pathetic deluded girls, too.'

Jerking poor Stina up and down again, she gestures to Riana standing beside her.

'Once upon a time I wanted to be in that band myself!'

Purrfect all give each other another one of their special looks, and you can't help but get the feeling they're imagining what it would be like to have her in the band. They've bunched up now and have taken each other's hands. Tess glances at them and then looks back at Michelle.

'And do you really think *this* is going to make you a star?'

You've got to hand it to her. The old bee is quick off the mark. I suppose that's how she got to where she is now, by being able to think on her feet. It's a gift, probably God's way of making it up to her for making her so unattractive.

'Shut up!' snaps Michelle. 'This isn't about me anymore! I've watched you for so long, Tess. You think you're so clever for the way you use people to get what you want, but I've got news for you, Tess – *the world uses you!* You're just the weapon it employs, in order to strike down the innocent for its own pleasure! It's hilarious, because you're more exploited than anyone and you don't even know it! You know what you are, Tess? *Do you?!*'

She pauses and looks around and then at the camera. You can't help noticing what a great pause it is. She's got everyone's undivided attention and she's milking it better than even a professional could. Every single one of us is holding our breath to find out what she's going to say next – and to see what she's going to do.

'*You're a piece of equipment!*'

She spits it out like bile. You can almost hear everyone's heart skipping a beat. Still not one of us dares to breathe as we wait for Tess to respond. This time anyone can see the panic on her face. Two little bulges of muscle have appeared on either side of her jaw and her eyes are more bug-like than ever, as if they're going to jump out and make a break for it any second without her. She's beginning to crack. In a weird way I find myself wondering if she's thinking that any second now she's going to die and that these are her last moments of being alive. I wonder if she regrets being such a mean and awful person.

'Michelle,' Tess quavers, practically hyperventilating from the effort. 'You've got problems, everyone can see that! But it's no use trying to pin the blame on me! It's a competition – that's all! So you got stung because you didn't get in. We've all been stung! You have to get over it!'

'You can't talk your way out of this, Tess!' snarls Michelle. 'All those souls you've destroyed and all you can say is "get over it!" What if they can't? *What if they just fucking can't?*'

'If only I could blame someone for all the times I've been put down!' exclaims Tess as if the whole thing was one big joke. She's trying to sound calm and ironic about it but instead she sounds desperate and scared. 'I'd have a list as long as my arm! But life doesn't work like that! You have to pick yourself up and move on – that's just how it works!'

Michelle stares at her so hard it's almost as if she's looking through her. The whites of her eyes are massive. It's chilling, almost as though she's been possessed by an evil spirit, maybe even the Devil himself.

'Look,' says Tess loudly – too loudly. 'I'm sure you don't really want to hurt anybody. You're obviously suffering from a terrible amount of stress. You need to talk to someone . . . Put the gun down and let Stina go, then we'll go somewhere quiet and have a long chat. Just you and me.'

It sounds a bit hopeful. Even Tess knows it. Michelle turns back to the camera, producing yet another moan from Stina.

'This woman is responsible for so much pain!' she cries, looking directly into the lens. 'So much hurt and so much hatred. She shouldn't be alive. She needs to be freed from her own self! Everyone needs to be freed from her!'

She squeezes her eyes shut suddenly, as if she's been overcome with pain. There's another long period of silence in which you could hear a pin drop. Tess is really trembling now. The cellulite bunched up under her armpits wobbles back and forth like jelly. From the corners of Michelle's eyelids tears leak and run their way down her cheeks in snail trails of silver.

'Michelle,' yells Tess suddenly. 'Don't try to make yourself out as some victim! The only person responsible for you is you! Not me! *You!*'

For a second I actually think her words have hit home. Michelle stops crying. It even looks like she's stopped breathing. The hand with the gun seems to relax and I almost expect her to drop it. The security guards start to edge towards her. But then her eyes ping open again, and now she's grinning like she's just won some kind of award. Without warning she unhooks her arm from Stina's neck and shoves her roughly away. Stina stumbles and trips over her heels before flopping down onto the stage, where she lies face up, slowly moving her arms and legs and feeling for the floor around her like an upturned beetle.

'A victim!' screams Michelle into the mic, blasting all our eardrums. '*I'll show you who's the victim!*'

She raises the gun, and points it at Tess.

Do it, I think. *Do it.*

'You think you got rejected because I'm evil?' cries Tess. 'If I rejected you it was for one reason – *because you didn't have the talent*! Deal with it, Michelle! *Just deal with it!*'

She's actually crying herself. Big podgy tears slip down her big podgy cheeks. It's one of the strangest sights I've ever seen, because not so long ago I didn't believe she was able to cry. But there she goes, sobbing away like a massive fat baby. A massive fat baby about to die. I wait for the bang, for the shocked silence and the sight of her body slumping forward and blood spewing out of a hole in her chest.

Then Michelle suddenly turns the gun towards her own head.

'Don't!' cries Riana. The idiotic bitch is obviously so desperate for attention she doesn't even have the sense to stay out of it. Why can't she just shut up like everyone else? 'Don't do it, Michelle!'

It's too much. I pray to God to make her pull the trigger, even though I know it will be horrible and gory, because at least then it will be over.

Nothing. Riana's shouting at her, telling her to ignore Tess because she's stupid and obese and just not worth it. She's saying all these awful things about Purrfect too, about how rubbish and pointless and fake they are, completely ruining her chances of ever being one of them. And yet the crazy effing bee stands completely motionless pointing the gun at her head, not saying or doing anything. She's just staring at Tess with her mouth wide open. She looks like an absolute dork.

Then Riana is on her, grabbing at the hand with the gun and trying to prise it away. Michelle lets out a scream and starts to fight her. They fall to the stage right next to Stina, who moans and pathetically starts to crawl away. Riana's almost twice the size of Michelle, but it seems like Michelle really has been possessed because she's got the strength of ten men. As they struggle the gun turns away from Michelle's head and towards Riana's face.

Then I'm running up the steps and onto the stage myself. I'm only half aware of what I'm doing because it's as if everything has slipped into slow motion. The security guards are running up the steps on either side too and so is a guy with a headset from the other wing. We're all racing towards Riana and Michelle, but even as we do I know that none of us is going to make it in time. Riana is trying to turn her head out of the way of the gun but she can't move it far enough because Michelle has rolled on top of her. Her face is strained in a way I've never seen it before, as if she knows what's coming and that she can't do anything about it. She looks frightened and suddenly I know, like I've had a proper epiphany, that the only thing I care about in the whole world is her.

Save her, God. If you're truly up there then save her. Do this one thing for me and I promise I'll never ask you for anything ever again.

There's a great, terrible, awful bang. It deafens me. As it goes off I trip right over Stina, who I'd completely forgotten about and who was halfway across the stage and directly in my way. I stumble over her body, hearing her cry out behind me as my shoe connects with one of her beach-ball breasts. I land hard on my knees, but the pain doesn't even register. I crawl forward into the puddle of red that's already spreading out around Riana's head and across the floor with sickening speed. It's warm and sticky under my palms.

A security guard has got to them before me. He ignores Riana and focuses instead on Michelle, who's now rolled to the side and is lying on her back facing the ceiling, completely still. He kicks the gun away from her through Riana's blood, creating a disgusting splash. Then he grabs hold of her and she starts screaming as he yanks her up and pulls her arms behind her back.

I finally reach Riana. 'Don't move her,' says the other security guard from behind me. He pulls off his jacket and folds it roughly up, pushing it against the side of her head. But it's no good because her face is unnaturally still and expressionless. Her eyes are shut and her mouth is slack and I know she's never going to smile again. And I know, too, that there is no God and never was.

Two medics arrive and I'm pushed away while they start doing chest compressions on Riana. It seems pointless but I stay to watch anyway. I'm suddenly aware of all this noise like I've never heard before, like every kind of sound is coming from every direction. It's the audience, shouting and screaming, calls being made and explanations being demanded. I shiver. A strange hollow feeling descends over me, as if all the colour has been sucked out of the world, leaving it empty, grey and lifeless.

'It's okay, Louise.'

Someone is pulling me up, turning me away from Riana's horribly still face and pressing me into their shoulder. I don't resist. 'That's my daughter!' another voice is yelling, and I know it's Dad, trying to get through security and onto the stage – 'Louise!' he's shouting, 'I'm over here!' but they won't let him past, and I'm glad. I bury my head in the person's shoulder and try to blot out his voice.

Then I look up, and that's when I discover whose shoulder it is. Ella. Ella, the snivelling whiny cry baby who left the competition because she couldn't hack it anymore. I pull back. After what's just happened you'd think nothing could affect me ever again, but what I see still makes me gasp. Her cheeks are spotted with red and there's lipstick spread across her mouth as if it had been applied by a five-year-old. Her hair is wild and tangled around her face, and tiny black hair clips are caught up in it willynilly. She's wearing one of the costumes, only it's half falling off her and doesn't look like it's been zipped up at the back. But it's not her appearance that makes me gasp, it's the look on her face. There's something so unexpectedly tender about her expression that it's almost angelic. I stare at her and as I do I feel tears spilling out down my own cheeks – tears I didn't summon and have no control over at all.

The second the bell goes I ignore everyone else and race down the stairs to the common room. The window here has a pretty good view of the drive and you can follow it virtually all the way up to the fence. I can hardly keep still with excitement. All day long I couldn't concentrate and Jackie, who I was helping with lunch because it's my turn, lost patience with me when I let the sausages burn and had a huge go at me about it.

My last visit was three weeks ago. Rita came down from London with Mimi, which was pretty nice of her since it meant taking time out of her schedule right in the middle of putting together *Fascinate!*'s five-year anniversary edition. I was touched, even if she did spend most of the time on the phone. The only problem was Mimi who kept asking me in a really loud voice every time we passed someone in the corridor if that person was crazy. But then to my surprise Rita snapped at her to shut up and stop being so bloody tactless, and then, to my further amazement, she apologised and said they were both looking forward to when I was coming home. She even smiled and pretended to be interested in my artwork. I decided things must be getting a bit strained now that it's just the two of them on their own. Unfortunately this niceness didn't last very long, because a minute later Carrie, who really is crazy, burst into the common room not wearing any skirt or panties and shrieking for Jackie because she'd gone and pissed herself again, at which point Rita suddenly remembered she had an urgent meeting back in London and whisked Mimi away. Since then she's sent me several short, blunt emails, which all say the same thing: that she and Mimi miss me, that she's snowed under, and that she hopes I feel better soon.

When I first got here I thought my life was over. Despite what Rita said about how wonderful it was supposed to be and what great success they have with their 'special students', I could tell she was thinking it too. It didn't come as a surprise to me that I was being shut up with a bunch of loons, or that everyone thought I was one, it just made me feel sad, that's all. I couldn't help wondering how Daddy would feel if he knew this was where I'd ended up. But then I settled in and got to know some of the others, and I started to see that it wasn't the end at all. In fact it's the complete opposite. Obviously everyone here has their problems, like Carrie and her incontinence, or Susan and her hysterical outbreaks, or Naomi and her urges to set fire to things. But essentially everyone here is normal underneath, they've just got stuff going on that they need to sort out before they're ready to be with the rest of the world. It's like Holly, my counsellor, keeps telling me: this is about rehabilitation and not giving up on people.

Just then my heart skips a beat because there at the end of the drive a figure is being let through the gates. It's got a pushchair and I know instantly that it's Joni. Even though you're supposed to check with someone first if you're going to go outside I can't wait, so I push the sliding door open and start running up the drive to meet her. I call out as I get closer. Joni looks a bit surprised when I throw myself into her arms. Then she starts laughing and hugging me tightly back.

'All right?' she says after a bit, pulling back. 'Let's have a squiz at you.'

She pretends to admire the punky haircut Susan gave me while I was asleep, then grabs at my midsection like she's checking to see if I've been eating enough and shakes her head and tells me I'm way too thin. I have a look at her. She's got a new hairdo too, a sharp bob with amber lowlights, and is wearing a pale pink jersey and an ankle-length white skirt with two pleats down either side. I'm so behind on fashion these days it's embarrassing, since the magazines we get delivered are always out of date, but I'm surprised at how chic she looks. It's still Joni though. I look down at the pushchair. Strapped into the seat is this massive fat child in a little blue and green tracksuit with an orange baseball cap wedged over his big head.

'This is Baby,' says Joni. 'Baby, say hello to Ella.'

Baby just stares at me. Children frighten me, but for Joni's sake I crouch beside him and say hello in the sort of soppy voice that always comes out automatically when you talk to small kids. From the look on Baby's face it's as if he's trying to figure out what species I belong to, but I act like I find him adorable, pretending to adjust his cap, and at least he doesn't start crying.

'He's nearly three,' Joni tells me proudly.

I tell her he's cute and she beams at me like I've just told her he's a genius. We start walking up towards the house. Joni can't get over the size of the place, and keeps joking if there are ever any vacancies to send her the application form. But I can see she's the tiniest bit unnerved really. That's to be expected, Holly says, because for most people coming here means stepping outside their comfort zone.

Since it's a nice afternoon instead of going in we take the path that winds round the side and leads across the grounds, past the tennis courts.

'Fuck me!' shouts Joni. 'You've got *tennis courts*? What the fuck *is* this place? There a jacuzzi somewhere round here too?'

I realise she's serious and I can't help laughing at her. She grins and starts to tell me about her life in Reading. She says she's finally moved out of her mum's place and into a flat of her own in another area, and that it's nice because there's a couple of other mums on the same block and they all help each other out with the kids and share the cost of a babysitter when they want a night out. Every few minutes she leans down and checks on Baby as if making sure he's still there, like she thinks he's going to have undone his belt and bolted while she wasn't looking. It reminds me of how she looked after me during the competition. You can see that she really loves him, and that she doesn't even care if he is fat.

I nod to everything she says and try to seem interested, but after a bit we fall silent. I was looking forward to showing her around and telling her what I'd been up to. I'd even planned to give her something – the bookend shaped like a swan that I made in one of our pottery workshops. But after hearing about life outside it suddenly all seems really stupid and small in here. I mean, what does Joni care about mood paintings or the fact that I got special privileges for not freaking out when Susan chopped off all my hair when I was asleep?

We pass the courts and go into the flower garden behind, where everyone has their own plot and is allowed to grow whatever they like. A lot of the girls opt to grow vegetables for some reason, but I've planted mine with lots of cornflowers because they grow easily and are so colourful. So far hardly any have come up though, which Gemma who loves gardening says is because I didn't rake the soil enough before I planted them. There's a bench in the middle of the plots which we plop down on. Joni reaches over and unbuckles Baby and we watch him toddle back and forth, trying to catch cabbage whites in his fat little hands.

'You hear about Riana?' says Joni after a bit.

I nod. It was weird how all the papers just forgot about her a couple of weeks after it was all over. I suppose they were busy with all the stories about Purrfect sacking

Tess as their manager, and the 'exclusive' interviews with Michelle that were supposed to tell the real story behind what happened. But not long ago there was an article in one of the papers about how the hospital wanted to switch off her life support, only because she doesn't have any family they can't get the permission for it. I was sad when I read that.

'I'm going to go and visit her when I'm out,' I tell Joni.

'What's the point of visiting a vegetable?' she snorts. 'What you gonna do cept look at her and prod her?'

I stare at her, appalled.

'What? It ain't like she's gonna know you're there or nothing!'

I just carry on looking at her. This is a trick I've learned from Holly, not to say anything but just to wait until someone starts to feel uncomfortable and rethinks what they've said. Sure enough after a minute Joni goes red and looks away.

'Well . . . maybe I'll come with you,' she says sheepishly.

I reward her with a big smile. No matter how tough she acts, Joni's still the sweetest person in the world, and always will be.

A gust of wind blows a cloud of dandilion spores across the plots. 'Cor, getting chilly, ain't it?' says Joni, rubbing her arms. I suggest that we go up to the house and hang out in the common room, which should be quiet now because everyone will be in the dining room having their tea. Joni nods and calls over to Baby, who's pulling up bulbs from Maria's patch. She buckles him back into the stroller and we return towards the house.

In the common room someone's left all the lights and the TV on. I tell Joni to sit anywhere and she throws herself down on one of the beanbags nearest the TV. I take the one beside her and pick up the remote, which has been left on the carpet. I flick the channels absent-mindedly, not particularly looking for anything. Maybe it's just a coincidence or maybe it's fate, but no sooner have I changed the channel than Louise's face fills the screen. Both me and Joni sit bolt upright and exchange looks. She's onstage with the other girls from Purrfect and they're singing their new single, 'This Is War (Don't Ya Know?)', the one with all the synthesisers and power chords in the background. They're all dressed in khaki and combats, like they're going to war, and Saffron's even wearing a red bandanna around her head, Rambo-style. The backdrop behind them is of a burning jungle.

'Jesus,' mutters Joni, rolling her eyes.

Louise has a whole solo to herself. Kharris, Monique, Saffron and Fina roll their bellies around her and sing the chorus while she runs her hand over her exposed navel and launches into a string of Oohs and Ahhs. She looks great actually, older than I remember and somehow taller too – though I suppose that could just be the angle they've filmed her from. But despite what hair and make-up have done, there's something hard about her face. It's like she's just going through the motions. It's not that I envy her: I've discussed this a lot with Holly and we've agreed that I never really wanted to be in the band in the first place, so it's not jealousy making me feel this way. It's just that there's something so hollow about it. There's a sort of blankness to her – to all of them. Maybe it was always there and I just never noticed it before, I don't know. I never listen to Purrfect anymore, apart from when their songs come up on the radio, but I know from the magazine interviews that Louise has settled in well and they all think of her as their baby sister and feel that the band has never been so tight. It's nice, I suppose. I hope she's happy.

'Looks like she's had her boobs done,' remarks Joni. I've got to admit it does look like her chest has filled out a bit, but then it's well hidden underneath her crop top and so it could just be chicken fillets. Joni carries on making little comments about how rubbish everyone looks right up until the song finishes and the next band starts to play. I can see that she's still bitter about the whole thing, but secretly I'm glad she didn't get it. I wouldn't want to be watching Joni on that stage and seeing that blankness in her face.

'Oi, Baby, put that down!' shouts Joni suddenly. I look over and see that he's found a pink crayon and has started scrawling across the wall with it. Joni jumps up and prises it away from him. Baby immediately bursts into tears.

'Shit, Ella,' says Joni. 'I'm sorry! It ain't gonna come off!'

She passes the crayon to me and starts working at the wall with the sleeve of her cardigan just in case, succeeding in doing little more than spreading the pink even further. When she raises her hand there's pink all over the sleeve as well. I start laughing, I can't help myself, and pretty soon Joni is laughing too. We stand there cracking up and every time it seems like we're going to stop one of us starts up again, setting the other one off. Baby stops crying and looks between our faces in wonder. Eventually we both collapse back on the beanbags, gasping. It's nothing huge, but it's probably one of the best feelings I've ever had.

'We gotta go,' sighs Joni when she's finally got her breath back. 'Got a train to catch, ain't we, Baby?'

It seems like they've only just arrived, and I'm about to protest, but then I look up and see they've actually been here nearly three hours and I remember the last train from town leaves at nine. I walk her up the drive, to the halfway point by the field which is as far as residents are allowed to go without supervision. Back at the house the bell is ringing again, which means it's time for evening activities for anyone who wants to participate in them. Joni kisses me on the cheek and gives me a wink, promising to come again soon. Then she walks off towards the gate, trundling the stroller with Baby in it and not looking back.

Once she's through the gate I turn and run back to the house. I can hear the other girls chattering away in the common room, preparing for whatever they're doing tonight, but I don't go in. Instead I carry on up the stairs to my room, which is on the top floor right beside the bathroom. I go to my desk and take out my writing pad. Then I switch on the lamp and sit down and try to think of something inspired to write. After a minute I put:

Dear Jack,
Today Joni came for a visit. It was lovely to see her after all this time, and she brought Baby with her, too. That's her little boy. You'd like him I think, since you always have liked children. Maybe we'll have some of our own one day. If we do I wonder who they'll look most like – you or me.

I pause and chew the pen, which is a disgusting habit that I'm trying to kick since it not only ruins the pen but also leaves a nasty taste of ink in my mouth.

What I want to know is when are you coming to visit, Jack? Every day I wake up breathless with anticipation, thinking that maybe today will be the day. But it never is.

It never will be. I'm not that stupid, I know he isn't coming. He's never going to get this letter either, or any of the others that now lie in a folded-up pile under my mattress. He probably doesn't even know what's happened to me, despite Rita's threats of legal action. He's probably living in a big house with that bronze woman. Maybe he's even married to her now.

Nobody knows I write these letters, not even Holly. I'm supposed to be over him, learning to let go and move on. I keep them a secret, because what Holly and everyone

344

else fails to understand is that I'm never going to move on. My love is for life. Those feelings I have for Jack are real, and they're the only thing I've got that I can believe in. That's why I'm holding on to them no matter what. Somehow, one day, maybe years from now, maybe even decades, we'll be together again, I know it, and I can wait. I'll wait for ever if I have to.

There's the sound of footsteps up the hallway outside, so I quickly slide the letter away under a text book and throw myself back on the bed, just as there's a knock on the door and Jackie pokes her head round.

'Ella? You okay?'

'I'm fine,' I say. 'Just a bit tired, that's all.'

Jackie nods like this is perfectly understandable, despite the fact that it's a Sunday and I didn't get up until ten thirty.

'How was your visit?'

'Great! It was so nice to see Joni again!'

'Good. Glad to hear it.'

She smiles and tells me that they're watching a DVD downstairs if I want to join in. I say I'll be down in a few minutes and she nods again and gently closes the door. As soon as she's gone a wave of tiredness hits me and I have to fight the urge to shut my eyes. I don't know, maybe you really can get exhausted just by people coming to visit you. After a minute of trying to find the motivation to move again I give up and close my eyes.

I find myself picturing Riana. I imagine her lying in her hospital bed surrounded by all these multi-coloured tubes and bits of machinery which bleep as they monitor the waves of her brain and heart. I try to imagine what her dreams are about, while she sleeps that sleep which they say she isn't going to wake up from. I wonder if she knows the difference between her dreams and real life. I wonder if in a way she isn't better off dreaming.